The Wicked Place

a novel of suspense

by

Zaner Grace

Sawdust Publishing

The Wicked Place

by Zaner Grace

Sawdust Publishing
P.O. Box 8328
Huntsville, TX 77340

Front cover design by Sandy Farris.

Author photo by Doug Masters.

Acknowledgments

Dr. Linda Joyce Byrd, thank you for reading and marking my manuscript in its infancy before I even searched for a publisher. Your advice and grammatical corrections were invaluable. Thank you for the precious time you spent when your time was already delegated to a thousand other obligations. I am honored to call you friend.

Sandy Farris, the cover you designed for this book captured its essence. You were able to see inside my wishes and make them so incredibly visual. Having you for a life-long best friend has been a privilege. Having you create this book cover and be a part of this journey has been one of those silver linings you have so often embellished my life with. Thank you.

Dr. Thomas Fensch, as my publisher, you have given me the opportunity to make my dreams come true. As a writer and a mentor, you have inspired me to seek a higher perch. As a friend, you have become part of that truth which gives life worth. I am grateful.

Luke William Masters, as you know, I developed the character of Reed in this book around you. So much of you has influenced everything I do, and I could not have asked for a more precious son. You have filled my heart with joy and love and oh, yes, fiddle music. Thank you.

Douglas Ray Masters, Thank you for helping me, encouraging me, loving me, and for not thinking I had lost my mind for spinning such a tale as this one. Because of you, I can write love scenes.

For Doug
❧ my Valentine ❧

Gargoyles chaperone the realms of darkness
    where Evil whispers its malignant refrain.
From lofty roosts of cathedrals they perch
    while their innocence they proclaim.
Fantastic facades averting demons from hell
    they flaunt an iniquitous face.
But when no one is watching and the devil comes 'round
    they visit The Wicked Place.

—Where Gargoyles Roost,
Linda Carol Masters

Thou shalt not bow down thyself to them, nor serve them; for I the Lord thy God am a jealous God, visiting the iniquity of the fathers upon the children unto the third and fourth generation of them that hate me; and shewing mercy unto thousands of them that love me, and keep my commandments.

— Exodus 20:5-6

Prologue

The pecking of her mother's shoes on the hardwood steps was getting louder with each passing tick of the clock. The loud tapping shoes were carrying her mother closer and closer toward the door to her bedroom.

They stopped.

The doorknob turned. She could hear it turn. She was lying on her stomach with a pillow over her head; her tiny hands held the covers taut. Still she could hear the doorknob turn.

The door opened silently, yet she could feel it open. She could feel her mother standing at the threshold to her room.

"Get up and get dressed," her mother said, curtly. Then the woman in the loud tapping shoes closed the door behind her as she left to go back downstairs. Tap, tap, tap . . . They were going to the wicked place again.

Chapter 1

"Look, this guy just got out of prison from your unit, Pretty. Listen!"

The Houston evening news was on television. An inmate, according to the reporter, had just been released on parole from the Estelle Unit two days ago and had already raped and murdered a woman in front of her eight-year-old daughter. He confessed to burning the dead woman with his cigarette to make sure she was dead just before raping the little girl. A neighbor had heard the child screaming and called the police. The police arrived before the suspect got away and was arrested at the scene.

"Pretty, did you know him?" Reed was sitting on the floor behind the coffee table doing his homework.

Hannah didn't want to answer his question. "Sweetheart, you know that the people I deal with are criminals or they wouldn't be in prison, and I don't tell you about them because it would just make you worry for no reason. Why don't you turn the television off and help your dad set the table?" It was a gentle command more than a question. Hannah had not abated Reed's concern one bit.

"You did know him, didn't you? He was in your class, wasn't he? Just tell me." Reed was adamant as he climbed up on the couch. William had stopped dead still and was waiting for an answer as well.

Hannah paused. "All right. He was one of my students, but sweetheart, he never tried to hurt me. They don't want to hurt anyone that works there because all their privileges would be taken away from them if they did. I am very safe when I'm at work." Reed was not buying her testimony and she knew it. The dog had gone over to him sensing something was not right. "The other inmates and the security officers look out for me. Besides, God isn't going to let anything happen to me at the prison. I pray about that every day."

Reed looked straight at her and replied, "Why didn't God protect that woman and her daughter from that crazy man?" A blush stained his skin.

"I don't know. I guess she didn't know to ask Him to," Hannah said with some hesitation, having absolutely no idea how to answer such a question.

Dragon jumped up on the kitchen counter where Hannah Douglas was cooking supper. The chinchilla Persian stared at her, daring her to make him move, as his fluffy tail swished back and forth before curling around his body and resting in front of his paws.

"Get that stupid cat off the counter," William said, knowing full well that Hannah wouldn't acknowledge that the man of the house had spoken, but he was grateful for the opportunity to change Reed's direction.

"I think I need to haul both of you to the pound," William said as he put his arms around his wife and squeezed her gently. He was still tough enough and toned enough and handsome enough to pose for a Marine Corps recruiting poster, even though his thick hair had silver streaks and he had passed the forty mark. But it was the gentleness within his strength that Hannah adored. Like his voice – it could sound authoritative, or it could whisper like the reeds along a moonlit river, and it was when he whispered to her that first time that she fell in love.

"Son, come in here and help me. You grab the cat, and I'll grab your mom." He began tickling Hannah. Reed picked up the cat. "Okay, I've got him. Let's go." Neiman jumped up and wagged his tail as though he didn't want to be left out. Reed knew his daddy was trying to ease the tension in the air, and he would have to play along, but nothing would suppress the fear that he lived with everyday. His beautiful mother taught school in a maximum security prison, and he would never get used to it. He didn't want to.

Not much of the meat loaf was eaten – thanks to the report about Hannah's ex-student. "It looks like Neiman is going to get a good supper tonight," Hannah said. William and Reed gave her their "don't you dare" looks. "Just kidding, guys. I'm only going to give him the scraps."

Reed kissed his mom and thanked her for the delicious meal even though he had barely touched it. William kissed her too. "It really was good. I've got to go feed the horses. Reed, do you want to go with me?"

"No, sir. I need to practice. I've got a contest in two weeks."

"So, I guess that means I'm cleaning up the kitchen tonight?" Hannah asked with a pout.

"Looks that way," William said and winked.

"Okay, okay. Go on you two, but don't be surprised if all the meat loaf is gone before tomorrow." She looked over at Neiman as he was gobbling up the scraps she had finally given up.

"Hannah?" William said.

"Just kidding. Go on. Get out of here, and hurry back."

"I will. I love you. You know that, don't you?"

"Yes, I know that."

It was just past nine o'clock when Hannah went into Reed's bedroom to kiss him good night.

"Pretty, I wish you would get another job somewhere else."

"I know you do, son, and I am so sorry that you worry about me, but I'm truly not in any danger at work – no more than you are at school. Remember last year when that kid brought a gun to your school and shot that thirteen-year-old boy?"

"Yes, ma'am."

"Well, what if I asked you not to go to school anymore because you might get shot?"

"I don't know." His large brown eyes seemed burdened beyond their years.

Hannah reached over and brushed the hair away from his forehead. "Reed, sometimes bad things happen to good people. That's just part of life. It's full of danger and sickness and sadness, but it's also full of beauty and happiness and excitement. If we were to hide ourselves away to prevent the danger and the sadness, then we would miss all the joy that life brings. We just have to have faith that God will protect us from the bad, but when our share does come, we have to ask God to help us deal with it and get through it."

Reed sat up and put his arms around his mother. "I love you, Pretty."

"I love you too."

Hannah stood to go but turned to look at her son one more time. His high cheek bones had become more prevalent it seemed to her in the last couple of months, adding strength to his young face, and he, already tall for his age, had grown almost too tall for the new blue jeans she had recently bought him. She could hardly believe he was twelve years old.

He rolled over in his bed and said, "Good night."

From her son's bedroom she went to the one she shared with William. The lights were off, but the room was sprinkled with the flames of sweet smelling vanilla candles. Kenny G. was playing his soprano sax on the CD player while William had drawn their bath and perfumed it with drops of the Shalimar bath oil he had given her for Christmas.

Without a word William began to undress his wife. His eyes held her in the candle-light as he gathered her glorious black hair and wound it around and around before putting pins in it to hold the long tresses on top of her head. He kissed her neck as he began unbuttoning her denim shirt. Even under faded blue jeans and large boxy shirts she wore erotic lingerie. She wore it to entice him, but it did more than that. They got into the oversized tub and let the warm water caress their already heated bodies. He whispered to her and then his hands, his powerful, gentle hands, moved with intent as he massaged her with Shalimar soap. He took her to that place where only William could, and they both got lost – neither of them aware that a storm was coming.

Chapter 2

Humidity hung in the air like a blanket of ghosts. You couldn't see it, but you felt its presence. Thunder had been rolling in the distance but was getting louder as she traveled north on Interstate 45. Lightning was dancing to its rhythms and added hostility to the atmosphere. Heavy rain would come soon. It had to.

Single loud drops began pelting her van – not pouring sheets of rain as the thunder and lightning had insinuated, but unrelenting globules pecking and tapping at her van.

Tap, tap, tap. She couldn't stand it. She had to get out of the van. Exit #116 was a half mile ahead. It was past midnight, but The Kettle would be open. "America's Kitchen" never closed. Tension in her shoulders caged and constricted her movement. The rain continued to peck, tapping against the metal. Single – loud – drops. Finally the exit; finally The Kettle. The parking lot was not vacant as she had hoped it would be. All the parking places next to the restaurant were taken, but she didn't care about that. Getting wet didn't bother her; it was the loud tapping on the hood and the roof of the van that made her want to scream. She pulled in, taking up two parking slots, and left the van unlocked.

As she made her way across the macadam, the sky ripped open with streaks of bright white light. Thunder ruptured the sky, releasing the torrents of rain it had labored so hard to contain, and she got soaked, but at least the tapping had stopped.

No one stared at her as she walked in and dripped all over the floor. The beads of rain that fell from her hair and her clothes didn't make her look helpless or in any way appealing, as it would have for an attractive woman. It only made her look stupid and pathetic. She wasn't the kind of woman who aroused compassion or sympathy in anyone.

The waitress came to seat her. "Table for one?" she asked.

The woman smarted back, "Trouble counting today?"

The waitress grabbed a menu and said, "Follow me." As she turned, she flipped her long blond braid of hair back, nearly hitting the customer in the face.

The booths were upholstered in a mauve vinyl and shielded on one side with panels of thick, dimpled, amber glass; the ceiling and walls were aqua. The result was cheap and tawdry, yet somehow inviting, and the food was good for the price.

The waitress handed her the menu. "Something to drink?" She already knew she wasn't going to get a tip from the woman because women seldom tipped her well – especially the ugly ones, and she knew why.

"I want a cheeseburger all the way, a large order of onion rings, a large chocolate milk, and a piece of pecan pie." Water was still trickling from her hair and down her face.

"We're out of pecan pie. We've got apple and lemon chiffon."

"Apple."

Twila Brooks leaned over the table to retrieve the menu, exposing her cleavage and name tag for the flat-chested woman in front of her. Twila was well aware of her petite, hourglass figure, long natural blond hair, and piercing aqua-blue eyes. Men were her best tippers by far.

After a few minutes, Twila served the burger, onion rings, and pie to her customer. "Ketchup's on the table," she said in a matter-of-fact manner.

Twila walked back behind the counter and perched herself on a stool. The rain was still coming down hard. She looked over at the woman she had just served – she was attacking her food like a starved animal. Her mouth was full, but she kept stuffing more into it, so much so that she was barely able to chew. It was repulsive.

Feeling someone watching her, she looked up and saw the waitress staring with her mouth open and a look of disgust on her face, and it made her furious. She hadn't liked the waitress to begin with – so arrogant with her long twisted hair. That was bad enough, but now the bitch was mocking her; found her disgusting, found her ugly. Oh, how she hated that! She hated Twila with all that was in her – her beauty and the way she flaunted it. Oh, but she shouldn't have mocked her. She would pay for that.

The woman finished her meal, got up to leave, and left a five dollar tip on the table.

Twila saw the five dollar bill and immediately felt ashamed. It was pouring down rain after all, and the woman had gotten soaked to the gills. No wonder she was in a bad mood.

"Was the food all right?" Twila asked politely as she rang up the woman's ticket. Her long blond braid fell over her left shoulder.

"It was real good. I hadn't eaten all day. I guess I was pretty hungry."

Twila smiled.

"You live around here?" the woman asked. "I haven't seen you before."

"Oh, I just moved here from Livingston. I'm trying to finish my degree and was tired of commuting."

"Are you living in the dorms on campus?"

"Me? No! Most of the girls in the dorms are freshmen. I'm twenty years old. No, I'm living in a little house on Fox Glen," Twila said.

"No kidding. I used to live on Fox Glen in a house with pink aluminum siding."

"For real? I know the house you're talking about. I live two houses down. Thirteen-twenty-six."

"Well, the rain stopped. I need to get home."

"Nice talking to you. Come back," Twila was being sincere.

An eeriness stole the woman as she walked towards the door. "My mother had long hair and wore it in a braid like yours." Droplets of water were falling from the roof of the diner, pecking the asphalt. Tap, tap, tap, tap, tap . . . She hurried to the van and drove away, but she didn't go home.

Chapter 3

Hannah Douglas's alarm clock beeped at 3:30 a.m. She rolled over and slapped the snooze button then rolled back over to cuddle her husband again. Nine more minutes before the next beep. Sleep reclaimed her immediately.

Beep - beep - beep - beep. 3:39. *Oh, good. Another snooze left.* And she slapped it again. William cuddled her this time. Even in his sleep, he fondled her bare breasts. The alarm infiltrated her dreams again. 3:48.

She got out of bed, reset the clock for William, then walked to the kitchen to brew some tea. Six cups of strong tea contained enough caffeine to help her stay awake and supplied her with the energy she needed to face the prison with all its trimmings.

After she washed her face, Hannah began to get dressed. A smile peeked out as she fastened stockings to her pink garter belt and thought about last night. Donning a robe, she went to the kitchen to pour her first cup of tea. Neiman was waiting for her. "Come on. You can come back to my dressing room, but you'll have to be quiet." Neiman looked at her as though he understood everything she said, and in fact, he did.

Neiman, big as he was, managed to crawl under the vanity, and Hannah rested her feet on him while she applied her make-up. In less than ten minutes she was ready to zip up her skirt and pull on her sweater. Neiman grunted when she got up.

Usually, Hannah wore her long black hair up in a bun or a French braid. Today she wore it up and used two lacquered chopsticks to hold it in place.

After turning out the dressing room lights, she kissed William lightly, went to Reed's room, kissed him, and finally to the kitchen to pour her tea in an insulated mug. The collie got his kiss too then kitchen lights out, coat and identification tag on, tea and keys in hand, and she was out the door by 4:25.

The night air was cold and damp, and it had obviously rained while she was asleep. February weather in southeast Texas could be eighty degrees, or it could be eight degrees, and it could manage both in the same twenty-four hour period. Hannah hadn't watched the weather report after Reed had made such a fuss about her ex-student on the news. They had turned off the television and not turned it back on, so she had no idea what this day had in store.

Backing out of the driveway, she noticed a dark van parked in front of the house next door. It was unfamiliar. Never one to muster fears without just cause, Hannah felt as though she was being watched, and it unsettled her a little bit. She looked to see if anyone was in the van, but she couldn't tell. Security lights were perched in every yard in the Westwood subdivision, but instead of providing a secure and protected atmosphere, this morning they gave the neighborhood a mystical, eerie look. *I am getting too paranoid.* Hannah drove down Westwood Lane toward Highway 30. Hannah never encountered traffic that early, except for bread trucks, but this morning she saw a vehicle turning off of Westwood Lane onto Highway 30 heading east behind her.

The first traffic light was red. Hannah stopped while the vehicle behind her got closer and closer. *I can't believe how spooked I'm acting.*

As the vehicle approached, the driver flicked on his bright headlights.

Hannah proceeded through the red light on an impulse and the large vehicle behind her ran the light too.

She was completely unnerved. She changed lanes; so did the person behind her. The next traffic light was green, as well as the next four. Hannah turned left by First National Bank, onto Maple Avenue, and when she turned , she could see that the vehicle following her was the dark van that had been parked in front of her neighbor's house.

Maple Avenue was not well lit. She was alone except for the person who was behind her.

Why is someone following me? Who could it possibly be? Surely its not an ex-convict or heaven forbid, a gang-member on the outside. Hannah continued to drive toward the next traffic light. *Thank God, it's green.* She drove past the Byrd Prison Unit on the left. A small strip center was across the intersection on the same side, and a park and ride was on the right, but of course no one was there – only vacant cars.

Few people worked the same shift as she did, 5:00 a.m. - 12:15 p.m., so she seldom saw any cars. *God, why weren't there any other cars?* It had never bothered her before now. She drove onto FM 980, one of the county roads that the state of Texas traditionally called a farm-to-market road. The narrow lanes with no shoulders, along with the many winds in the road, made it dangerous to travel at any time, but never so much as now – in the middle of the night – with someone following her in a van. Hannah was scared.

Eight miles down the road Hannah came to the FM 3478 turnoff. The van still followed her with the brights still on. It was three miles to the entrance of the Estelle Prison Unit. Finally she reached the guard shack, but no one was on duty. The unit was up to two hundred officers short at any given time, so they often left the front entrance guard shack unmanned. Hannah turned onto the drive that led to the employee parking lot, eased over the cement speed bump, and watched in her rear-view mirror as the van followed.

On nights such as this, when the clouds were heavy and the air humid, the lights from the prison did not illuminate the parking lot. It appeared as though the light was being shoved down and held back inside the maximum security fences; contained like the convicts within. But the lights that disturbed Hannah were the ones behind her. The ones on the van. The ones following her.

She backed into a parking space, afraid to get out. The van made a loop around the parking lot and left with no further ado. Hannah couldn't read the license plate because there was dirt or mud smudged across it.

She finally got out of the car and headed toward the front picket, the guard tower, where she would see or at least hear a security officer, anxious to get inside the walls of the maximum security prison and feel safe. *Okay, God, how bizarre is that?*

Meanwhile, the van went back to Huntsville. Downtown was still very quiet. A few houses she passed along the way had lights on, but not many. It was 5:15.

She drove back to Eleventh Street, crossed it, and drove through a residential neighborhood. The houses were old, but for the most part, well-kept. She drove down the street to where the pink house stood, parked in front of it, and waited for Twila to get home.

It was forty-five degrees outside, and the clearing sky had spaces where the stars were beginning to shine through. The air felt less heavy. She retrieved a blanket from the back then moved to the passenger side of the van where she could stretch out. It was still very dark as she waited, watched, and listened for Twila.

Night sounds floated across the moist air like specters in search of redemption. She hated the sounds of darkness, but she hated its silence more. In the silence she could hear her own tormented soul, and nothing disturbed her more than that — the memories of the past and the warnings of the future.

The house was dark when Twila pulled into her driveway. She got out of her car and walked toward the steps to the small concrete porch. A flood-lamp came on.

The woman wondered if perhaps someone else was in the house. She watched. The light did not go off immediately. It went out after a light inside the house went on, so she decided it must have a motion sensor. She continued to watch the waitress's house.

A light went on in a room where the window was small and frosted. Twila was in the bathroom.

The woman got out of the dark van and walked up the street to house number thirteen-twenty-six. The houses were all dark except for Twila's.

She went around to the back of the house to avoid the automatic porch light. There was a small brick patio off the back of the house. She pulled medical gloves out of a black bag, put them on, then tried the door, but it was locked. She felt above the door for a key — nothing — then under the doormat. No key. There were several flower pots around the patio containing dead plants. She looked under one pot at a time and found a key after the third try.

Quietly, she put the key in the door lock. It fit. She unlocked the door and went inside, carefully closing the door behind her. She was in the utility room. Another door opened up into a small paneled dining room. A bar separated this room from a small, but clean, kitchen. The wallpaper was yellow and orange plaid. The counter top was lemon yellow, and there were yellow knobs on the cabinet doors. Cutesy, just like Twila — cutesy. Next was a very small living room with a television, a gas heater, a couch and a love seat, with a square end table in the corner. How charming. She wanted to gag.

The door to the bathroom was not closed, and she could see that Twila was taking a shower. Steam was billowing over the clear vinyl shower curtain. Twila was washing her long blond hair. Her petite, curvaceous body was easy to see through the clear curtain. Even in the shower when she thought no one was watching, Twila moved sensually, as if she were a cat in heat performing for a male companion.

As she stood in the dimly lit living room watching Twila in the shower, she took the dagger out of her bag. Golden king cobras' heads flared out at the top of a cross hilt. The head of Satan, cast in gold, gazed from a red leather scabbard. Slowly she removed the dagger from the scabbard. The thirteen inch blade shimmered in the dim light.

Twila was too preoccupied with her body, her hair, herself, to realize that someone was watching her, stalking her, and preparing to kill her.

The woman waited. It was still dark outside, but she knew the neighbors would be waking up by now. It was six o'clock in the morning.

Twila threw back the curtain, grabbed a towel and wrapped her hair in it, then took a blue chenille bathrobe off a hook next to the sink and put it on. It was embellished with white daisies and a red and black ladybug.

Her comb was on the back of the sink. She unwrapped her mane of long blond hair and began combing out the tangles. She was very careful with it; the process took all of five minutes, maybe longer.

The woman continued to watch.

Twila bent over to get her hair dryer from under the sink, still unaware of the danger she was in. She tossed her head over and began drying her beautiful thick hair. After ten minutes it was dry. She picked up her bore bristle brush and brushed her tresses lovingly. It was resplendent and she knew it. She was beautiful and she knew it; the woman knew it too.

"Braid it," the woman said out loud.

Twila almost jumped out of her skin. The voice startled her so that a wave of dread absorbed the air in her lungs, and she had to gasp for a breath. She searched for the courage to look to see who it was.

"Braid your hair, I said."

When Twila got her wits about her, she realized it was the woman from the diner. "What are you . . ."

The woman held the fancy dagger with both gloved hands, in front of her chest as though she were acting in a B-rated movie and was trying to make the most of her one scene.

"What are you doing here? What do you want?"

"I want you to braid your hair," she said calmly but distinctly.

Twila looked at her like she was crazy, and it made the intruder mad — so mad that she could barely control herself from killing Twila right then and there.

Twila was shaking all over.

"For the last time, braid your hair!"

Twila gathered her hair and with fumbling fingers began braiding it.

"Not like that!" the woman yelled. Put a rubber band at the top, first."

Twila found a rubber band and put it around her hair and began again as the intruder watched.

"All the way to the end."

Twila did as she was told and banded it at the bottom. She was so scared that it didn't occur to her why the woman from the diner would ask her to do such a thing.

"Turn around."

"Why?"

"Because I said to."

"Are you going to kill me?" Twila was more afraid than she had ever been in her life. Nothing the woman was doing made any sense, and her brain wasn't able to counter attack the emotions being fired off in her nerves.

"No, of course not."

"Please don't hurt me."

"I'm not going to hurt you unless you don't do as I say. Now, turn around."

Twila turned around. The woman grabbed Twila's shiny rope of hair with one hand, lifted her dagger with the other, and cut off the braid above the rubber band that was next to her scalp. She put Twila's hair in her bag.

Twila wailed as if her heart had been torn from her chest.

"Oh, what's the matter? I told you I wasn't going to hurt you, and I didn't. What are you crying about?"

Twila turned back around to face the woman.

"Go into the bedroom."

"No, please," Twila cried.

The woman threw a look at her that was sharper than the dagger she was holding. Twila trudged into her bedroom, and the woman followed.

Chapter 4

6:15. The alarm raided William's dream. He reached over to turn it off. If Hannah had been there, it would have been harder to climb out of bed. "Jeez, it's cold in here," he said to Neiman. "Yeah, I know. You've got on a nice warm coat. Don't give me that devil-may-care attitude. I know you think I look silly naked, but don't forget who feeds you." Neiman cocked his head as if William was crazy. "Okay, okay, so Hannah feeds you. Why am I talking to a collie? Never mind."

William put on his robe and headed straight for the thermostat. Reed was still asleep, though some days he was awake by five o'clock and practicing his fiddle – but not this morning. He was in his bed all covered up, breathing slow and heavy, and he was sound asleep. William stood beside his bed for a minute and watched him. He looked so peaceful.

William nudged his son. Reed's eyes opened a little, focused on his dad's face, and his arms went up. William bent down to get his morning hug.

"Hey, big guy. Did you sleep good?"

"I would have if Lady Penguin hadn't made the house so cold."

"Yeah, I could see how much trouble you were having. Looked like to me you were really having a rough go of it."

"Dad!"

"What?"

"Nothing. What's for breakfast?"

"What would you like?"

"Anything but low fat stuff."

"You're giving your mom a pretty hard time this morning, aren't you?"

"No, you know I love her. She can't help it if she thinks skinny penguins look better than fat ones."

William started tickling Reed under his arms. He giggled and squirmed and begged for mercy. William bent down to get another hug then went to the kitchen to make breakfast.

Reed was right about the low fat food. Hannah had always been weight conscious and didn't want her son to grow up fat, so she never had very many sweets around the house, but now she was counting fat grams. If any kind of food came in a low fat, or better yet, fat free variety, she chose that.

William and Reed complained about it, but Hannah stood fast and reminded them about clogged arteries, heart disease, and obesity. They didn't have a prayer. They did, however, have real eggs in the refrigerator. They had the egg substitute also, but she gave them a choice about that, and they always chose the eggs that came in a shell.

William heated the griddle and popped low fat bread in the toaster and then put the low fat margarine on the bar.

Reed's tape player was playing old-time fiddle music in his bathroom. William could hear "Shuck - in - the Bush" from the kitchen, one of Reed's favorite tunes. Reed had been playing the fiddle since he was ten. He had liked the sound of the fiddle on country songs he heard on the radio, so one day he asked his mother what instrument was making that sound, and she told him it was a fiddle. Reed told her he wanted to learn how to play one. For Christmas that year, William and Hannah bought him a fiddle, a bow, and a case for one hundred and twenty-six dollars, and he was thrilled.

They found a young man, a college student, Matt Brice, who played old-time fiddle music. He had won every major fiddle contest title there was in the United States.

Matt taught Reed how to play using sticks and circles – a method called tablature. Reed picked it up quickly, and after just six months he entered his first contest and won first place in the zero to twelve age group. He was awarded seventy-five dollars and was hooked.

Hannah's grandfather had died when she was an infant but her mother told her that he had played the fiddle. She said he did three things every day: read the Bible, studied a page in the dictionary, and played his fiddle. Hannah's first cousin had inherited both of his fiddles, but after he heard Reed play, he sent one to Reed. It was very old and very fine and Reed loved it. One of Reed's great-grandfather's friends, Mr. Dudley, heard him play at a contest and was so moved that he gave Reed his oldest and finest violin. And, at Reed's last recital, his science teacher, Ms. Suzanne Stuckey, came to hear him. Reed was always affectionate with a fiddle when he played it, cuddling it with his chin as though it were a soft puppy. He moved as he played, like a willow tree in a spring breeze. It touched her, and that night she gave Reed one of her most prized possessions, a German-made violin that was the finest instrument he could ever hope to own. Along with that gift she gave him something even more valuable – the determination to be the best that he could be.

By the time breakfast was ready, Reed was clean and dressed. His hair, however, was still wet.

"Hey, Dad, this looks good enough to eat."

"So eat!"

"Okay, okay."

After eating, William went back to take a shower while Reed rinsed the dishes and put them in the dishwasher.

By 6:45 a.m., Reed was in his room practicing to a guitar track that Matt had recorded for him.

William listened to his son while he dressed. He was a sheriff's deputy for Walker County and had a lot more to put on every day than Reed did. First the T-shirt, then the bullet proof vest. The shirt had a badge, ribbons, and collar pins to attach. After the trousers were on, he had all the leather to deal with. The first belt went through the loops, then the other belt went over the first belt. It had the gun on it. Next he had the cuff case, then the mace case, and two extra magazine cases for his bullets. Leather keepers were snapped around both belts to keep it all secure. Finally his radio and shirt radio were clamped in place, and he was dressed.

Reed was proud of his dad. Every once in a while he got to ride in his police car and play with the lights if no one was around. He didn't worry much that his dad would get hurt on the job because he had been a Marine, and he knew how to take care of himself. It was his mother's job that troubled him. He couldn't get used to his mother teaching hardened criminals inside a maximum security penitentiary. Every night he prayed that God would protect her. He thought his mother was the most beautiful woman in the world. He had called her "Pretty," instead of "Mom," since he was three years old. He knew she was beautiful, and even his friends thought so. If the klutzy kids his age could see it, he knew that mean, dirty old men, who had been locked up for years, would see it.

His mother had taught the second grade in public school for eight years. But when Reed was six years old, she had the opportunity to teach for the prison, and she took it. The job paid a whole lot more, and she thought she could handle it.

Of course, Hannah's parents tried to talk her out of working inside a men's prison, and William begged her not to, but Hannah had made up her mind, and everybody who loved her just had to deal with it. They all adored her, even if she was as head-strong as a beef-master bull.

Hannah Douglas was an excellent teacher and she loved her job. It was challenging, tough, and even frightening at times, but it was also very rewarding.

Most of the time, when a student was placed in school, it made him angry. Hannah's students were all mandatory, which meant they couldn't read well enough to pass a fifth grade level test. Public school had been a failing experience for all of them. A lot of them came from homes where parents didn't care, or where parents weren't educated enough to help them. Many of the students Hannah dealt with came from poverty-stricken neighborhoods or from families with a history of criminal behavior for generations. School had not been a priority.

In the prison school system, a teacher gained students or lost students often. The program was not blocked into semesters. It was open entry-open exit. A new student would come in and he might be on kindergarten level or he might be on a fourth grade level. Some could read a little bit while others couldn't read at all. Some students could not subtract three from seven.

Hannah Douglas could usually turn the meanest, most verbally abusive inmate around in a matter of days. She had a way of calming them down and gaining their trust. Trust was something a convict seldom earned, and less often did a convict put his trust in someone else.

There were two prison guards in the education department. They shook down each inmate when they came in and again when they left out and marked off their names on a roster. If a fight broke out, they came running, or if a teacher hollered for help, they came running.

The education department was handled differently than the rest of the prison. In education the inmates were encouraged to achieve; to be somebody. They were motivated in positive ways.

The hospital was not so bad either. Doctors and nurses cared for the sick, while guards secured the facility, but the cell blocks, the day rooms, and the hallways were different. Stabbings were not uncommon. The inside was loud, and the halls echoed foul language. Officers, at times, had to body-slam an irate convict, and other bosses would rush to help. It was not unusual to see a naked convict hanging, like a monkey, from the bars above the crash gates either trying to get attention, or because he really went off the deep end, and there was no place to go but up. Crash gates, the bars sectioning off the hallways, had more uses than for psyches to climb, of course. They came in real handy when inmates became rowdy or if a riot broke out since they stood every forty-five yards or so. When closed off, movement stopped and trouble was isolated.

Hannah Douglas didn't like to go anywhere on the inside, except for the education department. The walk down the hall to education was long enough. She had seen more than she had ever wished to see of "the inside." On occasion, she had to go to the chapel for a mandatory lecture or seminar, and once she had to walk to the south gym at the very end of the building for a job fair with her students. She had been to the Officer's Dining Room a few times and to the commissary, and twice the teachers had a luncheon out in the vocational complex, which Hannah had to attend on in-service days. She had seen the entire facility, but the education department was the only place where she felt measurably safe. She knew the inmates in there and they knew her. Problems surfaced every week, but all jobs had their problems. That's why it was called work.

Chapter 5

Twila Brooks was terrified.

The woman took a black strip of cloth from her black bag and told Twila to put her hands behind her back.

Twila did as she was told, scared not to. The woman tied her wrists together.

"That hurts! It's too tight."

"Shut up, Bitch."

"Why are you doing this to me? I'm sorry if I was rude at The Kettle. I was just tired, and it had been a slow night. Please forgive me!"

The woman wasn't listening to Twila; her mind was focused on what she was doing.

"Lay down on the bed."

"Oh, God! No!" Twila cried, but she sat on the bed, then lay down.

The room was too sweet and delicate to harbor such a scene with its lavender walls and border of wisteria. White eyelet curtains, just the kind for a beloved little girl's room, dressed up the two windows. The shades behind them were pulled all the way down for the not-so-little girl's privacy. The bed had a white eyelet canopy, and wasn't it just the dream bed for the perfect little girl – who was oh, so naughty when nice? The bedspread and pillows and pillows and more pillows were a garden of wisteria, so thick you could smell their scent, and it made Ethel want to scream for fresh air. The white wicker furniture, the foo-foo girl stuff on the dresser, the full- length mirror for the little whore to see her perfect reflection . . . it wasn't so perfect now.

"Did your parents love you when you were little?"

Twila looked at her as though she were a frog on top of a wedding cake. "Yes. They still love me."

The intruder's face had a blank look, like the face on a mannequin, but her eyes were hot, searing, and alive. They weren't focused on Twila. They were focused on her own parents, reflecting the hate she held for them.

Tap, tap, tap, tap . . .

"What is that?" the woman asked frantically. Her trance was broken.

"What is what?"

"Shut up!" the intruder screamed as the slow, tapping beat continued.

"She's coming!" she whispered.

Twila lay there on her bed in a state of confusion and fear, and she thought for a fleeting moment about her hair. She had been so proud of her gorgeous long blond hair. Every day someone complimented it. People would touch it, stare at it, envy it, and now it was gone, viciously cut off of her head. She thought about all of her hair clips and head bands that she had collected over the years. Her hair had always been long, but all those things would be useless now. Her hair was gone. That crazy lunatic had stolen it from her. Tears rolled out of the corners of her large, aqua-blue eyes and down each side of her face.

"Shut up!" the woman screamed again. "I'm not going to listen to that. We've got to go. Get dressed."

Twila looked at her as though she were looking at the craziest person on earth. "Go where?"

"The wicked place," she whispered. Her face was there in front of Twila, but her spirit was somewhere else.

The tapping had turned into a steady shower of rain.

C3&O

William knocked on Reed's door. Reed didn't hear it over the guitar track coming from his stereo and the fiddle music he was playing along with it. He was focused on the music.

William flicked the light on and off a few times and got Reed's attention. "Son, it's 7:20. Your ride will be here soon."

"Okay." Reed hung his fiddle up on a plastic covered wire that he had suspended between two pegs. It was attached to the wooden shelf Reed had seen at a fiddle contest and asked his parents to buy for him. He was having to store his fiddles in their cases and put them under his bed until the shelf was bought. All four of his fiddles were hung on the wire, and they gave the room a look of importance and dignity. Reed had outgrown the way the room had been decorated before he became a fiddler. His yellow walls had to be painted a manly taupe color. Bright curtains and bedspread were replaced with paisley wine-colored drapes and bed comforter, and his school artwork hung on his walls instead of the posters he once thought so great. Bike- racing trophies cluttered the top of his chifferobe, but his dresser displayed his fiddle trophies. Those trophies just hadn't looked right in a kid-looking room.

After Reed hung his fiddle up, he turned off his stereo, kissed his dad, grabbed his book bag, and went outside to wait for his ride to school.

William went around the house turning out lights and making

final house checks then locked up the house.

Reed's ride was coming around the curve as William got behind the wheel of his Crown Victoria. It was a new car, and he was proud of it. No one had smoked in it, and there was no trash on the floor or in the door pockets. None of the equipment had been rearranged or tampered with. It was William's car, and only he would drive it. Finally, the department had given him a take-home car.

When Reed got in the car with his friends, William turned on his overhead lights and hit the siren. It delighted the kids.

Arriving at work early, as he always did, William had a cup of coffee with some of the officers finishing up the night shift.

Lately, some of the deputies were having to assume some of the cases from the detectives. The Sheriff's Department of Walker County was not large. There were twenty-one deputies, three sergeants, and four detectives, and the detectives were swamped with cases that had not been solved.

Over the past year, five young women had simply disappeared without a trace in Walker County. The women, ranging in age from eighteen to twenty-three, all wore their hair at least waist length, were attractive, and attended Sam Houston State University.

The campus police were putting in overtime and were stationed at every women's dormitory. Coeds had the officers escorting them to classes, to the library, to the cafeteria, or wherever they went on campus.

City policemen, sheriff's deputies, and the university police had joined forces to find whoever was kidnaping these young girls. Normally there were strict boundaries between the three departments. The city police did not work outside the city limits; the sheriff's deputies usually did not handle cases within the city limits and the university police only worked on the Sam Houston State University campus, but when five young women disappear, boundaries disappear as well.

None of the women kidnaped were from Walker County. One of the girls was from Ennis, Texas, Houston was home to two of them, while another was from Lufkin. The latest victim had been from Cleveland, Texas. All Texans. The cases had gained national attention and brought unwanted chaos to the small, quaint town of Huntsville.

Huntsville, Texas, was a beautiful place during every season of the year. The weather in the summer could be ferociously hot and humid, but the rest of the year it was mild with pleasant temperatures, except for a few spurts of freezing weather during the winter. Pride was evident in the old historical site. It had claimed Sam Houston its son and named the university after him. A sixty-seven foot statue of him stood south of downtown.

Oddly enough, Huntsvillites also took pride in the prisons that stood in the area. The Walls, standing since 1849, had confined some the most infamous criminals in the country. The structure had been used in several big movies. "Old Sparky," the term given to the electric chair, was located at The Walls until Texas declared it cruel and unusual punishment, surrendering to lethal injection, so now it rested in the prison museum.

Every execution that Texas carried forth was done at The Walls, and most were covered by Houston TV news stations. The most infamous cases attracted national and even world news coverage. It gave Huntsville a measure of importance, though morbid.

The five kidnappings gave Huntsville a sour and disturbing feel. Things such as that didn't happen in the small town. Huntsville was where the criminals of such crimes were punished and confined. It was a place where you could distinguish between the good and the bad, and the bad guys wore white in Huntsville, Texas.

ওঃ৪০

Wednesday could not decide on clear weather or rain. The rain was pouring as the kidnapper forced Twila towards her van in the early morning hour before daybreak. Across the street were housing units for married college students who wanted dormitory rates. On Fox Glen, the low rent end, people minded their own business and paid little attention to the comings and goings around them. Twila thought that was great before the monster came to her house, but now she would give anything if someone was watching her, spying on her. God only knew what would happen to her next, and no one would even know she was gone. No one would know for hours. She worked nights and kept her answering machine on so people wouldn't disturb her sleep, and she didn't get up until around noon. Her class-es were all scheduled in the afternoons.

The van was dark green and plain. The woman opened the back and told Twila to get in.

"I need help," she cried. "I can't get up that high with my hands tied behind my back."

"Shut up that sniveling," the woman spat as she got a step stool out of the van for her captive.

Twila managed to get in. There were no windows in the back and no seats – only empty space. Twila scooted over towards the side of the van and got as comfortable as she could. She heard her captor lock the door. It was so cold, she was wet, and her short, chopped hair kept falling in her eyes. Her face itched, and the beads of water rolling down it made her want to scream. She thought back to the first moment she laid eyes on the woman. When she had come into The Kettle, beads of water were dripping down her face, and she had looked ugly and spiteful. *How could I have been stupid enough to tell a complete stranger where I lived? I knew she was crazy the minute I saw her.* Then it hit her like a stray baseball crashing through a window. This was the person who had been kidnapping the girls at Sam. Long hair, young, college student, pretty. *Oh, God! I fit every single description. I'm one of the victims!* Every nerve ending in her body exploded in terror. *Some of those girls have been missing for months; one for nearly a year. They have not been seen or heard from. They vanished. Where were they? What had this monster done to them?*

The woman drove the dark green van through the rain and into the dawn of Wednesday morning. It was February the eleventh.

The eleventh of February was a special day. Twila knew it was if she could only concentrate for a minute. February the eleventh . . . An inkling of hope penetrated the bleak despair that had consumed Twila Brooks. It was her daddy's birthday, and her parents were driving over this afternoon so they could celebrate it together. They would realize she was missing and call the police. Thank God! They would call the police. She was sure of it.

Oh God, she prayed, *let someone find me.*

The rain was letting up again, and the woman in the dark green van headed to the wicked place.

Chapter 6

Madness had many faces, but few were as descriptive as that of Ethel Fletcher's. Protruding from the center of her face was a long and narrow nose. Her eyes were set too close together, and they were almost colorless, perhaps a shade of blue. Her cheeks were hollow and the cheekbones severe. Pallid, oily skin covered her face, and red, perm-damaged hair surrounded it. Red, usually, a healthy, vibrant color for hair, mocked this young woman. There was absolutely nothing healthy or vibrant in her appearance. There was nothing congruent about her facade. She was pathetic.

Beneath Ethel's head was an anorectic body, displaying starved legs with oversized feet and emaciated arms attached to scrawny hands. She had no bosom and no behind. Ice water ran through her veins, and her heart's only function was to disperse it.

At 10:30 a.m., February eleventh, Ethel Fletcher called Virginia at The Walls Unit to tell her she was sick and couldn't come to work. Her shift was from 12:00 noon until 7:00 p.m.

"What's wrong?"

"It's none of your business what's wrong with me, Virginia Deigo. You're just a lousy secretary, and I don't take orders from you, nor do I have to answer your nosy questions."

Virginia motioned to Earl Cowen, the principal, to pick up the extension from his adjoining office. She smoothed the front of her teal satin blouse that was stretched across her ample bosom.

"Yes, Ethel, I know you don't take orders from me, but I've been told to ask what's ailing you every time you call in sick because you call in sick so often."

"Like I give a red damn what an uneducated idiot like you thinks. Just get me a sub."

"Before you hang up, Miss Fletcher, this is Cowen. Don't bother coming to work tomorrow either. You are hereby suspended until further notice."

There was silence on the other end of the line.

"Did you hear me?" Cowen pushed his glasses back up and adjusted them as though that gave him more authority.

"You can't fire me for calling in sick. I know my rights," she answered, feeling the hatred for her boss seeping out of her skin like pus from an infected wound. Men were stupid and vile.

"No, I can't fire you. But I can suspend you for talking to my secretary the way you just did and for the many other reasons which are stashed neatly in your personnel file. Please be aware that your behavior on this unit leaves much to be desired, and the superintendent is looking into the matter. You are suspended until further notice without pay."

Ethel slammed the receiver down on the hook. She turned toward the bar in the kitchen and with her bony arms cleared the entire counter in one sweep. This new mess could easily have gone unnoticed in the steadily climbing debris in which Ethel lived. Wicca, her cat, began eating scrambled eggs from the floor. Ethel didn't bother to pick up the broken plate.

"I can't believe that woman!" said Cowen. He took his old fashioned black-framed eye glasses off and rubbed his face.

Virginia noticed a Masonic ring on his right hand but knew it wasn't the appropriate time to congratulate him on becoming a Master Mason. She was aware that Earl was going to "turn in" his oral work the night before at the lodge, and apparently he had passed. Instead, she said, "You should have been around when Hannah Douglas taught here. Ethel nearly drove Ms. Douglas crazy. But I guess you've heard all about that."

Earl Cowen had been transferred to The Walls Unit in August of the previous year from one of the northern units at his request. His wife had died and he needed a change from what they had together. The house, the lawn, the street, the town, all held too many memories of his life with her. They rose up like phantoms to haunt him everywhere he turned, and he simply could not live like that.

"I only know that Ms. Douglas was transferred to another unit, at her request, because of friction with Fletcher, but no one has really given me the whole story."

"Have you got a few minutes? I'd be glad to fill you in."

"Sure, let's go into my office. I'll get us a cup of coffee."

"Thanks. I take mine black." Virginia sat down in the inmate upholstered chair across from Earl's organized desk. He kept his office immaculate, free of personal items from home, except for one ceramic figurine of a horse.

Virginia Diego was five feet three inches tall and at least sixty pounds overweight. Her short teased hair was bleached and always looked orange next to her scalp. White oversized glasses framed her eyes, accentuating her puffy eyelids. Rather than dyeing her eyebrows a lighter shade, she colored them black with a heavy hand, and the light green eyeshadow she wore every day tended to make her skin sallow. She wore what some had referred to as bridesmaid clothes everyday to work. The fabric was usually shiny or lacy and formal looking in a cheap sort of way. All of her skirts and dresses were hemmed above her fleshy knees. Her hands were pudgy, but she proudly sported a watch ring on one finger and an assortment of gold rings on the others. If she hadn't been so self-satisfied, others may have considered her tacky, and even if they did, she would not have noticed. Her style, or lack of it, suited her.

Earl handed Virginia her coffee then pushed the door shut behind him. "I'm listening."

"Let's see, I guess I'll start from when Hannah first arrived at the unit. She was teaching at the Pack Unit but requested a transfer here because of that hour drive back and forth to Navasota. Anyway, Ethel had been here for just a few months. She was the only female on her shift and obviously liked it that way. It was probably the only time in her life that she got any attention at all for simply being a female."

"Yeah, I know what you mean," Cowen said, wondering how even a convict, who had been locked up for years, could see anything appealing about Ethel Fletcher.

"Well, when Hannah Douglas walked in that morning in January, after the Christmas holidays, you could see Ethel's temperature rise. It was a teacher preparation day. You know how we always have one of those after an extended vacation. The students didn't come till the following day."

"Yes, I know, Virginia." *If only she would stick with the details.* "What happened?"

"Oddly enough, Hannah calmed Ethel down in a matter of minutes. She went up to her and said, 'I'm so glad there is another woman to work with. Being around men all of the time is tough sometimes, isn't it?' Ethel agreed with her. Then Hannah complimented Ethel's clothes. She had a genuine way about her that made others just feel better about themselves. And she did that for Ethel. She liked Hannah in spite of herself.

"You've seen Hannah at in-service. People can't help but notice her. She's gorgeous. That long black hair and those emerald green eyes, you know."

"Yes, I've met her," said Cowen. "So what was the problem if Ethel liked Ms. Douglas? I didn't know she had ever liked anybody."

"Her fondness for Hannah turned into love. Not a friendship love, but a sick, distorted, jealous love." Virginia animated her face and accented the story with her hands.

"You mean to tell me that Ethel is a lesbian?"

"I don't know what she is, Earl, besides crazy."

"How did you find out about her 'love' for Ms. Douglas?"

Virginia re-situated herself in her chair while enjoying Mr. Cowen's undivided attention. "Ethel would leave love letters in Hannah's mail slot right in there in the teacher's lounge," continued Virginia, pointing. "She even signed her name to them. I'm telling you, it beat all I had ever seen. Hannah showed them to me. I'm talking sick stuff."

"What did Ms. Douglas do with them?"

"Eventually she turned them over to the sheriff."

"You mean the law had to be called in?'

"Yes, sir, but that came later."

"Later than what?" He took a sip of his coffee, feeling the need for a shot of caffeine.

"Well, Hannah tried to be kind to Ethel and handle the situation carefully. You know, she has a master's degree in psychology."

"No, I didn't, but go on, please."

"When Hannah didn't respond to the love letters, Ethel started buying her gifts and leaving them in the bed of her truck. Expensive stuff, I mean. A set of stainless steel silverware, a leather purse she had commissioned an inmate to make, all kinds of wind chimes. Just a bunch of stuff. I can't remember what all."

"Did Ms. Douglas keep the stuff?"

"No. That's when the you know what hit the fan," Virginia stated brightly. "Hannah tried graciously to return the gifts to Ethel, but Ethel would throw a tantrum every time; right here at work, I mean. Finally Hannah asked Ms. Bolton, she was the principal then, if the three of them could have a conference in her office and hopefully put an end to it all. Ms. Bolton agreed to it."

"Did it help?"

"No, not really. The gifts stopped, but Ethel's love turned to hatred." Virginia added her own touch of theatrics by stopping ceremoniously and taking a sip of her coffee. "She started doing things to harass Hannah; things that were disturbing but not illegal, if you know what I mean."

"Like what?" Mr. Cowen was loosening his tie.

"Well, for instance, if Hannah wore a pair of white slacks, a yellow blouse and a navy blazer on Monday, Ethel would have on white slacks, a yellow blouse, and a navy blazer on Tuesday. Hannah could wear a blue skirt and blouse with a colorful belt on Tuesday, and Ethel would come to work Wednesday wearing a blue skirt and blouse and a colorful belt. I'm telling you this went on for weeks. We figured Ethel went shopping after work every night looking for clothes as close to Hannah's as she could get. Of course Hannah looked darling and Ethel looked downright pitiful. We all talked about it. Even the inmates talked about it. You know Inmate Jacobe? He told Ms. Douglas one day real loud that she should start giving Ms. Fletcher a list of the wardrobe she planned to wear for the week and save her the trouble of having to go out looking for what to wear every night after work."

Earl couldn't help but chuckle. "Did she hear him?"

"Oh, yes," Virginia sang. "It made her so mad that she took her skinny little arm and cleared off her desk with it. You've seen her do that. We've all seen her do that."

"What other things did she do to irritate Hannah?"

The phone rang in Earl's office.

"You want me to get that?" Virginia said as she got up to reach for it.

He shook his head and answered. It was the law library lieutenant.

"This is Cowen."

"Can I call you back on that? I'm in the middle of something."

"All right. Thanks. Bye."

Virginia smarted, "That was short and sweet."

"Go on with your story," he said.

"Everyone knew how conscientious Hannah was about her job. Very organized. Always prepared. Everything in its place. Well, low and behold if her class rosters and lesson plans and graded papers didn't start disappearing. One day Hannah opened up her filing cabinet to get her students' permanent records out, and I'm telling you that every student folder was empty. All of those records gone just like that." Virginia had snapped her finger to make the point.

"What was done about it?"

"There wasn't anything that could be done. No one had seen Ethel take the contents of those folders. Of course, everyone knew that she had done it. There was no question about that. And what's worse, Hannah had to redo all that paperwork. You can imagine how many hours that took. Of course I offered to help, but she wouldn't hear of it."

Cowen shook his head. "What a role model for the inmates," he scoffed.

"Wait, that's not all. When she realized Hannah wasn't getting in trouble for lost rosters and student folders, she started doing illegal things to badger her."

"Is this when the sheriff was called in?"

"No, and it wasn't Hannah who called the sheriff." She crossed her legs and tugged at her skirt. Cowen waited patiently for Virginia to relish her self-importance.

Finally, she continued. "One day Hannah went to get in her truck. I'm telling you it wasn't a year old, and someone, we could all guess who, had taken a key and scratched from here to yonder on both sides." She gestured to be dramatic. "Ruined the paint job."

Cowen folded one arm over the other. He regarded her for a moment. "I'm surprised the guard in the picket didn't see her do it. Those guard towers are at least forty feet high, I'd guess. It's their job to look for anything suspicious going on."

"Yes, sir, I know it is, but the afternoon teachers can't generally find a park in the parking lot. By the time they come to work, all the parks are filled. They have to park clear over to the bus station sometimes. The guard can't see over to there."

"Yeah, I guess you're right, but didn't the other teachers who came to work at that time, spot her?"

"Now Earl, you know Ethel never gets to work on time, and she leaves early more often than not."

"All that is in my report," he said.

"Anyway, a few days later Hannah walked to her truck, and one of her tires was slashed. Cut to pieces, I mean. A couple of days after that, another tire, then another, till she got around to all of them. It got to where Hannah's husband, William, started bringing her to work and picking her up.

"Ethel started following Hannah out everyday, walking right at her heels, real close to Hannah, just trying to upset her. It beat all."

"When did the sheriff's department get involved?" He had to admit that this was the most fascinating story he had heard in a long while.

"You're not going to believe this." Virginia took another opportunity to add some flare to her tale and adjusted her legs to a new position then straightened her skirt again. "Ethel called the sheriff's department and filed a complaint against Hannah." She raised her eyebrows then took another sip of coffee, allowing Cowen to absorb what she had just told him. "Said she had stolen clothes from her. Told the sheriff she had let Hannah borrow the clothes, and she refused to return them. Also, get this: all the gifts Ethel gave Hannah, the silverware, wind chimes and stuff, well, she reported that stuff stolen and had the receipts to prove she had bought them. She told the sheriff that she had seen the wind chimes hanging all around Hannah Douglas's house."

"You mean Ms. Douglas hung them out?" asked Earl, astonished.

"Heavens, no! Hannah had collected wind chimes for years. They weren't the ones Ethel had given her."

"I see," said Earl. "Did the sheriff believe her? Ethel I mean?"

"No, sir, thank goodness, but it nearly scared Hannah to death when her husband called up here at work and told her a complaint had been filed against her and that she needed to come down to the office. She honestly couldn't believe it."

"I can't believe it either. That woman is a lot sicker than I thought," Earl said while rubbing his forehead.

"To make a long story short, the sheriff wanted to talk to Hannah in person. Since William's a deputy and all, Hannah wasn't likely to get into any trouble with the law, but it embarrassed her to no end, being complained on. Earl," Virginia leaned forward, "they found out that Ethel had been accused of vandalizing a car when she was in college. Other crazy stuff, too."

"Did anyone file charges on Fletcher?"

"No, sir. They had no proof or witnesses to verify that Ethel had vandalized those vehicles either time. It's just that everybody involved was certain that she was guilty."

"How on earth did Ethel Fletcher get a job teaching for the prison system? A person is checked out thoroughly before they are even considered for a job."

Virginia looked at her boss very seriously. "You are really not going to believe this." Not able to contain this bit of news a second longer, she blurted out, "Ethel used to live with Elaine and Jack Tyler."

"What?"

"You heard right," Virginia said coolly.

"God help us."

Chapter 7

Hannah's students could tell she was on edge even though she didn't act any different than she normally did. One of the things the inmates liked about her was that she was steady. They knew what to expect from her everyday; she didn't throw them curves – always fair, even tempered, courteous, and strict about the rules. The convicts knew that if one of them got out of line, she would write a disciplinary case on them. She did not waver, and they could respect that when so many other things in their enclosed, institutionalized lives were chaotic.

Long-time inmates developed a heightened sense of awareness. It kept them alive. Hannah's students could not physically see a difference in her, but they could feel it. On the inside she was tense, nervous, and ready to cry, but on the outside, she was as cool as an autumn breeze and was taking care of business.

"Hey, Ms. Douglas, what's up?" Inmate Skylark asked.

Hannah looked up. "Nothing. Everything is fine."

"Hey now. You know we ain't gonna buy no story. Somethin' goin' down," Skylark said, more concerned than curious.

"You know we aren't going to buy a story," she corrected. "I've taught you better grammar than that, haven't I?" She threw him a look that said she was teasing and serious at the same time. It was a talent she had that kept her students prone to respect her authority and view it as if it were their idea.

"Okay, okay. I get the picture. You're just goin' to ignore my question," he said.

The rest of the class sat quietly and waited for her to tell them what was wrong. They weren't going to let the issue drop.

Hannah looked at her class, all dressed in white, and decided to give them an answer. "I was harassed a little bit on the way to work this morning. Some other car sort of tailgated me and kept their bright lights on all the way out here."

"Well, hell, why didn't you get their plates and turn 'em in?" Inmate Jernigan asked.

"I tried, but the plates were covered in mud."

"You idiot, you know she's gonna try to get the man's number. She ain't stupid, you know," voiced another student.

"Did you see where they parked?" Inmate Moss asked.

"They didn't park. They left. I say they, but I really don't know how many people were in the van. The brights were on, and I think maybe the windows were tinted. Anyway, it was no big deal. Whoever it was is gone, and I'm safe inside this maximum security prison surrounded by convicted felons. I couldn't be any safer." Hannah grinned.

The students chuckled at their teacher's sense of humor. They knew she wasn't putting them down.

"Who's ready to read?" she asked.

Craft raised his hand.

"Thank you, Mr. Craft. Bring your book and come up to my desk. The rest of you work in your folders. And stop looking at me like that. I'm fine. Really!"

Craft sauntered up to her desk. His black bald head was a bit larger on the right side and it had a row of pronounced wrinkles on the back and center. His smile was crooked and revealed a row of rotten teeth. One eye was a bit cocked, and he had a speech impediment.

"We're on story nine," he said. She had learned to understand him.

Hannah followed each word with her pencil as Inmate Craft read orally to her. He stumbled, but she patiently helped him sound out the words that gave him trouble.

One at a time she listened to her beginning readers read. Others would come up for help with math or language. They each had an individualized lesson plan with assignments to work on at their level. Hannah Douglas was extremely organized in her classroom. Her students excelled. They gained self-confidence, and they learned respect; not only for themselves, but for her.

At 7:00 a.m. Officer Parrish came in to count. Count time was always between 7:00 and 7:30. They counted again at half past twelve noon, 7:00 p.m. and then at 10:30 p.m. It took approximately one hour to clear count. The totals were tallied and every convict on the unit was accounted for. If the count did not clear after two hours, the entire unit was racked up. Every convict was locked down in his cell and a recount done. If the count did not clear the second time a horn sounded which meant they had a runner; someone had escaped. Certain officers were assigned to go on the hunt. They used horses, dogs, even helicopters if necessary. County and city police officers, along with state troopers, were notified, and those officials set up road blocks, searches, or whatever they deemed necessary to capture the runner.

A convict escaping from a prison unit was not all that uncommon. In the Huntsville area there were eight penitentiaries and one state jail facility. There was also the county jail. The citizens of Walker County would hear the news of an escape on the radio or television or at one of the businesses in town, and not give it more than a minute's thought.

Convicts, dressed in white, were all over town. They had farms to work, livestock to tend, guard housing to maintain, and the prison facility itself to keep up. Trustees were in plain sight everyday in Huntsville, Texas.

At The Walls Unit, where inmates were released on parole and into the free-world, the new ex-offenders wore new prison-made pants and shirts. They were as easy for a Huntsvillite to spot as the inmates were, and even if the newly released were not dressed in such conspicuous attire, their behavior, their walk, and their grinning faces gave them away.

At 7:58 a.m. count cleared on February eleventh. Hannah's first class was dismissed at 8:20 and her second class began filing in at 8:30. The day was going by quickly with hardly a minute to catch her breath, much less think about the dark van that had followed her to work. Hannah's second class did not notice that their teacher had been upset earlier. She was quite normal by the time they saw her.

CB&O

8:30 a.m. William had been assigned the southern district to work for the day. He was in his car headed towards New Waverly when Julie, in dispatch, radioed him to come back to the office. The sheriff wanted to talk to him.

At 8:45 William was waiting outside the sheriff's private office. Sheriff Weldon Applegate came out to greet him a few minutes later.

"Come on in, William. Coffee?" the sheriff asked while pouring himself a cup.

"Sure. Thanks. Just black."

Applegate handed William a cup and sat down. He leaned back in his chair.

"What's up, Sheriff?"

"William, I know you like being a deputy, patrolling, handling calls, the 911 emergencies, and you do one hell of a job."

"Thank you, sir."

"The fact is, I need another full-time detective. I know you've never applied for that position, and I assume it's because you haven't wanted it, but the fact of the matter is, I need you. The detectives I've got are doing all they can do and more. We'll never be able to pay them back all the overtime they've put in. I need another man."

Applegate looked at William. The disappearances of the young women in his county had taken their toll on him.

"Sheriff, I'll work in any capacity you tell me to. I don't have a problem with that, but why me? Aren't there some guys and a couple of the women who have put in for detective?"

"Yes, several have."

William still looked puzzled.

"William, you're older than the others. You have a wife and a child, and that gives a person a different perspective on situations when they are dealing with people. And last, but not least, you were a Marine. I think you know that I was in the Corps myself."

"Yes, sir. I knew that."

"That pulls a lot of weight with me. I know what you're made of."

"I'll do the best I can. Will someone be able to show me the ropes?"

"Jeff Stone. He's a good man."

"Yes, sir. I know he is."

"Good. That's what I needed to hear."

"When do I start?"

"Hell, man. Right now. Jeff's waiting for you in his office. You'll be sharing that office with him. It'll be a bit cramped in there, but knowing the two of you, I don't think that will cause a problem."

William had to ask one more question. "Sir, does this mean I have to give up my take- home car?"

"Hell no. You earned that car. I'd give you an unmarked one if I had a spare, but I don't." His green eyes had softened somewhat. He offered his right hand. William shook it, smiled, and headed out of the office.

The sheriff spoke up one more time. "Detective?"

William turned around.

"Thanks."

"Sure thing," William said. Detective. That wouldn't be hard to get accustomed to.

Jeff Stone was on the phone when William knocked on his office door. He motioned for William to come in and sit down.

Stone was a couple of years older than William. He reminded William of his brother, Randy. He had sandy colored hair, a gentle and kind face, and blue eyes. His voice was steady with an East Texas drawl. William thought a lot of him. Jeff wasn't married and never had been. William didn't know why. He did know that Jeff dated fairly often, but never the same girl for long.

Jeff hung up the phone. "William, how's it going?" He stood up to shake William's hand – always the gentleman.

"Heck, if I'd known I was going to be a lowly detective today, I wouldn't have gotten so dressed up," said William.

Jeff laughed. "Yep, after today you can hang up those dapper green trousers and khaki shirt and dress like a real man."

Both men chuckled.

"Seriously, pal, I'm glad you're on board. We need the help. If we don't get a break soon in these disappearances, I'm afraid we're all going to be run out of town, if not the state."

"What have you got so far?"

"We've got zip. Of course, you know the profile: young, beautiful, waist length hair. Speaking of such, how is your gorgeous wife?"

"Hannah's great." All of a sudden, William looked like he had been drenched with a bucket of ice water.

"Oh, man. What did I say?"

William leaned forward in his chair propping his elbows on his legs and supported his face in his hands. "It's just that until now, I never really thought about how much Hannah fit the profile."

"Hey, now. Come on. I didn't mean to . . . Look, every one of those girls were students at Sam. They were between eighteen and twenty-three years of age. Hannah doesn't fit the profile." Jeff rubbed his face and slicked back his hair. "I mean she's beautiful, and she has long hair, but that's all she has in common with the victims."

William sat up straight again and tried to shake it off. "Yeah, you're right. It just startled me for a minute. I couldn't stand it if something happened to her."

"You're a lucky man. Everybody talks about it."

"I know I am. I still can't believe she married me. I can't believe she ever went out with me. I never dreamed somebody as pretty and smart as she is would go out with me, much less marry me. It's not like I had money or anything, and she treats me like I'm the greatest thing since sliced bread."

Sergeant Perry peered in the door. "Congratulations, William, I think."

William stood up to shake yet another hand. "Thank you. This all happened kind of suddenly."

"You'll do fine."

"I hope so."

Perry left.

Jeff got up and closed the door. "I need to fill you in on what we're doing and how you and I will be working together."

"I'm ready."

Chapter 8

It was one o'clock in the afternoon of February eleventh. Twila's phone rang.

No answer.

"What's the matter, dear?" Martha Brooks noticed a look of concern on her husband's face.

"Nothing. I was just calling Twila to see if we could bring her anything."

"Edward, it's your birthday. Not Twila's."

Edward Brooks missed his daughter desperately since she had moved to Huntsville. Livingston was only forty-five miles away, but Twila was working and going to school, so she rarely had the time to even spend a weekend at home. She was grown and needed to be on her own, but to him, she would always be his little girl.

"We're going to see her in an hour. I'll swear, you act more like a kid everyday." She shook her head and swallowed a chuckle.

"You're right. Are you ready?"

"Edward, fifteen more minutes." She could hardly appear domineering with that face. Her creamy complexion and bright blue eyes put a soft edge even on her worst anger fits, and her vibrant blond hair was like a halo in the sunshine. She was the envy of almost every middle-aged woman in town, and like Twila, she knew it and was proud of it.

Edward, the president of the Citizens State Bank of Livingston, was good-looking as well. His aqua-colored eyes defined him, and when he saw that his baby-girl's were just like them, he was more than a little proud. With his salary, along with some smart investments, Martha was able to stay at home for most of their marriage and tend to the house and, of course, Twila. She had been their pride and joy since the day she was born. Being an only child, she had been spoiled with material things and with lots of attention. Even so, she had been an easy child to raise and love, rarely causing problems for her parents.

At 1:10 p.m., they left the house. It had turned out to be a lovely afternoon. The temperature had warmed up to sixty-seven degrees, the rain had cleared out and the sky was clear and azure blue. The Brooks were planning to visit with Twila at her house for a little while, then drive to Houston and eat at The Olive Garden. Afterwards, they would go to a mall and shop for Twila some new clothes, even though it was Edward's birthday.

Edward knew Twila would have a chocolate birthday cake for him when they arrived. She hadn't missed baking him a birthday cake since she was ten years old. Oh, how he loved his baby.

The trip was uneventful. Martha looked out the window at the thick pine forests that flanked each side of Highway 190. She had grown up in Lubbock, Texas, where trees were few and far between. Still, after twenty-two years, the thickets in East Texas made her feel claustrophobic. Even in the dead of winter, the towering pines and dense underbrush remained green. Some of the trees, a lot of them actually, were bare for a while, but not enough of them that you could see past the bend in the road.

Highway 190 ran into Eleventh Street, and just up ahead was The Walls. Martha Brooks locked her car door. Edward looked over at her.

"Well, I don't want one of those convicts to drag me out of this car." She held her hand out in front of her husband to shield any remarks he might make. "And I know when we reach the traffic light that's right in front of the prison, it will be red. It's always red. Besides, I think it's one of those trustees who's dragging those girls off the campus. It's just right down the street. Who's idea was it to build a college right down the road from a state penitentiary anyway?" she rattled.

"I don't know, dear." He kept his eyes on the road.

"Lord, I'm so glad we rented that little house for Twila. If I had my way, she would have left Huntsville and gone to school in Nacogdoches when all this kidnapping started."

"Martha, Twila has never been one to run from trouble, and you know it. You're just getting yourself all worked up for nothing." He was saying that to appease his own anxiety as well as his wife's.

The light adjacent to The Walls was indeed red. She looked at her husband and raised her eyebrows. He acknowledged that her premonition had merit. Without hesitation, they both looked over at the old penitentiary. It had stood in that spot since 1849; the old clock tower, the steel bars, the red brick, the brass handrails that flanked the steps, all played equal measure in giving Texas's first permanent penitentiary its somber, yet curious, appeal.

After two more blocks, they reached the town square and the courthouse. The original courthouse, erected in 1888, was destroyed by fire on Christmas Eve night in 1968. Many of Huntsville's fine and grand old buildings had fallen victim to fire over the years, and with the flames and smoke went much of the historical town's splendor.

Surrounding Huntsville's modern and stark courthouse were buildings built from the 1860's to the 1930's, and were sites for many antique shops. Their architectural styles were varied, but to make the storefronts appear more quaint, the buildings had been painted to give the illusion of carved stone. The square could have easily been mistaken for an olden-days movie set.

Martha and Edward turned left on Sam Houston Avenue and hit every red light on the street.

Finally, they reached Fox Glen and turned right. Twila's house was the sixth house on the right, and they could see her red Mustang in the driveway. It was two o'clock on the dot, and they were there.

With the cloudless blue sky and sweater-perfect temperature, Huntsville looked and felt every bit the charming, picturesque town it had so often claimed to be.

Chapter 9

Magnolia Drive was the address for a row of old but unique houses that captured their personalities fifty years ago and refused to fade away. They were well kept, well manicured, and charming. Stella Perkin's little house boasted seven gables even though it was less than seventeen hundred square feet. Hunter green shutters, with a large white wooden heart in the center of each one, framed the paned windows. Fancy, New Orleans-style wrought iron supported the open end of the roof that covered the small front porch. Behind the white wooden fence that surrounded the narrow back yard, was a tiny one-car garage.

Stella was cute with short brown hair and brown eyes. She had learned how to apply her make-up well, highlighting her hazelnut colored eyes with eyeliner and eyeshadow, and fringed them with several coats of mascara. She wore blush to highlight her cheekbones and to give her some color, and she always wore red lipstick.

She stopped by Walmart and picked up a box of donuts on her way to Huntsville Memorial Hospital. The doctors and nurses at the hospital thought she was the best they had seen at dealing with frightened patients and their families or friends. Stella loved her job and it showed.

It had been a slow night; no shootings or stabbings, one minor traffic accident, but nothing serious.

"Good morning," Stella said with a smile.

Dr. Zachary Tobin poked his head out from behind a blue curtain that sectioned off a treatment room. "Mornin', sweetheart," he said. He was fifty-eight and completely gray-headed. His eyes were such a vivid blue that they almost stung you when they looked at you. He had a beard that was a touch darker than the thick mane on his head. His smile was warm and almost as healing as his hands. "What ya got there?"

"My breakfast," she said selfishly.

"You mean to tell me that you are going to eat a dozen donuts all by yourself?"

"Maybe." Stella looked at him through narrowed eyes then said, "It sounds to me as if you just might need something sweet to offset your sour disposition." She offered him the box.

"Don't mind if I do," he said while taking two of the pastries. Patting her shoulder, he said, "You're my girl."

Dr. Tobin worried about Stella. He watched her as she offered her donuts to Sarah, Eddie, and Reba. She was so sweet, so eager to please and be liked, but she wouldn't let anyone get close. She surrounded herself with an imaginary shield, not letting anyone touch her emotionally, yet when anyone else needed comforting or a shoulder to cry on, she was eager to lend herself to them. She could console others with a loving heart, but she could not accept compassion for herself. Someone must have broken her heart in a big way.

The doors flew open, jolting the doctor out of his reverie. Paramedics were pushing a gurney carrying a wounded man.

"He fell asleep at the wheel, as far as we can tell, doc," offered the paramedic.

Donuts were put aside. It was time to go to work.

Chapter 10

William had finished reading the files on all the kidnappings that had occurred in Huntsville over the past year. It sickened him. The description of each woman was so complete that he felt as if he had met her before, even talked with her. There were photographs of each victim as well. Each one of them had very long hair, as long as Hannah's. That had to be, of course, a major requisite for the predator that was taking them. Either this bastard loved long hair, or he hated it. The color of it varied and apparently was not important in his motive. They were all young, eighteen to twenty-three and enrolled in the university. Their backgrounds were not uncommon, but there was nothing common about them either as far as he could tell. It was an angle they should look into. Perhaps they had missed something there.

Detective Jeff Stone came back into the office. "Finished?"

"Yeah. I'm finished. Where do we start?"

"I want to go talk to a guy who was a friend of Mary Brown's. She was the girl that vanished on December the third." Stone had his hands clasped behind his head. He eyed William thoughtfully. "I've been trying to track down all her friends. I want to interview everyone that knew her. We might get lucky."

"Let's go," William said as he stood up and grabbed his hat.

They walked out to the parking lot. William looked over at Jeff almost sheepishly and said, "Let's take my car."

"Sure. You just got it, didn't you?"

"Yes, and I want to drive it."

Stone grinned. He liked William because he was the type of man that would stick his neck out for you – loyal and unselfish. He wasn't afraid to tell people what his opinion was, and not too close-minded to consider someone else's. Smart, honest, and he valued his friendships; nurtured them with care and consideration, but his family was his lifeline and came above and before anything else.

Stone knew that William was totally and completely devoted to his wife – that he adored her and wanted everyone to know it. It was obvious that he not only loved her, but he respected her, and when they were together, they enjoyed each other's company. They didn't put each other down or joke around about who didn't do what. When they spoke about each other, it was complimentary and sincere. It was a beautiful relationship.

Stone had almost gotten married himself sixteen years ago. They made it to the altar, she looking like a princess in a fairy tale dress, but when it came to the time for her to say, "I do," she said, "I can't do this," and ran back down the aisle and out the door of the church. She walked down the same aisle a year and a half later with his own brother.

Losing Debra broke Stone's heart. Losing Debra in front of all his family and friends crumbled his pride, but losing Debra to his brother shattered his soul. He privately compared himself to Humpty-Dumpty, truly believing no one could put all the pieces of his heart back together again.

Instead of wallowing in self-pity, he submerged himself in his work, giving himself to the Walker County Sheriff's Department. Obsessive about his cases, he went to work early and never quit at quitting time, putting in at least fourteen hours a day, and when he wasn't at work, he was mulling over them in his mind. He studied criminal behavior by reading every criminology book he could get his hands on. Huntsville had a good supply, too, since Sam Houston State University was considered one of the leading schools in the country for the study of criminal justice.

Stone had gotten his undergraduate and graduate degrees in criminal justice at Sam years ago. He planned to begin work on his doctorate as soon as the kidnapping cases were resolved, but for now, he had no time for anything else. The kidnappings were utmost on his mind, and he would not be able to rest or concentrate on anything else until he found out what had happened to five young women in his county and stop the freak who had taken them. He had to stop him.

Stone had resigned himself to the fact that love and marriage weren't in the cards for him, and he had learned well how to fill his time. Being happy was no longer his ambition – staying busy and being useful were the two reasons he woke up every morning.

William Douglas knew that Jeff Stone was a workaholic. He was aware, as was everyone in the department, that Jeff gave one hundred and ten percent of his life to the job, and William was more than a little concerned that he might expect as much of him. While William loved his job, it was not his main focus in life. His main focus was Hannah and Reed. Jeff would have to come to terms with that, and William was not going to be hesitant in letting him or the sheriff know it.

"This character, Mark Casey, works at Pizza Hut. He should be there now," Stone said as they were driving out of the parking lot. William headed downtown.

Stone scooted the passenger seat back to allow for his long legs. "You know, it's after one o'clock. We might as well eat while we're there. That way we can visit with Casey, and it won't seem so official. He's liable to open up more."

"Sounds good to me. You won't hear me complain about eating," William said. He looked both ways before crossing the intersection of Normal Park and Eleventh Street. Pizza Hut was straight ahead.

"From what I hear, you don't complain about anything." Jeff was adjusting his shoulder holster beneath his jacket.

"I don't know where you heard that. I can hold my own with folks."

"Oh," Jeff chuckled, "I know that. I just mean that you have a reputation for being easy to get along with." He raised his eyebrows and added, "As long as nobody makes any wisecracks or wife jokes around you."

"A man has to set his boundaries." William said, having no intentions of denying it.

William parked the car in front of the pizza parlor. He was already wishing he was in plain clothes.

The two detectives ordered the buffet, then Stone asked the waitress, a pretty brunette, if Mark Casey could give them a holler when he got a minute. Stone acted like they were old acquaintances, fending off any unwarranted notions that Casey was in trouble. The young waitress was pleased to relay the message, thinking she wouldn't mind knowing a cop herself, especially with the recent kidnappings.

They were eating when a twenty-year-old man came to their table. He had soft curly brown hair that showed no signs of ever having been tamed. His bright blue eyes introduced his personality – not the least bit hesitant in visiting with the officers. He assumed they had come to question him about Mary.

"Mark Casey," he said, offering a handshake, first to William, then to Detective Stone. "Are ya'll here about Mary?"

Stone answered, "Yes, that's right. We understand that the two of you were friends."

"Hard to believe, huh!"

"Why's that?" Stone asked before taking a huge bite of hot pepperoni pizza.

"Well, you know, she being so pretty and all. And me. I'm no Mr. Universe." He studied the detective as he took a long drink of Dr. Pepper.

"So, the two of you were involved?" William was watching him work. He knew Jeff was good at what he did.

Casey looked back and forth between the officers. "Oh, gosh no. We were just platonic friends. Heck, that was enough for me. I was just proud she liked me. Hell, I knew better than to dream someone like Mary could fall for me in a romantic way. You know."

Stone swallowed. "Why's that?"

"Well, like I said, she was so beautiful, and I'm not the kind of guy that attracts beautiful women."

"Why's that?"

Casey looked dumbfounded. "Take a good look, detective. I'm a jelly roll with fuzz on top. What do you want me to say?" He didn't get angry, just frustrated.

"Nothing. I'm sorry. It's just that I thought I was the only guy in the world who couldn't get a girl."

William watched and listened as Jeff continued to work this guy.

Casey cooled down immediately. He was beginning to like Detective Stone.

"What was she like?" Stone asked, continuing to eat while William motioned to their waitress for a refill of Coke.

Casey's eyes moistened, "She was as sweet as she could be."

"Was?"

"What I meant was, well . . . good grief, I haven't seen her in a couple of months. I didn't mean to sound like she was dead or anything. Is she dead?"

"We don't know."

Casey rubbed his face.

"When was the last time you saw Mary?"

"I saw her at the University Student Center."

"What was she doing?"

"She was coming out of the book store, and she saw me. I was about to go into the barber shop to get a trim."

"Did you talk with her?"

"Yeah."

"So? What did the two of you talk about?"

"I don't know." Casey searched his memory. "A research paper coming due. Finals. Going to the library. She didn't like going by herself, so I usually went with her. It's where we met."

"Then what?"

"I told her I had an appointment to get my hair cut and needed to go."

"And?" Stone asked.

"And, I went in the barber shop."

"Did you see her after that?"

Mark looked pensive. "Come to think of it, I did see her talking to that crazy girl. I saw their reflections in the mirror."

"What was the crazy girl's name?"

"Ethel . . . Ethel something." Casey shook his head.

"Was she a friend of Mary's?" asked Stone.

"Ethel? Hell, no. No one is a friend of Ethel's. She's as weird as they come. Ugly, too."

"How do you mean, ugly – looks or by the way she acts?"

"Both." Casey looked over at William as if for approval.

"Were they having cross words, or could you tell?"

"Best I could tell, Mary was a little agitated. Ethel was talking loud and making angry faces."

"Have you reported this to anyone before now?"

"No."

"Why not?"

"Because it was nothing out of the ordinary. Ethel's always like that. Everybody knows it."

"You don't know what she was mad at Mary about?"

"Nothing and everything. Ethel's just a mad person."

"So, how is Ethel classified? Do you know?"

"I don't think she takes classes. She's a teacher at one of the prisons. She's at the library a lot and goes in the bookstore, eats at The Grill, uses the pool. You know, an alumnus, maybe. Pays some kind of fee for student benefits."

Stone continued, "Do you know which prison unit Ethel works on?"

"No."

"What does Ethel look like?"

"Well, let's see. She's kind of tall; not real tall. About five feet seven. She's skinny as a hoe handle. She looks like she's got one of those eating disorders."

Stone broke in, "Bulimia, anorexia?"

"Yeah. One of those."

"What else?"

"Well, she's got red frizzy hair about shoulder length."

"Curly, like yours?"

"It's not curly like mine. It's frizzy. Like she stuck her finger in a light bulb socket."

"What about her complexion, color of eyes?"

"She's got a fair complexion, I guess. Shoot, I don't know. She has freckles on her face or something - maybe zit scars, but her eyes are the worst part about her."

Stone was surprised. "How so?"

"They are almost clear. I guess you could call them blue, but they are a real light blue. Like I said, almost colorless. She looks like some kind of witch-devil to me." Mark looked over at William again as if he needed his approval of the description he had just given. Often-times the uniform seemed to dictate that feeling in others.

Stone turned to William as well and said, "I don't know about you, but I want to get a look at this girl."

William nodded his head. He looked as though he wanted to say something but suddenly changed his mind.

Stone looked back at Casey. "You've been a big help. We appreciate it," he said, standing up to leave and offering him his hand.

"Hey, no problem. You come by anytime. I want to help any way I can. Mary's a real nice and decent person. Whoever is taking those girls has to be stopped." He looked convincingly sad.

There was some annoying laughter at a table in the back, and it got under William's skin. It seemed inappropriate somehow, having been witness to the conversation just now. Those people didn't know that they were discussing a missing girl or that Ethel Fletcher's name had been brought up. They were just having a good time, eating pizza. They didn't know that Mary Brown was gone, and perhaps they wouldn't even care. William picked up the check from the table.

"Here. Let me take that. The manager likes for cops to come in here. It's on the house."

"Thank him for us," William said.

Mark Casey nodded and the two detectives left Pizza Hut.

William said to Stone, "I know I've only been a detective for a few hours, but I'd say we may have gotten a good lead."

"I'd say you're right. Damn it, all this time I really thought the kidnapper was a man. Women just don't do that. They don't go out and kidnap other women again and again and again. I never even considered a woman. What if it is? What if it is a woman, and all this time I was too stupid to even consider that possibility?" He stood at the door of the squad car as though he didn't have the strength to open it.

"Jeff, it may not be a woman. Ethel may have nothing to do with anything." At least he hoped to God she didn't.

Jeff looked William square in the eyes. "She does," he said emphatically. "I can feel it."

Chapter 11

Edward and Martha Brooks waited on the front porch for Twila to answer the door. Edward knocked again.

No answer.

He called out, "Twila, it's me, Daddy. Baby?"

Still nothing.

"Wait a minute. I've got a key," Martha said. "She's probably drying her hair and can't hear us." Martha fished out the key from her purse and unlocked her daughter's front door.

"Twila, honey? It's Mom and Dad. Are you dressed?"

The house was silent and still.

Martha looked at her husband. "She must be in the back yard. I'll bet you anything she went and got that little puppy she's been wanting."

Edward followed his wife through the small house to the back door. They opened it and peered out.

"Twila?" Edward said as he checked the back yard.

"She's not here," Edward said to his wife candidly.

"She has to be here. Her car is outside," Martha said. She searched Twila's bedroom.

"Maybe she's next door. You check with the people on the left, and I'll check the house on the right."

After both had questioned the neighbors, they met on Twila's porch. No one had seen Twila all day.

They went back in the house and stood in the middle of the living room.

Martha could feel the prickly heat of fear climb her body like a burning flame consuming a bush. It grew hotter and more severe as it climbed higher, until it reached her head, and then her insides began to melt. She knew that Twila was in trouble. She knew it as sure as she was standing there. Her daughter had vanished like the other girls. She was gone.

The low animal scream that came from Martha startled Edward. He had been deep in thought, wondering what to do next. Then the wave of panic from his wife rolled over him. He felt her fear. He saw what she was seeing. Twila had been kidnapped.

Edward Brooks covered his face with his hands and cried out, "Oh, God! Oh, God!"

☙❧

On the way back to the sheriff's department, William looked over at Jeff. "I know where Ethel teaches."

Stone turned toward his new partner. "You know her?"

"Yes. Her last name is Fletcher. Everything Casey just said about her is true. She's crazy as all get out."

"Why didn't you say something?"

"I didn't want to interfere in your interrogation. I haven't been at this a whole day yet. I didn't know if you'd want me to butt in or not."

"Okay. So spill what you know."

"She teaches at The Walls, and Hannah used to work with her. She nearly drove Hannah berserk."

"How? What did she do?"

"She harassed Hannah so bad that she asked for a transfer. I had to take my wife to work and pick her up because of that crazy witch. We couldn't prove it, but I know that she slashed all four of the tires we had on a new truck. Did each one on a different day. She also put a key scratch all down the side of it."

"Good God, man, why didn't you try to do something through the department?"

"Oh, the sheriff knew about it. Ethel Fletcher had the nerve to call him and accuse Hannah of stealing from her."

"You're joking." Jeff's mouth went dry.

"I'm as serious as a heart attack. Hannah wanted it kept quiet. She was afraid that I would be embarrassed if it got out that she'd been accused of stealing. She was afraid that there would be a couple of people in the office that might believe it."

"So what happened?" Like always, Stone was impatient to hear the whole story faster than what it could be told.

"Sheriff Applegate never said a word to anybody about it. He ran a criminal history on Fletcher and found out she had been into some similar mischief when she was in college, harassing other women, and then accusing them of harassing her."

"What did he do about it?"

"He asked her to come up to the office and visit with him. When she did, I was there, too. He told her point blank that when she messed with Hannah Douglas, she was messing with one of his deputies, and when she messed with one of his deputies, she was messing with him. Then he told her that if she didn't put a stop to it, he'd have every deputy in the county following her every move. He said to her, 'Believe me, Miss Fletcher, I can make your life hell.'"

Jeff couldn't believe he hadn't known anything about this. "What did she say?"

"She just stared at him with those crazy eyes of hers and asked him if he was threatening her. He told her that's exactly what he was doing. Then he stood up and very plainly said, 'Now, get the hell out of my office.'"

"So did she stop bothering your wife?"

"Yes, but a week after that, Hannah was transferred to the Estelle Unit. She had requested the transfer when all the mess started, but I think the sheriff had a hand in getting her out of there so quick after he talked to Fletcher. He has friends in high places."

"William, be honest with me now. Do you think Ethel Fletcher is the kidnapper?"

"I think it wouldn't surprise me."

"Let's go to the office and find out what we can about her, then we'll . . .," the radio interrupted him.

"S.O. 826."

"826. Go ahead."

This is S.O., 826. Be advised. Check by Thirteen Twenty-six, Fox Glen. Reference, welfare concern. Will advise further when 10-60."

"826. 10-4."

The detectives were told that the complainants' last names were Brooks.

Martha and Edward Brooks were waiting inside Twila's house when William and Jeff got there. The front door was open. They were pale, holding onto one another to keep from literally falling to pieces. Together, they stood up when the detectives came in. Martha grabbed William's arms and shook him as one might have done a child who had disobeyed. Her eyes were filled with tears and her face was twisted in anguish.

"My daughter has been kidnapped. You've got to find her. Do you hear me?" Martha screamed.

William was very gentle with the woman who had latched onto him. "Now you've got to calm down a little bit. Try to pull yourself together and maybe we can figure this out."

Martha let go of William's arms and put her head on his chest. William hugged her, trying to offer whatever comfort one could to a grieving, heartsick mother.

After Martha cried for a moment, they were able to talk.

Jeff Stone asked Edward Brooks to tell him why they thought their daughter had been kidnapped.

Edward told the detectives that Twila had invited them over for his birthday, that she had always made a big deal about his birthday, and they were to meet her here at two o'clock. Her car was in the driveway, but Twila was nowhere to be found, and none of the neighbors had seen her since the day before.

"Have you called any of her friends? A boyfriend perhaps?"

"Twila doesn't have a boyfriend right now. She would have told us if she did. We haven't called anybody," Martha said.

"Well, now. I think that's a good place to start," William said.

"It's no use," Martha said emphatically.

"Why do you say that?" William asked, his voice rich with sincerity and concern.

Martha asked Edward for his wallet. She turned to the most recent photograph that he had of his daughter, and she showed it to the two officers.

They took one look at the photograph and could see why these parents were terrified. Twila Brooks fit the profile. Picture perfect.

Chapter 12

Supper was already on the table when William Douglas got home. Hannah and Reed were about to eat without him.

Hannah got up from the table to kiss him. "We thought you might be really late so we were about to go ahead and eat." It was 6:15 p.m.

Reed gave his dad a hug, and they all sat down at the table.

"You look tired," Hannah said.

"I am tired. I got a new job today," he said nonchalantly.

"What?" Reed and Hannah asked together. They both looked at him in disbelief.

"I am now to be referred to as Detective Douglas. I think it has a nice ring to it, if I say so myself." He was smiling in spite of himself.

"You've been promoted?" Hannah asked excitedly.

"Well, if you can call it that. I'll be working on unsolved cases rather than patrolling." He took a bite of his salmon patty. It was golden brown and crispy, just the way he liked them. He was astonished that Hannah had actually fried something, and he planned to enjoy it to the fullest.

"Dad, do you get to keep the car?" Reed's face showed some concern.

William laughed. "That was my question, too. The sheriff said I could keep it until they can give me an unmarked car."

"That means it won't have lights on top?"

"Yes, but it will have lights in the grill."

"Oh," Reed said with a touch of disappointment in his voice.

Hannah got up to get the water pitcher. "This means you won't be wearing uniforms anymore, doesn't it?"

"That's right. I'll have to keep them though, for special occasions, or in case I work an extra security job."

Hannah put the pitcher down after refilling everyone's glass and grasped William's hand. "Congratulations, sweetheart. Are you happy about this?"

"It looks like I'll have to be."

"When do you start, Dad?"

"I started first thing this morning. The sheriff called me in and told me to go to work with Jeff Stone."

"Have you solved any cases yet?" Reed asked around a mouthful of mashed potatoes.

"No, not yet, but it sure was a busy day. It's going to take some getting used to."

After dinner, Reed went to his room to practice his fiddle. Hannah began clearing away the dishes while William got out of his gear and uniform. He definitely would not miss the uniform.

His mind kept revisiting the little house on Fox Glen. He couldn't get Martha and Edward Brooks out of his mind. They had been so devastated over their daughter's disappearance, and it made him sick to see people so distraught and helpless, but what worried him more than the encounter with Martha and Edward Brooks was Ethel Fletcher's name being brought up and into his life again. At least this time it didn't involve Hannah. It was another case. He wouldn't have to worry about Ethel on a personal level. He wouldn't let his job affect his personal life and his family.

William and Jeff hadn't been able to reach Ethel. She hadn't gone to work that day, but this gave them some time to prepare in their minds exactly what they wanted to ask her and how they wanted to handle her. She would need to be handled with caution, as William knew only too well.

Hannah came into the bedroom, and as usual, broke his train of thought.

"I brought you a glass of wine."

"Hey, thanks! I can sure use this."

"Rough first day?"

"A little."

William was going to tell her about the sixth suspected kidnap victim and about Ethel Fletcher, but the phone rang before he could. It was Hannah's daddy, Henry. He called every Wednesday night at seven o'clock while Meredith, Hannah's mother, was at prayer meeting. That way he could visit with his daughter all by himself. Henry and Hannah acted like they were getting away with something, but Meredith knew all about it. She had known it for years but had no intentions of spoiling their little secret.

"Daddy, William was made a detective today," William heard Hannah say. Her father was apparently happy about it. She continued to brag about him. Henry must have asked about how her week was going and, as always, she told him everything was fine. She knew he worried about her at the prison, so never even hinted that she ever had a lousy day.

William went back in the den and left his wife to visit with her father.

Hannah had to wash and dry her hair, and it was already seven-thirty. William was helping Reed with his homework.

By eight-thirty Hannah was finished and finally able to snuggle down with William on the couch. She wanted to hear everything about his first day as detective.

A fire was crackling in the fireplace. Hannah walked over to the couch and cuddled up to her husband.

"God, you are beautiful," William said as he gently stroked her freshly washed hair.

"Thank you, Detective Douglas," she said with a beguiling look. "Now, I want to hear all about your day."

"You first," he said.

Hannah's face showed signs that there was indeed something he needed to know about her day, and she was about to tell him about the mysterious van that had followed her to work, when the phone rang again.

"Dad-gum-it. Hold that thought," he said as he got up to answer the phone. It was his brother, Randy.

William talked to Randy for almost twenty minutes. His brother was having marital problems with his third wife. He always called William for advice and then never took it, but William always listened patiently and offered his shoulder to cry on.

When he came back to the couch, Hannah was sound asleep. Reed was on the floor in front of the fireplace watching television, and Dragon was stretched out next to Hannah.

At nine o'clock, the show Reed was watching was over. He gave Neiman a hug, stroked the cat, gave his mother a kiss on the cheek, then patted her gently as though he were her caretaker. Finally, he kissed his dad and headed off to bed.

"I love you, Reed."

"I love you too, Dad. Goodnight."

After another two hours had passed, and Reed was fast asleep in his bed, William turned off the television, booted the cat off the couch and crawled over in front of Hannah. Her breathing was slow and even, and he wondered what was going on in her dreams. The flickering firelight danced on her dark silky hair. She couldn't possibly know how beautiful she looked to him at that moment, so peaceful and safe there in front of him. He wanted to touch her hair and let it glide through his fingers. He loved the way it felt in his hands, against his cheek, on his body. He loved the way it fell over her breasts when she made love to him, while he lay beneath her.

He bent down and whispered in her ear, "Sweetheart, it's time to go to bed." He wanted her so bad, but it wouldn't be right. She had to get up so early, and it was after eleven o'clock. She stirred a little, but did not wake up.

He put his arms underneath her and carefully lifted her from the couch. Her satin pajamas swaddled her and felt good against his naked chest. Oh, how he wanted her.

He laid her down on their bed and began to undress her. First he peeled off her socks, then he loosened the drawstrings on her pajama bottoms and slid them down her long lean legs. Her panties were lacy and delicate and came down easily. He unbuttoned her satin top. He wanted to kiss her breasts and nuzzle his face between them, but he shouldn't. He couldn't wake her up. It was so late.

He pulled the covers over her, undressed himself and slid into bed beside her. Like every night, he molded his body around hers and put his hand over her bosom, but it was like he had never touched them before. His heart was racing. He wanted all of her just for a moment, but he didn't want to wake her. It wouldn't be fair.

Tenderly he caressed her bosom and cradled against her. She sighed quietly, erotically. He caught his breath. She was so soft and warm, and she moved ever so slightly as though she was waiting for him to steal her. He wouldn't move, he told himself, he would not wake her. The thought of making love to her made him rigid with desire, and without realizing it he had squeezed her breast earnestly, passionately.

Without saying a word, his lover, his wife, his soul-mate, took him to her, and again he caught his breath. Was he dreaming? No. Yes! She was his dream come true, and she wanted to be one with him. And in that moment when she gave herself to him, he wanted her more than he ever had before.

He didn't know what had caused him to be so aroused this night. For fourteen years they had been married and slept together, but tonight his desire had been carnal. It was as though she were a forbidden fruit that he would never again be able to taste.

Not one word had been uttered, but it was some of the purest and sweetest moments he had ever spent with her.

Chapter 13

Twila Brooks was cold and scared. The February air chilled her to the bone, but nothing like how the coldness and hostility of her captor did.

When Twila was let out of the van, she could barely stand. Her limbs shook violently, her teeth chattered, and her heart beat like that of a fallen bird's. The sun was up, and its glare stung her eyes after having been in total darkness for goodness knows how long. There was an old Victorian house in front of her and a huge barn off to the side of it. Only trees and pasture land surrounded it. Secluded. She could scream until her tonsils exploded, and no one would hear her.

Grabbing Twila's arm, the woman said, "Let's go."

"What are you going to do with me?"

"It's a secret," the woman said. "We don't tell our secrets."

Inside, the house was ominous and foreboding. It emitted spooky vibes as though it had a life of its own, shrewd and haunting. The furniture was heavy and dark with intricate carvings of faces that were eternally twisted in grotesque poses of pain and sorrow. Red flocked wallpaper hung on the fourteen foot walls. Unlike a bordello, the walls in this house promoted a sense of repulsion rather than pleasure. Everything Twila saw frightened her. She wondered if a coven of witches haunted the house, or perhaps the devil himself.

They came to a room that was painted totally black – even the ceiling was black. To the left there was a long red table with chairs along one side. In front of each chair, and on the table, was a black candle. Across from the table stood some sort of demonic looking altar, and in the center of the black shiny floor was a white five pointed star with symbols painted around it.

"Get in the cage," the woman said, refusing to remove those dark glasses that perched on her nose like visors. Against one wall was a row of wire cages similar to those used to transport animals the size of a large dog if the dog didn't stand or sit up. The floor of the cage was not solid, but made of the same wire as the rest of it. There was no way any living creature could get comfortable in it.

Twila looked at the woman in disbelief. "I can't. I won't! It's too small."

The woman cocked her head as if someone had struck her in the face, then suddenly she seemed to recover. "Don't argue with me. Get in!"

"At least untie my hands, you crazy – you crazy – whatever you are!" Twila was screaming now. Tears of anger, fear, and humiliation pricked her face.

The woman pulled out the fancy dagger from her bag. "I will cut you with this if I have to tell you again."

"Go to hell!" Twila shouted as she lowered herself to the floor and managed to crawl into the cage. It was smaller than it looked, once she got in it. Her arms were numb from the cold and from being tied behind her back. All she could do was lie on her side with her legs pulled up to her chest. The wire was hard and cold, and it hurt every part of her body that was exposed to it.

"God, I wish someone would put you in a cage and tie you up!" Twila shouted.

"They have," the woman said.

With the door closed, there was no light at all. It was pitch black, darker than night or anyplace Twila had ever been, and it was so very cold.

Twila tried to think about the last time she was at home with her parents. It had been Christmas. Her mother had decorated their house with strings and strings of twinkling white lights, and the tree was adorned with the ornaments they had collected since she was born. The smells from the kitchen had been filled with the aromas of a lifetime of Christmases past. They were as much a part of the holiday season in their home as was the crackling fire in the fire-place, stockings hanging from the mantel, and gifts beneath the tree. All of Twila's Christmases had glistened in her memory. She remembered sitting on the couch next to her dad watching *It's a Wonderful Life*. And today was his birthday. She began to cry and sing. "Happy birthday to you. Happy birthday to you. Happy birthday, dear Daddy. Happy birthday to you." She sang it over and over and over again until she melded into the darkness that surrounded her.

Chapter 14

Thursday morning, February the twelfth, came too quickly for Hannah. She slapped the snooze button and rolled over to cuddle William, but William didn't turn over like he normally did. He lay facing her.

"Thank you for last night," he said dreamily.

Hannah smiled. "I love you," she said before giving way to sleep again.

William cradled her, cherishing her until the alarm stole her away.

Lightly she kissed him on the lips and got up. While brushing her teeth, Hannah remembered the van that had followed her to work the previous morning. She hadn't gotten the opportunity to tell William about it. She thought about telling him now but decided to wait and see if it was outside before doing that.

Neiman had already crawled under her vanity, waiting for her to put her cold feet underneath him. His furry body would warm them up while she applied her make-up.

Hannah got dressed a little faster than usual. She pulled her long black hair back with a barrette she had bought in the French Quarter last year when William had taken her to New Orleans. Her mind wandered back to the night they had watched the fireworks over the Mississippi River for the Fourth of July. Hundreds of people surrounded them, but they were quite alone in a world of their making. One of the most passionate kisses he had ever placed on her lips had been under those sprinkles of light on the river walk. She tingled at the memory of it.

From the bay windows in the music room, she peered through the blinds. There was no sign of the van, and everything looked normal, so there was no reason to wake him; it would just make him worry, and he did enough of that on her behalf already. She went back to their bedroom, kissed him on the forehead and whispered, "I love you."

Neiman preceded her to Reed's room. He knew the routine. While Hannah bent over to kiss her child, Neiman curled up on the floor beside his bed. Dragon was in the windowsill purring. Hannah stroked the cat, patted the collie and left her family for work.

Her drive this Thursday morning was without incident. The sky hosted a million glittering stars, and the air was cold and crisp. Hannah felt privileged to be a spectator of God's beautiful night sky, and thanked him for it. She thanked God for her family and all the love she had been given since the day she was born. She had a wonderful life.

Hannah had wanted to hear more about William's new position in the department. She couldn't tell if he was excited about it or not, but she did know that he would be good at being a detective. She worried, though, that he might get too emotionally involved in his cases. The kidnappings had really bothered him. The situation had the whole town in turmoil, but now that William was a detective, he would take it even more personally. He would get to know the families, feel their pain, grieve with them, and he would do all he could and more to find those girls. He would work himself to a frazzle after he got involved with it on that level because that's the kind of man William was. She would have to help him leave the worries at the office, not letting those terrible, ugly crimes eat him up. She loved him too much and would be there to help him through it, just as he was always there for her.

As usual, the prison looked oppressive and austere. The guard towers, the barbed wire, the bars, all cast morose currents into the atmosphere and into her psyche. But every day Hannah managed to walk inside, go through one crash gate after another, listen to the heavy steel doors slam shut and echo down the stark corridors.

The door to education was locked. Officer Dillon was inside by himself unlocking the offices and classrooms, so she would have to wait in the main corridor. Count had obviously cleared because inmates were already traveling. A few of them would make cat calls, whistle, or spout off crude and repulsive remarks at her as they walked by like they always did. Many of the convicts felt the need to degrade others, perhaps because it was the only way they knew how to make themselves feel significant or superior to someone else. Whatever the reason, Hannah hated it.

Mr. Shaffer walked up, to Hannah's relief. He taught Phase III. They chatted about the upcoming GED test until the officer unlocked the education door and let them in.

"Good morning!" he said cheerfully. "Sorry you had to wait on me. I'm here by myself for awhile. Officer Parrish isn't coming in this morning."

"No problem. No problem," Shaffer said.

"And how are you this morning, Ms. Douglas?" the officer asked.

"I am absolutely wonderful. How is your wife?"

"Doing great. The doctor said she would get to go back to work next week. And I just want to thank you again for the meal you and your husband brought out to us."

Hannah smiled. "We were glad to do it."

She didn't worry much about there being only one guard on duty. It happened that way often on the early morning shift.

Students began filing in at five o'clock, and the first thing they wanted to talk about was the van. Hannah assured them that the van had not followed her this morning, and she was sure that she simply overreacted yesterday morning. However, her students weren't so sure. They knew a whole lot more about the seedy side of life than she would ever know.

At ten minutes before six, Hannah's new student came to the door. His hard face was scrunched up in a scowl. Anger trickled off of him like sweat, and she would be the scapegoat for whoever had enrolled him in school.

"Come in," she said with a warm smile. "You must be Mr. Dunlap."

He walked into the room towards Hannah's desk and spouted, "Who the fuck put me in here? I'm fifty-four fuckin' years old. Ain't nobody gonna tell me I got to go to school like some damned kid, still be suckin' his momma's tit."

The other students sat quietly and watched, ever ready to intervene if necessary.

"Mr. Dunlap, the counselor put you in school because the parole board is going to deny you parole if you don't try to get your GED while you are incarcerated."

"I don't wanna hear none of that shit, like I be some pig-headed fool. I been down five fuckin' times and ain't had no trouble parolin' before. You ain't gonna talk some line of shit tellin' me 'bout no parole board. Who the hell you think you are?"

"My name is Ms. Douglas, and I am the lady who is going to teach you how to read and write and talk properly."

"Say what?" Inmate Dunlap looked at her like she had lost her mind.

"Mr. Dunlap, there isn't a man in this room who wanted to be put in school, but they have all gotten used to it and even enjoy it. Now, to be perfectly honest, none of us like having to get up this early, but that is something we have no control over, and we have learned to make the best of it."

The convict, looking as mean as a snake, didn't move. He just stared at her. A scar ran from his left ear to the top of his nose. Most of her students were scarred from knife wounds, gunshot wounds, or various other violent injuries.

"Come have a seat right here at my desk and let me ask you some questions."

"She-e-e-it," he said in an elongated slur.

"Mr. Dunlap, do you ever want to get out of prison?"

"What kind of fool question is that?"

"It's an important question that you need to answer. The people in this state are tired of people who commit one crime after another against them. The people of this state are tired of people, like you, who refuse to better themselves and try to make it in society, and those same people have pressured the legislature into doing something about it. So, here are the facts. If an incarcerated felon refuses to work, lock him down. If he refuses an education, lock him down. If he refuses to behave, lock him down. And here's the part that has changed – throw away the key. You see, Inmate Dunlap, Texas has built enough prisons to lock up as many people as it needs to. We don't have to worry about overcrowding. In fact, we have so much space that we can even rent out cells to other states. So, if you don't want school, the door is right behind you. You can walk out the same way you walked in. Frankly, I don't think a hateful, uneducated, foul-mouthed low-life like yourself needs to be unleashed in this state, only to commit more crime and fall again and again and again. The way I see it, you have two choices: stay in here and learn how to read and write, or you can keep doing what you've been doing and rot in your cell. Either way, I get my paycheck."

He didn't know what to say.

"What's it going to be?" Hannah asked.

"I guess I'm gonna have to stay today. That fuckin' son of a bitch won't let me out, what's he said. Thinks he's runnin' some-thin'." His face was still snarled, but bewilderment had replaced some of the anger.

Hannah smiled. "Good for you. Have a seat right here by my desk." The other inmates had begun working. "I've got some paper work I need to fill out on you."

"No need in me doin' that today. I ain't got no glasses. I could read if these sorry-ass doctors 'round here could fit me with the right glasses."

"I hate to be the one to break it to you, Mr. Dunlap, but glass-es aren't what you need to be able to read. I am what you need to learn how to read. I know you've used that excuse your entire life, but it won't hold water in my class. You can't read because you don't know how. I can teach you, like I taught the rest of these guys, but only under one condition."

"What's that?" he asked suspiciously.

"You'll have to leave your filthy language outside this depart-ment. I will not have it in here. Understood?"

"She-e-e-it," he said again, letting the word crawl out of his mouth like an earthworm.

"Mr. Dunlap, that is considered an ugly word. Apparently you have used obscene language for so long that you don't even recognize it anymore. So, what I'll do is correct you when an ugly word slips out, and before you know it, you'll be talking like one of us." She looked at her other students. They all grinned at the new arrival.

ଓଃଅଠ

Reed had a thousand questions for William when he got up Thursday morning. He couldn't wait to tell the kids at school that his dad was a detective, and he wanted to have plenty of information to go with his news report.

William patiently dealt with Reed then set out for the Sheriff's Office. He was dressed in navy Dockers, a white dress shirt and a green and navy tie. He wore his gun in a shoulder holster beneath a gray wool sports coat. This attire was much more comfortable than his deputy uniform. No bullet proof vest and no double belt packed with gear. He could move.

When he got to the office thirty minutes early, Jeff Stone was already there.

"How long have you been here?" asked William as he poured himself a cup of coffee.

Jeff was sitting at his desk just finishing a cup. His eyes brightened when he saw William. "Oh, not long. I was making some notes on what to ask Ethel Fletcher when we find her."

"Good deal." William went around the chair and sat in front of Jeff's desk.

"I found out where she lives. Woodhollow Apartments on Lake Road. Apartment thirteen."

"That's appropriate," William said peering over the edge of his coffee mug.

"I called The Walls Unit, and get this. She's been suspended," Jeff said.

"Well it's about time. What for?"

Jeff locked his fingers behind his head as he leaned back in his chair. "The secretary wouldn't tell me. She said I'd need to talk to a guy by the name of Cowen, the principal. Do you know him?"

"No. Suzanne Bolton was the principal when Hannah worked there."

Jeff nodded. "We've got an appointment to see him this morning at nine o'clock. Maybe we can track her down before then."

"Sounds good."

"Before we go, I've got some paper work to finish up."

"Good, that will give me some more time to look at the files we're working on."

"William, there's something I want you to understand."

"Shoot."

"I know you are concerned that I might expect you to put in as much time as I do up here."

William was taken back. He regarded Jeff seriously.

"Just for the record, I don't. This is my life. It's just your job. I want you to know that I do realize that and respect it, so don't feel like you have to get here thirty minutes early to appease me."

"No, I didn't. I mean . . ."

Jeff leaned forward and looked very frank. "If I had a wife and a kid like yours, this would only be a job to me, too. But I don't. This is all I have."

"Thanks." William felt relieved, but more than that, he appreciated Jeff's genuine intent.

Jeff nodded and William went to the filing cabinet.

After a few minutes Jeff said, "Let's hit the road. And let's go in my car today. It's less conspicuous."

William agreed.

A mockingbird was perched on the wooden table outside the jail. A trustee was tossing it little pieces of bread. *There's a story in that somewhere,* William thought.

The two detectives got into Jeff's sable colored county car. It was nice, but Reed would be disappointed when he got one like it because there wasn't a light bar on top. The emergency lights were in the grill.

Jeff Stone pulled out onto FM 2821. Across the street was the Wynn prison unit that housed over three thousand inmates. It was like a small town inside the barbed fences.

They came to the intersection at old Seventy-five. The approaching vehicle was in the right turn lane on Highway Seventy-five with his right blinker flashing. It was seven -forty in the morning.

Jeff's left turn signal was on, and they were going to the Woodhollow Apartment Complex where Ethel Fletcher lived. He stopped at the stop sign, then proceeded, assuming the oncoming car in the right turn lane would indeed turn.

It didn't.

Chapter 15

Martha and Edward Brooks couldn't eat or sleep. Their beautiful, sweet daughter had been stolen, and they both were sick wondering, fearing what was happening to her. Was she dead? Was she alive and being tortured? Had she been raped? Had she been shot or stabbed? Was she with the other girls that had been kidnapped? While those questions raced through their minds, they didn't voice them out loud. It was as if each of them was afraid if they asked their questions out loud, their fears might come true.

They had been married for twenty-six years, not every day of it perfect, but no matter what happened in their lives, they had always had their love to fall back on and to get them through. This unimaginable thing, though, that had happened to Twila, their only child, was more overpowering than anything they had come up against or even dreamed of ever having to face.

If Twila had been injured or even killed in a car crash, or if she had suffered a catastrophic illness, they would have found a way to deal with their pain and grief, but not knowing what was happening to her, yet knowing it had to be terrible and frightening, was going to eat them from the inside out. Their worry and fears would drown them and smother them. It would be like sinking in quicksand: dirty, muddy, thick and inescapable. And the love they had for one another wouldn't save them – the love for their missing daughter would destroy them. All they could do was pray and hope. They didn't know how to help her or each other. They waited.

CB&C

Inmate Dunlap settled down. He decided to give school a try since he didn't seem to have much of a choice. The other convicts looked as though they didn't mind it too bad, and the teacher acted like she could teach him how to read. Maybe it was time.

"Okay, Mr. Dunlap, I've got your folder ready. Come back up to my desk, please, and have a seat so I can explain this to you."

He did, hesitantly.

"I've put you in the Laubach Reading Series. We'll start with the green book. It looks like this." She showed the skeptical inmate the adult reader. "The first thing you'll learn how to do is recognize these six letters and the sounds they make. If you'll notice, they have pictures to help you make a connection between the sound and the letter. Do you see how this bird has been drawn to look like the letter 'b'?"

"This is some kind of baby book. I ain't gonna act like no baby, I don't care what you say!" He was getting angry again.

Hannah smiled as though she was very pleased. Her emerald eyes lit up. She said, "Mr. Dunlap, do you realize what you just did?"

Bewilderment replaced his anger. "No."

"You just spoke three whole sentences and didn't use one ugly word. You're going to do fine." Her sincerity was obvious to the convict.

"You know, I ain't stupid. I learn pretty fast."

"I can see that, and that is why I selected this book for you. It's not a child's book at all. You see, if I were going to learn some other language, like German for instance, I would need to start out in a book that had the German letters. I would also need some pictures to give me clues as to what sounds they made. There's nothing childish about that. It's really the best way to help your brain retain the new stuff you are learning."

"All right then," he said. "I'll give it a try."

"Good. And don't get the idea that it's going to take forever before you actually read a whole story." She showed him the next page in the book. "You'll be able to read this entire page in the next five minutes."

He looked at the page full of symbols that meant nothing to him, and then he looked at her like she had just fallen off a truck loaded with Thanksgiving turkeys.

Inmate Prescott grinned at Dunlap and said," I know it sounds like a bunch of bull right now, but listen to her. I started out same as you. Didn't even know my alphabets. I read that page your lookin' at the first day." Prescott held up a Louis L'amour book entitled *Silver Canyon.* "See this?" he said. "I checked this book out of the library on Monday, and I'm nearly through with it. And it's a chapter book."

Inmate Dunlap looked at his new teacher and said, "Oh hell, I'll give it a try."

Hannah raised her eyebrows.

"I mean, oh, good, I'll give it a try."

She smiled.

At eight o'clock, the principal, Lonnie Ray West, knocked on Hannah's classroom door. She motioned for him to come in. He motioned for her to come out in the hall. His demeanor was sober.

"Yes, sir?" she asked.

"You've got a phone call. You can take it in my office."

"A call? I never get a call. Who is it?"

"It's your husband. He's calling from the hospital."

Hannah's heart skipped a beat. She didn't wait for Lonnie Ray to finish. She ran to his office.

"William?"

"Hey, you sound out of breath. Is everything okay?"

"No, everything is not okay. My principal comes and gets me out of class to tell me that my husband is calling from the hospital."

"Oh heck, I'm sorry. Everything's fine. Jeff and I were in a little car accident this morning. We had to come to the emergency room for Jeff to get sewed up."

"You weren't hurt?"

"Not a scratch."

"Is Jeff all right?"

"Yeah. He's fine. I was afraid you may hear about it and get worried so I just wanted to let you know that I wasn't hurt."

"Thank God." Hannah was twisting the cord on the phone into knots.

"Really." he said.

"I wish I had a few minutes to talk to you. I want to know all about your new job."

"I know. We'll talk tonight, I promise. And if you fall asleep, I'll wake you."

"Like last night?" She knew he would smile at that.

"Don't do that, Hannah. You're going to get something excited here."

"Sorry."

"No you're not."

"Look, I'd better get back to class before the gang comes looking for me. Mr. West is in there with them. They don't warm up to him much."

"I don't know how you do what you do, but I'm proud of you.

You know that, don't you?" William could visualize her emerald green eyes in front of him.

"I'm proud of you, too, detective. I love you."

"I love you more."

"Bye."

"Good-bye, sweetheart."

Her inmates would want to know why she ran down the hall, and she would tell them.

Chapter 16

Twila woke up. Her neck was tight, too stiff to turn without a measurable amount of discomfort. Her back and shoulders were exhausted from the position they had maintained for no telling how many hours. She tried to shift her body to lessen the strain, but there was so little room in the cage. The wire made indentations in her skin where it was pressed up against her.

After fully realizing and absorbing the extent of her physical pain, Twila's mind began to interpret her fear of what was to come. If being locked up in a metal cage in the dark for hours was the first step of abuse, what was in store for her later? No, she couldn't think about that now. She had to push it out of her thoughts and concentrate on what to do when the monster woman came back. She must make a plan; figure out how to escape, but her parents crept into her thoughts. She could visualize their worry. Her mother would cry and shake, much like she had done herself, and her daddy would try to comfort her mother, but he would be burning inside. She knew how much they loved her, but back to her plan. When the monster woman came back, she would tell her she had to use the restroom. After she stood up and stretched a bit, she would have better luck in overtaking her. Even with her hands tied she could fight back, do something instead of just allow herself to be a passive piece of meat.

She had nerve. She had backbone, but oh, God, how her back hurt. If she could just concentrate for a minute on what to do.

The sounds in the darkness floated to Twila like ghosts and even though the sounds were haunting, they were a welcome relief to the silence.

Twila listened carefully, intent on grasping something that would make sense to her, but the sounds were like chants she had heard on scary movies, meant to enhance the suspense and make you feel uncomfortable. You knew that in the next moment or two some-thing awful was going to happen to the character in the movie, and your heart would race a little faster as the chanting became louder and more intense, and your breathing would follow along with shal-low quick steps. Then Twila realized that the chanting had indeed gotten louder, closer, and this was not a scary movie. She was the character and her name was Twila Brooks. *Oh, God, don't let them open that door.* Only evil, the worst kind of evil, could be behind it, and she did not want to see it.

"No!" she heard herself scream as light scorched the frame of the door while it opened slowly and with purpose.

Twila closed her eyes, determined not to succumb to the fear that was licking her with hot sharp tongues, in cadence to the chants.

CB&CO

"Some of these are going to need stitches, detective." Stone had sustained lacerations on the left side of his face all the way to his elbow when the driver's side window shattered on impact from the oncoming car. Stella used special tweezers to pick out tiny shards of glass from his flesh.

"I figured as much. There was a lot of blood."

"What happened?" she asked as she continued to clean him up."

"A car rammed into the side of my car – the driver's side. I was driving."

"I see," she said while preparing him for Dr. Tobin to come in and sew him up. "Have you had a tetanus shot in the last five years?"

"No, ma'am. I haven't."

"I'll need to give you one in that case. Since your left arm is already in pain, and likely to be sore, I'll give it to you in that arm."

"You're the boss."

"Oh no. I've never been the boss." Her expression was pensive.

She wasn't beautiful, thought Stone as she walked out of the room, but she was attractive in her own way, and interesting.

Debra was beautiful. At least sixteen years ago she was. He had loved to watch her walk, watch her eat, watch her sleep. She was the most exquisite sight he had ever seen the day she walked down the aisle on her father's arm, coming to be his bride.

Stella came back in with a needle, ready to give him the shot.

"Are you feeling faint?" Stella looked alarmed and felt his face with her skilled, but soft hand.

"No. Why the worried look?" Stone asked.

"It's just that your face is whiter than our sheets. Why don't you lie back against the bed. I'll raise it for you." Stella raised the bed and gently pushed him back against it.

He was looking in her eyes again. "Thank you," he said.

She smiled. "You're welcome,"

As she gave him the shot, he looked at her face. It was clear that she didn't want to hurt him. It appeared as though it almost sickened her to stick him with the needle. She was so careful and compassionate with him.

"There," she said. "I hope that wasn't too bad."

"Actually, I rather enjoyed it."

Stella looked at him quite strangely. "I didn't know anyone

enjoyed getting a shot."

"No. What I meant was, you are just so sweet. I'll bet you are the best nurse in this hospital."

"I doubt that." Stella was blushing.

"Dr. Tobin will be in to stitch you up in a couple of minutes."

"Will you stay in here and talk to me while he does?" Stone couldn't believe he was asking her to stay. He felt a bit ridiculous, but he didn't want her to get away. He found himself attracted to her.

"I'd be happy to."

A tall gray-haired man with piercing blue eyes walked into the treatment room. "Hello. I'm Dr. Tobin. I hope Nurse Perkins hasn't been too rough with you," he said, winking at his patient.

"I managed to survive it."

"I see. I suppose that's the reason you asked her to stay in here with you while I sewed you up."

"Ouch!"

"Haven't you ever had stitches before?"

"No. What are you doing? The nurse already gave me a shot."

"That was a tetanus shot. I'm having to deaden the area where I'm going to put the stitches." Tobin pushed up his glasses with his gloved hand. Stella had moved in much closer to put her hand on Stone's free arm. She stroked it to calm him down.

"Jesus! How about letting her do it." He looked up at Stella.

The doctor chuckled. "I heard you say you actually enjoyed her shots." He peered up at the detective over his half-framed glasses.

Stone was embarrassed.

"Tell me," the doctor said as he worked, "any leads on the kidnappings?"

"Nothing I can talk about."

"I see."

Stella interrupted, "You're the detective on those cases?" She sounded impressed.

"Yes, ma'am, I'm ashamed to say."

"Ashamed? Why?" Stella asked

"Because I haven't found the kidnapper."

Once again, Stella consoled him. "I am sure no one could be doing more than you are to find whoever is abducting those women. It's a terrible thing. The soul that is doing this must be very sick and disturbed."

Jeff couldn't believe it. She even felt compassion for the criminal that was terrorizing Huntsville, and it was genuine concern. She had to be the sweetest girl he had ever met.

For sixteen years, Jeff Stone had not even contemplated the idea of seriously dating another woman. He had picked up women at bars for sexual release when he needed it or wanted it, but he never even asked them their names. He had resigned himself to bachelorhood, never to have his life mangled again. No other woman would be allowed to make him vulnerable to love, then strangle him with it. He had successfully constructed a shield around his heart that, so far, had not been penetrated. At least, not until now.

Stone could feel his heart fluttering. It felt good.

CB⁊◌

Virginia, dressed in a floral print dress with a chiffon overlay, knocked on Earl's door. "Mr. Cowen?"

"Yes, Virginia."

"You aren't going to believe this."

"Try me, Virginia."

"Those detectives that were coming over here had a car wreck this morning." Virginia stopped, waiting for her boss to ask for more information. She poofed up her hair so as to look more presentable.

"Well? Were they hurt?"

"The lady at the Sheriff's Office, Kay Buckner, do you know her?"

"Virginia," he said in his tone of voice that meant get to the point and get to it now.

"Sorry. They weren't hurt bad. But they did have to go to the emergency room. Cuts and bruises, I'd imagine. Probably just scared 'em more than anything else."

"Thank you, Virginia."

"Yes, sir. Now, you'd better get going if you plan to make your principals' meeting on time."

"You're right."

Virginia walked over to him and fiddled with the handkerchief in his suit coat pocket. There was no intimacy in the gesture.

She asked, "Are you going to mention Ethel to Mr. Wagstaff?"

"Yes, as a matter of fact I am."

"Good for you. Don't you let that old buzzard butt intimidate you, either," she said as she patted the lapel of his coat, obviously pleased with her ability to fold a handkerchief.

"Virginia," in a tone that meant she ought to be ashamed of herself, "you can't go around calling our assistant superintendent a buzzard butt." He was beginning to adore his secretary, despite her quirks, but not in a romantic way. His feelings toward her were more like those someone would have for a favorite aunt.

"And why not?"

"Because, he's a jackass."

Virginia clapped her hands and laughed a little too loudly.

Earl grabbed his overcoat and left feeling a bit more dapper than when he had come in, thanks to Virginia.

The meeting started promptly at ten-thirty. They would have a lunch break, according to the agenda, at twelve-thirty. Earl had already made arrangements to eat with Lem Wagstaff.

Attendance rosters were the main topic of discussion. Then Wagstaff brought up teacher absences. "Folks, it's difficult to explain to a convict why he has to come to school when we can't get the teachers to show up. Some of you have teachers that use up their sick leave day every single month without fail." Wagstaff walked back and forth across the front of the meeting room with his hands folded behind his back. He looked at individuals for long moments at a time then broke the stare by gazing down at his wingtips. "Don't think I can't see the pattern when a teacher is absent the first Friday of every month or before or after a holiday. You people are suppose to be in charge of and responsible for the teachers who work for you. If you can't control your teachers, then it causes me to wonder if you can control the students. Without control, people, you might as well hang it up, and I will be more than happy to help you reach that decision when the time comes. And believe me, the time will come sooner than you think if I don't see some changes in teacher absences. Have I made myself clear?"

After a final survey of the Region I principals, Wagstaff took off his glasses then said, "Let's break for lunch. We'll resume precisely at one-thirty. Don't come in here late."

Earl walked over to the assistant superintendent. His gray owl-like eyes were moist with disgust for his boss. "I've got a table reserved for us at The Cattlemen Club."

"Do what?" Wagstaff asked smugly.

"Look, Lem. I need to discuss something with you, so I reserved a table at the most exclusive place in town, hoping that you'd be kind enough to accept." His face showed angst for the man in front of him. Clearly he didn't like him, and clearly Wagstaff could care less. "My treat."

"This must be serious."

Earl nodded. He was determined not to let Lem Wagstaff intimidate him. For once Lem was going to listen to what he had to say.

"All right. Let's go."

All of Wagstaff's features together could be described as handsome, but he was too anal to be considered sexy. His self-confidence, or lack there-of , was his most pronounced feature. Middle age had only made him less likable and more driven. He wanted everything done his way, not because it made the most sense, but more often than not, because he thrived on making decisions and having them carried out. He enjoyed making his subordinates suffer brutal admonishments and more especially when they were delivered in front of others.

Cowen, on the other hand, was a senior citizen. He was a good twenty years older than Wagstaff, making it all the more difficult for him to be on the receiving end of one of his hissy- fits. Cowen was mild mannered but decisive and the kind of boss most people enjoyed working for. He had never been good looking. Large gray eyes peered out of heavy black glasses, making his ruddy complexion seem less than healthy. His hair was still brown and was cut and styled the same as it was in the fifties, and fittingly, Jerry's Hair Tonic still kept it in place. He had never seen the need to alter his appearance. Age had a way of doing that without his assistance. His wife had never complained.

The Cattlemen's Club had once been home to the Leeber family. Their original ranch house had been turned into a restaurant and bar. It was constructed of massive wooden planks with mortar sealing them together. Inside the dining area, the partitions between rooms were constructed of the same kind of wood, only the mortar had been removed. The dining tables were all heavy and antique; no two alike. The chairs did not match either. There were other rooms not used for dining. Occasional poker games could be found going on in some, and it had been rumored that sex could be bought in the others. Only men were served in the Cattlemen's Club. It had been that way since the nineteen forties and would no doubt stay that way. Cowen had been a member since he had moved to Huntsville.

Wagstaff on the other hand, had never been to the club. It had never occurred to him to become a member, and no one had ever invited him there until now, so he was taking it all in.

After ordering, Wagstaff asked, "So, what was so important that you felt inclined to bring me here?"

"It's Ethel Fletcher."

Some men that Cowen knew came in and spoke to him as they walked by. Earl wondered if Lem knew anybody outside of work. He couldn't imagine that he would have any friends.

"I've got a disciplinary file on her two inches thick. What does it take to fire a teacher?" He took a long drink of the margarita he had ordered. "Hell, as often as you threaten your principals with termination, I figured you should know." It was as though confidence was in the glass and disguised as liquor.

The waiter brought out two bowls of cream of mushroom soup, and a basket of breads.

Undaunted by Earl's sarcasm, Lem said, "That's a catch twenty-two situation. This soup is delicious," he said while reaching for a small cornbread muffin.

Earl had gulped down another swig of his drink. "I want to know what it has to do with Elaine and Jack Tyler."

"Believe me, I'd like to know myself. The principal before you, Suzanne Bolton, tried every way in the world to fire her, but it never happened. Ethel Fletcher is the reason she requested to be transferred to another unit. Hannah Douglas, too."

"She called in sick again today and talked ugly to Virginia. I listened in on my extension. Lem, I suspended her." His face was stone cold.

"Oh boy," sighed Lem.

The waiter cleared the soup bowls for their main course: sixteen ounce T-bone steaks, cooked medium well, baked potatoes with all the trimmings, and mixed steamed vegetables. Lem was impressed. He thought for a brief moment that it might be a good idea for him to join the club, then remembered he had no friends to socialize with.

Earl broke the silence. "I want to tell you something. I have had enough. I will go over the Tylers' heads if I have to. Something is going on, and I intend to get to the bottom of it."

Lem looked up from his plate. "Earl, slow down. You could get yourself fired if you go too far." No true concern was implicated in the suggestion.

"If Ethel Fletcher can't be fired, then I know I don't have anything to worry about."

"Don't bet on it."

Earl's face flushed, not from embarrassment but from anger. He hated the man whose dinner he was buying.

"Hey you, do you think I could get some ketchup over here?"

The waiter, responding with the utmost class said, "Certainly. I'll have that out to you in just one moment, sir. Anything else?"

"That will be all." Wagstaff's tone and manner was complacent.

Feeling more liberated after having finished his margarita, Cowen said, "Lem, this place is for gentlemen. It doesn't cater to obnoxious, abusive, self-serving, egotistical sons of bitches such as yourself. So, if you think you can manage it, don't act like a horse's ass again to our waiter. It's a pitiful shame you wouldn't recognize class if it was rammed up your ass." He took a bite of his perfectly done steak.

Lem Wagstaff didn't know what to say. For the first time in a long while, he was stunned.

"Here you are, sir. Your ketchup." Looking at Earl, the waiter asked, "Will either of you gentlemen be having dessert this afternoon? We have peach cobbler, carrot cake, praline cheesecake, and a variety of ice creams, all homemade of course."

Lem held his finger up about to order one of the sweets. Earl spoke, "I wish we could, but we have to get back to a meeting. You see, we can't walk in late. My boss is a member of the anal retentive society and constantly feels the need to show his authority while showing his ass. I'm sure you've met the type. God forbid you ever have to work for one."

"I understand, Mr. Cowen." The waiter had an idea that the ass being referred to was sitting at that very table.

Lem couldn't say a word. For some reason he understood that in this club and at this table, away from work, he shouldn't.

"So, Lem, are you going to back me up on this business with Ethel Fletcher?"

Wagstaff looked at him squarely. "No."

"I figured as much. You know, you really are a bastard."

Wagstaff was finishing up his potato. "Part of the job. Part of the job."

"No, Lem. Being a bastard is not part of the job. Being a bastard is just a part of your personality; a part that you take great pride in. The sad thing is, you hurt yourself the most by it."

Lem shrugged and sopped up the buttery remains of his steamed vegetables with another muffin. He didn't need any friends.

C380

Jack and Elaine Tyler had been married for five years. They lived in a beautiful and spacious home in Elkin's Lake, a large subdivision south of downtown Huntsville off Interstate Forty-five. It was an exclusive residential area that was home to many retired people. Aside from the lake that the neighborhood was named for, Elkin's had a respectable golf course, swimming pools, stables, a club and manor house, tennis courts, playgrounds, and bicycle trails.

Jack and Elaine Tyler had little time to use the amenities that gave Elkin's Lake its prestige. They were both workaholics.

Director for the Texas Department of Corrections, Jack Tyler earned his title the old fashioned way. He worked his way up the ladder. He began as a correctional officer working the wings. While taking college classes around his shifts, he became a sergeant. Graduating from Sam Houston State University with a degree in criminal justice helped him get his lieutenant bars. In a few short years, Jack had earned a master's degree in criminal justice and had made the rank of major. Two years after becoming a major, he became an assistant warden, then six months later he became the senior warden for the Ellis Unit where death row, along with a large number of general population inmates of the hard-core type, was housed. There, he remained senior warden for six years, then was promoted to director for TDCJ.

Jack's wife, Elaine Tyler, had climbed a different ladder to the top of the TDCJ institution. Hers was the stairway in the educational arena. Her journey took her to the office of Superintendent of the Windham School District, the prison's school system. Like Jack, Elaine worked long hours, devoting herself to the job. She never made time for romance. For five years the Tylers had shared a home and a bed but seldom their lives. Even though they had always been ambitious, they had loved each other. At least they had loved before Ethel came.

CBED

Jeff Stone and William Douglas missed their appointment with Principal Cowen, but they had the afternoon to try and run down Ethel Fletcher. Her residence was listed as Woodhollow Apartments. On the way there, William noticed that Jeff was in an extremely good mood to have just come out of a wreck, emergency room treatment, and worst of all the ribbing he had taken at the Sheriff's Office from the deputies.

William said, "Why don't you let me drive you home? I can look for Ethel Fletcher."

"No, no. I'm fine, really." Jeff was tapping his foot and bobbing his head to a song that was apparently in his head because the radio was not on.

"You're sure?"

"Never been better," Jeff said, continuing to tap his right foot.

"I don't mean to pry, but I am a detective now, and I detect a change in your personality since you came out of the emergency room." William raised his eyebrows and cut his eyes toward his new partner.

"Really?"

"Did they give you some funny pills in there?"

"No."

He knew Jeff wasn't going to say any more on the subject, so he decided to leave it alone. He was glad Jeff was so jubilant, but he certainly could not understand it.

The weather was turning cooler. Skies were gray and a north wind was blowing.

William parked his car across the street from the Woodhollow apartments. Unfastening his seat belt he looked over at his preoccupied partner. "Jeff, you coming?"

Jeff snapped out of his reverie. "Do what?"

"Are you really all right?"

"Sure. I'm fine. Just in a good mood."

"Let's go then."

"Apartment thirteen. I'll say it again. That fits her."

"This girl really spooks you, doesn't she?" Jeff said while zipping up his jacket.

"She spooked Hannah, and that's what spooked me."

The two detectives walked down the sidewalk and paused before Ethel's front door. Jeff looked over at William and finally knocked.

There was no answer. Jeff knocked again. Still no answer.

"Sheriff's Department, Miss Fletcher. Open up," Jeff called out.

The manager, who lived next door in apartment twelve, came out.

"She's not home," he said.

"How do you know?"

"Because I always hear her when she comes and goes. She's not there. Hasn't been a peep in there since yesterday."

"Does she have a boyfriend?" William asked.

The manager looked at him strangely. "You ain't never seen her, have you?"

"Yes, I've seen her." William glanced over at Jeff. He understood full well what the man was implying.

"How about any girlfriends?"

"None that I know of."

"Thank you," Detective Stone said. "We'll be back with a search warrant."

"Sure. Okay. What's she done?" the manager asked. He looked like he needed a bath. His scalp was crusted over with dandruff and a thin layer of oily hair.

"We just want to talk to her," Stone said.

"Should I tell her when I see her?"

"No thanks. We'd like to surprise her." Stone winked at him as if letting him in on an important secret.

The manager stood taller, sucked in his chest, and crossed his furry arms in front of him. He put on his "I understand" look as though he were now a major player in a cop drama.

"We appreciate your help," Detective Douglas said as they turned to leave.

On the way to the car Jeff asked William, "How long did it take you to trust Hannah after you met her?"

Without hesitation William replied, "About a minute."

Jeff didn't say anything else.

William broke the silence. "Let's get something to eat. My treat."

"You treat, you pick."

William drove to El Chico.

Both detectives ordered the deluxe nachos and iced tea with lemon.

There was Spanish music coming out of the sound system. No one was within hearing distance when Jeff leaned over the wooden table and asked, "How did you know you could trust her?"

"Who? Hannah?"

"Yeah."

"Everything about her made me feel like I could trust her. She never once acted like she wanted anything from me but love and loyalty. If that's what she wanted from me, then I had no reason to believe that she wouldn't give me that in return."

"I was engaged once," Jeff said in a deep voice.

"What happened?"

"She left me standing at the altar in front of over two hundred people." He picked up a bottle of Tabasco and unscrewed the cap. He looked into the bottle as though he were trying to find a place to bottle the humiliation that still consumed him. "She made her entrance in a flowing white dress and veil." He paused, reliving the experience as he had a million times. "She said, 'I don't,' turned around and walked out. That was sixteen years ago."

"That must have been tough."

"That's not the worst part. She married my brother a year later. I don't know if she wore the same dress. I didn't attend the ceremony."

"Do you ever see them?"

"No."

"What made you fall in love with her?" William asked.

Jeff wasn't expecting that question, and it threw him off guard. "Well, detective, I don't really know. She was beautiful, popular in school, smart."

"Those are reasons to admire someone. What made you love her?"

Jeff looked back into the bottle of hot sauce he was still toying with and tried to think of one good reason. "I don't know." Looking back at William he said again, "I really don't know."

"Are you sure you really loved her then?"

For the first time in sixteen years he contemplated that question honestly. "No," he said, "I'm not."

"Then no love lost. Maybe it was pride, just pride, and the fact that your brother got the girl. Sounds to me like maybe they deserved one another. I mean, I don't know either one of them, but if your brother could marry your bride?" He stopped for a brief moment. "Well, maybe you came out the winner."

"Then why have I felt like a loser for the last sixteen years?"

"Heck if I know. But I think it's time you look at it from a different angle and get on with your life. Not all women are like the woman that left you, just as all men aren't like your brother."

"Yeah, I guess you're right."

"I know I'm right," said William. "I would stake my life on Hannah's loyalty and her love for me, and I know for a fact that she trusts me just as much as I trust her."

Jeff recapped the bottle of hot sauce and put it back in its place alongside the salt and pepper shakers. "How did you get so lucky?"

"I have no idea."

"You know, people talk about you two behind your back," Jeff said.

"How do you mean?"

"Oh, you know, about how you act together, and that it's genuine. You can see that, you know, that it's genuine. I think most people are even envious of it."

"You think so?" William asked.

"Don't look so surprised. How many people do you know who have a marriage like yours?"

William shrugged his shoulders. "I've never really thought about it."

"Yes, you have."

The waitress brought out their nachos. A lettuce and tomato salad was surrounded by crisp tortilla chips that were layered with refried beans, seasoned taco meat, and smothered with chili con queso. Sour cream and guacamole topped the salad. It was as good as it looked.

Conversation turned to a lighter subject.

Chapter 17

"Hello," a voice said sweetly. It came from someone draped in a black robe and hood. "Would you like to get out of the cage?"

The voice was masculine, dreamy, almost a whisper.

Perhaps she was dreaming.

"Yes, please," Twila heard herself say.

After unlocking the cage he reached in and took her by the shoulders to help maneuver her body out and onto the floor. Twila found herself to be grateful even though this person was obviously one of her captors.

"Here, let me untie you. I know you don't need that anymore, now do you?"

"No, I don't." Twila was willing to do almost anything just to be able to stand up and stretch. Any haughtiness she had possessed was all but gone.

"My, you are such a beauty," he said, while helping her to stand.

Her body was so unyielding that she couldn't maintain her balance, and she grabbed hold of him for support. He felt strong.

"Just lean on me. The feeling will come back. It won't take long."

"I hurt all over. Will I have to go back in there?"

"No, I don't think so." With his hand he nudged her head to his chest and let her rest it there. "Now, now, don't cry. You must be brave. You have been chosen. You don't realize it yet, but it is a very high honor to be chosen and brought here."

Twila lifted her head and looked into the man's hooded face.

He smiled. "Only the most beautiful and flawless young women are brought here."

On hearing that, Twila cried harder. "My hair was cut off by some crazy witch."

"There now, don't cry. It's all for a higher purpose. You'll see. You'll see." He held her in his arms much like a father would do and comforted her, and in spite of herself she let it make her feel better.

As soon as she was strong enough to walk, the man led her to another room. In the center of the room was a deep porcelain tub filled with warm water. She could see the steam rising in the chilled air. Around the tub were flickering candles, and there was soft music playing, from where, she could not tell. In one corner there was a white fluffy bathrobe; in another corner there were towels and wash-cloths. Across one mirrored wall was an antique Victorian vanity table, and on top of it were exquisite crystal bottles filled with oils and perfumes. Across another wall was a table like those used in massage parlors. Next to the tub was a silver platter spilling over with many different kinds of fruits, cheeses, and crackers, and there was a bottle of chilled wine next to one very beautiful crystal goblet.

The man rubbed Twila on the back. "This is for you, my dear."

Almost in embarrassment she said, "I need to use the restroom."

"Of course. Right through there," he said pointing to a door.

She went through the door and closed it behind her, thinking the strange man would leave while she was in the restroom, but she didn't know if she wanted him to or not, and that in itself bothered her; it made her feel guilty.

When she came back out he was waiting for her, only he had

disrobed. He was wearing a loin cloth; the rest of him was naked. His dark brown hair was thick and combed straight back, and it hung to his shoulders. His eyes were the color of the sea after a storm and set deep into his chiseled face. He looked strong and in spite of her situation, she thought he was quite possibly the most attractive man she had ever seen.

"I'm going to help you to relax. First I'm going to bathe you, and then I will work out the soreness in your aching muscles." He could see the apprehension in her face; he had expected it. "Don't be afraid of me. I'm not going to hurt you. I'm here to make you feel better. Trust me, Twila." His voice was compelling and tantalizing.

She couldn't speak. All of her sensors were going haywire, and she somehow felt disconnected from her body.

He walked over to her, and using great care and finesse, undressed her. He lifted her petite body effortlessly and placed her into the tub. He picked one of the crystal bottles from the vanity, and Twila watched as the candlelight danced on the cut glass. He poured some of the liquid from the bottle onto her shoulders. It made a sensuous lather that felt good on her skin. The scent was exotic and strong. First, this angel of mercy, as Twila had considered him, washed her neck, her back and then her chest. She was uncomfortable with his touch at first, but soon she realized, at least she felt like, he was not going to hurt her.

"Lie back." He took one of her legs and washed it from the tips of her toes up to the top of her thigh, and then he did the same with the other one. Next he washed parts of her that were completely private, but she did not stop him. He had not hurt her, and his eyes told her not to be afraid.

"Let me help you up so you won't slip," he whispered. He reached for one of the towels and helped her out of the tub then dried off her body with the velvety towel. "I'll get your robe. Can you eat something?"

"Not right now," she said. Her emotions were smothering her. Fear, confusion, and perhaps even lust was not a combination she had ever experienced, nor did she think it proper to feel lust in her predicament.

"Well then, lie down on this table and we'll get started on your massage."

He took back the robe, and she lay down on the table. Her face was flushed from the heat, the candlelight, the bath, but most of all from this man and the way he had touched her and gazed at her. She felt that he could see into her future and also into her past. He was removing the pain that had wracked her body, but the fear that had infected her was still tangible.

He reached for another of the crystal decanters. This time he poured the liquid into the palm of his hand so as to warm it with the heat from his body. His movements suggested no hint that he was planning to rush through whatever was in store for her.

"I'm going to stand behind you," he whispered. "Don't be afraid."

She remained silent and submissive.

As his hands slid down each of her arms, she could feel the heat from his body radiate into hers. The twinkling candles with their intoxicating scents intensified the pleasure she was feeling as he rubbed her sore muscles. Her nudity no longer embarrassed her.

"You are so beautiful," he whispered again as he walked around to the front of the table. Her eyes guarded his every move.

He poured more of the soothing oil into his hands. He took her left foot and worked magic into its sole then took her other foot and did the same. Expertly he worked up and down her legs until the soreness and pain from her confinement had been erased.

When he poured the oil again, he poured it directly onto her chest, between her breasts. It was cold and exhilarating. Her heart was racing and her bosom was heaving. His hands worked her taut stomach muscles and then around and underneath her torso to her back. He pulled his hands, while titillating each side of her spine with his fingers. She could hear the vertebra in her back pop as he moved up and into her neck. Even while sheathed in fear, she had never been so relaxed.

Coming around to her chest again, he massaged her voluptuous breasts. The heat within her began to rise. Her breath was short and pinched again.

Walking around to the foot of the table, he asked her to turn over onto her stomach.

Her buttocks were smooth and firm, and she couldn't help but lift them slightly as he kneaded them. His hands moved up to her waist and then underneath and around to her stomach. His fingers were moving and sliding and heightening every sensation within her, and just as she hoped he wouldn't, his fingers found her most private place. Her conscience said no, but in her frightened and confused state of mind, her body yielded to the sensuous fondling.

As she lay there unclothed, ashamed, vulnerable, and still very much afraid, she could only wonder what would come next.

Chapter 18

Ethel Elizabeth Fletcher had graduated with a degree in elementary education from Stephen F. Austin State University after doing her student teaching twice at Riley Elementary School. Her first go around in the classroom revealed her inability to maintain her temper and interact professionally with students, deeming her an inappropriate candidate for teaching. She was ultimately allowed a second chance and passed student teaching barely, no thanks to Leona Mizell, her supervising teacher.

The first thing one noticed about Ms. Mizell was her streaked and perfectly teased hair. At forty-seven she was five feet nine inches tall and still slender with an arrogance about her that was attractive rather than haughty. Being happily married to the same man for twenty-five years had given her a wide berth of comfort, and teaching had been something she enjoyed since their two boys had enlisted in the army.

Leona Mizell had a no-nonsense attitude and was not the least bit pleased when her principal told her that she would be supervising Ethel Elizabeth Fletcher that semester for her second try at student teaching. Dottie Saxon was her best friend in the whole world, and she knew every detail about the previous semester and Ethel's behavior under her supervision.

The sixth grade students in Ms. Mizell's class were none too pleased about Miss Fletcher's assignment either. They knew of her reputation from their school friends from the year before, but they didn't have a choice about the decision any more than Ms. Mizell did. They were stuck with her for twelve weeks, and they would just have to make the best of it.

Ethel hated the little brats in the class as soon as she saw them. They were obnoxious, selfish, and totally self absorbed as far as she could tell. Discipline was what they needed, and she was the one to give it to them.

Careful not to be too impatient or abrasive when Ms. Mizell was watching, she would not tolerate disrespect from one single child. Any inappropriate behavior from them would be handled in her own good time.

As the semester progressed, students in the class started having accidents. Howard fell out of his second story bedroom window one night. Doctors assumed he had been sleep-walking. He broke both legs, his right arm and his jaw. Kathy was hit by a car while riding her bicycle home from school a week later. Her neck was broken, but would eventually heal. Cindy fell from the bleachers at the first football game of the season. Her head hit several of the steel braces that supported the tiered wooden planks on the way down, causing a serious concussion. She also broke an ankle and sustained deep bruises. Robert was walking home from soccer practice two weeks later when a dog he had never seen before attacked him, biting him on the face, neck, arm, buttocks, and left side of his torso. The dog was never found. Robert had to be hospitalized and required the rabies vaccine and ninety-seven stitches.

The other children in Ms. Mizell's class began getting the message loud and clear that you didn't do anything to anger Miss Fletcher. Howard had talked back to Miss Fletcher at school, and she slapped him. He told Ms. Mizell about it, but Ethel denied it and said he was just trying to get her in trouble.

Cindy and Kathy were whispering and giggling about how ugly Miss Fletcher was, and she walked up on them before they realized it.

Robert had drawn a picture of Miss Fletcher that actually resembled her. He was showing it to some of the other kids before class and she caught him.

Now those four students had been seriously hurt and would be out of school for the remainder of Miss Fletcher's stint.

After Robert's altercation with the dog, Ethel only had six more weeks of student teaching to complete. Ms. Mizell was assigning her more and more of the daily lessons to assume as well as lesson plans and duties such as lunch time and bus duty. Ethel did not mind teaching the lessons. She was very smart and did her homework preparing for each subject. Interacting with the children, listening to what they had to say, watching them eat, waiting for them to get on the bus – that was the part she hated. Ms. Mizell was all too aware of Ethel's feelings of animosity towards the students, and she didn't see how she could give Ethel a satisfactory report if her attitude toward the girls and boys did not change. The children were afraid of her.

The weeks passed and Ethel's disposition did not get any better. The children were extremely cooperative with her and resolute in doing whatever she said to do without question. They did not talk about her or to her unless she asked a question. Ms. Mizell found the atmosphere of the class to be stiff and constrained. It was not normal by any stretch of the imagination.

Leona Mizell had talked to Ethel repeatedly about her relationship with the students and earnestly tried to give her advice about how to treat them and gain their admiration, but Ethel would have none of it. She did not want their admiration. It was not her job to be their friend. It was her job to make them behave and to teach them the subjects mandated by the state of Texas, and she told Leona as much.

In good conscience, Leona Mizell could not give Ethel a passing grade for her student teaching. It was a hard decision to make because she knew that if she failed her, Ethel could not become a certified teacher in the state of Texas. Ethel had gone through four years of college only to fall short of the finish line. Leona had to do it though. She could not put her signature on a report saying that Ethel Elizabeth Fletcher was a qualified candidate to teach people's children and be responsible for them seven hours a day. Ethel was not qualified because she had no feelings, at least no human feelings.

Ethel broke into Ms. Mizell's desk drawer to read the report that she knew Leona had filled out on her. She had to see if she had passed or failed. The report was there, and it was clear. Leona Mizell had failed her.

Only one week was left before Ethel was to complete her student teaching. She acted as though she knew nothing about Leona's decision to fail her. It was Friday afternoon and Leona was anxious to leave school because she and Dottie Saxon, the lady who failed Ethel the year before, were going Christmas shopping in Tyler.

Ethel watched the two women get into Leona's car. She even waved to them. Both women were surprised by that. She could see the looks on their faces. They were so high and mighty, so proud of themselves.

Ethel watched them until they were out of sight, then got in her car and followed them. The streets that led from the school were brick. Nacogdoches was, after all, the oldest town in Texas. The streets were a part of history that the townsfolk had been smart enough to preserve. It gave their town authenticity, and even Ethel saw some dignity in that. The ancient red bricks led all the way to North Street where Leona turned to head out of town. If they noticed Ethel behind them, she could not tell. They were too busy talking about and making fun of her to notice anything, even the surprise that Ethel had put in the car for them that morning.

The sun was very bright and had warmed the day considerably for a December afternoon. The pines looked like preening statues, still frocked in green while the other trees stood nude and unpretentious.

The women continued to gab, enjoying the beautiful weather and each other's company. Teaching elementary school facilitated the Christmas Spirit to its loftiest heights, partially because of all the decorating and activities that accompany those grades, but mainly because the children's appetite for the season was simply infectious. They were eager to get to the mall and spend their hard earned money on people they loved and to revel in the hoopla that the mall would provide.

Neither of the women noticed Ethel following behind them. Ethel had never gone Christmas shopping, she had never had a friend, and she honestly could not recall ever having a good time. For all those reasons and more, she resented the two ladies in the car ahead of her.

Leona was telling Dottie about the letter she had received the day before from her son, Paul, when she felt something crawling up her right leg underneath her pants. She thought at first that it was a bug or something and slapped at it. When she did, she could feel the bulge under her pants leg and the shape of it. Instinctively she knew what it was. Dottie saw the expression of absolute terror on her friend's face and looked to see what Leona was grabbing at underneath the steering wheel. Then she saw it. The end of the snake was coiled up on the floor board, and she instantly knew where the rest of it was. Dottie screamed, and as if the scream were catching, Leona started screaming. Panic unleashed its beast within Leona as she lost control of the car, swerving over to the oncoming lane of traffic. Fear of a head-on collision paled in comparison to the horror in the car with a snake coiling around her leg and gaining ground. It was up to her knee.

Dottie tried to grab the steering wheel. She hollered at Leona to slow down, but the snake was advancing up her right leg, and the gas pedal was at the bottom of it.

Leona's car ran head-on into a gasoline tanker truck that was traveling south going seventy miles per hour. The explosion was colossal.

CঙৎD

Monday morning Ethel offered to complete the year for Ms. Mizell, who had died so tragically. She had already altered Ms. Mizell's report to say that she had done an outstanding job and was highly recommended to be certified as an elementary teacher.

The principal knew, of course, how Leona and Dottie had both felt about Ethel, and also how the children feared her. She was asked to leave immediately, and under the circumstances they would not dock her for her inability to finish her last week of student teaching. The principal could not prove that Ethel had altered her records and therefore allowed her to pass her second stint of student teaching. She would not, however, be given an appointment at their school or any other school in Nacogdoches, Texas.

Ethel was going to find a teaching job. She had a teaching degree, and she was going to teach. No one was going to tell her what she could and could not do ever again. Four years of hard work and straight A's, and then those two bitches gave her a hard time student teaching. They thought she was too hard on the children. They thought she wasn't attentive enough to their needs. They thought her discipline was too rigid. Wonder what they're thinking now, she asked herself.

Those brats did not know what tough was. They were all spoiled rotten and had everything they ever wanted. What were they going to get for Christmas? What was Santa going to bring them? That had consumed their empty heads for weeks. Discipline was what they needed. None of them would have been able to endure even one Christmas she had spent as a child – not one. They didn't have a clue. They didn't know anything. I hate them all. I hate them all! I hate them all! I hate them all!

She packed her belongings and headed to Huntsville to find a job. She had grown up in Walker County, and the house was still there. She hadn't gone back to the house since she had moved to Nacogdoches. There had been no reason to.

Finding a teaching job in Huntsville was just as hard as finding one in Nacogdoches. Sam Houston State University graduated as many education majors as Stephen F. Austin, so Huntsville always had an abundance of applicants. Those who had student taught in the school district had a better chance of obtaining a job there than someone who hadn't.

Ethel Elizabeth Fletcher went to every public and private school in the county only to be turned down after they contacted Riley Elementary in Nacogdoches.

She had to find a place to live, but she couldn't live in her parents' house; she wouldn't. They were dead and buried, but the memories weren't. The memories would never die.

She bought a Huntsville newspaper to look for an apartment. While she was turning the pages, a shiver ran up her spine when she thought she saw a picture of Mother. She looked closer. The woman was the spitting image of Mother, but the name was different. Her mother's name was Elsa Johnson. The woman in the picture went by the name Elaine Tyler. Ethel's stomach did a somersault.

Reading the article, Ethel discovered that the woman in the picture was the superintendent of the Windham School District. She was being honored at a dinner that night for her outstanding accomplishments of reducing recidivism of inmates in the Texas Department of Criminal Justice. The Governor of Texas was coming to present the award himself, and teachers of the Windham School District from all over the state were invited to attend. The article said that Elaine was the wife of Jack Tyler, the director of TDCJ.

Ethel knew this woman wasn't her mother. It couldn't be. She was dead. She had watched as her casket and her father's casket were buried in the family cemetery behind the house. This woman had to be a relative. No two people could look that identical without being related.

She went to a phone booth and looked up the name Jack Tyler and found that it was not listed in the directory. She called information and learned that their number was unlisted, and after a verbal assault on the operator, discovered that there was no way they would release it to her.

The dinner was being held at the Lowman Student Center Ballroom on the Sam Houston State University campus at 7:00 p.m.

At 5:15 p.m. Ethel went to the college campus, parked her car outside the library, and walked to the student center. There was a fast food eatery inside on the first floor, so she ordered tater tots with chili and cheese and a Sprite then sat down at a table with a book.

At 6:30 she went outside to the parking lot to wait for the Tylers to drive up. Ethel was certain that one of the reserved parking spaces would be for them, and of course one for the governor. She wouldn't have any trouble recognizing Elaine if she looked anything at all like her picture.

People were already arriving for the banquet, but the Tylers would probably arrive right at seven o'clock.

It was a humid winter evening with a chill that hung in the air. Ethel's coat was heavy enough for the weather, but the anticipation of seeing this look-a-like of Mother caused her to shiver as if the temperature was in the twenties rather than the fifties.

A late model Cadillac drove into the parking lot followed by a white limousine. Both cars parked in the reserved spaces after which several men got out of the limo and then the governor. The Tylers emerged from the Cadillac.

Ethel's throat closed up for a moment while her heart pumped hard and fast. Her shivering escalated, making her knees buckle. It couldn't be. She had seen the bitch dead, along with her father. They were dead! Dead! Dead! Dead! Dead!

Elaine Tyler stood by her husband as they greeted the governor, both acting as though they knew the governor well.

After they all walked into the building, Ethel had walked to her car. She would wait and follow the Tylers home. She knew well how to wait.

Chapter 19

After the principals' meeting, Earl Cowen decided to visit Elaine Tyler in her office. He was sure she would still be there because she usually worked late. The secretary had already left, so he knocked on the superintendent's office door.

"Come in." Elaine was sitting behind a massive oak desk that had been made by an inmate. She was wearing a green suit trimmed in navy, looking very capable with pen in hand.

"I hate to disturb you this late in the afternoon, Ms. Tyler, but I desperately need to talk to you about one of my teachers."

Elaine could guess who he wanted to talk about. She motioned with her hand for him to have a seat across from her desk.

"Oh really, who?"

"Ms. Tyler, it's Ethel Fletcher." Cowen was determined not to be nervous. The margarita from lunch had about worn off, however.

"What seems to be the problem?" Elaine cleared her throat and tried to keep her composure.

"The same problem Ms. Bolton had. She hasn't gotten any better. In fact, she's worse. I have a file on her two inches thick. She comes to work late, leaves early, talks ugly, teaches poorly, has temper tantrums, calls in sick half the time, and I'll tell you the truth, I'm at my wit's end."

Elaine concentrated hard on what she wanted to say, but the words seemed to dam up in her throat. She took a deep breath and leaned forward in her chair. "As a principal, Mr. Cowen, in a penal institution, I would think a man of your stature should be able to control his teachers. If not, then how can I assume you could possibly control convicted felons?"

He looked at her pointedly, "It's not the same, and you know it. And I believe, along with others, that were it any other teacher, he or she would have been terminated a long time ago." He shoved his glasses back up his nose in a way that showed his irritation.

Elaine wasn't ready for Cowen to cross her like that.

"Who do you think you are talking to?" Elaine spewed indignantly in a hard voice that Earl had never heard come from her. She clinched her manicured hands.

"I'm talking to a woman who has something to hide, and I intend to find out what it is. And don't bother threatening me with my job. If you won't fire Ethel Fletcher, then you sure as hell won't fire me."

"Oh? And what makes you so sure?"

"The look in your eyes, Ms. Tyler." Cowen got up. "I think you are in some deep dung, Madam Superintendent, and I intend to find out exactly what kind. Good night."

Elaine bit back an angry response. She looked at the photograph on her desk of the governor presenting her an outstanding achievement award. Had it just been a year ago? No, she thought, it had been an eternity.

Elaine buried her face in her hands and tried to remember her life before Ethel mangled it so. She couldn't cry anymore. All of her tears were gone, used up. She was thirty-nine years old, but had aged fifteen years in the last twelve months. Her hair had lost its healthy sheen and so had her eyes. She looked dried up and used up, and she had turned into something she had promised herself she would never become.

Slowly she picked up her head and looked at the clock. It was already ten minutes after seven. She needed to go home to her big beautiful house, the house she used to love. She needed to go home to the husband she used to love. If only she could love something, someone, even herself. She thought back to the day Ethel had called her to meet her out at the lake house. She remembered walking in and finding Jack having sex with the maid. What happened next changed everything, but she couldn't think about that now. What was done was done. The girl had made her own bed.

She straightened up her desk, turned off the green banker's lamp, locked up and headed home in her new Mercedes that had been a birthday present from Jack. His gifts had been lavish and plentiful over the past year as he tried desperately to reach her, but she was unreachable.

Pulling into the drive, she realized Jack wasn't home yet. The house was dark. Maybe he's fooling around, she thought. Honestly, she doubted he would ever do that again, and either way, she really didn't care anymore.

After entering the house, she went into the kitchen for a glass of White Zinfandel. Mechanically she pushed the button on her answering machine to hear her messages.

After a few minutes and another glass of wine, Elaine took a hot bath, then read herself to sleep. Alone.

Chapter 20

He handed Twila the robe again. Her face flushed, she was embarrassed that she had allowed this perfect stranger, one of her captors, to touch her the way he had. What was wrong with her?

Twila looked up at the man. "Who are you?"

"I'm someone who is going to take care of you."

"What do I call you?"

Carefully, stoically, he looked at her and said, "My name is Jona."

"What's going to happen to me, Jona?"

"That's not for you to worry about. Let me show you to your room."

She followed with caution. He presented the room with a wave of his hand as if it were an offering from a Greek god. The whiteness of everything in the room was blinding. Twila literally could not speak as she entered her prison. The plush white carpet melted into the white- on-white flocked wallpaper. The white painted furniture was delicate and intricate; the bed was as decorated as a virgin bride. In front of the dresser mirror stood a crystal vase of perfect white roses, the stems and their thorns bringing the only color into the room.

Twila walked over to the flowers and bent down to smell them.

For one brief and precious moment, they reminded her of home.

CB80

While Martha packed, Edward Brooks went to his office and explained to his co-workers what had happened, at least as much as he could surmise. He didn't know when he would be back, and they would be staying at Twila's house – doing everything they could think of to find their daughter.

The television was on. Martha wasn't watching it, but the noise was a relief from the thick silence of the house. She would have been all packed and ready to go when Edward got home if the news had not come on. She heard her daughter's name. It was the lead story for Thursday, February twelfth.

She had feared that Twila had been abducted by the person who had kidnapped the other women in Huntsville, but hearing it on the news, having her daughter's name, and oh, God, her picture, on the news, validated her suspicions. It was no longer just her fear, it was reality. The world would know now, and she wouldn't have those tiny fragments of a moment to think that perhaps she was mistaken and that Twila was just out with a friend and had forgotten her daddy's birthday. She couldn't use those morsels of peace to sustain her any more because the anchor on the news just took them from her. With one sentence he robbed her of what little hope she had left, and she despised him for it. It wasn't his place to take that from her.

When Edward got home, he found his wife on the floor curled up with one of his shirts, sobbing deeply.

He kneeled down to the floor and reached out to her. "Martha, honey, you've got to get a hold of yourself. We've got to be strong so that we can help her. She's out there somewhere, and we are going to find her." He rubbed his wife's arms, then held her close to him.

"But you don't understand, Ed. It was on the news."

He choked back the lump that had firmly attached itself to his throat like a cancer and whispered, "It's all right, sweetheart. Everything's going to be all right."

Chapter 21

With her work day over, Hannah finally reached the gate that opened up to the free-world. She was always tired by Thursday and usually succumbed to a nap on Thursday afternoon. Today, however, she had to go shopping for Valentines. Her enthusiasm for giving and receiving Valentines was like that of a wide-eyed child opening gifts on Christmas morning.

Pushing back the sandman, she turned on the radio in the car and sang with the Bee-Gees. The traffic was light on FM 980. The clouds in the sky were scattered and thin. The weather was supposed to turn much colder by tomorrow with a chance of freezing rain.

She had a standing lunch date with her best friend, Sandy, the day before Valentine's Day every year. This year they were going to meet at Chili's at one o'clock to eat and then go to Bare Necessities to buy some sinful lingerie; something that would hopefully exceed their husband's fantasies. They had grown up together and were closer than most sisters. Hannah had to get her Valentine cards and treats today so she could spend Friday afternoon with Sandy.

She would have to remind William to pick Reed up from school and take him to his fiddle lesson tomorrow. She just hoped that would not be a problem now that he was working with Jeff Stone. William knew that she and Sandy had precious little time with one another and that seeing each other that day every year was not too much to ask. She knew that somehow he would find a way to handle picking up Reed.

Texas Ranger Waylon Abbot was in with the sheriff when William and Jeff got back to the office. The secretary motioned for them to go on in.

"Ranger," Jeff said, extending his hand, "I was hoping to see you today. You know William Douglas."

"Sure do. How's it going?" he asked William, with a handshake.

"Not so good, I'm afraid. My first day on the job and another girl gets kidnapped, or at least we think that's what happened."

"You boys sit down," the sheriff said. "You need to fill us in on what you know about this most recent girl. Twila, isn't it?"

Both detectives removed their hats and took seats. William let Jeff speak first.

"The girl's parents said they were supposed to meet her at her residence at two o'clock p.m. on February the eleventh to celebrate her father's birthday. Supposedly they were all looking forward to it, but when they arrived at their daughter's house, she wasn't home even though her car was parked in the driveway."

Ranger Abbot spoke. "Do you suspect either of the parents at this point?"

"No sir, we don't. William and I just got back from Twila Brooks's residence. Her parents are staying there until they find out what happened to her. We questioned them at length and feel that they are in no way responsible for her disappearance."

"What about the father?" Sheriff Applegate asked. "Wonder if he could have been molesting his little girl while she was coming up and got to missing her now that she's moved out of the house. Maybe he's got her holed up somewhere for his own private use. Or, maybe she got up the courage to take off on her own to get away from him."

Jeff ran his fingers through his short sandy colored hair. "No, sir. I don't think so."

"William, what do you think about him? You're a good judge of character."

William looked up to the ceiling as if the truth were up there and he knew exactly where to find it. He chose his words carefully and finally said, "Well, I'll tell you. Just for a few seconds I tried to imagine what it would feel like to find my child missing, gone without a trace. Those two people, Martha and Edward Brooks, personify anguish, and I don't think we should waste precious time suspecting either of them, especially since there are five other women missing who have so many similarities to Twila Brooks."

"That's good enough for me, Ranger. What about you?" the sheriff asked.

"All right. I'll go with that for now. Tell me what you do have. Anything new?"

Jeff spoke up. "Ethel Fletcher's name was mentioned when we questioned Mark Casey about victim number five, Mary Brown."

The sheriff sat up straight. He looked over at William.

Jeff noticed the sheriff's response and said, "William told me how Fletcher harassed his wife, and that's what makes me think she may have something to do with all this."

The ranger asked, "How so?" Applegate nodded his head and glanced at Ranger Abbot, letting him know he would fill him in on the harassment of William's wife later.

"Well, Mark Casey said that Ethel Fletcher was having a heated conversation with Mary Brown the day she disappeared, and now, finding out that she has a history of irrational behavior with other women, I think it might be a good place to start."

"Look into it. Does she still work at The Walls?" Sheriff

Applegate asked William.

"Yes and no." He looked first at the sheriff and then at the ranger. "She's been suspended. We were on our way to talk to her principal when we had that minor traffic accident yesterday." William grinned at Jeff.

"Oh, yes. Yes. Yes. Yes. I heard about that." The sheriff winked at Abbot. "How are your injuries, Detective Stone? Few, I hear, considering you ran out in front of an oncoming car."

"Yes sir." Jeff's face turned the color of raw hamburger being prepared for the grill.

Sheriff Applegate stood up. The seriousness of the previous discussion was back in focus and printed across his weathered face. "Fellows, you can pretty much guess how much shit has been hitting my fan. These girls were nabbed in my county, damn it, and so far we have turned up squat. Everyone from the FBI on down has rammed a rod up my ass wanting to know what I'm doing about it." He looked down at the floor and rubbed the back of his neck as though that might relieve some of the tension that had sequestered his body. "Shake that Fletcher woman till her teeth rattle if you have even a sneaking suspicion that she might know something about these missing girls." He looked first at Jeff and then at William. "You know what I mean, don't you?"

Both detectives nodded their heads then Jeff stood up and William followed suit. "We're on it." Jeff said.

The detectives exited and went to their office.

"That was so embarrassing!" exclaimed Jeff.

"What?" William asked.

"That friggin' car wreck."

"Well, get used to it. You know the guys are going to ride you pretty hard about it." He elbowed his new partner in the ribs then put his hat back on his head.

"I know. I know."

William noticed a look of amusement on Jeff's face. "What are you thinking about?"

"Oh, nothing."

"Come on. What gives?"

"I was just thinking about that little nurse in the ER. She was, well, I don't know. I just keep thinking about her. She was so sweet. I mean, I know it's her job and all, but she really seemed to care. You know what I mean?"

"Sure do."

"Did you see her?"

"No. I'm sorry to say that I didn't. Why don't you call her?" William wasn't going to rib his new partner about this newfound interest. He wanted Jeff to get a life – a personal life.

"What?" He gave William a dumbfounded look. "Now?"

"No time like the present."

"I don't have her number."

"Call the hospital. She's probably at work."

Jeff reached for the phone and it rang, startling him for a second. "Hello, this is Detective Stone."

Jeff's face broke out into a genuine full-fledged grin. "Oh, I'm fine," he said to the caller. "The stitches don't hurt a bit."

He cupped his hand over the phone, "It's her," he whispered to William.

"You probably aren't going to believe this, but I was just about to call you when the phone rang."

"No, really, I was. I was wondering if maybe you would like to go out some time for dinner and a movie or something."

William wished he could hear the other end of this conversation. Jeff was more nervous than he had ever seen him.

"Great. How about tomorrow night, say six o'clock?"

He smiled. She must have said yes.

"Okay, six sharp. See you then. Well, oh, wait a minute. Where do you live?"

Jeff laughed out loud. She had obviously teased him.

"I'll be there. You just wait and see."

"Bye-bye."

William had to ask, "So, what happened?"

"I've got a date."

"I know that. What were you laughing about?"

"Oh, when I asked her where she lived, she told me that if I was a good detective, I should be able to find that out on my own."

William felt good for Jeff. He slapped him on the back. "Come on. Let's get out of here, Romeo."

Chapter 22

Pleased with her Valentine's Day purchases, Hannah went home. She would have to hurry to get the fudge made before Reed got out of school.

Neiman was waiting at the door.

"What's the matter, Neiman? Am I late today? Do you need to go out? Okay. Here we go." Dragon was trying to loop around her legs while she walked toward the kitchen.

She put her sacks down while the collie went outside to take care of his business. He was back inside before she even got her coat off. No matter how little time she had, Neiman would have to be petted and talked to because he would not be denied. He knew what time she was supposed to get home, and he pouted whenever she was late.

The fudge had cooled just barely enough for Hannah to hide it in her closet before Reed got off the school bus.

"Hey, Pretty. How was your day?" Reed asked as he bounded through the front door.

"Just great. And yours?"

"Good, except John Coker Babbit made me drop my tray in the cafeteria, and I didn't have time to get back in line for another tray. The creep wouldn't even share his lunch with me after he caused me to drop mine." He put his book bag down on the couch and hugged his mother. "Sarah Park gave me her apple."

She patted his cheek. "That was nice." Hannah picked up Reed's book bag and carried it to his room. "I missed lunch myself today, so why don't we go pick up some KFC?"

Reed didn't hesitate. "Wow! Real fried chicken with the skin and crust and grease?" He made a fist and yanked his arm down in victory. "Yes! I'll meet you in the car. Come on, Neiman."

Shaking her head, Hannah grabbed her purse and keys.

"So, what else is going on at school? Anything I need to know about?"

Reed buckled his seat belt. "No, not really."

"Not really. What does that mean?" She looked questioningly at her son.

"I just don't like my history class. That's all. Ms. Manry wants us to memorize the date if somebody important went to the bathroom."

Hannah laughed.

"It's not funny. How am I going to learn all those stupid dates by tomorrow and get ready for my fiddle lesson?" Neiman stuck his head between the seats for Reed to pat him.

"Are you having a test tomorrow?"

He nodded.

"And how long have you known about it?"

"I don't know. A week maybe."

"A week!" Hannah exclaimed. She peered at him and he gave her that pitiful help me look.

"Well, I guess I know what we'll be doing tonight."

"Stuffing those dates in my head. Right, Pretty?"

Hannah tousled his hair. "Right."

William walked through the front door at five o'clock. "I'm home."

Hannah and Reed were in his room studying. She looked at her watch.

"Goodness gracious. Are you home already?"

"I am. Can you believe it? Come here and give me a hug, both of you." Neiman scooted in for his. "Not you, Neiman." The collie looked hurt. "Oh, come here. I'm sorry." Neiman licked his hand. Dragon weaved in and out between everyone's legs. Even the dog's.

"Hey, dad. You'd better wash you hands. We've got Kentucky Fried Chicken, and it is finger lickin' good."

"How do you know it's good? Have you already eaten yours, you little pig?"

Reed laughed. "Yes, and so has Pretty."

"What, you guys aren't going to wait for me anymore?" He took off his jacket and shoulder holster.

"Sorry," Hannah said, "Neither of us had lunch today, and we were starving. Reed, go fix your daddy's plate."

"Why? It's already in a box."

William answered him. "Because I want to kiss your mother all over her face and neck, and I don't want you to see me." He winked at Hannah.

"Yuck! I don't want to see it. Hurry up. Yuck!"

"Do you think we might be able to visit tonight?" Hannah asked.

"Maybe, if you'll turn on the answering machine and make Reed promise not to answer the phone."

While William ate, Hannah finally got to tell him about the dark van that followed her to work the morning before. Somehow, it didn't seem as big of a deal as it had then. She felt silly mentioning it, but William didn't think it was silly at all. He wanted to know what color it was, the license number, and the year and the make.

"You're going to be a better detective than I thought," Hannah said after not being able to answer any of his questions.

"I'm sure it was nothing, and quite frankly, it all seems kind of silly now. No one followed me today."

But William could not let it go. He wanted to follow her to work the next morning.

"William, we are not going to start that. I'm fine, really! No one is going to hurt me. I just over-reacted, that's all, and who could blame me after living with you and Reed? Both of you are so over-protective, and if that isn't enough, Neiman got all bent out of shape because I was late getting home today. Honestly!"

William just looked at her.

"By the way, don't forget that I'm meeting Sandy for lunch tomorrow and then we are going to do a little shopping. Can you still pick Reed up and take him to his fiddle lesson?"

"Sure I can."

"There won't be a problem with Jeff?"

"No. He knows I've got a family. We've already discussed that. You go out and have a good time. Tell Sandy I said hello."

"I love you."

"I love you, too," he said.

"Do I dare ask how your day went?"

"It went fine. Jeff and I talked to the sheriff and to Ranger Abbot about the latest victim. We talked to the girl's parents earlier this morning. That is so sad."

Hannah rubbed his cheek with the back of her hand.

William said, "I'm going to your old stomping grounds tomorrow."

"Where?"

"We're going to The Walls to talk to the principal there."

"Really? Why?"

He hated even mentioning her name in his house. "We have to

ask him about Ethel Fletcher."

Hannah looked surprised. "You're kidding."

"No. She's been linked to one of the victims that was kidnapped, and we have to check it out."

"What?" Hannah's heart skipped a beat, remembering all the trouble she had endured with Ethel.

"Yep, she's been suspended. I'm surprised you didn't hear about it at work."

"Well, it's about time. So, do you think she could be involved in the kidnappings?" She ran her fingers through her long thick hair and wrinkled up her forehead in deep consideration.

"I don't know what to think at this point. I'm just thankful you don't have to deal with her anymore."

"Me, too."

Reed came into the room. "Okay, Pretty, I think I'm ready."

"Ready for what?" William asked.

"Pretty's helping me with my history. I've got a test tomorrow. She said I couldn't practice my fiddle until I learn all the dates for the test tomorrow."

"I thought it was awfully quiet in this house."

"Dad, you're not funny," Reed said rolling his eyes.

"I'll tell you what, let your daddy and me go take a bath, and you can practice your fiddle. When we're finished, I'll come in and help you with your history again."

"Deal."

Hannah did as she promised, but when she came back into the den from helping Reed, it was William who had fallen asleep on the couch.

Chapter 23

Her scream was long and terrifying as though it came from some
haunted berth deep inside her soul. Dr. George Biscamp had put
Blair Compton into a hypnotic trance that had taken her back to her
childhood. He was very tempted to wake her from the nightmare she
was reliving. Nothing in his twenty-three years as a psychiatrist could
have prepared him for the tales that would come from the anguished,
disturbed woman on his couch.

Dr. Biscamp's office was on the twentieth floor of a sky-scraper
in the middle of downtown Houston. It had a warm and cozy feeling
about it even though the outside of the building was glass and steel.
The walls were the color of coffee that has a touch of cream in it,
and dark wood molding set off the ivory colored ceiling. Rich, ornate
bookshelves lined one wall and housed a distinctive display of books,
including three that he had authored. A few tasteful and expensive
curios were placed strategically about by an interior decorator who
had been told to make the office have an untroubled ambiance. The
room, in fact, had more personality than the doctor, and the woman
on the leather couch did not seem an appropriate visitor for the
serene surroundings.

"One of the devils is coming. I can hear him! Oh, please. I don't
want to go in there."

Dr. Biscamp tried to steer her. "Where is the devil taking you?" Sweat was popping out of his forehead even though the room temperature was set at seventy-two degrees.

"He's taking me to the black room." She struggled, apparently trying to detach herself from whoever was dragging her to this room.

"What's in the room?"

"The cages!" she screamed. "Please don't make me go in there," she cried. "Please make them stop. Please!"

"How old are you?" asked the doctor.

"I'm ten and I don't know how to do the dance. They'll kill me if I don't do the dance."

"What dance?" he asked, feeling as if he were in an urgent hurry for the answer.

"The covenant dance. Momma made me take my clothes off. The devil put me in one of the cages and I'm naked," she shrieked. "Oh, no! I need to go to the bathroom." She was squeezing her legs together and crying.

"Tell me what's happening. Is the devil still there with you?"

"No. He's over with the others at the table where all the black candles are."

"What does he look like? Can you remember?"

"They all look alike. They all have on masks, and I can't tell."

"All right. Now, tell me what happens next." Dr. Biscamp didn't want to put his patient through this, but it was the first time in nearly a year of therapy that she had shown any kind of a breakthrough. This could help her to heal, he thought, only to realize there just might be no healing from an experience such as the one this poor woman had apparently gone through. And she had been just a little girl, for God's sake, when all these horrors took place. Just a little girl. Focus, he said to himself.

The room, she remembered, was painted black, and there were

tall black candles everywhere. There were so many candles that the room was almost bright. Yet, the brightness was eerie rather than comforting. She would rather have been in the dark. She couldn't have witnessed the evil if she had been in the dark.

"Oh, good. They picked the girl in the middle cage to dance first," she said, very relieved.

The woman remembered the scene so vividly that it could have been playing in front of her on a stage at that very moment. *That girl is so scared. She can't dance any better than me, and she's skinny as me, too. I know you hate being naked in front of everybody – all embarrassed, but you'd better stop that crying if you know what's good for you. Shut up or you know what's gonna happen. Please stop crying.*

The woman had stopped talking, but her facial expressions showed signs of horror and disgust, and then just pity.

Biscamp waited a few moments for her to continue. Watching the godforsaken and thwarted life in front of him brought a forbidding and undeniable depression upon his own psyche. Doctors of psychiatry were to remain above the melancholia that their patients brought with them, but this patient had cast a moroseness over the entire room.

"Is she dancing?"

His patient eventually spoke, but very softly. "She didn't dance good. They made her lie down on the altar." She was contorting her face again as sheer terror consumed her countenance. "The biggest devil stabbed her with his knife!" she screamed. This scream was not loud; it was almost hollow, almost translucent.

"Stay with me. Tell me what happens next," he prodded.

"They're picking another girl." She looked shocked, almost as if she had seen a revelation that had taunted her for ages, yet the thought of it was inconceivable.

"Do you know this girl?"

"I don't know. I can't see her face. Wait, it can't be."

"What? What's happening?"

His patient still looked bewildered. She was seeing something that confused her, baffled her, and horrified her. "The girl. It's me. No. Wait. It's my sister. My twin sister."

"Is she dancing for them?"

Looking as though she were still perplexed, she answered, "Yes, she dances real good. They like her. She's dancing over towards them. She's putting her hands on the big devil. I can't watch." She turns her head as she said it.

She stops speaking for a moment. "No. No. Oh, no! He's putting her on the altar next to the dead girl." Panic gripped her again.

"Is the devil killing her?" Biscamp asked. He was breathing too hard.

Her face relaxed. "No, but one of the devils is going up to the altar."

"What is the girl doing? Is she crying or screaming?"

"No."

Biscamp was sickened by the scene that this woman was painting. He had to continue. "Are you still in the cage?"

"Yes. I hate the cage. It's too little to sit up straight in, and my back and neck are hurting, but I don't want to be on the altar with the dead girl. That one devil is going back to his chair. The next one is going up to my sister."

Dr. Biscamp, trying to rush her past the horrifying picture she must be witnessing in her mind, said, "The devils are all back in their seats."

"Yes."

"What's happening to your sister now?"

"They're putting a real pretty robe on her and taking her to the special chair. The big devil is telling her that she did well and now she is a high priestess and that she is Satan's daughter. She looks proud, but I don't think she really is."

"Why do you think that?"

"I think she just didn't want to get stabbed with that knife so she pretended to like what they did to her. They'll pick me next time, won't they?"

Chapter 24

Any Friday the thirteenth was a hectic day for policing agencies, and the Walker County Sheriff's Department was no different. If superstition of harrowing events wasn't enough to create chaos, the nasty weather forecast was. Rain would fall first, eventually turning into sleet. The streets would ice over for the most dangerous of driving conditions, and the natives of Southeast Texas would insist on skating their unweatherized vehicles into anything and everything and each other. By nightfall the trees would be frosted with ice. Pine needles would glisten with sharp points and tinkle like Japanese wind chimes. If enough ice formed, the tops of hundred foot trees would snap like firecrackers, knocking out power lines on their way down, but that was only if this storm proved to be anything like the one three years ago.

Hannah, William, and Reed had gone to bed before the ten o'clock newscast and had missed the six o'clock report as well. Hannah had no idea how bad the weather was forecast to be when she left for work Friday morning.

By the time William and Reed woke up, the rain had begun to fall. The temperature had dropped ten degrees since four o'clock that morning.

Reed checked the utility room. "Dad, Pretty didn't wear her

drizzle boots. Why don't you take them to her?"

"I'm not a patrol deputy anymore, son. I'm working on a case with Jeff."

"So?"

"So, what do think Jeff would think if I told him I needed to take some drizzle boots to my wife all the way out to the Estelle Unit?"

"He'd think you care about your wife," he said.

William had no come-back for that remark.

"When I get my driver's license," Reed said, "I'll do things like that for Pretty, and I won't care who is with me."

"And I think you should. You're a good kid, Reed Douglas, and I love you, buddy."

Reed hugged his dad. "I'm hungry. Do we have any toaster waffles?"

"I think we do." William walked towards the freezer.

"Fix Neiman one, too. He looks hungry to me."

"That dog is always hungry," William said as Dragon jumped up on the counter.

"Uh-oh! Dragon's jealous. He wants one if Neiman gets one," laughed Reed.

"Neither of them are getting waffles for breakfast. Take that stupid cat and mangy dog outside where animals belong."

"Dad, it's raining."

William popped four waffles in the toaster. "Trust me, they won't melt."

"Pretty isn't going to like this." Reed picked up the cat lovingly. Neiman whined, wanting the same attention.

"She'll get over it. Scoot!"

"Come on guys. Detective Douglas has spoken. Out you go. Don't look so sad, puppy. I'll probably be next."

The phone rang. William answered it while Reed ate breakfast.

"William, it's me. I wanted to remind you that I'm having lunch with Sandy today and then we're going to do some shopping, but it will be here in town."

"Hannah, I've been listening to the weather report and you might ought to reschedule."

"A little rain never hurt anybody. Besides, I won't melt."

"Funny you should say that. I was telling your son the same thing about the cat and dog when I made him boot their furry butts outside." He was grinning from ear to ear.

Reed was making a face while pointing to the word "lite" on the syrup bottle.

"You what? Don't leave those babies out in this weather. It's supposed to freeze tonight."

"I know. That's why I wish you would come home after work."

Hannah had to think quick. "I'm not going to be out all after-noon, sweetie. We're just going to Chili's and then to Bare Necessities." She wound the phone cord around her finger. "Honestly, you are such a worry-wart, and Reed's getting just as bad."

"I know. I know. He wanted me to bring your drizzle boots to you this morning."

"He did? That sweet thing. Let me talk to him. I love you."

"I love you, too. Here he is."

"Hey, Pretty," Reed managed to say with his tongue wrapped around a chunk of waffle and lite syrup. "What are you up to?"

"Oh, just working. Did you eat a good breakfast?"

"Yes, ma'am." He swallowed. "Waffles. Dad wouldn't fix any for Dragon or Neiman. They look pitiful, too. They're out in the rain looking at the back door." He made it sound truly woeful.

Her voice was just as sympathetic. "Your dad told me. I'll let them in when I get home."

"Don't forget I have fiddle lessons today."

"I'm glad you reminded me. Let me talk to your dad one more time. I love you. Make it a good day. It's Friday the thirteenth, you know," she said, changing her sympathetic voice to a spooky one.

"I know. You be careful, too, Pretty."

"I will, sweetheart."

"Hey," William said, taking the phone back.

"Hey. Don't forget to pick Reed up for his fiddle lesson."

"You guys treat me like I have Alzheimer's. I won't forget."

Hannah laughed. She had to get back to class. "See you both tonight. I love you."

"I love you, too, more than you will ever know." His message was urgent and sincere. Reed rolled his eyes again. "Bye-bye."

Finally, he hung up the phone. For some reason it was hard to do this particular morning.

Hannah's day was challenging, but not unusual. Her students had arrived, wearing their whites and brogans, at 5:00 a.m. She greeted each student as he entered the room trying at the same time to read each face and disposition as they went by her desk to get their work folders. The inmates had been frisked at the door before being allowed to enter the education department. That was just one of the jobs performed by the correctional officers assigned to the department.

Hannah had to be ready for foul moods, depression, or sometimes elation and over- excitement, never knowing what the men had been through or had put others through from the time they left her classroom on one day and entered it again the next. She had developed a sixth sense to judge, by their demeanor, how to respond to each of them on any given day.

The unit was piloting the new SOTP program. The letters stood for "Sex Offender Treatment Program." Behavioral and clinical psychologists were hired to develop group and individual therapy for inmates who were imprisoned for any kind of sex crime.

The Texas Department of Criminal Justice needed programs such as these if inmates were going to be rehabilitated; otherwise, they would be released, commit more heinous acts against society, ruin lives, and land right back in prison and await the date they would be released to do it again. It had been a never-ending cycle for some of these men. While being locked up and punished for their crimes, their minds, the source of their sick and repulsive behavior, had been ignored by the officials of the prison, and worsened by the other convicts. Sexual activity of the most salacious kind was prevalent on the inside of a penal institution, and sexual deviants were taught to be even more perverse while locked behind bars.

Hearing the outcry of the people of the state of Texas, TDCJ had to start doing something to try to rehabilitate the sex offender, and so SOTP was established. All the sex offenders in the Central Region were sent to the Estelle Unit for treatment. They were housed in separate wings from the other inmates and immersed in intensive psychological counseling. It was considered their assigned job to attend these sessions. Those who did not have a high school diploma or a GED, were forced to go to school around their therapy schedule.

Hannah had thought the program was much needed in the prisons. She was not thrilled, however, to learn that the program would be located on her unit and that every known sex offender, sexual deviant, debauchee, and pervert would be housed, fed, and schooled where she worked everyday. Her classes had already been infiltrated by them, and then, of course, there were the regular psychotics who lived on the psychiatric ward. They had always kept things interesting.

Before the hour of six that morning, one of her students had beaten another student to a bloody pulp for masturbating while in her class. A little after seven another student had fallen out of his chair from high doses of Thorazine, a drug administered to convicts who were often prone to violence. Approaching nine-thirty, her second class was working diligently when one of the schizophrenics started hearing voices. The voices were telling him to pull his left ear off his head and then eat it. Thankfully, the two officers responded to Hannah's call in time to prevent the inmate from carrying through with those orders from his so-called head monsters. It was Friday, she had a date with Sandy, and she wasn't in the mood to watch as some lunatic chewed on his own ear. By eleven twenty-five a.m., Hannah's classes were over. Most of her students had accomplished the work assigned to them and had actually learned something.

As she was walking down the well lit corridors to the teacher's lounge, she saw Officer Dillon. His gray and navy uniform was looking a bit faded, but it was starched and ironed to perfection. The inmates who worked in the laundry and handled officers' uniforms took a great deal of care in their work, not because of pride, but because it was one of the better jobs in the prison, and they didn't want to lose it.

"Hey, Mrs. Douglas, about Inmate Fuller, they put him in solitary confinement for fifteen days. Now that creep can be a pervert twenty-four hours a day and nobody will care." He rubbed the back of his neck as if it were tense. "I just wonder if his psychologist will try to make him feel better about himself while he's in there," he said sarcastically.

Hannah sighed and shook her head. "Who knows."

Officer Dillon said, "That's all right. He seems to be capable of making himself feel good all by himself."

"Dillon!" shouted Officer Parrish. "They're on their way. Let's shake 'em down."

"Got to go. Listen, don't waste your time thinking about that jerk for another minute. He won't be put back in your class. There's no way he's gonna beat the case you wrote on him even if he is under the SOTP blanket, so to speak."

"Dillon!" Parrish shouted again.

"I'm on my way," he shouted back.

Hannah smiled. "I appreciate you getting to the room so quickly after I blew my whistle. Fuller looked pretty bad after Inmate Steadman got through with him. Steadman won't get in trouble, will he?"

"No, ma'am, I don't think so. He was just looking out for you. Most of them don't like it when some idiot like Fuller shows disrespect for his teacher like that. Hell, Fuller couldn't hit Steadman back because he was too busy trying to get his pants up. That sure as heck wasn't Steadman's fault."

"Damn it, Dillon." Parrish hollered while looking around the corner. "Get the lead out. They're here."

"I'm talking to Mrs. Douglas, damn it. Grab one of those rookies out in the hall to help you shake down till I get there." Dillon was red-faced. He wasn't leaving until he was finished with his conversation.

"You just go home and take it easy." He patted Hannah gently on the shoulder. "Your day will get better the minute you walk out of this crazy place." He couldn't help but wonder why someone as beautiful, smart, and nice as she was would work in a prison, especially one like Estelle where all the certifiable lunatics lived.

"It couldn't get any worse," she said with a tired but reassuring smile. "Thanks."

"Well I'd better get down there before Parrish has a stroke. He's scared to death he's going to have to do more than someone else."

Hannah chuckled.

As she continued toward the teacher's lounge, she realized once again that the department she worked in wasn't as dreary as it always appeared in her dreams. The cinder block walls were painted white, the floors were as glossy as those found in any hospital, and fluorescent lighting illuminated the department. Except for the teachers' restrooms and lounge, large windows spanned the width of every room, giving an unobstructed view from the hallway, even the inmate restroom. Hannah shielded her face as she walked past those facilities.

The other teachers were talking and snacking in the lounge when Hannah entered. Popcorn was dancing in the microwave and emitting a buttery fragrance that was once confined to the likes of movie theaters and carnivals. The atmosphere of such places, however, eluded the stark, institutional looking room that was considered a sanctuary for the teachers.

"I heard your pervert alert this morning. Are you okay?" Ms. Grimmer, one of the GED teachers, tended to sing her sentences rather than just speak them.

"I'm fine. You'd think I wouldn't let that bother me so much after all these years, but it does. I hate it. And I hate having all those sex offenders in my classes." Hannah was on the verge of tears. In the back of her mind she could hear Reed asking her to get a different job. She could see the look on his face when he asked her if the ex-convict on the news the night before last had been one of her students.

"Lord, I hate it too. I think I'm going to get me one of those whistles." She offered Hannah some cheese crackers that were shaped like fish. "One of my new guys said he thought that was a fire drill when he heard the whistle blow three times. I told him that it was and that more than likely you had extinguished the fire."

Hannah turned around to put her rosters in the appropriate slot.

"Stand still a minute," Ms. Grimmer said. "Let me see what you've got in your hair today." She examined the sterling silver pony tail holder. It was a three-dimensional combination of a giraffe, lion, zebra, hippopotamus, and cheetah. "That is so neat."

"Thank you. Reed gave it to me for Christmas. He picked it out and bought it with his own money – money he won at fiddling contest." She turned back around. "I just love it."

The principal walked into the lounge to get his popcorn out of the microwave. "Ms. Douglas, did you hear the news last night, or was it night before last?"

"Yes, I did, if you are referring to the segment about one of my former students," Hannah replied.

"Yep, that's the one." He crammed a handful of popcorn into his mouth.

"I taught that guy how to read," Hannah said as though it sickened her. "That's why I don't want to know what crimes they have committed. I couldn't teach them if I knew. I do better just thinking that they are all in prison for writing hot checks or for public intoxication."

He nodded. "I know what you mean. Speaking of which, I hear you had some trouble with one of the sex offenders this morning." He opened the refrigerator and grabbed a Dr. Pepper.

"Nothing I haven't had to deal with before." Her face was drawn. Hopefully her boss would see that she didn't want to discuss that for the third time.

Luckily the door opened and the secretary looked at Mr. West. She held her hand up to her ear and mouth like it was a telephone and went back to the office.

"I like her," he said, referring to his new secretary. "She's quiet and reserved, but efficient. I like that." He headed to his office.

12:15 p.m. finally approached and Hannah hastened to leave. She said good-bye to Officer Dillon as he unlocked the door for her to exit the education department. Now in the main thoroughfare of the prison, she found herself humming "Amazing Grace" as she walked down the middle of the hall. Inmates on both sides, in straight lines, not daring to cross the yellow stripe that separated their lane from free-world people, hollered and whistled and made ugly, crude remarks. "Amazing grace, how sweet the sound, that saved a wretch like me," she sang in her head, thinking of how beautifully Reed played the melody on his fiddle. "I'll get him to play that for me tonight," she said to herself, trying to ignore the gestures and expressions resounding in the resonant artery of that insane place she called work.

Chapter 25

Elaine turned off the bath water and stepped in. Almost immediately she felt the stress and tension in her body begin to subside. Carefully, she lowered herself into the warm water and laid her head against the back of the porcelain tub. She was almost relaxed when Ethel crept into her mind again. Her niece had occupied her thoughts, her job, her life, for well over a year now. She could barely remember life before Ethel came.

Ethel had been waiting for her when she got home from one of the most fulfilling nights of her life. The Governor of Texas had presented her with an outstanding achievement award for her work. It had been a perfect evening. Jack had been so attentive and proud of her. The news media was there: radio, newspaper, and even television. She had worn a beautiful Chanel suit that flattered her, and the governor himself told her she looked beautiful. Many of the teachers had come. That pleased her as much as anything, to be appreciated by the people who worked for her. It had indeed been a splendid night until she got home and saw the car pull in behind them.

At first she had no idea who it was, and then the stranger spoke. "Mother, is that you?"

Elaine was startled. Jack had said, "Who are you? What are you doing here?"

The person behind the voice stepped out of the shadows and into the light. The young woman looked harmless and was, in fact, almost pitiful to look at. She didn't respond to Jack's questions, nor did she look at him. She couldn't take her eyes off Elaine.

Elaine felt compelled to run and hide because something in her psyche told her that the life she had built was going to crumble. A puzzling fear saturated her all at once.

Jack tried to decipher his wife's despair. It was written all over her face. "Honey, do you know this woman?"

"No. I don't know who she is."

The voice even sounded like Mother's. Ethel got closer to get a better look and said, "The question is, who are you?"

Jack answered, "Her name is Elaine Tyler. She is my wife and you are on our property. Now why don't you leave, or I'm going to call the police."

"Go ahead. I'm sure they'd love to hear some of the stories I could tell about this woman, your wife, if she is who I think she is."

Jack looked at Elaine and saw dread in her eyes. "Honey, do you know who she is?"

"No."

Ethel asked point blank, "Did you know someone by the name of Elsa Beth Johnson?"

Elaine could not respond.

"Answer me!"

Jack put his arm around his wife. "I'm taking you inside."

"Yes," Elaine said almost in a whisper. Her eyes were fixated on the creature standing in their driveway. She was trembling.

"I thought so. You look just like her, so much so that you could be her twin, an identical twin even."

Jack looked at his wife. "Honey, what is she talking about?"

"Yes," Elaine whispered again.

"Yes, what?" Jack had turned her toward him face-to-face and held both her arms with his hands.

"Yes, Elsa was my twin sister." Tears had formed in her eyes and were now rolling down her cheeks.

"I never knew you had a sister, much less a twin."

Finally Elaine looked at Jack. "I didn't want you to know. I didn't want anyone to know."

"Why?"

"Tell him, Aunt Elaine," Ethel said vindictively. "Tell him why you didn't want anyone to know about your twin sister."

Elaine could not speak. The words were in her throat, but she could not release them. Jack would not understand. He could not find out about Elsa or her life back then. He must not find out.

"Well, Elaine, tell me. I'm listening." Jack's concerned look warmed her heart but at the same time made it more difficult for her to tell him about her past. She couldn't. She wouldn't.

"Jack, I . . . I . . . I'm tired. We'll talk about it tomorrow."

Ethel crossed her arms and drew up her eyebrows. "Aren't you even going to ask me my name?"

Elaine shook her head. "No. Not tonight. Just let me have the rest of this night. You can call me tomorrow." She turned around and started to walk to her door.

"Your number is unlisted."

"Jack, please, give her our number."

Jack fished out a business card from his pocket and wrote their private number on the back of the card and handed it to the young woman.

"Thank you, Uncle Jack."

Ethel put the card in her pocket, got back in her car, and drove away.

The water in the tub seemed to chill the more Elaine thought about Ethel. She was worse than a cancer that robbed your body of its strength and vitality. She had turned Elaine's job, her marriage, her self-respect, her life, into muck. All the years she had worked and strived to climb out and away from the life she had been born to and a twin she had learned to hate were for naught. It was as though none of that mattered now.

Downstairs the door opened. It would be Jack, but he wouldn't come up to tell her he was finally home. He would head straight for the liquor cabinet and mix himself his first drink, and after he drank enough to deaden his senses, he would drag himself into the guest room and sleep until morning. He hadn't touched her in months — not that she wanted him to. She hated sex, but she had tolerated it with Jack for the sake of her marriage, and it had helped that he had never been too demanding of her.

os so

"You'll have to check your weapons at the outside picket, detectives." The new TDCJ officer was fresh out of the academy and still anxious, nervous, and arrogant about his new position of authority, especially over cops.

Jeff and William walked back down the brick steps, flanked on both sides with polished brass rails, and put their hand guns, at least the ones in their side holsters, in the gunnysack. The officer in the tower pulled up the rope attached to the bag.

William called up to the guard. "I don't want you handling my gun. I don't want you to look at it, feel of it, take it apart, or unload it." Jeff looked at his partner with incredulity. "I'm telling you, when you take it out of the bag, use a cloth, a napkin, or your shirt if you have to, because when I get it back, I'm having it dusted for prints. And if yours are on it, I'm coming after you. You got that?"

"Yeah, I got it, dirtbag."

"What was that?"

"Nothing. I won't touch your pistol."

"Good. That's real good." William turned around and started for the brick steps again. Jeff followed.

"Hey," the guard shouted. "How do I know which one of them is yours?"

"You don't," William said.

Jeff didn't know what to say, so he said nothing. William was just a little more aggressive than he had figured, but that was good. That was good.

Virginia Deigo was wearing a pink crepe de chine princess dress that was a size too small. The matching top dress was made of cheap lace and hiked up on her hips. Feeling very pretty, she met the two detectives at the double glass doors.

William could see Virginia when he started up the cement ramp, but Jeff was too busy complaining about the steep ramp to notice anything but the task ahead of him, and that was to make it to the top. He asked William, "What idiot designed this monstrosity?"

"Inmates. What did you expect?"

"I didn't know what to expect, but certainly not this!"

"You've never been inside The Walls before?"

"Nope."

Virginia had opened the door and was babbling at William. "Come on up here, you sweet thing. How in tarnations have you been?"

"Fine, Virginia. How about yourself?" William hugged the secretary that had been so kind to Hannah.

"I want you to meet someone. This is Jeff Stone."

"Hey, Sugar. How you doing?"

Jeff smiled. "I'll tell you in a minute. That ramp just kicked my butt."

Virginia hooted. She splayed her hand over her bountiful bosom and laughed without inhibition. Then, without notice, she hugged Jeff, too. Surprised by her overt display of affection, Jeff winced at William, but good-naturedly hugged her back. Her disposition was infectious, in spite of her wedding party attire. William winked at Jeff, glad that he was treating her with kindness.

"Mr. Cowen," she said knocking on his door, even though it was open, "We've got some mighty fine gentlemen visiting us today. Would you just look at this?" She took William by one hand and Jeff by the other. "A sight better than looking at those convicts day in and day out. Wouldn't you say?" She didn't wait for a reply. Her face was lit up like a Coleman lantern. "This is Detective William Douglas and Detective Jeff Stone." To William, she whispered, "Congratulations on making detective. I'm proud as punch of you." She pinched his cheek. "I read about it in the paper. I'm just glad I didn't know it was you in that wreck, or I'd have been beside myself with worry."

"Well, gentlemen, come in and have a seat." He offered his hand, first to William and then to Jeff. Tactfully dismissing his secretary, he said, "Thank you, Virginia."

"You're welcome." She remained at the door.

Earl Cowen raised his bushy eyebrows above his heavy black glasses, but she had decided not to take his subtle hint. "That will be all, and if you don't mind, close the door, please, ma'am."

Making a face at William, as if to say, I never get to be in on the juicy stuff, she bowed out and closed the door, but not before waving at both of them sheeplishly.

Earl chuckled, "Forgive my secretary. She means well and does a hell of a good job." He shook his head. "But she takes some getting used to."

Jeff nodded his head and grinned. William, however, blew her a kiss over his shoulder. She made great strides to catch it and apply it to her heavily made-up face.

"Well, now. How can I help you boys?"

William took the reins. "We need to discuss Ethel Fletcher with you. We understand that she has been suspended."

He nodded.

"Can you tell us why?"

"Same old stuff. From what Virginia tells me, you have had some first hand experience dealing with her."

"Yes, sir, I have."

"She hasn't changed one iota. In fact, I'd be willing to say she's gotten worse, or at least her attendance has gotten worse. She's always late. Tries to leave early. Throws hissy-fits in her class. Treats the inmates like scum-bags. Do you get the picture?"

"Yes I do."

"I've written her up umpteen times and not a damn thing is ever done about it, and my ass is in a crack right now for suspending her."

"Why's that?" Stone asked.

"I went to the superintendent, Elaine Tyler, and told her what I had done, and she was none too happy about it. I even accused her of having something to hide. She all but threw me out of her office and possibly would have if she'd thought she had the tough to do it. She did say that I might need to worry about my job, and I told her that if Ethel Fletcher couldn't get fired over the kind of stuff she's been pulling, that I certainly didn't have anything to worry about. She told me not to be so sure." He raised his bushy eyebrows over his eyeglass frames and pursed his lips together.

"Do you know why Ms. Tyler is reluctant to discipline Ethel?" William asked.

"I just know that Ethel used to live with them."

Jeff crossed his leg and looked at William.

Cowen noticed the serious look and asked, "Do you mind me asking why you boys are interested in Ms. Fletcher's problems at work? She hasn't been harassing your wife again, has she?"

"Oh, no, sir. We're just trying to check out all the people who had contact with any of the kidnap victims immediately before their abductions, and Ethel's name was brought up. Just a stab in the dark, but eventually we hope to hit on something."

Cowen's owl-like eyes peered sharply through his heavy black glasses. He propped his elbow on his crossed arm and rested his finger on his pale lips. "God almighty."

"It's nothing to get alarmed about. It's merely routine," William said, trying to douse the fire behind Earl Cowen's face.

"There is nothing routine that involves that crazy woman. I've been a principal for twenty-five years, and I have never seen anything that would even compare to her. I hate to say it, but if evil had a face, it would look like Ethel Fletcher."

Chapter 26

The door, of course, was locked, and the window had bars on it. Both the bars and the window panes had been painted white to match every thing else in the white, white, room. Twila was still trapped, but at least she was out of the cage.

Her guilt for allowing Jona to give her pleasure was taunting her. The fact that she had so easily succumbed to the pleasure he gave her made her feel like a whore, less than a whore. At least a whore knew what she was in the game for.

She lay down on the fantastic white bed, closed her eyes, and let sleep rescue her for a while.

ༀ

While still humming *Amazing Grace*, Hannah came to the control-picket and grabbed the handle of the massive steel door but did not pull.

"Ms. Douglas, is something wrong?" questioned the guard in the control-picket room.

"Oh, no, ma'am. I guess I was daydreaming."

Hannah pulled the door open and made her way toward the next one. It slammed behind her. On the right was the room where lawyers visited with their clients who were in prison there. A woman was talking with an inmate through the barred and screened window, but Hannah paid no attention to the inmate. She was caught off-guard by the woman who was apparently an attorney. The woman was swinging her leg as though she was preparing to kick someone with it, and the motion was continuous. She felt as if she should know the woman, even though she couldn't see her face under the stunning hat the woman was wearing. A strange feeling swept over Hannah. The door in front of her unlocked electronically. She pulled it open wishing she could get used to the loud heavy slam it would make on closing shut.

Finally, Hannah came to the main lobby. She felt like it had taken her an eternity to walk from the education department to the front door. She had spent nights before dreaming that she was walking through a dark, bleak tunnel that never came to an end, and she wondered now if those dreams stemmed from the journey she had just made.

The parking lot was straight ahead and only two more gates to go through. Seeing the sky and trees and feeling the free-world air saturate her lungs gave her a sense of relief. She always felt like God was blowing her a kiss when she exited the confines of the steel bars, cement walls, and oppression.

Now if she could only find her car.

⊂ℬℰ◯

The inmate visiting room at the Estelle Unit was to the left of the front lobby. It was a long narrow room with a row of chairs down each side.

"Can you handle this?" The visitor demanded through the screen while her leg continued to sway back and forth.

"Yes, I can handle it," Leo Trinket said, brimming with confidence, but looking so very inadequate in his wrinkled white uniform that distinguished him as a criminal. His false teeth were in his shirt pocket. Leo scratched his chin and thought for a minute as though an intelligent question was coming to mind.

"Well? she asked impatiently.

"There's just something I don't understand about all this."

"Oh, really," she said sarcastically.

"Yeah. What exactly do you need me for? You could do this job without my help." Leo's mental reasoning was slow due to the medication he was taking, but he was not retarded.

Her leg began to move more swiftly. "I just thought you would want an opportunity to get out of the joint. You scratch my back, and I scratch your back sort of a thing. That's all."

"No. You were thinking I wouldn't figure it out by you just springing this on me so quick and all, but I know what you're up to. You're thinking the police will blame all this on me, just like the last time I helped you." His stare was so penetrating that the black iron mesh separating them seemed to disappear. "They'll all think I kidnapped that woman and stole her car. You want me to be your patsy. You don't think anyone will suspect you, and all the while the entire state, shoot, the entire country, will be out looking for me. That's why you're here pretending to be my lawyer, using a different name and all disguised up." Leo wasn't angry. The medicine he was on didn't allow his brain to administer anger impulses. He was just more or less pleased with himself for figuring out her scheme.

"All right!" she exclaimed. "But just look at it from your side." She tried to look convincing and sincere. "You're doing life without parole. You have absolutely nothing to live for or to look forward to except one day after another in this hell hole. Aren't you sick of it? Don't you want to live again?"

"Live again?" He exhaled indignation through his nostrils like a bull standing before a matador. "I've never lived at all." His eyes grew red and moist.

"Look, I'm offering you a way out of here for what I'm getting in return. I'm taking a risk, too, you know. Besides, what's the worst they can do to you if you do get caught? You are in here for the brutal murder of two people. They didn't send you to death row because of the circumstances involved. You wouldn't be this time either. You'd just be brought back to prison, maybe with more time added, but what's more time for a lifer?"

She made a good point. Leo was listening.

"And if you don't get caught, hey, it would have all been worth it. Just getting out of here for a little while would be worth it, I would think."

Leo Trinket thought for another minute and said, "You're right. What has a lifer got to lose?"

"I knew you would come to your senses."

"Time is up. Form a line for strip search," yelled the guard.

"What's the lady's name?" asked Leo.

"Hannah Douglas," she whispered, getting up to go.

ᴄ৪৪ᴆ

Hannah couldn't remember where she had parked that morning. She had been preoccupied with thoughts of Reed and his begging her to get another job. She felt kind of stupid for a minute. William had told her to try and park in the same place every day since she had a habit of forgetting where she parked in any parking lot, but that was easier said than done. The security officers had different days off and therefore people didn't have regular parking spaces, except of course the warden, his assistants, the principal, the doctors, the handicapped, and the employee of the month. She began walking down the rows of cars looking for hers. She was beginning to wonder if perhaps her car had been stolen, but then she decided that someone would have to be pretty brazen to steal a car from a prison unit parking lot.

Hannah was on the last row of cars when she heard a vehicle driving up behind her moving very slowly.

She turned her head to look as she moved out of its way. It was the dark green van with tinted windows. Hannah's heart skipped a beat. Her sweat glands sounded a red alert even though the weather was cold and wet.

"Looking for something?" the voice from inside the van asked after lowering the window.

Hannah looked in through the window to find the lawyer from the attorney counseling room she had just passed. Then she looked more closely. The woman was wearing oversized tinted glasses. Her hair had been stuffed up under a large brimmed hat and she was wearing heavy makeup, but underneath the hat and makeup was no lawyer. It was Ethel Fletcher.

"Let me give you a lift."

"No, I mean thanks, but I don't need one. I have my car here."

"Oh really. Where?" she asked derisively. She looked over the parking lot, unable to keep a satirical grin off her heavily made-up face.

Hannah felt her own face turn a deep shade of red. "It's over there. I just remembered. I parked over there this morning."

"You know, Hannah, I'm hurt. You act as though you're not happy to see me. And it's been months."

Hannah, her brain searching for the files that contained her knowledge of psychology, took a deep breath and let it out. "You're right. I'm sorry. I was just surprised to see you here, and you look so different that I didn't recognize you for a minute." Trying to muster some composure she said, "You look splendid. You really do."

Ethel smiled through garish fuchsia lipstick.

"Thank you."

"Hey, it was nice seeing you, but I have really got to go, but it was nice seeing you again." She turned to leave when she heard a sound. A pistol hammer being cocked.

"Get in the van, sweet Hannah." Having the gun in her hand aroused her. It made her feel dominant, in charge, in control.

Hannah stopped dead in her tracks and slowly turned around. "Ethel, you aren't going to use that. There is a guard up there in the picket-tower. He'd see you." Hannah felt her knees trembling beneath her skirt. The situation seemed like it was happening to someone else and that she was just an invisible bystander watching it all take place.

"I said, get in the van, bitch!" Ethel's voice was hostile.

Hannah looked around. Was there not one person coming or going other than herself? What were the odds?

Ethel, reading Hannah's thoughts, said, "It's Friday the thirteenth. Not your lucky day." She smiled. "Thirteen is my luckiest number."

"I'm not getting in the van with you, Ethel. I'm not that stupid. I know you aren't going to shoot me in broad daylight in front of a prison guard." Hannah turned to walk away, trembling violently on the inside as well as on the outside of her body.

Ethel laughed sadistically. "Whatever, dear, sweet Hannah. I'll tell your son that you just don't give a hoot and a holler about him."

The sky seemed to bear down on Hannah as if it was trying to push her directly into the ground. She turned to face her adversary. The look of astonishment and fear in her emerald green eyes gave Ethel much pleasure.

"That's right. I have Reed. And if you ever want to see him again, then you will just have to come with me."

The slightest cool breeze stroked Hannah's cheek as though everything was all right, but it wasn't. Nothing was right. "I don't believe you," Hannah finally managed to say.

"Well, I was afraid of that, Hannah Banana, so I brought this along to convince you." Ethel tossed a hand-tooled leather wallet at her. It had a fiddle on the front of it along with the name Reed. Hannah had commissioned one of her students to make the wallet for one of Reed's Christmas presents. With trembling hands, she opened the wallet and found his school ID card, his lunch card, and a picture of William and her that he had taken of them the previous summer in Galveston.

Hannah got into the van.

Chapter 27

Jeff had almost as much trouble getting down the steep ramp as he did climbing up. " I'm glad I'm not in a wheelchair," he spouted. "They could haul this thing to Astroworld and seriously have something to brag about." He cupped his hands over his mouth like a megaphone. Attention all wheelchair patrons. Line up for the ride of your life."

William laughed.

"I'm not kidding. I know that prison is no country club and isn't supposed to be, but this is cruel and unusual punishment for those poor guys in wheelchairs. Man!"

"Would you cut it out?" William said as he slid down the last couple of feet in his new loafers. "I'm trying to summon my ugly side for that jerk in the tower-picket."

Reaching the ground, Jeff said, "Well, you sure didn't have any problem finding it before."

They entered the holding area for transient inmates, soon to be ex-mates. The bars on both sides of the walkway were solid brass and shined to a high gloss.

"I'm ready to get the heck out of here," Jeff said.

They showed their badges and ID's to the officer in the booth.

"This place bothers you, doesn't it?" William asked.

"I wouldn't want to work here. I don't know how your wife stands being locked up all day, but I do know how she got those sexy legs of hers."

"Oh, yeah? How's that?"

"That frigging ramp."

Finally outside, William approached the tower-picket. "You can send our weapons down."

"Let me see some ID," the guard retorted.

"I'll show you some ID up close and personal." William started for the iron staircase that went up the tower.

"What the hell are you doing?" the guard asked, noticeably getting nervous.

"I'm coming up to get my weapon and show you just exactly who I am."

Jeff just stood there dumbfounded.

"Wait, hold on! I'm sending it down. I'm sending it down."

Carefully, using a paper towel he placed both guns in the gunnysack and lowered it to the ground.

"Thank you. Have a nice day," William said.

"Yeah, well same to you, jerk-face."

Jeff had to ask. "What's with you and that tower boss?"

"Nothing with him personally. It's just that I've had to go to a lot of units to pick up prisoners for bench warrants, and it never fails, the fools in the pickets get your gun and think they ought to get to play with it. They think they're some kind of cop because they wear a uniform and corral convicts."

"You're exaggerating. Right?"

"Nope. I got my .45 back one time and the idiot in the picket had taken it completely apart. He didn't know how to put it back together, so he just sent it down in the bag in a dozen pieces. I had a convict with me, in cuffs, to transport to The Walls. I was so mad

I wanted to wring that fool's neck."

"What did you do?"

"After chewing him out, I told the guard in the ID booth to call the warden to come out there."

"Did he call?"

"He didn't want to, but I told him I would arrest him for obstruction of justice if he didn't, and that he would lose his job right along with that fool in the tower. He changed his mind and called the warden."

"What did the warden do?"

"He fired the guy on the spot and sent for a major to come out and hold the prisoner while I went into the visitors' waiting area to put my .45 back together."

"And that's happened more than once?"

"Not quite that bad, but I've had it come down with the magazine out, and one time I got it back, checked it, and found that the guard had removed the bullets and hadn't replaced them."

"You're kidding."

"I am not."

"Why would he have done such a thing?"

"He had sent himself through the police academy and couldn't get hired with the city or the county. He was a cop-wanna-be. Resentful, I guess. Got him fired too."

They were driving to the Sheriff's Office. "So, to change the subject, are you ready for your hot date tonight?"

Jeff grinned. "I haven't been this nervous in a month of Sundays."

"Why are you so nervous? You've been on plenty of dates."

"I know this girl's name."

"Oh."

CЗ୫Ͻ

Jona took a tray up to Twila. The meal, on a delicate china plate, looked as though it had been prepared in a fancy restaurant. The T-bone steak was an inch thick and cooked medium well. There was rice, steamed vegetables, hot buttered bread, and sautéed mushrooms in butter and wine sauce. Italian cream cake was for dessert. In crystal glasses were water, iced tea, and red wine. And in a crystal bud vase was a single red rose. RED.

He put the tray down on the table outside the bedroom door and knocked before unlocking it.

"Hello, Twila. I brought you something to eat. You must eat to keep up your strength." He paused and looked at her compassionately. "And a red rose."

Twila looked at the meal, and her stomach growled. She hadn't realized she was hungry until now, but the blood red of the rose amidst all the whiteness took her breath away. "That looks wonderful."

"I'm glad." He started to leave.

"Wait, please don't go."

"I must."

"Will you come back in a little while?"

"Yes, I'll be back in a while."

"When?"

"You'll see. It won't be long. Enjoy your dinner."

Twila ate heartily, but fear of the unknown diluted the taste of the meal.

CЗ୫Ͻ

"Jeff, I need to pick Reed up this afternoon from school and take him to his fiddle lesson. Hannah usually does it, but she's had a long standing date with her best friend, and I didn't ask her to break it."

"You don't have to ask me for permission to pick up your kid."

"Yeah, I know. I just didn't want you to think it would be an everyday thing. It's just that this detective business sprang up kind of sudden, and we had already mapped this week out at home."

"William, it's not a problem."

"Okay. That's good then. I'll just . . ." The phone rang.

"Hello, this is Detective Douglas."

"Hello. This is Edward Brooks. We were wondering if you had any news about our daughter."

"We're following a couple of leads and doing everything we know to do to find your daughter, sir. I wish I had something positive for you, but I don't."

"I see." He sounded wounded.

"How is your wife?"

Edward looked at Martha before answering the question. "Maybe it would help if you could come over and talk with us for a few minutes. Just tell us what you've done on the case."

"Sure. We'll come right now."

"I'd appreciate that. We'll see you in a few minutes then." He hung up the phone and looked again at his wife. She looked much older somehow. It was as though desperation had spread through her body and into her cells, strangling her skin.

Martha asked, "Do they know anything? Anything at all?"

"Nothing definite. But they're coming over to talk with us."

"Good. If I could just talk to them."

"I know, dear. I know."

03 80

"What have you done with my son, Ethel? Is he all right?" Hannah knew Ethel was emotionally disturbed down to the core of her soul, and it absolutely scared her to death to think that she had done something to Reed.

Ethel ignored her questions. She just smiled.

"For God's sake, tell me what you have done to my child. If you've hurt one single hair on his head, I'll kill you. I mean it, Ethel. I'll kill you."

"Ooooh! I'm so scared. You are really feisty when you're mad."

Psychology textbooks would instruct that you stay calm when encountering a person such as Ethel, but Hannah's heart was playing tug of war with her Adam's apple, and textbook logic wasn't a match for a mother's fear or anger.

"What have you done to my son?" Hannah yelled.

Ethel relished the moment. The thought of Hannah being frightened titillated her, and she wasn't about to tell her anything.

"Answer me!"

"Shut up!" Ethel scolded. "Now, take these handcuffs and put one side around your left wrist."

Hannah just stared at the hideous creature next to her.

"Do it!" Ethel screamed. Her lipstick was thick and went beyond her lips to make them look fuller. Instead, it made her look crazy, like the character Bette Davis played in *Whatever Happened to Baby Jane?*

Hannah took the cold metal bracelets and did as she was told while the demented person next to her stuck a pistol in her face.

"That's better. Now, put the other one around the door handle."

Hannah obeyed.

"Good girl. We're going for a little ride."

Ethel drove down the drive that led from the employee parking lot to the road that was the only paved entrance into the Estelle

Prison Unit. The three mile road had fenced-in pasture land on both sides. Cattle were on the right hand side; the hoe squad was on the left. Field bosses watched as the convicts swung their hoes in unison while high riders, atop state owned horses, surveyed the spectacle at a distance. If only they knew what was happening in the van passing by them.

"Ethel, where's Reed? Why are you doing this?" Hannah asked sincerely.

"You treated me like dirt, Hannah Douglas. I tried to be nice to you, but no, you wouldn't have it. You threw it back in my face like I didn't even exist. I really cared for you, and where did it get me? You tried to get me fired. Now you're going to see what it feels like to be hurt like you hurt me."

"But that's not how it happened. You were making advances toward me that went beyond a normal friendship. I'm married. I'm in love with my husband. You couldn't expect a relationship with me, not like you wanted."

"You don't know anything about what I wanted or how I felt," Ethel shouted. Her body was stiff and straight as her hands gripped the steering wheel the way a strangler might choke his victim. "I hate you, Hannah Douglas. I hate you. That's all you need to know for now."

"What did you do with my car?" Hannah asked.

"It's in a safe place."

"How did you move it without the keys?" Hannah asked, trying to get her to talk and perhaps eventually expose some information about Reed.

"Oh, I've had a set of keys for awhile. I borrowed your set during in-service and had a set made of my very own during one of the sessions. No one ever missed me. I had them back in your purse before lunch. You're such a nincompoop." She took her eyes off the road long enough to glance at Hannah. "I took them right out of your purse, from right under your uppity nose and you never had a clue. I am so much smarter than you. Don't you wish you could be half as smart as me?" She was puffing up with arrogance.

Hannah thought back to the teacher in-service training. She remembered trying to avoid Ethel, but Ethel watched her and went to every session that she attended except for one. She never missed her keys, but her state ID card had disappeared. She thought she had simply lost it. She had to have a new one made, and it had cost her twenty dollars.

"Yes, I do wish I was as smart as you. Tell me, are you really a lawyer?"

"I am a lot of things. But why do you care? Are you looking for one?" Ethel sneered.

"Well, no. I was just wondering how you got into the prison and into the attorney counseling room if you didn't have the proper identification. That's all. I'm just curious. Intrigued really."

Ethel was elated that Hannah noticed how clever she was, but she wasn't going to tell her everything. "You have to know the right people, and I know the right people."

Hannah knew Ethel was smart – brilliant even, and that's what made her so dangerous. "God, please let Reed be all right," she prayed.

Ethel turned left on FM 980. She was taking Hannah to Hell.

Chapter 28

Dr. Biscamp was not at all sure how to deal with Blair. In all honesty he was frightened of the case. He was frightened of what else he would learn from her. The atrocities she suffered at the hands of adults, her parents for God's sake, made him want to puke. He found himself wondering if indeed they were true or if she had made it all up. But who could make up such a story? And who could do so under hypnosis? He rewound the videotape of their session on Wednesday.

Dr. Biscamp watched himself on the video as he hypnotized Blair, sending her mind back to the farmhouse.

"Blair, where are you?" he asked.

"Momma's pushing me. She's pushing me into the house and telling me to go into the dressing room. She's going to make me get naked again."

"What happens next, Blair? Tell me what's happening. Is your mother still in the room with you?"

"Yes, but she won't talk to me when we're in the little room. It's like she is dead behind the face. She just stands there after I'm undressed and waits for the devil to come."

Blair's body trembled as she waited for the devil. It was as though she were experiencing the past in reality once again, and

Biscamp did not know whether he should let it continue or stop it. Would it help her to remember, or would it destroy her?

"I'm so scared," she said as she waited. "He's coming. I can hear him. He's coming to get me." Blair resettled on the couch, trying to make herself invisible to the devil that was coming after her. She drew up her knees to her chest and clasped her arms around them, interlocking her fingers. She buried her face under her knees, with her chin as close to her chest as she could get it. It reminded the doctor of a young toddler playing peek-a-boo, thinking that if he covered his face then no one could see him.

Blair started screaming. Biscamp was about to stop the session when she suddenly stopped and her whole demeanor, her entire personality, changed right before his eyes. Her facial expression altered and she opened her eyes. She sat up on the couch. He thought she had brought herself out of the hypnotic trance.

"Blair, are you all right? he asked.

"My name isn't Blair," she said.

"Oh? What is your name?"

She straightened her skirt and fussed with her hair. "My name is Leena."

Biscamp had studied Multiple Personality Disorder, but he had never treated a patient who had suffered from that psychosis. He had found himself wondering at times as to whether or not the illness truly existed or if some people with vivid imaginations only pretended that it did, and so convincingly in fact, that some of their therapists believed them.

"Well, aren't you going to talk to me?" the woman asked in a very distinct and assertive tone of voice. There was no childlike quality about the voice and certainly no hint of Blair.

"Yes, of course I'm going to talk to you. What would you like to talk about?"

"I would like to talk about Blair."

"All right." Biscamp said, "What about her?"

"I happen to know that you are trying to help her, but I do not think that is a good idea."

"That's interesting. Why?"

"For one thing, the questions that you are asking her could very well kill her. I am completely surprised that she is not already dead."

"Why would the questions I have asked her, kill her? I'm afraid I don't understand."

"Of course you do not understand. You weren't there." She was smooth and very sophisticated.

"I wasn't where?"

"At the farmhouse where they operated on her."

"Why don't you tell me about it. I wouldn't want to hurt Blair, and I would appreciate anything that you could tell me that might help." He felt like he needed to go back to school to deal with this patient. He was not ready, even after all of his years of experience, to handle a patient like this. He could hear his father telling him that he wasn't made of the right stuff. He would never make anything out of himself, and then when he became a psychiatrist, his dad told him that shrinks weren't real doctors. That was the pussy way out for guys that couldn't handle the blood and guts. Anybody could listen to some loser spout off about his problems.

Leena crossed her legs in a very lady-like fashion and smoothed her skirt again. Her entire physical body looked different, more cultured, more refined, as though it did indeed belong to someone other than Blair.

"Blair told you about the cages and the dances, but she can't tell you about the other things that happened to her. It would kill her."

"You don't think she's strong enough to talk about those things yet?" he asked, thinking he was beginning to understand why this personality had presented itself to him.

"No, that is not the reason."

"Then what is the reason?"

"She will literally explode before your very eyes if she answers too many more of your questions."

"Well, that is an interesting way to put it." he said.

"I am not here to amuse you, doctor, I am here to save Blair's life." She looked annoyed.

"Leena, I promise you that I am not going to hurt Blair, but if you think I am overloading her psyche, then I will listen to you and be less insensate in my questioning; give her more time."

"You have not been listening to me, doctor. I said she would explode, blow up, disintegrate, if she gives you information that they do not want you to know."

"How is that possible?"

"A bomb was planted inside of her, and it will go off if she tells things they do not want her to tell."

She looked so candid when she made the preposterous remark that Biscamp wished he could believe her, but he couldn't, of course.

"And how would the bomb know if Blair told me things that they didn't want her to tell?"

"She has eyes in her stomach that see everything she does."

He shifted in his chair and propped his elbow on its leather covered arm. Removing his glasses, he asked, "And how did those eyes get there?"

"They made her swallow them at one of their ceremonies. They had a ceremony for everything. They can see everything that she does, hear everything that she says, and know every thought that she thinks. They literally see her soul."

"They actually made Blair swallow eyeballs?" Biscamp was finding the story ridiculous and seriously wondering if the whole thing weren't some sort of ploy to make a fool out of him, but then he looked in the face of this woman and realized that she truly believed what she was saying.

"I can tell that you are finding my story hard to believe, but I am speaking the truth. Blair was seated, along with five other children, at a table. The room was dark except for the candles that were burning in the middle of the table. You could smell the flesh of the babies from the candles. You see, the candles were made from the fat of the babies that were sacrificed to Satan. Nothing was wasted. Nothing."

Biscamp was feeling sick at his stomach. It was too warm in the office. Beads of perspiration trickled down from his hairline at the nape of his neck and rolled down his back.

"Go on," he said. "Where did the eyes come from that Blair and the other children had to swallow?"

"Like I said, nothing was wasted."

The doctor looked close into the television screen to examine the facial expressions, the eyes, the mouth, anything that might give a hint that the patient was fabricating the story she was surrendering to him.

"Tell me one more thing, Leena."

Her face was stone, separate from the rest of her.

"Where did they get the babies?"

"Really, Doctor. Can't you figure that out?" Leena said in an acrimonious tone.

"Perhaps, but why don't you go ahead and tell me?"

Leena reached inside the purse that Blair had brought in and took out a cigarette. Her mannerisms were so sophisticated. He lit Leena's cigarette.

She drew on the cigarette, held it in her lungs for a few seconds and exhaled. "The devils impregnated the young girls when they raped them. After the babies were born, they were taken and used almost immediately in ceremonies." She drew on the cigarette again. "Like I said, they had a ceremony for everything."

Biscamp asked, "Where did they get these young girls?"

"The government brought them." She took another drag on her cigarette and glanced at the doctor under raised eyebrows and a halo of smoke.

"The government? I don't understand."

Leena looked at the antique grandfather's clock. "It's about time for Blair's session to be over. I have to go."

The woman put out her cigarette in the hand-painted china ash-tray that adorned the table in front of the couch. She then closed her eyes and lay down.

Dr. Biscamp asked the patient, "What is your name again?"

"You know what my name is, don't you?" a little girl's voice asked.

"Of course I do, Blair. I'm going to count to five and you will wake up. One, two, three, four, five."

"How did it go?" a grown-up version of Blair asked.

"I think we made some progress." It was all he could manage to say.

He turned off the video player.

Chapter 29

Ethel is smart. I'll give her that, thought Leo as the officer searched his exposed body. She had figured out an escape plan that just might work. It just seemed so simple, maybe too simple. When the letter came from an attorney's office saying that a lawyer was coming to see him, he didn't have a clue what it was about, but he never dreamed that it would be Ethel. Besides, she wasn't a lawyer, or at least he didn't think she was. Anyway, that get-up she had on sure made her look better than her normal self. *She kind of looked like a lawyer today,* he thought. On second thought, he wasn't sure what a lawyer was supposed to look like.

Leo was the orderly for the front offices, the lobby, visitation room, rest rooms, and laundry pick-up room. After his visit from Ethel, he had to go to work. It was his job to clean the floors, dust, wash the inside windows, and empty the trash.

Leo was about to empty the trash container by the front lobby door when Lieutenant Grady came up behind him. "Trinket, did you decide to get yourself a new lawyer?" he asked.

"Yes, sir, boss. I sure did."

"What do you need a new lawyer for? I mean, what can she do for you that your other one didn't do?"

"Well, sir, she's gonna try and get my sentence reduced some."

"Mercy, Trinket. Your first lawyer kept you off death row. That was a miracle, a miracle he performed. I doubt God had anything to do with it." He snickered at himself. "After all, you did kill your parents in cold blood, and from what I hear there was a lot of blood."

"That's what they tell me, boss. That's what they tell me."

Leo was twenty-five years old, but like most convicts, he looked at least ten years older than what he was. Having no teeth, other than the false set he carried in his pocket, added to the look of being older than he was. His furrowed face had a harshness to it that made his faded brown eyes insignificant.

Leo emptied the trash and headed for the next container while Lieutenant Grady answered the phone on his desk. Quickly the inmate searched for the ID card Ethel had put in the trash. He found it and slid it inside his wallet. Next he went to the officer's laundry pick-up room, hoping Lieutenant Grady would be on the phone for at least a few more minutes. The inmate who worked in there was busy making number markers for the hangers. He didn't pay any attention to Leo. Leo had been doing the same job for months, and as far as that guy knew, today would be no different that any other day. He grabbed a laundered shirt and some slacks that looked to be his size and put them in the extra trash bag he had hidden inside the other one, then went right on working.

He knocked on the assistant warden's office door.

"Come in," Warden Skinner said.

"It's me, Warden. Just gettin' the trash."

"Go ahead." Warden Skinner responded without looking up.

Leo got the waste basket next to the warden's desk, emptied it in his bag, went straight to the door, lifted a cap from the hat rack and tossed it in with his other findings.

The count whistle blew signaling a clear count. There would not be another count until seven o'clock that night.

At ten minutes after two Leo said to Grady, "Boss, I'm going outside to toss the trash, and then I've got a lay-in to see the eye doctor." He didn't have a lay-in, but he knew that Grady would not check. Leo had never lied to him before.

"Okay, Trinket. See you tomorrow." He was working on the daily crossword in the Houston Chronicle. He would be totally absorbed in the puzzle for at least another hour.

The dumpsters were located in the rear of the building behind the inmate dining hall. Leo had to go through the control picket, down the main hallway, and make a right turn at the vocational turnout exit. Two officers would be at that door. One would frisk him and then let him through.

Vocational students were beginning to line up at the doorway for their two-thirty vocational classes. The officers would be busy patting them down and signing them in. Leo doubted they would notice if he went back through or not. His heart was racing. He could do this. He knew he could. He was just glad that he had not had time to think about it, or he might have gotten too nervous. He wondered if Ethel had considered that too.

He took the bag of clothes out of the trash then tossed the trash in the dumpster. Vocational students were now walking out to the vocational shops. The boss on duty never noticed Leo fall in line with the others. They passed the textile mill and the greenhouse. The hospital was off to the right and fenced in separately. Vocational trades were straight ahead. Electronics was in the first building, then next to it was drafting, walls and floors, brick laying, computer applications, and finally diesel mechanics. Leo knew that each department had a teacher's rest room. He had to see which teachers were at the officer's desk in the commons area, then go to one of their rooms.

Mr. Turner was the instructor for the walls and floors trade. He was talking to Officer Cunningham and appeared to be upset. Neither of them noticed Leo walk into Turner's classroom with the other students.

Inmate Minifree noticed Leo immediately. "Hey, man, what you doin' out here?"

Leo didn't hesitate for a second.

"Stopped up toilet in Turner's private rest room. You know he ain't gonna fix it."

"Yeah, man, I know that's right." Inmate Minifree was satisfied.

As Leo reached for the doorknob to the lavatory, he realized it would probably be locked. It wasn't. It locked only from the inside. He went in, closed the door and locked it behind him.

He slipped his white shirt easily over his head, but he had to remove his shoes to take off his pants. The blue free-world shirt fit Leo fine, but the black trousers were a couple of inches too long, so he had to roll them under at the cuffs. He slipped his state issued black belt through the loops and put on the warden's state cap that bore the Texas Department of Criminal Justice seal.

Leo looked in the mirror. He hadn't seen himself in any color but white in seven years. Color made a difference. Then he remembered his teeth. He fished them out of his uniform pocket and put them in his mouth. He got his wallet and found the ID card Ethel had altered for him. He rolled up his prison garb, put it in the trash bag he had brought the free-world clothes in, and put it in the waste basket.

He clipped the ID card with his picture on it to his shirt pocket. The name read *Douglas, Hannah.*

He opened the restroom door, praying no one would notice him. It had taken him less than two minutes to change clothes, and Turner's class wouldn't start for another ten minutes or so. He kept his head down, the TDCJ cap positioned low over his eyes, and walked out of the room.

Inmate Minifree noticed the man who came out of the rest room, and he knew who it was. He also knew the codes on the inside. A man could live by them or die by them. He kept silent.

Officer Cunningham saw Leo come out of Turner's room and stopped him immediately.

"Can I help you?" Cunningham questioned.

"No, not really. I was sent out to check the air ducts for the air conditioning system, but since they've got class going on right now, I'll just grab a bite to eat then go on over to CRMF and check those first. I'll be back when they're out of class," Leo said calmly.

"No problem," Cunningham said. Leo walked away, but the officer touched his shoulder. "Hey wait a second. Let me see your name tag."

Leo thought his heart would burst if it didn't slow down. It even caused his shirt to flutter slightly from its pounding. He was certain the "gray suit" would notice.

"Your name is Douglas Hannah?" asked Cunningham.

"Yes, sir. Why?"

"You're not going to believe this, but we have a teacher in the education department by the name of Hannah Douglas."

"You're kidding!" Leo tried to look astonished.

"Isn't that something?" Cunningham continued. Then he noticed that the comma came after the Douglas on his name tag. "Hey, they put your first name first and last name last on your ID. It's backwards."

"You know, I wondered how the people in personnel could make a mistake like that, but with that teacher having the same two names as me, I guess it's understandable." Leo felt good about his answer.

"Yeah, I guess so," Cunningham said.

"I'll see you later, man. Nice talking with you," Leo said, then walked towards the main building.

The vocational officers would not have recognized Leo Trinket as an inmate since he had not been in any vocational classes and never went out to the vocational buildings. With almost three thousand inmates on the unit, it was like a small town. You might recognize someone's face, but not be able to place him if he were out of his element, and the way inmates were constantly being switched from one unit to the next and always being shuffled, it was a wonder anyone learned anybody's name.

He went past the dumpsters, through the door, and down the hall from where he came. The same two officers were standing at the other end. They were deep in conversation with one another, so Leo tipped his cap and went right on by them. They didn't look at his face.

He was now in the main hallway. This time he walked down the middle of the hall while the inmates remained behind yellow lines.

Some of the inmates looked at him. He could sense their stares. *Did anyone recognize him? Would they snitch? Would the lady in the control picket open the door for him? Was Ethel's deal worth all this?* A roach scurried across the floor in front of him.

The hallway seemed a mile long. The cement floor was as glossy as a fresh water lake. Leo could see his reflection in it and wished wholeheartedly that he could immerse himself beneath it as if it were lake water indeed. The walls on either side of him stretched more than two stories high. Light from the outside poured through the small square windows across the top of those walls. There were no trees, no heaven, no birds, nothing but light coming from the windows. The way the structure was designed allowed for none of the free world to peek in and none of the confined to peek out. Cement, steel bars, and light. That was all.

Leo finally reached the control picket, thankful no one had

stopped him thus far. He grasped the door handle, saying not a word. Three officers and the head warden were in the control pen between the two massive barred doors and heading in his direction. The lady at the control panel opened the door. The four men came through, and Leo went in the pen. He walked to the other door, hoping his legs would continue to hold him up. The door buzzed and Leo pulled it open.

He entered the lobby where twenty minutes earlier he had been bagging trash. If he could get past Lieutenant Grady he could go all the way. The lights seemed much brighter than Leo remembered.

Bob Grady was an intelligent individual. Leo once asked him why he wasn't working somewhere that paid more money and offered more prestige. Lieutenant Grady confessed he had once had a very prestigious job in television. He had co-produced a talk show in California, but by the age of fifty-five he had grown tired of the rat-race and retired to Texas. Huntsville was where he grew up, and he still had family there. Working for TDCJ provided him with extra money and something to do.

As the lieutenant worked on his crossword puzzle, Leo walked right out the front door. The officer looked up but only saw the man's back and realized he was a contract worker. He was having trouble thinking of a ten letter word for cessation.

Leo traveled toward the front gates. Some black birds were roosting on the coiled barbed wire that secured the fourteen-foot high chain link fence. Why, he wondered, would something as free as a bird, choose to rest on a barbed wire that secured a prison? As he continued to think about it, he decided that the ugly black-winged beasts were there only to mock those that were confined to the inside. He reached the front gates. A red enameled sign with yellow letters read "DO NOT SLAM THIS GATE." Right beside it was a blue sign that said "HAVE A NICE DAY." The gate buzzed and

Leo pulled when the lock was released. He stepped toward the last gate and waited for the officer in the tower to buzz it open. She didn't.

"Sir, what is your name?" the officer shouted from forty feet up in the air.

Oh, no. "It's Doug Hannah." Perspiration spilled out of every pore in his body in spite of the cool forty degree weather.

"Are you new here?" she called.

"Yes, ma'am. Is there a problem?"

"I just didn't recognize you, that's all. Oh, please close the latch on the gate behind you, then I'll buzz you through."

"Sure thing," Leo responded politely. He ardently wished that he had made use of the toilet where he had changed clothes. He was worried that he just might wet himself in his stolen trousers.

Ethel said the car would be in the parking lot in front of the BLQ. Leo walked in that direction and passed several officers coming from the bachelors' living quarters. No one even noticed him.

The car was a silver Nissan. She said the door would be unlocked and the keys would be in the ashtray, and sure enough, there it sat. *This is too easy. Ain't nothin' this easy.* Leo opened the door and sat down.

He figured out how to adjust the seat and mirrors after he found the keys. Driving was an activity he had missed terribly for the past seven years. He was glad the little car had a standard transmission.

Leo turned the ignition, put the stick in reverse and backed out of the slot.

It was two-forty in the afternoon, and Leo Trinket was a free man.

Chapter 30

Reed was waiting for his dad on the curb across from the old ceme-tery. He frequently wondered why any town would build a school across from all those dead bodies, but today his mind was elsewhere. Reed had been preoccupied since lunch time. For one thing he had lost his wallet that he had only had for two months, and Ms. Sullivan had hollered at him to stop daydreaming in class. He hadn't been daydreaming. He was troubled but didn't know why, unless it was because he lost his wallet, but he didn't think that was it. Maybe it was because it was Friday the thirteenth and any normal person should feel a little weird on that day, or maybe it was because the weather was supposed to get real bad. He didn't know for sure exact-ly what was troubling him, but at any rate he hadn't paid attention to his lessons.

Lessons. He had fiddle lessons today! Where was his dad? Reed couldn't wait to play "Tugboat" for his teacher. Matt had only assigned it to him last week, and he had it memorized already. He was wanting to perform the new tune at his next contest, but Matt wasn't going to hear it at all if his dad didn't hurry up.

"Reed," someone shouted. "Reed Douglas!"

"Yes, ma'am. Here I am."

It was Mrs. Davis, the secretary.

"Reed, your dad called and said he would be a little late, but not to worry. He didn't forget about you."

"Yes, ma'am. Thank you for telling me."

Noticing his chagrin, the secretary asked, "By the way, how's the fiddling going? Won any more contests lately?"

His eyes lit up. "Yes ma'am. I won my last two in the zero to seventeen age division."

"You did? That's wonderful. Did you win any money?"

"Sure did. I won a hundred dollars at one and a hundred and twenty-five at the other one."

"My goodness. Have you spent it already?"

"No way. I'm saving it to buy me a new bow."

"A new bow? How much does a bow cost?"

"The one I want costs eight hundred dollars."

Mrs. Davis gasped, "Eight hundred dollars?"

Reed grinned. He knew that most people would not know the difference between a superior bow and a cheap one. They just knew that a bow was a piece of wood strung with horse hair. The average person wouldn't even know that some cheap bows even used synthetic hair. He looked down at the ground and kicked some dirt with his boot.

"Well now, I'll just bet you get that new bow in no time." She patted him on the back. "You have a real talent, Reed. I hope I can hear you play again real soon, and I sure do want to hear you play when you get that dandy new bow."

"Yes ma'am."

"I need to get back to the office, besides, it's cold out here. I do believe we're going to get some sleet after all." She looked at Reed one more time. "Your dad won't be long. See you tomorrow."

"Okay. Bye. And thanks."

"You're welcome."

Mrs. Davis is a nice lady, but not as pretty as my mom.

Reed couldn't think of anyone as pretty as his mother. He had called her Pretty rather than Mom as long as he could remember. She didn't look like the other kids' mothers or act like them for that matter. She had the most beautiful hair in the world, and she dressed so neat, at least she did when she didn't have to go to work. She wore those gypsy-looking skirts and great big hats. People were all the time looking at her – even his friends at school. He figured every kid in junior high envied him for having such a great mom. He would not have traded her for the world, even when she fussed at him.

His mother had been on his mind all afternoon. He hated that she taught in that prison. He was only six years old when she started teaching convicts. It scared him then and even more so now. He was always relieved to see her every afternoon. He tried not to dwell on his fear that one of those crazy convicts would hurt her some day, but today his mind seemed destined to harbor that train of thought. *What if* . . . He imagined a hundred different scenarios.

Reed was in deep thought when William sounded his siren for a quick second to get his attention. It startled Reed. He trotted toward the police car.

"Dad! Why did you do that?" I hate it when you blow that siren at me like I'm some stupid criminal! And where have you been anyway? I've missed my fiddle lesson. I hope you're happy!"

"Hey. Wait a minute, here. You need to back up and regroup."

Reed started crying. He cried hard. William waited.

"Son, what's wrong?"

"I don't know, Dad. I had a lousy day. I couldn't concentrate on nothin'. I got yelled at in science class, and I couldn't find one of my tennis shoes in PE. The coach is going to take seven points off my grade because of it, and I'll bet someone stole it out of my locker. And if that's not enough, I lost my wallet. Somebody probably stole it, too. I hate thieves! I hate 'em. Why does Pretty have to work with 'em? What's wrong with her?"

"What's wrong with her?" retorted William. "What's wrong with you? Reed, everybody has a lousy day once in a while, but don't blame your mother. She teaches at that prison so we can have more. I don't like it any more than you do, but she is a free spirit and doesn't always view the world the way everyone else does. She has worked for the prison for six years, and nothing has happened that she couldn't handle."

"But Dad, she'd quit if you told her to. Why don't you make her?"

"Does this have something to do with that guy you saw on the news a couple of nights ago?"

"I don't know. Maybe. Not really."

William searched his heart to find the right words. "In a marriage partnership, one shouldn't control the other." He put his hand on the back of Reed's neck and squeezed it gently. "I respect your mother and her decisions, and I want you to do the same. She's a smart lady. She knows what she's doing. Why all this concern about your mother's job all of a sudden? Did someone say something about it at school?"

"No. Let's just go home, Dad."

William backed out of the parking space. They passed Sam Houston's grave-site. Reed looked as they went. He always did.

"Since we missed your lesson, we could stop by Dairy Queen and get a Blizzard."

"Sure. Okay."

"You don't sound too excited."

"I'm just upset about missing my lesson. We need to call Matt and tell him what happened. What did happen?"

William turned into Dairy Queen and got in line at the drive-through. "Another girl got kidnapped two days ago."

"Yeah, I know."

"Jeff and I are working the case. Her parents called this afternoon and asked if we had found out anything."

"Have you?"

"No, not any hard evidence. Anyway, they wanted us to come by and talk to them."

"Why? Didn't you tell them that you hadn't found her yet?"

"Yes, they knew that, but they just needed someone to talk to about it. They are terribly worried and upset. So we went."

"But why were you late picking me up? Couldn't you tell them that I had a lesson?"

"I could have, but Mrs. Brooks – that's the missing girl's mother – had her head on my chest crying her heart out, so at that moment it seemed more important for me to hold that grieving mother than it was to get you to a fiddle lesson on time. Can you understand that?"

Reed glared at his dad. "Of course. I'm not totally insensitive."

"I know you're not. What kind of Blizzard do you want?"

"Oreo."

They ran a few errands and got home at five minutes after five. "Dad, call Matt and tell him what happened."

William called and explained everything to Reed's teacher. He understood and rescheduled him for Monday.

"Dad, where's Pretty?"

"I don't know where she is. She's probably still with Sandy, thinking we are at your lesson."

"That's just great," Reed said in a huff.

"Son, what has gotten into you? Your mother doesn't need your permission to go to town or anywhere else."

"I know she doesn't. It's just that the weather is looking bad, and

I've been worried about her today. What if something happened to her?"

William shrunk back. He knew he was overprotective of Hannah and worried obsessively about her. Now he had succeeded in transferring those emotions to his twelve-year- old son, and that was a burden too heavy for him to have to bear in his young life.

"Reed, I think you and I both need to lighten up a bit where your mother is concerned. I think we worry too much. Nothing is going to happen to her, and we have got to believe that. Deal?"

"No, Dad. No deal." Reed went to his room and turned on his tape player.

William went to the kitchen and checked out the contents of the refrigerator. He found a package of chicken breasts and decided on chicken and rice casserole for dinner. That was one of Reed's favorite dishes. He looked in the pantry for the mushroom soup and found it behind the cat food. It was low fat, of course. Not the cat food.

Meow.

"What do you want, you stupid cat?"

Meow.

"I'm not giving you any of that canned food. You can eat the dry stuff in your dish or none at all. Besides, that canned stuff makes your poop stink worse than it usually does."

Dragon brushed his furry body hard against William's leg and wrapped his tail around it like a snake. *Meow!*

"You know I hate that. That's why you do it, isn't it?"

"Talking to somebody, Dad?" Reed asked with a grin. "I thought you didn't talk to stupid cats."

"You must have been hearing things," he said, thankful Reed was in a better mood. Puberty was trickier than he thought it was going to be.

"Sure, Dad, we believe you. Don't we, Dragon?"

"I was not talking to that stupid cat, and for another thing, I don't want that mangy dog in this house either."

Reed cocked his head, realizing he had forgotten to let Neiman in. He went directly to the back door and called him.

William just shook his head. "Why don't you wash your hands and set the table? Your mom will be all surprised when she gets home and sees dinner in the oven and the table all set."

"Sure. Hey, I saw some daffodils and tulips blooming in the front flower bed. Can I pick a few and put them on the table? She'll love it."

"Okay, but not too many. You know how your mother is about her yard."

Reed came in with more than a few flowers. William glared at him like they might both get in trouble. "Gee, Dad, it's already colder that a witch's titty out there, and it's sprinkling rain. They'd just freeze."

"A witch's what?"

Reed hadn't realized what he had said. "Nothing."

William got tickled. "Where on earth did you hear that?"

Reed shrugged his shoulders. "From you." He scooted his dad away from the sink. William was rinsing the lettuce.

"Don't be pushing me around unless you want some serious trouble," William said.

The two of them shoved each other until William gave in.

"Get me a vase."

William handed him one from the cupboard above the refrigerator, then went back to his salad while Reed fussed over the flowers. "You'd better get the table set."

Hannah had five sets of dishes. Her china was given to her by her grandmother. It had been hers from when she got married. There were twelve full place settings and every one of the serving pieces. It was called Blue Dawn and had been made in occupied Japan during the war. She had let Hannah eat off it as a little girl because she had thought it was so beautiful. She also gave Hannah her Blue Willow set. Since she already had china, she got every piece of her chosen bridal registry pattern, Sculptured Daisy, when William and she got married. A few years later, her mother, knowing how she had always loved dishes, bought her a set of stone-ware with a colorful jungle motif, and if that weren't enough, William's aunt gave her a set of fine German made Waechtersbach mugs. They were fiery red with white hearts around the top. Valentine's Day had always been Hannah's favorite holiday, and those mugs were one of her favorite gifts. A few years later she found the matching dishes in a Hallmark shop. The dinner plates alone were twenty dollars a piece, so she couldn't buy them. Besides, she certainly didn't need them, but William and Reed knew she wanted them, so they bought her a few pieces at a time for "present days." Meredith, her mother, gave her the cookie jar one Easter and the large platter for Halloween. William bought the cream and sugar bowls for this Valentine's Day. It had been hard for him not to go ahead and give them to her early.

"Reed, let's give your mom her Valentine's present tonight at dinner. I can't wait till tomorrow."

"Then what will we give her on Valentine's Day? You know that's her favorite day, and she's romantic about that kind of stuff. You know she is, Dad."

"Well, you made her a card, and I bought her one. We can give her those and take her out to eat."

"Just don't forget to make reservations this time." Reed put the place-mats down and then the napkins. "You remember last year, don't you? We had to wait for hours for a table, then another hour for our food."

"No we didn't. It was more like forty-five minutes."

Reed rolled his eyes while laying out the silverware.

The phone rang, and William answered it. Reed reached for the red Valentine plates.

"Sandy, hi. How are you doing?"

"Fine, but I was wondering what happened to Hannah?" Her soft voice reflected a hint of concern. "I've called your house several times this afternoon, but there was no answer."

"I have no idea. I thought she was with you."

"We were supposed to meet for lunch and then do some shopping." Sandy knew this wasn't like Hannah. She was one of the most dependable people she had ever known, and she would never have kept her hanging, wondering where she was.

"I know. Are you sure you went to the right place?"

"Well," said Sandy, "I went to Chili's. That's where we had decided to meet."

"She told me she was going to meet you at Chili's, too. Gee, Sandy, I don't know what to tell you, unless she got held up at work."

Reed was standing as still as a tin soldier listening to his father's side of the conversation.

Sandy said, "I just heard on the radio that someone escaped from that unit this afternoon. But that wouldn't cause her to have to stay late, would it?"

"No, I don't see how. Besides, she gets off a little after twelve. She would have been gone before any of that went down if it was this afternoon. I hadn't heard about it."

"You're kidding! I would have thought that all the local authorities would have been notified to be out looking for him."

"They are, and I would have been, but I guess Hannah hasn't told you yet. I was promoted to detective the other day."

"Well, congratulations!"

"Thank you. Listen, I'll have Hannah call you the minute she comes in." He wound the cord around his finger, a habit he had picked up from Hannah. He could not imagine what had happened, but he was beginning to get worried himself, very worried.

"Thanks. Tell her she can reach me on my cell phone. I'm just sick that I missed her. I have really been looking forward to seeing her." Sandy had needed to see Hannah. A husband and three kids are great, but there's nothing like a long visit with your best friend in the world – just the two of you.

"It's all Hannah's talked about. In fact, she called me from work this morning to remind me to pick Reed up from school. So I know she didn't forget."

"Well, tell her I'm not mad. Scrap that. She'll know I'm not mad. Just tell her I miss her and will talk to her tomorrow, or if it's not too late, have her call me tonight. I don't like this worried feeling. I just want to know that she's okay."

"Sure thing. You take care."

"You too. And give Reed a hug for me."

"Will do. Bye."

"What did she want, Dad?" Reed had not budged from his spot.

"She said your mother never showed up for their lunch date."

"What else?"

"Nothing, really. She just wondered if the escape from the Estelle Unit would have had anything to do with her being late."

Reed dropped the red plates with the white hearts. They broke into a thousand pieces.

William jumped. Until that moment, he had no idea how concerned Reed was about his mother. It was obvious by looking in his son's face that the boy truly believed something awful had happened to her, and now he was wondering if Reed had some sort of sixth sense that had caused his unusual behavior all afternoon.

Trying to mollify the thoughts racing through his young son's mind, William said, "We'd better get this cleaned up 'fore Pretty gets home. She'll have a stroke if she sees her favorite dishes like this, but don't worry, we'll get some to replace them tomorrow and she'll . . ."

"Stop it, Dad! She's not coming home!" he cried. "Something has happened to her. Why can't you see it?" Reed was as serious as William had ever seen him. His young innocent face was drawn tight with worry and had surrendered to a fevered flush.

"I'll call her principal and see if he knows anything." William put his arms around his child and hugged him tight. "Don't you worry. We'll find her. I'm sure she's all right."

Chapter 31

Stella changed outfits three times. She couldn't remember the last time she had been so nervous. Finally, she decided on a long denim skirt, an oversized blue cable knit sweater, and brown leather boots since the weather was so cold and wet and turning icy. At work, the ER staff noticed her anxiety but didn't question her about it because she had always kept her private life isolated from them and never wanted to talk about herself. Her shyness though, never hindered her dealings with the patients who came through the emergency room doors. With them she was outgoing, confident, and caring. She was born to be a care-giver.

Looking in the mirror one more time, she decided she needed some jewelry, so she went through her jewelry box and found a necklace with stars and moons hanging from it. It would do. If only she had bigger breasts, she thought. That would have done a lot more for her than the necklace. Oh well, she had never claimed to be a beauty, nor had anyone ever accused her of such. Why was she going on so over a date? It was just dinner and a movie. She fluffed up her hair again. The phone rang and her heart sank. He was calling to cancel.

With anguish she managed to get to the phone and pick it up. "Hello?" she said, trying not to sound too disappointed.

"Stella?" This is Reba."

Stella's heart started pumping again. "Reba, hi." Her relief was apparent.

"Listen, I'm not feeling too well. Would you mind working my shift for me tomorrow? I know it's your day off."

"No. I wouldn't mind at all."

"You are such a sweetheart. I owe you one, girl."

"No, really. It's all right. I don't mind. I'm glad you called. I'm just sorry you feel bad. Is there anything I can do for you?"

"No. I just need some rest. I think I've just got a touch of the flu. With the way the weather has been, it's a wonder we aren't all sick with pneumonia."

"Yeah, I know what you mean," Stella said.

"Was that your doorbell I just heard?"

"What?"

"I thought I heard your doorbell, or maybe it was on my television. My head is kind of stopped up."

"Doorbell? Yes, yes, I think it was. Listen, I've got to go, but don't worry about tomorrow. I've got you covered."

"You're a doll. Thanks."

"You're welcome. See ya."

Stella opened the door. Sandy blond hair, windblown. Gray eyes, deep and honest. A small scar above his right eyebrow, sweet. Stitches from his car accident, softening. For a moment she didn't say anything. She couldn't. He looked like a movie star standing there on her porch. Her porch!

From behind his back, Jeff produced a bouquet of flowers. Stella was overwhelmed. She gasped, "They're beautiful. Thank you. Oh, my gosh. I need to put them in water." She turned around leaving Jeff on the front porch. Realizing what she had done, she twirled back around to apologize. "Please, forgive me. I don't know where my manners are. Come in."

Jeff was glad to see that she was apparently as nervous as he was. Ironically it made him feel a little more at ease. He looked around the room while she searched for a vase. Her house, at least the part that he could see, was clean enough to do surgery in. "I figured as much," he said under his breath.

"Excuse me," Stella said, coming out of the kitchen.

"Your house. It's neat and clean. Very clean. I'll bet there isn't any dust or grime anywhere." He appeared to be looking for some. He bent down to get a closer look at the floor. "No, I don't see any."

Stella smiled. "What can I say? I'm a nurse, and in my line of work cleanliness is very important." She looked almost apologetic.

"Well, I'm very impressed."

"The flowers are beautiful. I don't remember the last time I was given any flowers."

"I'll bet you get them all the time at the hospital."

His eyes. They are going to be the death of me.

"Occasionally, but that's different. People give me flowers at the hospital because they're grateful for me helping them, and usually they're bouquets that someone else has given them while they were in the hospital. I don't know why they bother since I'm just doing my job. I'm paid for what I do."

Jeff gently took her by the shoulders then dropped his hands again. "It's more than that. It's the way you do your job. There is just something about you that puts people at ease when they're at their most vulnerable. Of course you couldn't tell it by me at the moment. I'm as nervous as a cat in a room full of rocking chairs."

She giggled. "Me too. I changed clothes three times," she confessed.

"You look just great. But since you're confessing, I guess I'll have to, too."

"What?"

Jeff sat down on the edge of her sofa and lifted both legs of his blue jeans. He had on one tan sock and one blue sock.

"How did you manage that?" She cuddled herself with her arms, trying to calm down her excitement about being in the same room with this gorgeous hunk of a man.

"I do not know. But I am pretty certain that I have another pair just like this one in my laundry basket at home."

They both laughed.

"So, where would you like to go eat?"

"Surprise me."

"Okay, Princess. Get your coat."

Princess. He called me Princess. For a moment she couldn't take in enough air for one small breath. The oxygen in the room had turned into a liquid that was thick and deep.

"Are you all right?"

"Yes, just excited. That's all."

౭౩౮౦

"Hello, I need extension 2022 please."

Reed listened intently to everything William said.

"Education. This is West."

"Lonnie Ray, I was afraid you would already be gone. This is William Douglas."

"No way. Lem Wagstaff's monitoring team is coming out here tomorrow, and I'm going through all my records one more time to make sure everything is in order."

William smiled. He had heard Hannah talk about Wagstaff, and even she had never said anything good about him.

"Listen, Lonnie Ray, I'm worried about Hannah. Did anything

happen at work today that was unusual?"

"Hell's bells," he said, reaching for another cookie. "There's never a day that goes by that something unusual doesn't happen at this God forsaken unit." He took a bite of the peanut butter cookie that he had smuggled out of the officer's dining room. He continued to talk while chewing. "Why, is Hannah upset about something? Let me talk to her."

"That's the problem, Lonnie Ray. I don't know where she is. She skipped a lunch date with her best friend that she's been looking forward to for days, and I haven't heard from her. That's just not like Hannah."

"You know how women are. She's probably out shopping or something and forgot about the time."

"That's just it. She and her friend, Sandy, were going to go shopping after they ate lunch. She wouldn't have missed that date with Sandy for the world. They get to see precious little of each other as it is."

The principal began to feel a bit concerned himself. He put the cookie down.

William said, "Tell me what you know about the escape today."

"His name is Leo Trinket, but he wasn't a student, and besides, that happened after your wife left."

"Are you sure?"

"Yes, I'm sure. The inmate was present and accounted for at the twelve thirty count. They said the lieutenant up front talked to him after that and so did the assistant warden when he went in to empty his trash. They just discovered him missing a little while ago."

"I would have heard if she had been in a wreck. All of those calls are dispatched through the Sheriff's Office. They would have gotten hold of me immediately." William paused and stroked his forehead. "I've got to tell you, I'm getting more worried by the minute."

"Oh, I'm sure it's nothing. Aren't you overreacting just a little bit?" There was a knock on West's office door. "Hang on just a minute, William. Someone's at my door." He put a piece of paper over the plate of cookies.

"Come in, Cunningham. What do you need? I'm on the phone."

The officer from the vocational shops walked closer to the principal's desk. "There was a contract worker out in vocational that I didn't know this afternoon."

Sounding a bit irritated, West said, "So?"

"Mr. West, his name tag said Douglas Hannah. I asked him about it because it made me think of Hannah Douglas who works in here. And his ID had the comma after the Douglas part. He said they had printed it backwards, and he figured it was because his name was Douglas Hannah and they got it mixed up with Hannah Douglas. Anyway, with the escape and all, I just thought I'd let you know since you were gone most of the afternoon." He licked his thin lips and swallowed with some difficulty.

A porcupine suddenly manifested itself in Lonnie Ray West's stomach. It pricked and poked at the lining of it and threatened to do a somersault. "What was he doing out there?" He opened the desk drawer for his Tums.

"He didn't do anything. He said he would be back when classes were out, but he never showed up."

"Oh, Lord," West said with difficulty. "This could be bad."

"Shouldn't we tell the warden?"

"Yes. Wait in my secretary's office for me. I'll be right out. We'll go together."

"Sure thing." The officer walked out and closed the door behind him.

Lonnie Ray West could feel the blood drain out of his face and into his toes, and he was sure that some would leak out where the porcupine in his stomach had punctured him. He had to tell William.

With dread he lifted the phone and repeated what Cunningham had told him. "Now, William, I don't think we need to jump to any conclusions here. This could all just be a matter of coincidence."

William was silent – unable to speak.

"I'm going to check to see if we have a contract worker by that name, and if we do, then that problem will be solved. And if we don't . . . I'll let you know either way."

Panic gripped William's soul with such force and totality that he thought for a split second that his brain was going to overload and shut down everything in his body. Realizing that Reed was watching his every move and listening to his every word, he managed to take control of his emotions. "How would someone end up with my wife's ID card? Her picture is on it." He was careful not to say convict because of Reed, but he knew that Lonnie Ray was thinking the same thing that he was thinking, and that was that the escaped convict used Hannah's ID card to get out. But what had he done with her?

"Let me go talk to the warden. We'll get this all straightened out. I'll call you back as soon as I know something. I am certain that your wife didn't help that convict escape from here today. I know . . ."

"What? How could that notion even occur to you long enough for it to pass from your mind to your mouth?" William was livid. He now had wound the cord around all his fingers.

"Hold your horses. You know that other people are going to be asking questions. I just want you to be prepared, and tell Hannah to call me the minute she gets home. I'll be in the warden's office, I'm sure."

"I will." William hung up the phone. But he knew she wasn't

coming home. He knew it, and Reed knew it. Somehow, Reed had known it all along.

CB80

Rain was falling as well as the temperature. Jeff looked at the thermometer on Stella's porch and reported, "Thirty-three degrees." He helped her down the steps in case they were already beginning to freeze over, and also because he found himself just wanting to touch her.

He opened the truck door on the driver's side and motioned for her to climb in, hoping she would want to sit next to him, and she did.

They went to The Junction, one of the nicest restaurants in town. Jeff asked the hostess for an out-of-the-way table.

After ordering fried shrimp for both of them and a glass of wine, their conversations turned to their jobs. Stella was fascinated with all Jeff's stories about crimes he had solved, people he had arrested, and people he had helped, but Jeff wanted to talk about her, and that was like pulling teeth. "I want to know about your life – where you grew up, what kind of a kid you were, your favorite color."

"I'm afraid my childhood was not very interesting." She looked woeful as she spoke. She was looking into her past as though it were right in front of her. "I didn't have many friends because we lived way out from town. I was very shy, and I guess I still am in a way." She giggled sweetly. "I mean, I'm not shy at work. I really feel alive at work, but everywhere else I feel unimportant and in the way. It's like I'm breathing air that belongs to someone else, and I have no right to it." Her brown eyes were looking in Jeff's direction, but they were still focused deep within herself.

He didn't know what to say for a minute, so he said nothing at all.

Jeff took her hand from across the table and caressed it with his thumb. "You have to be one of the most unselfish people that I have ever met." She looked away as if embarrassed. "No, I mean it. Believe me, I know the queen of selfish." He paused for a few seconds and then continued. "I almost got married once."

"What happened?"

"She left me standing at the altar." His eyes moistened just thinking about it again. Stella took the hand that he wasn't holding and put it on top of his – a natural care giver. It was so easy for him to talk to her. The humiliating story of Debra and his brother poured out, and afterwards he felt as if a two hundred pound weight had been lifted from his shoulders.

When their meal came, they ate and talked some more. The wine softened the edge on their nervousness.

After paying the check at the table, Jeff stood and lifted her by the elbow. He continued to support her as they made their way down the old staircase and out to his truck, where again he had her sit next to him.

"Is there a particular movie you want to see?" he asked.

"I don't even know what's playing."

"We'll go by and see. I want you to select the movie, since I had to pick out where we ate."

"Okay," she smiled widely, obviously pleased that he truly wanted her opinion and that it mattered to him. Her heart had not slowed down, even though she wasn't quite as nervous after the wine. For the first time in her life, she felt like she could learn to trust someone and perhaps even love someone, and for the moment it felt great.

CR80

William felt completely helpless and stupid and scared to death.

In Recon, the elite of the tough-guy Marines, he had learned to deal with fear, stress, panic, and even the possibility of death, but they had not prepared him for the likes of this.

"Dad, what's wrong?" Panic seized Reed once again, but he did not surrender to it this time. He had to be strong.

"I honestly don't know, but I'll do everything in my power to find out."

"Pretty's not coming home, is she?"

William put his arms around his son, not knowing what to say.

Reed went to his room and closed his door. He took down his great-grandfather's old violin and played it hard and fast and angrily. The emotions that had swept through him were unlike anything he had ever felt, and he didn't know how else to deal with them, so he turned to his fiddle.

William dialed Jeff's home number, but there was no answer. Then he remembered that he had a date with that nurse, and there was no telling where he was. He would have to deal with this on his own for awhile. Maybe West would call him in a few minutes.

Chapter 32

The movie lasted for two hours and ten minutes. Jeff took Stella home at ten-thirty. The temperature was below freezing now, and her cement steps had iced over. The leaves and pine needles from the trees in her yard were making a clickety-clack sound that was romantic. Soft. Captivating.

He hopped up onto the wooden porch and extended his arms to pull Stella up. When he did, her body touched his. The cold made her breath form a cloud around her face. He said, "You are breathing someone else's air. You're breathing mine," and then he touched her lips with his. Placing his hands gently on each side of her head, he looked deep into her eyes and melded his lips onto hers again. Patiently, carefully, he parted her lips with his tongue and entered her mouth. He felt her arms around his body and ached to have them against his bare skin. He pulled her closer to him.

The feeling of a strong, handsome, sweet man against her in such a way was intoxicating. It aroused feelings inside her that she never knew existed – lust, she supposed, but more than that. Her heart felt like it might explode if it didn't slow down. She wanted to grab him. She wanted to pull him closer and move herself against him. But she couldn't. What was she thinking? What was she doing? He must think she was easy and cheap.

She pushed herself away. She felt dizzy. The sound of the leaves whispering in the wind, the warmth of his body next to hers, the smell of him, the taste of him, was all surreal. She was in a fairytale, and he was the prince who had come to rescue her from loneliness. But fairytales were not real.

"I'm sorry, Stella. I didn't mean to go too fast." He looked directly into her eyes. They were the most unusual shade of brown he had ever seen. They were beautiful. The color of clover honey. "I couldn't help myself for a minute."

"No, it's all right." She was breathing as hard as if she had run all the way from the Cinema. "It's just that I'm not used to that," wondering as she was speaking if she had done it right. She had never been kissed like that before.

"I've never felt like that before when I've kissed anyone," he said. "Like I said, you take my breath away."

"Jeff, you don't have to say that. I'm inexperienced." Her head was down. "I'm not very sophisticated when it comes to romance."

He tilted her head up to meet his gaze. "Like I said, you take my breath away." He bent down and kissed her softly on the cheek. "Good night, Princess."

Jeff leaped off the porch and with great strides made it to his truck. He turned around once to look at her, then blew her a kiss and he was off.

Stella almost collapsed when she made it inside her house. Everything in the room seemed brighter, more vibrant, even beautiful. All her senses were alive and swarming in and around her. She needed to go to bed, though she doubted she would sleep.

CB EO

Jack Tyler was sitting in his office after hours as he often did, not wanting to go home and face Elaine. He could not stand what she had done. He could not stand what he had done.

Taking the key that opened his private cabinet, he took out a bottle, slowly unscrewed the lid, and poured the whiskey into a glass. After taking a drink, he leaned back in his leather chair, closed his eyes, and tried to imagine angels coming for him, but as always the entities that came were demons and they wore the faces of Elaine, Ethel, and Libby.

The demons took him back to the night when Ethel was waiting in their yard for Elaine to come home after her award dinner with the governor. Elaine wouldn't answer any of his questions that night. He had wanted to know about her twin sister. He had wanted to know what frightened her so about her past, but she wouldn't tell him. She would not tell him anything.

The next day Ethel came back to their house and moved in with them. Elaine would only say that she was family and had nowhere else to go, and that it would only be for a little while, but that little while destroyed their marriage.

Elaine changed when Ethel came. He could tell she didn't want him to touch her anymore. Even though their marriage had never been saturated with romance, it had been comfortable. They had both traveled the fast track in their careers and had landed at the top, respectively. Being at the top took time and effort, leaving little time for lust-filled nights and breakfasts in bed, but they had been content in the life they had cut out for themselves. They had loved one another, respected one another, and trusted one another, but Ethel changed all that. Right from the very start, the sex stopped. Elaine could not relax with her in the house. Ethel began preparing their evening meals for them, and Elaine no longer enjoyed eating out as they often had before. She even fired Libby because Ethel didn't like her.

Jack would never forget the day that their housekeeper, Libby Angus, called him at work. He answered the phone and was surprised when he realized it was Libby. "What can I help you with?" he had asked.

Libby said she needed to talk to him alone and would he meet her somewhere for lunch.

"I'll pick you up at your apartment. I know the perfect place where we can eat and visit, and no one will bother us. I'll be there around 12:30." That had been so unlike him, he thought.

"That sounds great," she had said. "I'll be ready."

Jack had made a few flirtatious advances toward Libby in the past, but she had always respectfully dismissed them. He couldn't help but desire the pretty young woman. Elaine had not touched him in weeks, and he was still a strong and virile man with needs. He loved Elaine dearly and had never cheated on her, but having Libby around had certainly tempted him after his wife started ignoring him.

Jack called The Sandwich Shoppe and ordered two of their specialty sandwiches, chips, and a bottle of wine in a basket to go. He picked the order up on the way to Libby's apartment.

Sensational would pretty much describe how she looked as he remembered it. She wore a simple black dress that hugged her body like a bandage, emphasizing the fullness of her breasts. Her dark hair hung down past her waist. She wore black stockings and black high heels; her legs were gorgeous, and she smelled like a breath of spring. The whole package was completely different than when she was in his house working for him as a maid. She definitely did not look like a maid – not that day, and it was obvious to him that she did not want for him to think of her as one – not that day.

When she got in the car he called his office from his cell phone and canceled his afternoon appointments.

He remembered saying, "Why don't we go out to the lake house? Any objections?"

"No, that sounds perfect." He knew what that meant. She looked so beautiful, and her skin was young and smooth and looked as soft as satin. Dark lashes fringed her huge brown eyes. She was wearing make-up. He had never seen her in make-up. Her lips were full and moist, and the color of the lipstick she wore made him want to suck them like a lollipop. And her hair – he wanted to get lost in her hair.

She said, "Before we leave, I have to tell you something that happened today."

"Tell me while we're driving." Jack felt like a pimply-faced teenager on his first date. Libby was so young and taut; his body wasn't what it used to be. The skin beneath his shoulders sagged a bit, and his once flat stomach was now round and swollen, but even so he couldn't wait to hold her next to him and feel her ripe young breasts against his chest. He wanted to put his hands in her hair and nuzzle it with his face. It wasn't stiff and fixed like Elaine's. It was enticing with a fragrance of honeysuckle rather than the smothering smell of lacquered hair spray.

Libby was pouring her heart out to him, and he had not heard a word she was saying.

"What should I do?" Libby asked.

"About what?" he asked.

"The pearls, and Ethel, my job, everything!"

"What about your job?" Jack asked, confused. Libby was terribly upset and he didn't know why. "Start from the beginning. I was so excited about being with you that I wasn't paying attention to any-thing but the feelings you have stirred up in me. I'm sorry. I had no idea you were so upset. Tell me what's wrong. I'll listen this time."

Libby repeated her story about Elaine finding the pearl necklace in her purse and how she had fired her on the spot. "I know Ethel planted it there. She had such a smirk on her face when Ms. Tyler was confronting me. She stood there, behind her, with her skinny arms folded in victory. You should have seen her. She's evil, Mr. Tyler, evil."

"Did you try to reason with Elaine?"

"She wouldn't listen to me. She wanted me out of the house. She'll report it, and I won't be able to get a job anywhere."

Jack reached over and patted Libby gently on the leg. "Don't you worry about a thing."

Libby interrupted, "I have to worry. I'm paying my way through college. I have rent to pay, and I have to eat. I don't know what I'm going to do." Her angelic face looked so sad. Something that beautiful should never have to look so sad.

"I'm telling you not to worry. One of the secretaries at the personnel office is leaving at the end of next month to have a baby, and she's not coming back. I can make sure you get the job."

"I don't have enough money to pay bills until then. I wasn't counting on losing my job with you, Mr. Tyler."

"I'll take care of your bills. Let me take care of you, Libby," he heard himself say. "Let me take good care of you." His eyes were glazed over with sweet anticipation of what was to come. He began caressing the leg he had patted before. He moved his hand back and forth over the black stocking that covered her tanned skin. With each movement he went just a tiny bit higher, his hand now underneath her dress. It was becoming difficult for him to swallow, and his breathing had become heavy and labored. His eyes were on the road, but his mind was under Libby's dress. His hand finally reached high enough up her thigh to find a garter securing the stocking in place. He gasped. Moving his hand higher, he felt the soft skin of her upper thigh. He remembered the car was swerving on the road. He breathed deeply and evenly and kept his hand still while trying to regain control of his body and his car. When he felt it was safe to continue, he moved his hand again back and forth, ever so slightly, each time gaining a fraction of an inch on the sinewy long leg. Finally he reached the top and discovered that she was wearing no panties.

Jack spotted the green "Isaac Jones Cemetery" sign a few yards up ahead, and without a second thought turned down the dirt road that led to the lonesome burial ground. He had never taken his eyes off the road, and he had not taken his hand off Libby.

Jack finally stopped the car, put it in park and turned off the ignition. Only then did he dare to look at Libby.

Jack opened his car door and got out, but Libby did not move. He walked around to her door and opened it, then took her by the hand and urged her carefully out of the car. When she was standing next to him, he closed the car door behind her. She backed up against the car and Jack moved toward her.

Libby slowly unbuckled his belt, careful not to touch him. Jack's hands were on her waist and moving slowly upwards.

Jack remembered them both adjusting their clothes before getting back into the car. They had spoken not a word.

Finding the highway again, he proceeded to the lake house. Thirty minutes later, they got there. Jack opened the car door for her while still remaining silent, took the basket of sandwiches and wine from the back seat, then led her into the house.

They ate quietly, studying one another in a new light, absorbing one another. The wine subdued their inhibitions and left them hungry once again for each other.

This time Libby took Jack by the hand and led him to the bedroom she had cleaned only one week before. First she pulled back the pink satin spread then went up to him and whispered, "Don't touch me." She unbuttoned his shirt. Next, she unbuckled his belt, determined not to make contact with his skin. She pulled the belt through the loops of his trousers and threw it on the floor. Backing up she lifted her dress just high enough to reveal her garter belt. She unfastened her stockings and slid them down and took them off. She reached back to unzip her dress.

Jack remembered saying, "Let me help you with that," because he thought the words sounded like they came from someone else – and indeed they had. He didn't know this side of himself.

"No," she whispered. "Don't touch me."

Jack was almost in pain from desire. He wanted to rip her clothes off, but she wouldn't let him touch her.

Libby managed the zipper and let the black dress fall to the floor. She stood before him wearing only a black garter-belt and a black lacy bra.

"Let me," Jack tried to say.

"No," Libby said, stopping his plea.

She unhooked her bra as Jack stood there motionless, helpless. Leaving the garter-belt on, she stepped up to Jack and unbuttoned his trousers. He reached for her but she stopped him and once again whispered, "No. Don't touch me, not yet."

He couldn't take his eyes off her. The agony of not being able to touch her, caress her, was almost more than he could bear. She was perfect.

"I can't stand it, Libby. I've got to," Jack tried to say, but she stopped him.

"Yes you can. Just a little more," she said, her voice husky from emotion and desire.

Jack mustered all of the self-discipline he could find to keep from letting go. He didn't want it to end. It was torture and he loved it.

The things Libby had done to him put him in a higher place of eroticism than he had ever dreamed existed, but he willed himself to maintain control. He had not wanted it to end, but when he realized that she was losing herself in the pleasure, he could hold on no longer, and he still wondered if perhaps that afternoon of ecstasy was worth everything that happened afterward.

C3 80

The phone rang and startled Jack back into the present. It was the warden from Estelle.

"Jack, I've got bad news," the warden said. "An inmate by the name of Leo Trinket escaped a little after two o'clock this afternoon."

"How did it go down?"

"He was using an ID tag that belonged to one of our teachers named Hannah Douglas. His picture was on it."

"Did the teacher help him?"

"We don't know. We are checking into that possibility. I have someone trying to locate her this very minute."

"I'm on my way," said Jack, thankful for a reason to get his mind off his personal problems.

Jack buzzed his secretary. "Sally, look up the inmate Leo Trinket, from the Estelle Unit, on the committed screen and make me a hard copy please."

"Yes sir. Right away." She went back to her office. Most people who had hair as orange as hers would have sea-green eyes, but Sally's were small and dark brown. She didn't have many clothes, but what she did have were always neat and clean, and she always looked professional. The fact that she was soft-spoken and articulate made her an asset to the office. Jack didn't trust himself to have a beautiful woman work for him, and Sally wasn't beautiful. That made her all the more attractive for the job she was hired to do.

Sally typed in "COMM" on her computer, then she typed in the inmate's name. A couple of seconds later Leo Trinket's crime came up on the monitor. She pressed the print button.

"Here's your printout, Mr. Tyler. He looks like a rough customer."

"Really?"

"Yes, sir. It says here that he killed his foster parents. He was sentenced to two life sentences."

Jack stroked his chin and leaned forward. "I remember the case. It got a lot of publicity. He didn't get the death penalty."

"Why didn't he get the death penalty? Texas is seldom that lenient," Sally said.

"The way I remember it, he was involved in a cult that his foster parents were the leaders of. A lot of abuse went on there." Jack rubbed his neck and closed his eyes. "His lawyers went for insanity and the jury bought it."

"It looks like it will be a long time before he comes up for parole."

"Not anymore, it doesn't" Jack said.

"What do you mean?"

"He paroled himself a little while ago."

Chapter 33

The old Victorian house with its turrets, gables, and gingerbread stood atop the hill giving validation to the realms of darkness and hauntings and witches on a Halloween night. It was grand and fantastic, yet grotesque, like a gargoyle. Hannah could feel her soul dying as she breathed in the malignant air.

Ethel pushed her on the back. "Move!"

"Is Reed in that house, Ethel?" She couldn't bare to think that her sweet son was inside. It was too frightening. The dark clouds behind and above the house covered it like a shroud around a corpse. Reed was too alive, too full of sunshine to be taken inside a place that reeked of iniquity.

"Ethel, answer me!" she screamed.

"Shut up!"

The closer they got to the door, the more smothered Hannah felt. Never could she have believed that an edifice could foster such an animate energy, but this one did. It had a life of its own. And it was wicked.

The screen door squeaked on its hinges. Ethel pushed her inside. Red flocked wallpaper, the color of stale blood, saturated the walls and the atmosphere in despair.

"This is your new home, Hannah," Ethel said sweetly. "I hope you like it. I fixed up the green room just for you – green to match those beautiful eyes of yours."

Hannah could hear chanting from deep within the house, but she didn't know if it was real or if it was just her imagination, and in fact, she wondered if it mattered.

While being led through the house, Hannah felt like she was being watched. The furniture, like the house, seemed to possess life and flaunted carved faces of evil. Hannah was terrified, but more for her son than for herself.

"Ethel, please tell me where Reed is."

"If you ask me that again, Hannah dear, I'll have to tell Mother, and Mother doesn't like whiny babies."

Hannah wanted to scream. Her anger and fear had commingled into something greater than herself, and hatred for Ethel Fletcher consumed her. She had never truly experienced the feeling of raw and unadulterated hatred before now, and whether it would empower her or destroy her, Hannah couldn't tell.

Ethel paused and took a large brass key from her pocket then inserted it into a door that was framed with dark rich wood. Perched on the top was a gargoyle looking down at Hannah, and Hannah had the feeling it had every intention of eating her for supper. She shivered.

The gargoyle was nothing compared to the room. You could not tell where the floor connected to the walls or where the walls ended and the ceiling began. It was entirely black, except for the white five-pointed star in the middle of the floor. Along one side was a red table with red chairs. A black candle was in front of each chair. On the other side of the room was what appeared to be an altar with demons luring from its facade.

Absorbing her surroundings, Hannah failed to see the cage. It lay in the farthest back corner and was made of black sturdy wire.

"I know I promised you your own bedroom, but you'll have to stay here for awhile. Just until you get used to your new home." Ethel smiled wickedly. "Mother likes for the new arrivals to get a feel for the place." She pointed to the cage that Hannah had not yet seen.

"Get in like a good little girl." She led her towards it.

"What? You can't be serious."

Ethel opened the door to the cage and pressed down on Hannah's back. "Watch your head."

With her hands cuffed, Hannah tried to push Ethel away from her. She was not going in without a fight.

Ethel backed away and pulled out her gun. "We can do this the easy way or the hard way. It matters not to me." She had taken off her glasses, exposing those hideous eyes. They looked even more bizarre in a solid black room.

Hannah bent down, ashamed of her lack of confidence, and crawled into the cage.

Ethel closed and locked the door.

"Ethel, will you at least un-cuff me?"

"No."

"Why are you doing this to me?"

"It's all part of the big picture. You'll see soon enough." Ethel walked toward the black door and turned out the lights. When she stepped out of the room and closed the door, total darkness stole Hannah.

She tried to get comfortable, but the bulky coat and the handcuffs made that impossible in the cramped space of the cage.

I have two choices, Hannah thought, trying to calm herself. *I can become hysterical and fall apart, or I can hold myself together and reason my way out of this.*

The worst part of the whole ordeal for Hannah was agonizing

over what had happened to Reed. She knew William would be worried to death, but at the moment, he probably didn't even realize they were missing. *Oh, God,* she thought, *please don't let anything happen to my son.*

Hannah bowed her head in the darkness and prayed. "God, I've been taught to have faith in you. All my life I have believed that you answered prayers and that you would watch over me and my family. It was easy to believe that because my life has been so uncomplicated. I realize now that I never really needed my faith like this before. Now that I do need it, I'm having a hard time finding it. God, I want to believe that you are going to get me out of this cage and these handcuffs. I want to believe that you will help me find my son and that he is all right. Oh God, I'm scared. Please help me."

Hannah woke to the sound of two voices. One was Ethel's. Without turning on the light, they walked over to Hannah's cage.

"How are you doing?" Ethel asked as she bent down to peer into the cage, as if Hannah were some wild animal in a zoo.

"I need to go to the restroom."

"I think we can arrange that." Ethel unlocked the cage.

Relieved, but still scared, Hannah crawled out. She had no sense of how long she had been in there, but if her back and legs were any indication, it had been hours. William must have some indication that something was wrong by now.

She could barely stand. The person with Ethel held Hannah up until the circulation began to come back to her legs. She could not see the person's face or even tell if it was a man or a woman.

"The bathroom is this way. Follow me."

The small amount of light that came from the open door allowed Hannah to see well enough to follow Ethel's form. The other person stayed behind.

Hannah's hands were still cuffed. They made their way down a bleak corridor and finally to the bathroom at the end of it. "Take these things off of me so I can use the bathroom. I'm not going anywhere, and I'm too tired and sore to fight you, Ethel."

"I tell you what. You give me something in trade."

Hannah looked at her suspiciously.

"Turn around and sit on this stool. I want to brush your hair."

Hannah knew that Ethel had lost touch with reality a long time ago, but Ethel never ceased to amaze her with the odd ideas that crossed her mind at any given moment. And if letting Ethel brush her hair would allow her the privilege of relieving her bladder, it was worth it.

Ethel took a small ivory handled brush and began brushing the ponytail that was banded with the sterling silver ornament that Reed had given her. "My, my, what a pretty ponytail holder you have. Let's see. There's a lion, and a giraffe, a hippo, and a cat of some sort. What is that? A panther?" She put the brush down and started braiding Hannah's black silky hair.

"A cheetah, I think."

"Sure, that's what it is. A cheetah. And where did you find such an interesting piece for your lovely hair?"

"My son gave it to me for Christmas."

Ethel took a rubber band from a dish that was sitting on the vanity table. Hannah watched her in the mirror. She put it around the bottom of the braid. "There. That looks splendid."

Hannah started to stand.

"Wait, wait, wait. I'm not quite finished." She took some scissors from the drawer beside the sink, put them to Hannah's head and cut off the braid behind the sterling silver ponytail holder, next to her scalp. The sound was crisp and final. Ethel held the long black braid in her hands almost lovingly.

"Now you can tinky-wink. I'll take those miserable cuffs off."

As Ethel unlocked the stiff metal bracelets, Hannah felt like a balloon had been inflated in her throat. It took her a few seconds to realize what had just taken place. All the while Ethel was chattering endlessly.

Finally she left Hannah alone in bathroom. The scream that Hannah released could be heard all over the entire house.

Chapter 34

William tried Jeff's number again. No answer. Feeling the walls of the house closing in on him, he walked outside on the deck. The boards were slippery. The weather was terrible and steadily getting worse. Damn it! Where was she? He went back inside and ended up at the refrigerator. He grabbed a coke, opened it, and took a long swallow. It stung his throat going down. He poured the rest down the sink, and crumpled the can.

The reconnaissance division of the Marine Corps taught William to be the best in hand- to-hand combat, and he was a trained weapons expert. Learning survival skills in the deadliest regions of the world had made him strong, confident, and tough, and he could hide and slide with the best of them, but he had not been trained in how to deal with what faced him now.

Reed was still hammering away at his fiddle, trying to cope with his fear the best way he knew how.

William walked into Reed's room. Reed put his fiddle down in his lap and looked at his father expectantly.

"I'm going to drive out to the unit and talk to your mom's principal. Maybe if we put our heads together, we can figure out what's happened."

"Okay."

The buzzer on the oven alerted William that his forgotten casserole was done. He went to take it out, then came back to his son's room. Reed was sitting there expressionless, his face unable to reflect the angst he was consumed with inside.

"Will you be all right here by yourself?"

"Yes, sir."

"I could call someone to come over."

"No. I don't want anyone. I'll be fine. Just go try to find Pretty."

William felt a tear trickle down his face. He turned to go, hiding his face from Reed. Not because he was ashamed for his son to see him cry, but because he had to stay strong for a young boy who may have just lost his mother.

"Dad?"

"Yeah."

"I love you."

"I love you, too, son."

Reed went to his father and put his arms around him. He cried hard and so did William. William realized in that undiluted moment that strength was not always tough. At times like this it was a sharing of grief and the hug of a father and his child. It was tears and unblemished, gut- wrenching emotion . It was just getting through one minute at a time.

The drive out to the Estelle Unit generally took twenty-five minutes at least, but William took his police car and ran with his emergency beacons turning and flashing all the way. He got there in ten. There was a guard in the check station to the entrance of the prison unit. He motioned for William to come to a halt. Irritated, William stopped.

The guard bent down. "Could I see some identification, sir?"

William pulled out his ID wallet that also contained his badge.

"Are you William Douglas?"

"Yes."

"Hold just one moment, please."

William was getting more agitated by the second.

The guard came back out of the booth.

"Officer Douglas, there will be a TDCJ officer waiting for you at the front gate-picket. The warden is expecting you."

"The warden?"

"Yes, sir."

"Okay, thanks."

William drove through the parking lot looking for Hannah's car. It wasn't there. He knew it wouldn't be. Finally he drove up to the front row in the parking area reserved for emergency vehicles. *By God, this is an emergency, and this is an emergency vehicle. Just let them try to say something about it.*

He got out and was met by a young female officer at the picket.

"Are you carrying a weapon of any kind, sir?"

"No."

"Good. Come with me, please."

William felt uncomfortable with the greeting he had received. It was too official.

The TDCJ officer knocked on the warden's door, and Lonnie Ray West opened it.

"Come on in, William. I'm not surprised that you're here."

Warden Safford stood up to shake hands with William. Too soft for a man – his hands bore no calluses and looked to be professionally manicured. He greeted William with disdain.

Safford began. "I assume by your presence here that you still have not heard from your wife." Looking from Lonnie Ray to William, he said, "Oh, forgive me. Mr. West told me about your call to him."

"That's right."

"Has she ever done anything like this before?"

"Like what exactly?" William did not like the tone in the warden's voice. It almost insinuated that Hannah was cheap and loose.

"Not come home at night. Fool around. Run off with another man. You know," he said cynically.

William lost it. He stood up and got in Safford's face. "I don't know what kind of cheap trash you surround yourself with, but don't you even dare to presume that my wife is some two-bit hussy that fools around just because your sorry prison can't keep their convicts in line and locked up." He took a deep breath. "I doubt you'd know class if it stood up and bit you on the ass. And if you have ever met my wife, you have stared class right in the face, you son-of-a- bitch."

Lonnie Ray had gotten up and put his hand on William's shoulder. "Come on, William. Calm down."

"Calm down?" He looked around the room and back at Warden Safford who was too offended to speak. "Calm down? I honestly don't think this guy could tell shit from shinola." A mist of spittle landed on Safford's face.

"How could you even conceive of the notion that Hannah Douglas would leave her son and her husband for a sorry-ass convict? She is beautiful, she is smart, and she loves her family as much as her family loves her. The very idea that she would put her life in jeopardy to help a convicted criminal escape from prison, a prison where she works, is the most farfetched pile of crap I've ever heard."

William put his hands in his pockets to keep from knocking the shinola out of Safford.

"How in the hell am I supposed to calm down when some idiot is in charge of this thing, and all he wants to do is make it sound like my wife is some dumb slut that would take off with a no-good sorry convict?"

"He's not in charge. I am."

Everyone in the room turned to look at the door. Standing there was Jack Tyler, the director of the Texas Department of Criminal Justice, looking tall and confident. A crisp and expensive black suit made him appear to be even more significant than he was. William sat back down at West's insistence. Jack shook some hands then took a seat as well.

"I understand that the escaped convict had a teacher's ID card. Is that how he walked out the front gate?" His question was straightforward. No accusations.

The warden nodded his head, looking a bit smaller than he did before the director walked into his office, and before William Douglas told him off. He was wearing a gray sports-coat, a pink shirt, and a cheap yellow and blue striped tie, or rather, it was wearing him. What credibility he had left after William finished with him, waned fast the minute Tyler entered the room.

Jack Tyler had been compared to the actor, Robert Wagner, down to the gold ID bracelet and pinky ring, on more than one occasion, save for a slight belly pooch. He was suave and debonair and wore expensive clothes in good taste. His posture stemmed from pride in his accomplishments, not from his looks.

"Are we to assume that this teacher gave it to him?"

William spoke up. "First of all, her name is Hannah Douglas, and she is my wife. Second, you cannot assume any such thing. And third, I want to know what's being done about trying to find her."

Jack stared at William for a long minute before answering him. "I can assume anything I want as long as I don't have evidence to the contrary."

"Oh. I see. The law doesn't apply here. Is that it?"

"What law?"

"The law that says you are innocent until proven guilty. I can quote you some other laws as well like . . ."

Lonnie Ray cut in. "Mr. Tyler, William Douglas is a deputy, excuse me, a detective now, with the Walker County Sheriff's Department."

"Oh, I see." Jack clasped his hands together and popped his knuckles, a habit that had grated on Elaine's nerves of late. "I didn't realize we were dealing with another law officer here. I apologize." He sounded sincere.

"Aren't any of you concerned that my wife has more than likely been kidnapped by that maniac who escaped today? What possible motive would she have for helping him? What possible reason would she have for running off with him of her own free will? Hell, Lonnie Ray, you've known Hannah for years. Has she ever done one thing to make you think she is capable of helping one of these thugs escape, and then running off with him?" Tears stung William's eyes again.

"No, I know that Hannah is not capable of anything like that."

"Then what's the problem?"

"The problem, Detective Douglas, is that Leo Trinket walked out of here today wearing an ID with your wife's name on it beneath a picture of himself," the warden said sarcastically. "And your wife and her car are nowhere to be found."

William clenched his teeth so hard it made his jaws ache. He looked at Lonnie Ray and asked a question he had been thus far hesitant to know the answer to.

"Who are we dealing with here, anyway? Tell me about Leo Trinket."

Warden Safford looked at Jack Tyler. Jack nodded his head. "He's twenty-five years old. White. He's serving two life sentences. He's been locked up for seven years. Here's his mug shot." He bent over his desk to hand it to William.

William held the picture of Leo Trinket in his hands and studied it. "What did he do to get two life sentences?" he heard himself asking, scared to death to hear the answer.

The director swallowed hard, then said clearly, "He butchered his foster parents to death with an ax."

William, his face waxen, stood up to leave. He stepped behind his chair and started for the door.

Lonnie Ray West asked, "William, what are you going to do?"

"I'm going to the Sheriff's Office, and then I'm going to round up every deputy and detective, every city police officer, every university cop, every Texas Ranger, DPS trooper, and FBI agent that I know to help me find my wife before that crazy son-of-a-bitch finds his ax."

"I need that picture of Trinket," the warden said.

"I need it more." William left and took the image of Leo Trinket with him.

Chapter 35

Twila Brooks heard the scream. It chilled her to the bone. She walked to the door and tried the knob for the hundredth time, but of course, it was still locked. She put her head to the door, listening for something – anything. She closed her eyes to shut out the whiteness of the room. It was beginning to consume her. If not for the single red rose that Jona had given her, she might have gone mad.

There were voices coming up the stairs, muffled at first but becoming clearer as they got closer. She heard wailing from a woman. *Oh, no, they've kidnapped someone else. What are they going to do with us?* The sound got closer and went right by her door. It was easy to hear the new captive's labored breathing. Twila's heart went out to her, and she began to cry herself. She hadn't realized that her body could produce so many tears. It seemed like she would have used them up already, but they continued to flow and sting her face.

Finally a door slammed and she heard it lock. Footsteps came to her threshold and stopped. A key was thrust into the lock. Twila backed up swiftly.

It was Jona.

"Are you all right, Twila? Do you need anything?"

"What just happened? I just heard someone screaming and crying."

"That's not for you to concern yourself with. It has nothing to do with you." He walked up to her and put his hand on her shoulder.

She put her hand on top of his. "Jona, could you stay with me for a while? This room, all this white. There's nothing to do here. I'm going crazy. Just stay with me for a little while."

His expression did not change. His face looked as though there was no feeling behind it.

"Jona, did you hear me?" she whispered genuinely. She rubbed his cheek with her right hand. It was warm and strong. He was real. There was a person behind the front. If only she could reach it.

"I must go."

Twila reached for the other side of his face with her left hand and brought him close to her, so close that she could feel his breath. She ran her fingers through his long hair and heard him gasp ever so quietly. She was reaching him. His eyes closed for a long second. She put her lips to his. At first he didn't respond, but then he could not help himself. He put his arms around her and tilted her body back slightly, kissing her with a passion that was riveting. His tongue swept the softness of her mouth slowly and intensely. He explored it as though he were searching for her soul, or perhaps he was searching for his own.

When he ended it, he looked at her again with the same blue eyes, but there was something else. They had a glimmer of life in them.

She wanted him to touch her again like he had before after he had bathed her, only this time she wanted to touch him back. She wanted to make him feel. She unbuttoned his shirt and pulled it out of his jeans, never letting her eyes drop from his. She untied the sash on her white robe and let it open up to her bare body. He had seen it before. He had bathed it and massaged it, but it was for her pleasure, not his. She wanted him to feel her on him, next to him. She put her full breasts against his smooth chest. She sensed that he wasn't supposed to, but he let her anyway. He let her rub herself against him like a cat. And he liked it.

Abruptly he pushed her away.

"I can't do this," he said. "I'm sorry."

"But why?" She closed her solid white robe and tied the sash.

"I can't get involved with you. It wouldn't be right."

"Wouldn't be right?" Twila cried. "Is keeping me here, locked in this room against my will, right? Is being kidnapped out of my own home, right? Is being handcuffed and squeezed into a cage like a wild animal, right? All of a sudden you're concerned with what's right?"

Jona felt tortured. He wanted to touch her, hold her, and make the fear and pain go away but he could not. It wasn't part of the plan. He had to keep the vision in mind, but she was so beautiful. If she weren't so beautiful and delicate. He turned around and left the room because if he stayed he would get lost in her.

The hot white walls closed in around Twila, pushing at her, pulling at her. Was it the heat from the room, or was it the heat from within her? A war was being waged between her heart and her brain. She was in some Godforsaken place, perhaps hell, and she was falling in love with one of its demons. Was she losing her mind? Maybe that would be best.

Remembering the woman she heard crying, Twila went to the wall and wrapped softly. After a few seconds the knock was returned.

Hannah wondered who could be in the room next to her. Could it be Reed? Oh, God. Maybe it was Reed. It had to be. She knocked again, this time to the rhythm of one his fiddle tunes. The person behind the wall wrapped out the same rhythm. Hannah beat out the next phrase, hoping that if it was Reed, he would beat out the phrase after that. The person mimicked what she had done. She tried again.

Once more the person behind the wall mimicked her. Still, it could be Reed, she told herself. It was something to cling to, a ray of hope.

CRESTED

Leo Trinket had second thoughts when he came to the road that led up to the house. It was getting colder outside. It reminded him of the afternoon of the murders, before the blood bath. He turned onto the obscure road that would go unnoticed by people just passing by. The trees formed a canopy over the road, and the branches of the post oaks seemed to reach out at him as he drove through. Were they welcoming him home, or were they warning him of things to come? He didn't know. He had never known. The drive was long and winding. The wind outside was picking up. He had not been to the grounds in over seven years, but he had not missed it. Coming around the last bend, he spotted the house. The barn stood just behind and below it. The barn. Leo's mind began to pulsate in slow thick waves. He shook his head trying to clear it, but all he could see were the images of that last night he spent there. The night when hell came down and swallowed him whole.

The car had kept moving without Leo realizing it, and before he knew it, he had come to a complete stop in front of the house where evil lived. He took slow deep breaths and tried to summon the courage to get out of the car. The waves hit him again. He needed his medicine. He had missed his last dose. Ethel would have to get him some medicine or he couldn't compete with the house. The front door opened. He closed his eyes and rubbed them, trying to erase the vision he had just seen. He opened them and looked once again at the front door of the house. Mother was standing at the threshold. It couldn't be. Was this some kind of sick joke? She was dead. He had killed her. The waves carried him away.

Chapter 36

Leaving the warden's office, making his way through the lobby and out the front doors, William tried to imagine what had gone through Hannah's mind when she left there today. *Was she frightened? Did she have any idea about the danger that was about to be forced upon her, or did she feel happy about going to meet Sandy for lunch? Did she think that the afternoon ahead of her was going to be fun and carefree and a day about childhood memories with her best friend? When was she taken? How was she taken? What was she wearing? How was her hair fixed? God! Where is my Hannah?*

The officer in the front picket buzzed the gate open. William went through the first and then the second gate. His eyes scanned the dark parking lot. It was what Hannah saw every morning when she came to work. He looked around him – so bleak – so dismal. Yet, every morning she came to this place, filled with the worst kind of scum that the state of Texas had to offer, and she tried to make a difference. She took her heart and her soul into that dreary prison and offered hope, understanding, and kindness mixed with an education that no one else had been able to provide them and one of the sorry scum-bags took her. Just took her.

He backed out of the *emergency vehicles only* parking space and radioed dispatch.

"S.O. This is 826. Advise 801 to meet me at his office. It's urgent. E.T.A. fifteen minutes."

"826. This is S.O. 10-4."

The sheriff was eating supper when Nate from dispatch called him on the phone.

"Sheriff Applegate, this is Nate. William just called on his radio and said to advise you to meet him at your office and that he would be here in fifteen minutes."

"Did he say what this is about?"

"No, sir. Only that it was urgent."

"I'm on my way. Thanks."

"Yes, sir."

William got to the Sheriff's Office in ten minutes rather than fifteen. It gave him time to call Hannah's parents.

After the third ring Henry Richey answered. "Hello?"

"Henry, this is William. I've got some bad news."

Henry's throat squeezed tight. "What is it?"

"Hannah's been abducted. We think by a convict by the name of Leo Trinket."

"Oh, my God."

"I'm going to get every law agency in the county working on this. I'm at the Sheriff's Office now. I don't know when I'll get home, but I need for you and Meredith to come stay with Reed."

"When did this happen?" Henry reached for his wife's hand.

"We aren't sure. She never came home from work, but the inmate didn't leave until after two o'clock this afternoon. I think someone else could be involved, but at this point everything is just speculation. She was supposed to meet Sandy for lunch, but she never made it."

"Did you find her car?"

"No, sir."

"We'll pack and be there as soon as we can, and if you find out anything, you have our cell-phone number."

"Yes, sir. I have it." William swallowed hard. "I'd tell you not to worry, but I . . ."

"I know, son. I know. Bye now." Henry looked into his wife's face. How could he tell her this?

The sheriff hadn't made it yet. William needed to call Reed anyhow. Reed answered on the first ring.

"Pretty?"

"No, son. It's me."

"Dad, what did you find out?"

William knew this would end up on the news. He wanted to be the one to tell his son what had happened. "Your mother has been abducted by an escaped convict, Reed."

"What?"

"We know his name and who he is. I'm at the office and am about to meet with the sheriff. We're going to get everybody with a badge out looking for her. We're going to find her, Reed. We won't stop until we do."

"I know you won't."

Reed didn't know what else to say, but racing through his mind was the ex-con on the news – the one who had raped the woman and her daughter. The one who had burned the woman with a cigarette after he had killed her to make sure she was dead. The one who had been in his mother's class.

"Listen, your grandparents are coming to stay with you. They'll be there in a little while. I just called them. They have to pack some things and then they'll be on their way."

"Okay."

"Reed?"

"Yes."

"I love you."

"I love you, too, Dad."

William hung up the phone in time to see Applegate walk through the door.

"What's this all about? You look like something the cat drug in."

William told him everything he knew. The sheriff listened carefully and then got on the horn and called the chiefs of police for the city and the university. He called Texas Ranger Waylon Abbot and asked him to notify The Department of Public Safety. He called the chief deputy and told him to get in touch with every deputy on the force and bring them in now. And then he called the FBI.

Within the hour the Walker County Sheriff's Office was packed with enough law enforcement officers to lead an attack against a small country. Applegate herded them all into the squad room after he had opened the partition between it and the dining area, and explained the situation.

"Ladies and gentlemen, we need your help. One of our own, Detective William Douglas, has found out tonight that his wife, Hannah Douglas, is missing. She is a teacher at the Estelle Prison Unit where an escaped convict, Leo Trinket, used her state ID card to walk out the front gate. The warden and the TDCJ director have indicated that they think she possibly aided this criminal in his escape, but we know better. Those arrogant asses are embarrassed that one of their convicts can just walk out the front gate without being noticed, so they're wanting to blame somebody. I'm here to tell you, if you don't know this woman, then it's your loss. She is one of the finest human beings I have ever had the privilege to know, and she has been happily married to one of my detectives for the past fourteen years." He looked at his audience and felt a camaraderie that permeated the room. It was palpable.

"Leo Trinket was serving two life sentences for the murder of his foster parents. He butchered them to death with an ax. It was calculated and unmerciful. I worked the call seven years ago. I found this lunatic hiding in the corner of their barn with the bloody murder weapon still in his hands.

"I can't emphasize enough the urgency of this situation. Hannah Douglas is a member of this family." He stretched out his arms as if to embody the whole group. "We have to unite and find this young woman and bring her home.

"We will use this office as a post. Every shred of evidence, speculation, or just plain old hunches will be forwarded here immediately and shared with every law officer on this case. At this point we have no reason to believe that they have left Texas. We don't have much to go on except our collective years of experience and a good measure of expertise. And people, we're going to need everything you've got.

"The information in your folders contains a recent photograph of Ms. Douglas, the make and description of her car, and the license plate number. It also has all we have at this point on Leo Trinket. We will have more information on him by morning. Check back often for updates."

He looked across the men and women from every field of law enforcement in his county. "God speed and God help us. Thank you for coming."

William slipped quietly out the back door of the squad room to keep from being bombarded with people wanting to offer condolences. There wasn't time for that. His feelings weren't the issue here. Finding his wife was.

He tried Lonnie Ray West at home again. He answered finally.

"Lonnie Ray, this is William. I need you to get everything you have on Trinket: his birth certificate, previous residences, schools, hobbies, jobs, everything. I even want to know his favorite color."

"William, I can't just . . ."

"Lonnie Ray, I don't have time for this. I know they keep records like that in the RIO office. I'm an officer of the law, for God's sake!"

"You are a grieving husband, and you aren't the least bit concerned about rules and regulations."

"Would you be if you were in my place? Tell me you wouldn't be digging in his file if he had just stolen your wife."

Lonnie Ray knew he was right. "Look, if I go in tonight it will look suspicious. I'll go in early in the morning and get everything I can find on him."

"Fuck suspicious! Don't make me waste time getting a court order."

"All right. All right. Where do I fax it?"

William gave him the number.

"I'm just as worried about Hannah as you are. She's one of my teachers, one of my friends."

"You can't even begin to know how worried I am, Lonnie Ray. But thanks. I know you mean well."

Jeff Stone burst through the door of their office like a bull. William hung up the phone.

"Oh, Jesus, William. I just heard."

☙❧

It was almost eight o'clock when Earl Cowen got home. He had stopped for some barbecued beef over on Old Houston Road. He loved to go there. It was next to a small church, attended by mainly black Christians, and the restaurant in fact was owned by the church and run by three of its most faithful women. Out in front were two enormous barbecue pits tended by an old black man who was a genius at making magic with beef, chicken, ribs and sausage. He was famous state-wide for his barbeque. Considered to be a blessing to his church, he was a blessing to the community as well.

The mesh on the screen door was torn in several places and it was warped. Earl opened it, listening for the familiar creaks it always made, and was not disappointed. The mismatched tables and chairs were mostly occupied by white people, some dressed in business attire, others in jeans and tennis shoes.

The hands that sliced your beef and served your order were the same hands that took your money. Folks didn't seem to mind. The big old pots on the old gas range were full of beans, potatoes for potato salad, and barbecue sauce. Pies were in the oven. Earl had ordered the "all you can eat" plate for six ninety-five that came with three kinds of meat, potato salad, beans, sandwich bread, pickles and onions. The meat was served on a platter, and you took what you wanted. It was heavenly.

Since Joyce had died, it had been difficult for Earl to eat at home. She had been an excellent cook and that may very well be the thing that killed her. She died in her sleep of a heart attack.

Joyce couldn't have children and they never adopted any. Earl's parents were long since dead, and he had no brothers or sisters. He was all alone at the age of fifty-nine.

After a hot shower, Earl put on his old bathrobe and sat down in the recliner Joyce had given him for his birthday a couple of years ago. He zapped on the TV with his remote control and settled on the HBO channel only to doze off inside fifteen minutes.

At ten o'clock he woke up just in time to change the channel to catch the Houston news.

"Leo Trinket, a man who chopped his foster parents to pieces with an ax seven years ago, is on the loose tonight and is possibly holding Hannah Douglas, a prison school teacher, hostage. He escaped this afternoon some time around two o'clock from the Estelle Unit near Huntsville. He was wearing civilian clothes he allegedly stole from the officers' laundry and a state ID tag with his picture on it. The name on the tag was Douglas, Hannah. Ms. Douglas has not been seen or heard from since twelve-fifteen this afternoon. Her car, a late model silver Nissan Sentra, is also missing. The license plate number on that car is 420-LCM." A picture of Leo Trinket was in the upper right hand corner of the screen. A picture of Hannah Douglas beneath it.

"If anyone listening tonight has seen either of these people or the car, please contact the Walker County Sheriff's Office or this station. Both numbers are on your screen. We will give you those telephone numbers again a little later on in the broadcast."

Events from the day immediately resurfaced. Earl thought about what Virginia had told him that morning about Hannah Douglas and all the grief Ethel Fletcher had given her. *Why couldn't someone have kidnapped Ethel instead of someone like Ms. Douglas?* The ring of the telephone startled him.

"Hello."

"Earl, this is Virginia. Have you seen the news?"

"Yes, I was just watching it."

"That man, Trinket, used to be an orderly on our unit. Good God Almighty, I know him. Can you believe it?"

"No, Virginia. I can't." He knew to just listen and agree when Virginia was in a tizzy such as this.

"I guess you've heard the rumors about Ethel and Trinket," she said.

"No. What rumors?"

"Well, the talk was that they had a thing going. That's why he was transferred to another unit."

"What kind of a thing?" asked Earl. He searched for his glasses while holding the phone.

"There's only two incidents I know of for sure because I saw it myself. Do you remember when the inmates used to get their picture made if they had perfect attendance and good test scores?"

"Yes."

"Well, Trinket got his picture made. A couple of days after the pictures were given to the inmates, I saw Trinket giving his picture to Ethel, and she put it in her pocket. And if you think that's something, wait till you hear this. About a week after the picture business, I went to the supply room to get some copy paper, and I heard a kind of knocking noise coming from the broom closet. Thump, thump, thump, thump. I went out in the hall and waited to see who was going to come out of there. Guess who it was."

"Who, Virginia?"

"First Ethel came out of there. Her face was all flushed. She stopped and asked me what I was looking at, then she went to the restroom. Not more than a minute or two later, Leo Trinket came out of there. I can't believe you didn't know about that."

"Did you tell someone?" questioned Earl.

"You bet ya! I went straight to Ms. Bolton."

"What did she do?"

"She questioned Ethel, but Ethel lied and said she was in the supply room getting some paper. She didn't have any paper when she came out of there, and besides we don't store the paper in the broom closet. Anyway, Trinket was shipped to another unit the next day."

"I can't believe Ethel wasn't fired for that."

"Me either, Earl, but she wasn't. It's like everything else she's done that got swept under the carpet. Makes you wonder if she didn't have something to do with Trinket's escape and Hannah and all."

"Virginia, surely Ethel isn't that crazy."

"Oh no? Well I wouldn't put it past her."

"I guess I'd better tell someone about all this. You try to get some sleep. I know you were friends with Ms. Douglas. Maybe we can help her somehow."

"I hope so."

"Good night, Virginia, and thanks."

Some puzzle pieces were fitting together that made Earl feel sick. The news reported that Trinket's picture was on the ID tag. It could very well have been the picture he gave to Ethel, and she could have put it on Ms. Douglas's ID tag. Of course this was all speculation, but nevertheless, he had to tell somebody who would listen, and it would definitely not be Jack or Elaine Tyler. He knew better than to go over his superiors' heads, but on the other hand, he was a citizen that possibly had information that might prove to be helpful in an escape and kidnapping investigation. He decided to go down to the Sheriff's Department. Jeff Stone and William Douglas had questioned him about Ethel, and they were the ones who were going to hear this.

Chapter 37

There were enough police cars at the Sheriff's Office to avert an invasion of the body snatchers. Earl, of course, knew why, and he couldn't blame them. One of their own had been taken and they took that personally. Theirs was a brotherhood not to be messed with: the largest, the tightest, and the most sophisticated street gang in America. They had the means and the power to fight back, and it looked as though that was exactly what they were planning to do. They had been earnestly looking for the six women who had been kidnapped, but that was business; it was their job. This, however, was personal.

Entering through the front doors, he saw deputies, FBI agents, Texas Rangers, city police, university police, DPS Troopers, and even Huntsville School District police officers. It was awesome. A chill ran through Earl Cowen that, for a moment, made him wish he were a part of the group.

Scanning the lobby he searched for Jeff Stone and finally asked one of the uniformed officers where he could find him.

"Detective Stone has an office around the corner, two doors down on the left," the officer said. "I think he's in there." Earl managed to inch his way through the sea of officers, all strapped with gun belts, radios, pepper spray, and handcuffs.

He saw Detective Stone's back inside the door. Earl knocked and waited to be invited in.

Jeff didn't want to be interrupted at that particular moment. He wanted to talk to William, but he clenched his jaws tight and turned around. Earl Cowen stood there.

Jeff looked back at William before opening the door. "It's that principal. I'll get rid of him."

"Hello, Mr. Cowen. Look, I appreciate you coming down here, but this isn't a good time for us. If you could go and talk with one of the deputies, they'll be glad to take down whatever you've got to say." He drew his face into a pose that asked for understanding.

Earl Cowen pushed his way in and closed the door. "You'll want to hear this. Both of you.

"My secretary called me tonight after she heard the news about Ms. Douglas. She said Leo Trinket used to be at The Walls. She caught Trinket and Ethel Fletcher coming out of the broom closet after hearing some noises in there. Virginia thinks they were, you know."

"And?"

"And she also saw Trinket give Ethel a photograph of himself."

"Holy Toledo," Jeff said.

"Anyway, Trinket was transferred after Virginia reported the broom closet incident, but apparently nothing was done to Ms. Fletcher."

Memories of Ethel's harassment of Hannah flooded William again.

Earl continued. "I – Virginia and I that is – were thinking Ethel could be involved with your wife's abduction, seeing as how she knew Trinket and all."

"The van! The dark van!" William exclaimed.

"I don't follow, pal, " Jeff said.

"Hannah said that someone in a dark van was parked outside our neighbor's house the other morning when she went to work. You know she leaves the house around four-thirty and it's still dark out. Hannah felt a little skittish about it being there. She said the van followed her all the way to work."

"Did she see who it was?" Jeff asked.

"No, the windows had been tinted and she said the bright lights were on. It stayed directly behind her all the way out to Estelle and then left."

"What morning was that?"

William looked at the calendar on the desk. "The same morning I became a detective, and the same morning Twila Brooks disappeared."

Jeff patted Earl Cowen on his shoulder. "You may have just helped us crack this case and all the others. That would make you a hero in my book."

"No, sir. That would make Virginia Deigo one."

"If this leads to anything," Jeff said, "I'm going to buy the both of you a medal."

William felt a faint smile crease his face for the first time since he realized Hannah was gone. Virginia, the unlikeliest of heroes, had just given him his first ray of hope.

William barreled out and went straight to the sheriff's office. He walked in without knocking, too preoccupied to worry with protocol. "I need a background on Ethel Fletcher."

"Ethel Fletcher? William, she may have been involved with those other women, but I don't see how . . ."

"Sheriff, I need to know where she grew up, how she grew up, where she went to college, where she was born, her birth certificate, criminal history, and juvenile history."

Sheriff Applegate remained silent.

"She knows Leo Trinket. Intimately."

"Well, I'll be damned."

Jeff interrupted. "Channel Eleven in Houston wants some photographs of Hannah. Several, in fact. They're going to put her all over TV."

William nodded to Jeff then looked squarely at the sheriff.

"Ethel Fletcher has my wife. I know she does."

The sheriff looked out his window and into the lobby.

"I don't think I'll have any trouble finding some people to take care of that list for you. Go home, take Jeff with you, and get some photographs of that beautiful wife of yours. I can handle things from this end." He took William by the arm. "You need to be with your son right now, at least for a few minutes. Go on home."

"All right. But you call the minute you have any information at all."

"I will. I will."

When he walked back out into the lobby everyone stood still and silent, and in their silence they conveyed more sentiment than anyone could have spoken.

Jeff followed William in his car.

The lights were burning when they got to William's house, but they didn't look as bright as usual.

Reed opened the front door before William managed to get to it.

"Any news?" he asked anxiously. Henry and Meredith were right behind him.

"We've got a lead." William brought his son up as close as he could to him and gave him a hug.

After a long few seconds he hugged Meredith and then Henry.

"Thanks for coming." They both nodded, unable to speak.

William introduced his in-laws to Jeff.

"We need some photographs of Hannah for the media. Jeff's

going to take them up to the office and fax them to channel eleven."

"Dad, we can fax them right here. Pretty has a fax machine on her computer. I'll go set it up." Reed was anxious to do anything to help, and William was relieved that he had found something important. He needed to feel useful.

Jeff answered him. "Reed, that's fantastic. The sooner the better." Reed darted off to Hannah's study.

"I'll go get those pictures. They're in our bedroom."

Meredith offered Jeff some coffee. He walked through the den and noticed the portrait of Hannah and her horse above the credenza. Henry offered an explanation.

"That was taken on a cold and windy November day. It was in the low thirties. William got outside and bathed that horse, dried him and brushed him until he gleamed like a fifty dollar gold piece. He and Reed gave Hannah that horse for her birthday that year and all she could talk about was having her picture made with it for Christmas. That's what she wanted."

His eyes filled with liquid. "William saved two years to buy her that horse. Hannah named him Gabriel's Trumpet."

"It's beautiful, the horse, I mean.

"Yes it is."

"What kind of ring is that she's wearing?" Jeff asked.

Reed was back in the room by then. "I call that her spaceship ring. It's a gray pearl."

"Pearl? I've never seen a pearl that big."

"It's a mabe pearl," Meredith chimed in. It belonged to her grandmother."

"It looks blue, not gray," Jeff said, taking a closer look at the portrait.

"I know," Reed said, "and sometimes it looks lavender."

"I have never seen anything like it," Jeff said, "and I notice jewelry." He paused. "That's really pretty."

"What is?" William had come back into the room with the photographs.

"We were just talking about that pearl ring."

William handed Jeff the pictures. "Will these do, you think? They're more of her with her horse." There were twelve beautiful pictures of Hannah dressed in different outfits, from jeans and boots, to an old Victorian dress and hat.

Jeff looked at each picture. "They're perfect." The photographs made the whole ordeal seem even more horrific. In those pictures he saw a beautiful, sweet, and intelligent wife, mother, and daughter standing there with a horse that William had saved for two years to buy for her.

"Where's the fax machine, Reed?"

"This way, Mr. Stone." Reed headed towards Hannah's study. "We can scan them first and fax them right out if you have the number."

"It's right here in my pocket. And Reed, since we're partners now, why don't you call me Jeff?"

A smile gripped Reed's face. A much needed second of diversion. "Okay, Jeff."

William was behind them in the hall thinking that was one heck of a nice thing for Jeff to do. He walked back into the kitchen. "Meredith, did I hear you say you had some coffee? I sure could use some."

"Yes, and I have some snacks here. You need to eat something."

William started to decline. He was in no mood for food.

Meredith continued. "I want you to have all the strength you need to find my daughter, and you won't on an empty stomach. Please. Just a few of these finger sandwiches."

Henry sat down beside him at the bar. "Hand me a couple of

those, honey." They were all trying to dance around the hysteria that was tangible in the air. If each person could maintain his emotions, then perhaps they could trudge their way through this thick muck of despair.

Jeff sent the photographs via Hannah's computer to Channel Eleven News. He thanked Reed for his help, patted the young boy on the head and for an instant wished that he had a son to go home to – anyone to go home to, and then he thought about Stella. He felt guilty for having selfish feelings at a time like this. He had read somewhere that the greatest heights of passion were often achieved in the midst of tragedy or danger, but it didn't seem right.

"William, I'm going to go. I want you to try and get some sleep. You know what kind of force is working on this case as we speak. You can't do anything until we get all that information you asked for, and they said they would call if anything came up." He rubbed his hands through his hair. He wanted desperately to help William find his wife.

William looked at Reed and then at his in-laws. "I'll try to catch a nap, but I don't know for how long – not while Hannah is God knows where."

"It's just that you don't want to use up all your strength when there's nothing for you to do right now. Take care of yourself and be ready for in the morning bright and early. All the agencies that we need assistance from are closed. Most of the information you're looking for on Ethel is going to have to wait until morning."

"I know. I know."

Jeff hugged his partner like a brother – no, more like a best friend. William was nothing like his brother. William would never do to him what his own brother had done. He said good-night to the Richeys and left. On the way to his car, he wondered if Stella was still awake.

"I'm going to take a shower. Reed, I want you to crawl in bed.

I'll come tuck you in when I'm done. Okay?" William coaxed him with his eyes.

"Okay, Dad." Reed kissed his grandparents good-night, picked up Dragon, and patted his leg for Neiman to follow him into his room. The cat and the dog had both sensed the anxiety in the air. The cat would sleep with the young boy all night and Neiman would lie beside his bed.

Meredith busied herself doing laundry, trying to occupy her mind to keep from going crazy while Henry sat in the recliner and surfed the channels on television feeling helpless and empty.

Before getting into the shower, William felt pulled to Hannah's closet. He wanted to be close to her, get a sense of her. He opened the door and gathered some of her clothes up to his nose. He could smell her Shalimar. The stockings she had worn the day before were laying across the top of her hamper. He picked one up and pulled it through his hand, then rubbed it against his face. The stubble on his cheek snagged the silky lingerie. It brought closer to mind the softness of her skin against his. Putting it back he noticed something on the floor pushed up under her hanging dresses. He got down on his knees and pulled it out. There were two heart-shaped tins. He didn't open them. He knew that her home-made chocolate fudge was in each one. He and Reed loved it. On top of each container was an envelope. He picked up the one with his name on it and opened it even though he knew he should wait. Valentine's Day wasn't until tomorrow, but he needed to communicate with her, hear her voice – feel her. He sat down Indian style in the middle of her closet, surrounded by her clothes, shoes, hats, and stockings and he opened the card. It was a poem in her handwriting that she had composed just for him.

Colors of a Valentine

256

Red is the color of love
Pink is the shade of a kiss
White is the symbol of purity and the promise of faithfulness.

Growth comes in greens
And warmth wraps us in yellow
Blues pull at our heartstrings to make us feel mellow.

Deep purple radiates passion
Making love on a stormy night
Flames of orange dance about with intoxicating light.

Copper reminds me of fun in the sun, and gray - a cold winter day
Black seduces our hearts when we're sad
But silver linings push it away.

Gold gleams in each of our wedding bands
It's precious, exquisite and rare
Gold is the color of marriage vows, the color of showing you care.
No matter where I go
You can see my love for you
In every color on this earth, my heart beats out its hue.

And on this special day of the year
When red and pink reign sublime
Remember they don't begin to color my feelings for you, Valentine.

I love you, and Happy Valentine's Day!
Hannah

The tidal wave of tears and emotion that he had managed to hold back to a sufferable degree would no longer hold. *Dear God, please give this a silver lining.*

Chapter 38

TDCJ Director Jack Tyler went home. Elaine was not there and he hadn't expected her to be. She was at the lake house again, where she spent most of her nights. He couldn't bear to spend another night there since Elaine and Ethel walked in on him and Libby having sex.

Elaine looked as if someone had drained all the blood out of her body and replaced it with a thick white glue to hold her together. She didn't shout or cry or even turn around long enough for the two of them to get out of the bed and put some clothes on. She just stood there.

Ethel, however, was different. She had plenty to say — viscous, mean things. She wanted Elaine to feel hatred for him and the woman he was having an affair with, the woman who had once been their housekeeper. Ethel hissed, "Not only did she try to steal your jewelry, Aunt Elaine, she had to try and steal your sorry husband as well, and it looks like to me she may have." The pink carpet could not even tone down Ethel's appearance. She looked as hard and mean as a witch.

Jack couldn't get up or move. He knew that Libby felt humiliated. He couldn't look at her. Ethel broke the spell.

"Come on, Aunt Elaine." She pulled Elaine out of the room.

Jack and Libby got dressed without a word; they both knew it was over. What they had wasn't love, at least on Jack's part, it was lust and the need for a relationship. It had been exciting, even dangerous. Jack's reputation could be damaged by an illicit affair – not to mention his marriage – and Libby, well, she was using up her youth and beauty on an older man she couldn't have.

Jack never saw Libby again after that afternoon. With a tear-stained face, she walked out of the lake house and drove away. She did not say a word – not one word.

Elaine asked Ethel to leave and the two of them stayed for the biggest fight of their marriage.

Elaine called him every vile name she could think of. He let her rant and rave for a few minutes and then he had his say. He had told her that since Ethel came, she had been different, and that she no longer had time for him. She was obsessed with Ethel and he couldn't understand why. She never once made love to him after Ethel came. But Elaine would not take the blame for his infidelity. She spit words at him like sparks from a fire. She hated him.

He wondered what happened to Libby after that. He tried to call her, but she wouldn't answer the phone. He even went by her apartment once, but her car wasn't there, and then after several days she was reported as missing. No one knew that he was having an affair with her, except Elaine and Ethel. He didn't think that Elaine would say anything about it to anyone because she wouldn't want the embarrassing publicity, and he was sure she had sworn Ethel to secrecy as well.

If he had been implicated in Libby's disappearance, his career would be over. The director of the Texas prison system could not be in a scandal of that magnitude. The governor would have his balls in a slingshot.

He could not grieve over her disappearance, and he could not look for her, and to make matters worse, he had no one to talk to about it. He had to keep it bottled up inside him.

He worried at first that Ethel had done something to Libby, but after the abduction of the other young women in town, he knew it had to be a coincidence. Some lunatic who had a thing about beautiful girls with long hair had gone off the deep end. Still, at times, he wondered if that lunatic could possibly be Ethel, but one of the girls was kidnapped on a night when he and Ethel had a huge blowout, and another one was kidnapped while she was at work. Besides, the police never suspected her.

Jack knew a little about how William Douglas must be feeling even though the circumstances were different. Funny though, from the picture he saw of Ms. Douglas, she had hair as long as Libby's and all the other girls who were missing. That, of course, was just another coincidence. Leo Trinket was still behind bars when they were abducted. He had checked Trinket's visitation list, and the only visit he ever got was from his lawyer.

Jack fixed himself a Tom Collins and called it a night – another lonely night, but oh, did he have his memories.

CℨℰↃ

One light was on in the back corner of Stella's house. Like a thief in the night Jeff made his way back to the lighted window. His feet made soft crunching sounds on the sleet-covered ground. He peered in and saw her turning down the bed covers. She was still awake.

The doorbell startled her. She pulled the sash of her oversized robe tight around her waist. She was afraid to answer the door this late. Her thick wool socks made no sound on the floor as she tiptoed to the front door. The clock in the kitchen was ticking loudly. Strange how normal everyday noises seemed ominous when alarm loomed in your head.

Stella rested herself against the door and peered out the peep-hole. She didn't turn on the porch light. The tall figure turned around. It was Jeff. She turned on the light and opened the door.

"I know it's way late, but I saw your light on and thought you might feel like talking. It's just that it's been one hell of a bad night since I left your house. Is this a bad time? I know it's too late." He looked down at his feet. He felt like a big oaf.

Jeff felt her hand on his arm. The one that wasn't stitched up from top to bottom. She rubbed it up and down.

"How do you do that?"

"Do what?" she asked.

"Make somebody feel better with just a touch."

She smiled. "Come on in. I'll make us some coffee."

"What I really need is a drink."

"Wine?"

"Sounds great."

He sat down on the couch and she came out of the kitchen with two wine glasses, a bottle of wine, and a cork screw. She handed the bottle and cork screw to him.

Pouring the wine, he told her about his partner's wife. Stella curled up on the couch beside him, bundled up in her robe. She listened as he told her the details of the minutes and hours since leaving her house. She could see the pain he felt for his friends. It showed a compassionate side to him that most men didn't have; at least the men she had known. It warmed her the way he talked about William and the love he shared with his wife, and now the pain he was going through at the hands of an escaped convict. Life wasn't fair.

The glass of wine seemed to take the edge off, but Jeff still looked tense and emotionally exhausted. Stella poured him another glass and told him to take off his jacket. "Let me rub your shoulders. I think it will help you to relax."

She rubbed his shoulders and back with expert skill, and in her touch he felt not only tenderness, but perhaps even desire.

He grabbed her hands when they reached the top of his shoulders and held them for awhile. "I should go. You need to get some rest, and so do I. It's going to be a long day tomorrow."

Stella came around to the front of the couch and told him she could stay up as long as he needed to talk. Jeff knew he could stay up, too, only it wasn't his brain that he was thinking about. It had been years since he had made love to someone he truly cared about.

"Thanks, but I've imposed enough already. The wine and especially the back rub loosened me up. I feel better. I really do need to go."

"Okay. I'm glad you came. I'll walk you to the door."

What if he never came back? She couldn't think like that. Not all men were alike.

Jeff bent down to kiss her good-night. He brushed her cheek with his lips. She was a bit disappointed. She was hoping for one like he gave her when he brought her home from their date, but she understood. He was so down about his partner.

He knew better than to kiss her full on the mouth because he wouldn't be able to leave, and he couldn't stay. The time wasn't right. They had only been out one time, and she would think he was too zealous if he threw her down and went for it on their first night out. She deserved more than that. He could wait. He didn't want to scare her off.

"Call me if you can't sleep," she said sweetly. *Please call,* she thought.

"I'll be fine. Thanks for the wine." *I'd love to call,* he thought. "Good-night."

"Good-night."

He walked off her porch and she closed the door.

Jeff got to his truck. She watched him from the window.

He started to open the door. She didn't want him to leave.

"To hell with it," he said and ran back to her porch. She threw open the door as he slid on the thin layer of ice and into her arms. His lips seared hers as he parted her mouth with his tongue. He explored it frantically, hungrily. She wanted him to. He could tell.

Jeff picked her up in his arms and kicked the door shut behind him. He carried her into her bedroom. She was still all bundled up in the cuddly fleece robe. Stella reached for the bedside lamp and turned out the light. Sleet was falling again, hitting the roof with a soft steady beat.

"I'm not very experienced at this," Stella whispered. She wasn't sure what to do.

"Let me," he whispered back. "Let me unwrap you."

"Okay."

He untied her sash from around her waist, and opened her robe. She was small – almost as fragile as a china doll. He didn't want to hurt her. He felt huge next to her. He would take it slow.

"Unbutton my shirt," he pleaded. "I want to feel you on my skin."

Stella's fingers were clumsy; Jeff could tell she was nervous. "Don't be afraid," he said. "I'm not going to hurt you."

"I'm not afraid of you. I'm just worried that I won't be what you're used to."

"Oh, Stella. You're what I need. I don't want what I've been used to. I want you to let me make love to you. I don't want you to feel like you have to perform for me. Just go with it and feel me."

Stella's body was on fire with lust and desire for this gorgeous man in her bedroom. She got his shirt open and pulled it out of his jeans. She kissed the downy soft hair that covered his chest.

"My turn." Jeff found the buttons on her flannel night gown and undid them slowly. He kissed her neck. He placed his hands over her chest through her gown and held her while he kissed her softly on the lips.

Stella thought she would die. She wouldn't survive this. Her heart was beating too fast. She would go into cardiac arrest. This couldn't be normal.

His hands got heavier on her small breasts as he caressed them gently, lovingly.

"Let me touch you," he whispered.

"I want you to."

With all his heart he did not want to hurt her. He would be careful.

"Are you ready, Princess?"

"Yes."

Chapter 39

Valentine's Day was cold and gray. The trees in the county were frosted with icicles, and the temperature was forecast to stay below freezing at least through tomorrow. Most of the roads were passable, but there was little traffic on this Saturday morning.

William was at the office by dawn, and Jeff got there just a few minutes later. The place was crawling with law enforcement from all the departments that were there last night, but this was the day shift.

Some of the information that William had requested was on his desk and already being looked into. Ethel Elizabeth Fletcher had gone to college at Stephen F. Austin State University. She had to do her student teaching twice. The school district would not give her a reference. There were extenuating circumstances.

"Hey Jeff, I wonder what this means by extenuating circumstances? It doesn't say what they were."

"Let me see." Jeff looked over the document. "I don't know. Didn't you tell me that she had harassed some women while in college."

William replied, "Yes, but that wouldn't have anything to do with this. The children she worked with were in elementary school. This must be something else."

"I'll get someone to follow up and see exactly what they are referring to."

"Why does this have to be a weekend? Everything is going to be closed on Saturday and Sunday." William laid his head down on his desk.

"We're not closed, pal. We've got people working on this twenty-four-seven."

"I know we do. That means a lot."

"What else do we have?"

"Her fingerprints and her criminal history ."

"Anything else?"

"Just the harassment thing. Like with Hannah. She did the harassing and accused her victims of it."

"What about a juvenile record?" Jeff asked.

"Nothing yet. We'll need a court order for that. Jesus! It's going to be Monday before we can get that." William leaned forward on his desk and rubbed his head. "What the devil do people think happens on Saturday and Sunday? Do they think that everything just stops for the weekend?"

Jeff said, "Come on, partner. Don't go off the deep end on me."

William stood up and clasped his hands behind his back. "My wife is God knows where, and there is no telling what is happening to her, and we just bide our time so all of these pansy- ass agencies can have their lousy weekend."

Jeff knew he was operating on grit and will. He had to get him out of there. He had to be doing something that made him feel as though he were accomplishing something. "Let's go over what we need to ask the Tylers."

William's face relaxed a little. His bloodshot eyes focused intently on Jeff. "Yes. Hand me my notebook."

They were about to stir up a hornet's nest. They were going to question two of the state's most upstanding citizens. One of them ran the Texas Department of Criminal Justice, and the other ran the school district for that same institution, and oh, yes – they just happened to be married to each other.

Kay, the secretary that held the Sheriff's Department together, tapped on their office door before walking in. She was in her late fifties but as stout and spry as any twenty-year-old. She was supposed to be barrel racing at the Astrodome this weekend. It was what she most looked forward to every year.

"What are you doing here?" William asked. He looked at his watch. "It's five-thirty in the morning and a Saturday. Besides, I thought you were supposed to be riding at the Houston Livestock Show and Rodeo this weekend."

"If you'll shut up for a minute I'll tell you what I'm doing here." She widened her eyes and tipped her head. "This fax came in for you last night after you left. No one was in my office to receive it until I got here this morning." She handed him the information that Lonnie Ray West sent about Leo Trinket. "And I think it should be obvious why I'm here."

"Kay, you can't miss that rodeo. It's all you have talked about for weeks. And all the training you've put in." He looked down at the floor and shook his head. It was pounding.

"William, look at me," she said. "John and I were in a hotel room across from the Astrodome last night. We went up early so I would be well rested for tonight. He turned on the television. Can you guess whose picture I saw on the news?"

He drew his mouth tight.

Kay continued. "I saw Hannah's picture and some crazy convict's picture up above it. Do you honestly think I could stay there in that swanky hotel room and act as if nothing had happened? Do you think I could just saddle up my horse and ride those barrels today knowing that your wife has been kidnapped?" She tried not to cry but she couldn't help it.

William put his arms around her and squeezed her tight. "Thanks, Kay."

She backed up and wiped her face. "Now let me get back to work. I've got my hands full with all of these gun totin' officers of the law acting like they work for me – as if the Sheriff and his deputies aren't enough, I've got DPS, Rangers, UPD, HISD PD, FBI – they're the real pains in the butt – and the city PD. I think that's everybody. I tell you one thing, if we don't find her, it won't be because nobody tried." She winked.

"Yes, ma'am."

Jeff said, "Let's have a look at that info."

"I've got a copy of Trinket's birth certificate. Born right here in Huntsville Memorial Hospital. The mother's name is Jane Doe."

Jeff grimaced. "Looks like he was jinxed from the get-go."

"Sure does. But it looks like the hospital managed to get her thumb prints. I'll get DPS to run them."

"Thumbs aren't much to go on. It could come back to four or five, maybe even more. And Jane Doe may not have her prints on file. It's a long shot."

"I'll take what I can get."

"What else?"

"He was adopted at birth by Wanda and Otis Trinket. They were killed in a car accident when Leo was six years old. He was then taken into Child Protective Services and spent the rest of his child-hood in foster care."

Jeff had to ask, "Is there anything in his file that says whether or not he tried to hurt any of his other foster parents?"

"No. Those records would be sealed anyway if the crime occurred before he turned seventeen."

"So all we know for sure is that he murdered his last set of fos-ter parents?"

"The Johnsons. Yes."

Jeff was taking notes. "What else?"

"The previous jobs he has listed here are hauling hay, taking care of cows, and yard care."

"Well," Jeff said as he stretched his back until it popped, "I guess you don't have much time to build a work history if you've been locked up since you were seventeen."

"Guess not. Hey, listen to this. He had the gall to list as one of his hobbies: chopping up things with an ax. He is demented if he's crazy enough to put that in his RIO portfolio. I'm surprised they let him." William's eyes continued to scan the file on Trinket. "For Pete's sake." He almost snickered.

"What?"

"Last night when I called Lonnie Ray West to get this file, I told him all of the things I wanted on Leo, including his favorite color. It's red."

Jeff said, "Wise guy."

"Yeah. Listen, I'm going to run these thumb prints over to DPS and see if they can come up with anything. Do you want to come?" William asked.

"No. I'm going to try to get in touch with the Tylers."

"I want to go with you when you question them."

"I think it would be better if I went alone. You're too close to this. I'd probably get more out of them if you weren't there, and besides, I thought you told me that Jack Tyler came in when you went to see Warden Safford."

"That's right."

"It just seems to me that he already feels like he's got the upper hand on you. He's wanting to blame this whole thing on your wife. I'll be going in with a whole different perspective."

"You're right. I just want to feel like I'm doing something."

"After you drop off those prints, why don't you go have breakfast with Reed? He could probably use your company right about now. He looked mighty depressed for a twelve-year-old boy last night."

"Did I tell you that yesterday, when I picked him up from school, he was really cross?"

"No. What happened?"

"Nothing much, but he was in a foul mood. I asked him what was wrong and he said he had been worried about his mother all day, and when we got home and she wasn't there, he nearly blew a fuse. Then Sandy called and said Hannah had missed their lunch date. It upset Reed so much that he dropped the plates he was carrying to the table. He was certain something had happened to his mother, and I just brushed it off as puberty. If I had listened to him, maybe we would have already found her."

"That's crazy and you know it."

"Yeah, maybe. But that kid of mine knew something was wrong, and I didn't listen to him. Instead, I lectured him on giving his mother some space."

"William, you are the best dad around. I've seen you with that kid. He adores you. Don't go putting yourself on a guilt trip. You've got enough on your plate without that."

William just nodded.

"Go on home, partner. Spend some time with your son. He needs you. All of this other stuff is coming together. When it does, we'll be ready."

"I just feel like I need to be out driving around looking for her."

"William, I couldn't count all of the officers that were here last night. We've got people searching this county inside and out. They've got a description of her car, of Trinket, and of Hannah. Let them do their job. This county is literally crawling with cops."

"You call me if . . ."

"Go on. Get out of here."

Jeff tried to reach Elaine Tyler at home and at her office, but there wasn't an answer either place. He really didn't expect anyone to be at the office on a Saturday. Jack Tyler was out of pocket as well. Maybe they were together. He decided not to leave a message. He wanted the element of surprise when he questioned them. He always got better answers that way.

William got home just as Reed was crawling out of bed. He had been up late the night before and was exhausted from the stress of worrying about his mother.

"Hey Champ. How about the two of us eating some breakfast together?"

Reed rubbed his eyes trying to get rid of the sandbags the sand man had left behind. "Okay, but then I want us to go out looking for Pretty."

"There are dozens of people out looking for your mother, son."

"This is a big county. I'll go get dressed."

William couldn't deny him this. "Dress warm. There's still some sleet on the ground." Perhaps it wasn't the smartest thing to do, but Reed needed to feel like a part of the search, and by God, William was going to take him.

CஓBௌ

Leo Trinket and Hannah Douglas were gone without a trace.

Saturday and Sunday led them no closer to an answer than they had Friday night. People who needed to be questioned were out of town. Agencies that had information they needed were either closed because it was the weekend or because of the weather. It was maddening.

CB&O

Hannah prayed more earnestly than she had ever prayed before. There was an evil surrounding her that pulsated. It was in the air and the water and the food. It was in the walls and the furniture. And it was most assuredly in Ethel Fletcher. She worried about William, knowing he would be frantic, wondering what had happened to Reed and to her, and she felt so helpless. There was nothing to do but wait. The boredom would drive her crazy before Ethel could, and the green room was freakish. Green everywhere you looked. She was surprised that Ethel had not been up to torment her, but she had left Hannah alone since she cut off all her hair. Thinking about it, Hannah rubbed her head. It was a very small price to pay if she and Reed got out of there alive and unhurt.

CB&O

Meredith cooked bacon, fried eggs, grits with butter, and biscuits for breakfast. Reed could smell the bacon all the way into his bedroom. When he came out and went into the kitchen, he saw his dad and grandfather already at the table.

"Is that real bacon?" Reed asked.

"Well, of course," his grandmother answered.

"Where did you get it?"

"At the store. I couldn't sleep so I went to the grocery store early this morning and picked up some things you were low on."

"Really? What else did you get?" Reed asked as he filled his plate with the loaded-with- fat breakfast.

"Oh, just a few things. Butter, milk, eggs, pancake mix, syrup, some hamburger meat."

"The real stuff? Not low fat?"

"The real stuff. Why?" Meredith took a sip of her coffee, then added a touch of real cream.

"It's just that we're not used to real food. Pretty buys us fake food and tries to make us think it's real, but we know better, don't we, Dad?"

Meredith looked at William to see if he knew what Reed was talking about.

"It's not that bad," William said. "Hannah buys the low fat or fat free variety of everything. You can ask him, but I don't know if Reed even knows where real bacon comes from."

"Sure I do. It comes from a pig. It's Pretty who thinks it comes from a turkey." They all actually laughed.

William said, "That's Hannah, all right. She thinks if we eat right we'll live forever." The breakfast lost its flavor, but they all continued to eat because they didn't know what else to do. There were no rules or advice for a family who had just been faced with the disappearance of a loved one at the hands of a crazed escaped convict. There were no scripts to review, or choices to select from. It was all new territory, and each had to tread over it the best way he could, and it was rough going.

Reed kissed his grandparents and he and William set off to hunt for his mother. He pulled his cap down over his ears, and William opened the front door. To his surprise, there were television crews, radio crews, and newspaper reporters all over his front lawn. Microphones were jabbed up in his face. Neiman heard the ruckus and charged out the door, leaving the delicious and never tasted before bacon in his dish. Reed grabbed him before Neiman grabbed onto one of the reporters. The Richeys came out to see what was going on.

"Detective Douglas," one reporter spouted. "Is it true that your wife, Hannah Douglas, may have left the Estelle Penitentiary with escaped convict, Leo Trinket, of her own free will?"

William was too shocked to even make a reply.

They began crowding each other, to get closer to William. "Is it true, sir, that her car was used in the escape and that Leo Trinket left approximately two hours after Mrs. Douglas's shift was over?"

William tried to fend them off but they had him surrounded.

"We understand, Officer Douglas, that your wife's official state ID card was used in the escape and that she knew the inmate. Do you have a comment on that?"

The words and accusations got louder and louder. The microphones were jammed in his face. William turned around, but they were everywhere – all over him. "Reed? Reed? Where are you?"

"I'm right here, Dad," Reed hollered. The Richeys had put Neiman in the house and closed the door.

William tried to get to his son, but the reporters were intent on getting a statement and some answers to their questions. He didn't want Reed to see this. He didn't need this after all he had been through. It was too much, and then he heard him.

"Listen to me!" Reed shouted. "Listen to me!" His voice was strong and determined.

A couple of the reporters who were closest to him held their microphones to him and then the others followed suit.

"I have something to say. My mother was stolen by that crazy man. He took her. He just took her, and she couldn't get away from him. And I'll bet you didn't know that this is her favorite day of the year. Do you want to see what she made for me and my dad? Wait, and I'll show you." His eyes had beaded with tears. He pushed his way into the house to retrieve his Valentine from Pretty. William didn't speak a word while he was gone. He watched the reporters.

Anything for a story, a news flash. Right or wrong, they wanted something juicy to print. Something to get the public's attention. If it recklessly ruined someone's life, so what? And if it turned out to be different, they would print a retraction on page nineteen. Or if on TV, they would tell the correct version with as little enthusiasm as possible.

Reed came out carrying his Valentine tin of fudge that Pretty had made for him. "Dad has one, too. Here, take a piece. All of you." He was crying. No one reached for the candy. He took a piece out and forced it into the hand of one reporter and then another and another. "Take it. Take it. She made this for us for a surprise. For today. Dad found them in her closet underneath her dresses. And read this." He opened the card that she had made for his dad. The poem she had written for him was inside. With a tear-streaked face he choked out the words. "Read this and tell me my mother ran off with a convict that killed two people with an ax."

The crowd was silent. The cameras were rolling and focused in on Reed.

"You don't want to read it? Then I'll read it to you." Reed began her poem of colors and read each line with the melody of a musician and the heartache of a grieving child. The reporters had come there for blood, and a twelve-year-old boy had given it to them, only it wasn't what they had expected.

When he finished he looked directly into their faces. "My mother is in trouble. She's scared and she's homesick, and if I were you, instead of trying to be mean and make her sound like a crazy woman, I'd try to help and find her. What if it was your mother?"

He put the lid back on his Valentine heart and handed it, with the card, to his grandfather. "Come on, Dad, we've got to look for Pretty." Reed took his father's hand and urged him toward his police car. They got in and drove away.

Chapter 40

Leo woke up in familiar surroundings; he was confused though. The lamp by the bed still had the devil under it, looking at him, peering at him while he slept. He rubbed his eyes and his face with his hands, trying to remember how he had gotten there.

Oh, yes. He had driven there in a car. Ethel had gotten him a car. But why wasn't he in prison anymore? He couldn't bring it all into focus. He got up out of bed and noticed he was still wearing his clothes. On closer inspection he realized they weren't his clothes. Whoa, they weren't his clothes. All of his clothes were white. He had to go to the bathroom. There was a bathtub in there. It had been a long time since he had been in a bathtub. He ran the water. He had been in that bathtub before. He remembered the claw feet. It was deep. It would feel good.

Before stepping in, he tested the water – hot but not too hot. Carefully, slowly, he lowered himself into the water. It crawled up his skin soaking up some of his fears. He had been afraid, but he couldn't remember why.

He knew this room. The blood red walls. The gold framed mirror. The tub with the gold claw feet. He had been in this tub. He remembered the feeling. He remembered . . . what did he remember? Something. He wouldn't think about that now. The water felt too good. He didn't want to think. He closed his eyes. He could relax.

"Leo."

His eyes popped open. Terror crept over him like snakes writhing around his body. Snakes actually appeared in the water. Everywhere. He was afraid to move. Afraid not to.

He should jump out of the tub, but the snakes would bite him. They were everywhere. Everywhere. All colors, all kinds. He was petrified.

The door opened. "Leo."

"What?" he shrieked.

The figure in the door was more terrifying than the snakes. It was Mother.

"How are you, Leo?"

He looked down at himself. He was naked. He didn't want her to see him naked. He looked back at the tub. The last of the snakes were slithering down the drain with the water. He wanted to go with them.

Sounds came out of his mouth that were blood-curdling. Wails, moans, sobs. He could scarcely breathe.

What was Mother doing here? And then it came back to him. He had seen her at the front door when he got there. *Where had he come from?* He couldn't remember, but he wanted to go back. Mother had not been where he came from.

"Get dressed," she said. "You've got work to do."

Mother looked at him as if he disgusted her, as if he wasn't human. There was no fear of him in her eyes. Her gaze was filled with hate. Hatred for him.

"Well?"

"I'm coming."

He thought she was dead. He had chopped her into bits and pieces. The devil must have glued her back together, but he hadn't seen Father. Maybe he had become the devil.

Leo was in trouble, and Ethel had put him there. Why had she done that? He did not know.

Mother turned and left him standing there completely naked and dripping wet. He was ashamed. She shouldn't be looking at him when he is naked. She had done that before, or at least he thought she had.

Leo Trinket dried himself off with the thick towel and went to the closet where his clothes were hanging. He didn't know why he thought they would all be white, but none of them were white.

He got dressed and started for the hallway. He didn't want to go, but he had to. Mother had said.

The hallway seemed a mile long. The polished wooden floors were the same as before. They were the pathway to the wicked place.

The doors along the way were closed. He tried turning the doorknob to one of them. It was locked. He knew it would be locked.

"Who's there?" a female voice asked. Leo didn't answer.

"Jona, is that you?"

"No," Leo said. He continued down the hall to the stairs. He didn't turn anymore knobs.

❀

Twila wondered why Jona had not come back. She wondered why she cared, except that he was a diversion from all the white, and he was someone to talk to.

Who was she kidding? She had been enamored by him like some bitch in heat. God, she was disgusted with herself for wanting him. What would her daddy think if he knew how she had acted? He would be repulsed just as she was. Her mother would die if she knew.

They must be frantic with worry by now.

This waiting was driving her insane. Boredom waited for her to have a lucid moment so it could swallow it up and leave her mindless. Mindless might be better, then the anxiety would be gone, the fear of the unknown would be gone; the incomprehensible thoughts of Jona would be gone.

The turn of a doorknob had highlighted her day. Perhaps that was the plan, to let her die a long slow death from nothingness and whiteness. Part of her had already died: her self-respect.

CB80

Hannah knew it must be Saturday, Valentine's Day. She wondered if William found his Valentine candy and the poem she had written for him. Probably not. He would be too busy looking for Reed and her to even think about Valentine's Day. She would not have included the color green in the poem had she written it after a night in this room. Who in their right mind would paint an entire room, walls and ceiling, green and then put green carpet on the floor? She didn't know you could even buy green furniture. It must have been custom-painted. She knew for a fact that she had never seen a green door knob. Green lamps, green sheets, a lavish green bedspread, a green headboard. Ethel would fit right it. She is green with envy for my life and my family, Hannah thought. Hannah could actually visualize Ethel being as green as the witch in *The Wizard of Oz*, but this room sure as hell wasn't part of the Emerald City. It was no fairytale, no fantasy. *Funny, I never pictured hell as being green.*

CB80

Leo felt sorry for the girls in the bedrooms. They didn't know what was coming. They didn't know about the wicked place. They would find out soon enough, though. Mother had sent him to the barn. He had to get it ready, just like before.

The ax was hanging up on two nails where he had found it the day he killed Mother and Father. He had to get it down to chop the wood. It was good for chopping wood, but it wasn't good for killing Mother and Father. Even though he hadn't seen Father, he knew he had come back with her. He would be at the ceremony behind the devil mask. Or maybe it wouldn't be a mask. Maybe he really had turned into the devil. If he had, Leo was in trouble for sure.

He hated getting the barn ready, but it wasn't as bad as the wicked place. Nothing was as bad as the wicked place.

જ્જી

The thumb prints came back to two possible women. Trooper Brent Eckland drove the results over to the Sheriff's Office. He carried them in to Kay. "William wanted these as soon as we got them. Is he here?"

"No, Brent. He's out combing the county, but dispatch can reach him. He's in his squad car."

"Should I leave these with you?"

"If you want to make sure he gets them." She smiled. She wasn't being sarcastic. It wasn't in her nature.

"Are any of the other detectives here today?"

"Are you kidding? All of them are here. Well, maybe not in the building, but they are working. Everybody is just sick about Hannah. They're not even putting in for overtime."

"Are you?" he asked with his eyebrows lifted high as if he already knew the answer.

"No, I am most certainly not."

Trooper Eckland squeezed her shoulder. "I'm going to stroll down the hall and see who's here. Any of the other detectives could look into this the same as William. The sooner the better."

"Okay, but tell dispatch to inform William. He'll want to know."

"I will. Thanks."

"You're welcome." Kay went back to typing up notes and reports from all the officers who had filed any. The sheriff wanted to know every detail of what had been done, what was being done, and what was going to be done.

Eckland found Cody Dickerson in his office talking on the phone. He motioned for Brent to come in.

Cody hung up after a couple of more minutes.

"Another wild goose chase," he said. "We are talking to anyone and everyone who may have seen the car or her or Trinket. Something is going to have to break soon. The longer Hannah Douglas is gone, the less likely . . ."

"I know. I've got the thumb prints that were taken from Trinket's birth certificate. He was adopted and the birth mother was a Jane Doe. It came back to a possible match of two."

Detective Cody Dickerson leaned back and rested his cowboy boot clad feet on his desk.

"Let's have a look-see."

Trooper Eckland sat down in the only other chair in the small cubicle of an office, cluttered to the point of being claustrophobic. "You know," he said," I don't see where it would do any good to find who Leo's birth mother is. Talk about a long shot."

"That's why you're a trooper and I'm a detective. Sometimes the most minute and off- the-wall pieces of evidence can break a case wide open." Dickerson swung his long legs off the desk and back onto the floor.

"I guess."

"Tell you what, Smoky Bear, I'll find out who the bad guys are, and you can haul ass in your black and white after them. Deal?"

Brent stood up and tipped his hat. "That's a deal, cowboy."

"Hey, thanks for bringing this by. I'll get right on it."

"Sure thing." Brent got a call on his side unit.

"Walker County S.O. 2532."

"2532 go ahead."

"2532 Need you in route. I-45, north bound, 105 mile marker. Reference 10-50 major. Two car roll-over. Multiple injuries. EMS and first responders are in route."

"10-4. Show me 10-33 traffic."

"Blare them and scare them, Smoky."

Brent tipped his hat and shot out.

Detective Dickerson did not recognize either of the names on the list, and Brent Eckland was probably right. It was a shot in the dark at best, but it was a shot.

He started with the first name. Elsa Beth Johnson. No criminal history. *Odd that she would have prints on file.* He looked for job description. None listed. Next to comments it said: foster parent. *That would explain it.* Date of birth. *Gee, she would have been barely fourteen years old when Leo was born. Possible.* Next to it was her date of death. Seven years ago. *Well, one thing is for certain. Leo didn't run to her.*

The other name was Elaine Blair Compton. No criminal history, but she had a state job. *Boy, does she have a job!* He whistled. Superintendent of Windham School District. Date of birth. *Wait a minute.* He looked back at the other one, the one who had died. Same birthday. Same first two initials. *They were twins.* Twins, even identical ones, don't have the same fingerprints. But they can be similar enough for the computer to give a hit. Especially if all you have are the thumbs. It's hard to get a match at all with just thumbs.

The odds that either of those woman were Leo's mother were highly unlikely. They were only fourteen when he was born. It was more likely that the birth mother's prints were not in the computer bank.

At any rate, the Superintendent of the Windham School District, the school system for incarcerated felons, was not going to break somebody out of prison and most certainly not kidnap a teacher in the process. Why would she? If she didn't like Hannah Douglas, she could have fired her. She wouldn't have to kidnap her. No, Elaine Blair Compton had too much to lose to be involved in this. He would bet his badge on it.

Sometimes a coincidence really is just a coincidence.

CB BD

Before taking Reed home, William went by the DPS office to check on the thumb prints. He was told that Trooper Eckland had taken them by the Sheriff's Office. That irked William. No one from the department had bothered to tell him, and he had been waiting all day. He was ready to chew somebody about this.

He drove to the Sheriff's Office and before he could ask, Kay said, "William, you got the word about the prints, didn't you?"

"No, ma'am. I've been wondering what was taking so long."

"Trooper Eckland hand-delivered them. Since you weren't here, he looked for another detective to give them to."

"Who was here?"

"Sweetie, detectives have been in and out all day. All of them are working on this case."

Shame rolled over William. "I know they are, and probably not putting in for overtime."

"Would you?"

"No, I guess I wouldn't."

"I know you wouldn't."

"I'm going to see who I can catch here."

"I asked Brent to tell dispatch to call you. Something must have happened."

"I'm sure it did."

Kay knew that stress was about to get the best of William because he never lost his temper or his cool. But who could blame him for it now? His whole world had been blown apart.

William asked the two detectives there about the prints, but neither of them knew anything. He walked down to dispatch. "Eckland had some fingerprints for me. Did he tell you who he left them with, Nate?"

"No, he didn't. But I do remember dispatching him to a major wreck on the interstate awhile ago."

"I'll bet that's what happened then. I wish I knew who had them."

"You want me to call Eckland?"

"No. He worked all night. Don't bother him at home. If something shows up, the detective who has them will call me."

"Yes, I'm sure he will, and if not you, the sheriff," Nate said. He looked at Reed standing bravely by his dad like a little soldier. His heart went out to them.

William rubbed Reed's head. "Come on, son, let's go home. I know you must be starving. We skipped lunch, didn't we?"

Reed nodded his weary head.

William wished he could take his son's pain away; William wished he could find his son's mother.

CR80

Jeff called Stella late Saturday night. She answered in a groggy voice.

"Happy Valentine's Day, Princess."

"Hey, I was hoping you would call."

"I've been calling all evening. I didn't think your shift lasted that long."

"Normally it doesn't, but we had a major wreck on the interstate today. Lots of hurt people. It's been hectic."

"You sound tired."

"Not too tired to talk to you."

"Remember, I'm a detective and I detect exhaustion in your voice."

"I guess making love all night and then working fourteen hours straight has just worn me out."

"Does that mean you are too tired to look on your back porch?"

"My back porch? Why ?"

His warm rich voice said, "I think Cupid has been back there."

"Cupid?"

"The Valentine angel!"

"Oh, my word. Until you called I had forgotten that it even was Valentine's Day."

"Well, I didn't forget. Go on, look."

"You mean right now?"

"Yes. Right now. I'll hold."

Stella scurried to her back porch to find a dozen red roses, a heart-shaped box of chocolates, and a stuffed bear the size of a five-year-old child. Squealing with delight, she brought them in and ran to the phone.

"I love it. I love it. I love it." She was out of breath.

"Do you really? I wasn't sure what you would like best, so I got all three."

"It's the first Valentine I have ever gotten in my entire life." Her voice was shaky.

"The bear's name is Jeff too. You can cuddle up to him when I'm not there."

"I wish you were here," she said in a longing voice.

"Me too. But you need some rest, Princess, or you'll end up in the emergency room yourself."

"I've missed you today."

"You were too busy to miss me."

"Never."

"I'm going to let you go, but I'll call you tomorrow. Do you have to work?"

"Yes, but hopefully not for fourteen hours."

"They need more nurses. They shouldn't work you like that."

"You're one to be talking. I know what kind of hours you keep."

"That's different."

"Don't even try it."

"Okay. I surrender."

"Call."

"I will."

"Good-night and thanks for my Valentine."

"Thanks for making me want to get you a Valentine. Good-night, Princess."

If she wasn't careful, she could fall in love with this guy.

ᏣᏁ

Sleep eluded William. He had dropped everything but his obsession to find Hannah. He knew now how Martha and Edward Brooks felt. He saw the same devastation in his in-laws' eyes as he had seen in theirs, but losing your wife, a wife that you made love to, made a child with, tackled the world with, was like losing yourself. No one had gotten as close to him as Hannah had, and no one ever would. She was his soul mate, his angel from God, but God couldn't have her back. Not yet.

He felt guilty crawling into their bed without her. Where was she sleeping? Did she have a bed? Was she cold? Was she hurt? Was she hungry? Was she dead? The only thing that he could be certain of was that she was scared if she was alive, and he knew she was still alive. He could feel it. He would know if she wasn't. He would be able to feel that, too, and if he knew Hannah, she would be worried about what her disappearance was putting her family through.

William got out of bed and knelt down beside it. He hadn't done that since he was a boy and said his prayers with his mother. *"Please God, help me find my wife. Keep her safe. Please God, keep her safe."*

He pulled the comforter off the bed and wrapped up in it on the floor. He couldn't sleep in their bed again until he found Hannah.

A sound as lonesome and haunting as any William had ever heard came from Reed's room. He was drawing the melody of "Amazing Grace" out of his violin like a ghost searching for heaven. The sadness of it was all-consuming. It was the sound of grief and despair.

And Sunday began like that. No one had called him in the night with news, good or bad. Hannah was still gone.

William looked at the clock. It was six a.m. He called Jeff Stone.

"Did I wake you?"

"No, man. How are you?"

"Not worth a damn. Any word on Elaine or Jack Tyler?"

"No. Jack Tyler is in Austin and his wife must have gone with him because I can't track her down. Seems odd, considering he has an escaped convict running loose and Elaine has a missing teacher. Makes you wonder how they got to the top."

"Doesn't it though?"

"What about Ethel Fletcher? Any word on her?"

"No. It's as if she became invisible."

"Well, she hasn't. We've just got to find her."

"Meanwhile I'm going to talk to the guard who was in the picket when Hannah left the unit Friday. He's already been questioned, but not by me, and then I'm going to talk to the guard who worked out in vocational and actually talked to Trinket when he was in free world clothes."

"I want to go with you."

"Sure. I'll pick you up in an hour."

"I'll be ready."

Meredith had cooked another huge breakfast. Ham and cheese omelets, hash browns, buttermilk biscuits, and orange juice. Reed and William smiled at each other, knowing that they were both thinking they would gladly settle for fat free food for the rest of their lives to get Hannah back, and not complain about it. Meredith couldn't get the floors any cleaner if she had a genie in a magic lamp. The house was spic and span. The freezer had been filled with home-made casseroles ready to heat and serve. William wondered if she had rested for five single minutes in a row since she had heard the news of her daughter.

William knew that Henry wanted to go out with him. He had cleaned up the yard, every stick, every pine cone, had kept the dog brushed, and the deck swept off. He had done all he could do, and William knew it. He tried to put himself in his shoes. *What if it were Reed?* Wouldn't he want to be in the middle of it, whether he was a cop or not? Hell yes!

While the juice was being poured, William said, "Henry, I'm going with Jeff to the Estelle Unit today. Go with us."

Henry's eyes spoke volumes. "Thanks. I won't get in the way."

"I know you won't. He'll be by to pick us up around seven."

"I'm ready."

"Good."

"What about me, Dad?"

"I need you to stay here in case somebody calls. You can tell them where I am and take messages."

Reed looked disappointed. His head dropped.

"Son, I know you want to go, but I can't take you inside the prison."

"I hate that prison!" Reed shouted. He banged his fist on the table, unsettling the orange juice. Some of it spilled onto the table. Meredith quickly got up for a paper towel.

William wanted to scream. They all wanted to scream and in fact, it would probably do everyone of them some good.

"Try to eat your breakfast." William stroked Reed's arm gently.

"Okay."

When William ate all he could, he excused himself to make a call. Trooper Eckland was working.

"This is Eckland," he said when his phone rang.

"Brent, this is William Douglas."

"Hey! How are you?"

God, he wished people would quit asking him that. *How in the world do you think I am?* He decided to ignore the question. "Brent, I haven't heard anything on those prints. Who did you give them to?"

"Oh, heck, man. I'm sorry. Kay told me to tell dispatch, but I was called out on a wreck and forgot to."

William's patience, normally endless, was wearing thin. "Who did you give them to?"

"Cody Dickerson. He went right to work on it."

"Do you remember the name?"

"There were two possibles. One was Johnson and the other one was Compton."

"He didn't call me," William said.

"Look, William, if Cody didn't call, it's because he didn't find anything that related."

"Still, I want to see it for myself."

"I understand. Man, I am sorry for not telling dispatch to call you."

"That's okay. I know that my wife's case isn't the only thing going on. It's just that it is the only thing I can see." William rubbed his face.

"We are all pulling for you and your family," Brent said with heartfelt sincerity.

"I know you are, and I do appreciate it. Jeff and I are going out to the prison to talk to some people, so I need to go."

"Okay."

"Thanks." William hung up the phone. He called Cody Dickerson's house. He got the answering machine. "Damn it!" He tried the office. No answer there either. He then dialed the non-emergency number for the dispatchers.

"Walker County Sheriff's Office. This is Julie."

"Julie, it's William. Have you heard from Cody Dickerson this morning?"

"No, but I just came on."

"Damn!"

"What's the problem?"

"I'm just trying to track him down about some fingerprints."

"Is it urgent?"

"To me it is, but no, it's not."

"I tell you what, if I can track him down, I'll call you. Wear your side unit."

"That will work. Thanks, Julie."

"Sure." She had to go. A nine-one-one call was coming through.

Jeff knocked on the door. William let him in. He could smell the scents of breakfast foods in the air. Boy, could he get used to that. His coffee-coated stomach growled in protest, but nobody noticed.

"I'm bringing Hannah's father along," William said.

"Fine by me. How are you, Mr. Richey?"

"Wearing down, Jeff. I'm wearing down."

The three men made their way to Jeff's car. The sky was still gray. No sleet had fallen during the night, but it looked promising for today. Huntsville was in a deep freeze. Tree limbs that couldn't withstand the weight of the ice that had formed on them had broken and fallen to the ground. The pines were not accustomed to being frosted with icicles, and they looked weighted and weary, much like William felt. *It's fitting,* he thought, *that Hannah's abduction came during the coldest spell Huntsville has seen in two decades. Even Mother Nature mourned her.*

It was a hassle getting Henry Richey into the Estelle Unit. The picket guard didn't want to let him through. Security was supposed to be tight, but when one of the convicts was on the loose, it was extremely tight.

"Call the warden. Tell him my name is William Douglas, and I'm bringing my father-in - law with me onto this unit."

"Call him yourself," the young black woman spit back. "I ain't callin' no brass on Sunday. More especially the warden."

"Damn it to hell." William mumbled under his breath.

"I'll just wait in the car," Henry said. "Let's not waste time on this."

"No, by God. I'm getting you in."

Jeff looked at Henry. "It's a thing he has with the picket guards. One of them took his pistol apart one time and he hasn't been the same since." He grinned at William.

William exhaled. "I'm sorry. I don't know what's wrong with me. I'm not usually like this, Henry."

"The hell he's not. He eats picket guards for lunch."

Jeff used the telephone in the ID booth. He called the switchboard and after identifying himself, asked for the head ranking officer on duty.

The operator told him that would be the major and to hold.

The major agreed to let Henry in with his driver's license number and signature.

Walking inside, having the heavy loud gates slam shut behind him, seeing convicts in white uniforms parading around, stretched Henry's nerves.

Entering the main hallway, he saw a long line of stark naked inmates waiting to shower. He could not believe that his beautiful daughter worked in this place. Why would she? He found himself getting angry with her. She had placed herself in jeopardy. What did she expect? He had begged her not to take the job with the prison. She had always listened to him before, but not about this.

The vocational shops were outside. He felt a little better out there, but not much.

Officer Cunningham answered all Jeff's questions. He had been questioned again and again by Internal Affairs. He felt a little responsible for what had happened because he had, after all, talked to Leo Trinket and seen the ID tag.

William could not let it drop. He had to ask, "Didn't you think it was just a little suspicious that this idiot would be wearing a teacher's ID tag?"

"Yes, sir. I said I did."

William continued, "Maybe I'm different, but I think if some man was wearing a woman's name tag inside a maximum security state penitentiary, and I was a security officer of said facility, I would do more than just think it was odd. I would have checked it out. That is your job. Right? Security officer?"

"Yes." Cunningham was getting upset, too. "He told me his name was Doug Hannah. It sounded like he was telling the truth." He folded his arms in desperation.

"So, if I tell you I am the frigging tooth fairy, are you going to believe me, just because I have some teeth?"

Cunningham didn't answer.

"Where do they find you people?" William asked, not expecting an answer. He had already started towards the building.

"What's his problem?" Cunningham asked.

"Hannah Douglas is that man's wife and the mother of his twelve-year-old son. And this is her father," Jeff said indicating Henry Richey. "So, cut him some slack."

Cunningham channeled his anger to a different place. He truly felt sympathy for the man who had just chewed his butt. He was surprised that he wasn't fired, and in fact, he still might be. He had screwed up and others were paying the price – a big price.

Jeff and Henry caught up to William.

"That is exactly why cops should not work on their own case. Talking to that man that way didn't help matters one bit," Jeff said.

"It made me feel better," William said.

This thing was going to destroy William. Jeff didn't know if his partner could survive it, at least not in tact. It was a hard pill to swallow, losing someone you loved. Jeff knew only too well how it felt. It had taken sixteen years for him to quit choking over Debra and his brother. It was her choice to leave him. Rejection and humiliation. He didn't think it could get much worse than that, but this was. William not knowing if his wife was being tortured, raped, maimed or killed was a lot tougher than losing your bride to your brother.

Nothing about this situation compared to losing Debra. It really brought it down to size – a size he could cope with – now that Stella was in his life.

Chapter 41

Ethel had been preparing for Monday night for months, for finally it was her turn; she was the high priestess. The baby had been born. The moon would be full. Seven women were in rooms upstairs being groomed for the ceremony. The cult had come full circle and she had been responsible. It had died, but she brought it back to life and now it was stronger than it had ever been before.

The house was in good shape. The masks had been made. The candles had been dipped and were standing in place. The altar had been cleaned and made ready for the sacrifices. The braids of hair had been hung. Everything was right.

Jona knocked on Hannah's door. She did not respond, so he unlocked the door and entered.

"It is time to be groomed," he said in his stoic manner.

Hannah looked at him as if he were crazy. "Excuse me?"

"We have many things to do. I must cut your hair, massage your body with oils, give you a manicure and a pedicure. We need to get started. I have others." Jona's face was incredibly handsome, but lifeless.

"In case you haven't noticed, my hair has already been cut."

"I just need to clean it up and make it look more presentable. You would like it better."

Hannah didn't know what to think. All of her sensors told her to balk, but this man did not seem threatening and in truth did not seem to be anything at all, inanimate. "All right," she heard herself say.

"My name is Jona, Hannah, and I don't want you to be afraid of me. I won't hurt you."

She believed him, not because she was naive – she worked with hardened criminals for heaven's sake – but because she needed to.

Jona went into the adjoining room to draw her a bath. "Hannah, you'll need to come in here."

"I can bathe myself."

"Yes, but I must cleanse you."

"What do you mean?"

"I'll show you. I won't hurt you or touch you in places that you do not want me to."

"I don't want you to touch me at all."

"I will only wash your hair then."

"You can wash my hair, but nothing else."

Jona could see that she wasn't going to be like the others. They had relaxed with him and allowed him to touch them, caress them, and make them feel better, but this woman wouldn't. It was her decision. It was too bad, though. He could make her feel wonderful if she would only let him.

She untied her robe and stepped into the bubble-filled bath. He came up behind her with a pitcher of warm water and some shampoo. She relaxed a little.

"Have you seen my son?"

"Son? How old is he?"

"He's twelve years old."

"What makes you think I would have seen him?"

"Isn't he here?"

"There are no children here."

"Are you sure? Are you absolutely sure?"

"Yes, Hannah. I would know if there was a boy here. There are no secrets kept from me."

As Jona massaged the muscles in her back and shoulders, he could feel the tension and strain dissipate in his hands.

"What made you think your son would be here?"

"Ethel. It's how she got me into the van. She told me she had Reed."

"Don't trust Ethel."

"What about you? Can I trust you?"

"I haven't lied to you, and I won't hurt you."

She wasn't sure that was a good answer, but her fear had been cut by half. Her son wasn't here, and she chose to believe that. It had all been a trick to get her here without a scene, and it had worked.

Hannah felt better after her session with Jona. He kept to his word about being professional with her and in no way violated her, but mostly because of the sincerity in his voice when he stated for a fact that her son was not there.

Back in the green room, Jona locked Hannah's door. Twila was next.

Twila was asleep in her white robe on her white bed in her white room when Jona knocked on her door. At first she thought the knock was in her dream, hoping that it was because she did not want to awake from it into the white world that had become her reality. The knock came again, louder this time.

Twila lifted her head from the pillow and waited.

"Twila, it's Jona." He unlocked the door and came in.

"Twila, I'm here to groom you."

"For what?"

"For tomorrow night."

"What is happening tomorrow night?"

"The ceremony."

"What kind of ceremony?"

"You'll see. But we must get you ready."

"What are you going to do to me?"

"I'm going to fix your hair."

Twila reached for her hair and realized once again that the long beautiful tresses that she had always had were gone.

"I can make it look much nicer."

"All right."

"Will you come with me into the bathroom?" he asked.

"Yes." She was almost in a trance.

As he bent over to run the water for her bath, he said, "I'll wash your hair in here."

His face looked so solemn, so sad, as if it would shatter if ever forced to smile.

"Jona, have you ever been happy?"

"I am happy now, being here with you."

"Smile at me, Jona."

"Let me help you with your robe."

Twila stood up and let him untie the sash on her robe. It fell to the floor. He tilted his head towards the tub and she got in it. The water was warm and soothing. Sinking low into the deep tub, Twila let the water consume her. She closed her eyes.

Jona took the pitcher and poured water over her head. The shampoo smelled like gardenias, and that, along with the strokes of his fingers against her scalp, was intoxicating.

When he was done he lathered a sponge with soap and applied it to her neck, shoulders, arms, and finally her breasts. Lathering the sponge once again, he lifted one of her legs out of the water and washed it, cared for it. He lifted it higher and forced the sponge lower and lower. Just his mere touch gave her a strange sort of pleasure that she could not have explained. Her face tingled with desire for this peculiar, beautiful man. He was so careful with her.

Standing up, he reached for an oversized white towel from the white counter to wrap her in. The massage table was against the wall. "Are you ready?"

"Yes." She had dreamed of this.

He dried her off and helped her onto the table indicating she should lay on her stomach first. Just as before, he took oil and rubbed it in his hands to warm it, then he massaged her with expert hands and fingers, working the soreness and tightness out of her back, shoulders, arms, and legs. He worked his way up and down her body supplanting pain and fear with an odd, tangible sensation of pleasure and exhilaration.

Twila turned over onto her back, anticipating Jona's magic touch with his oils as he began rubbing the front part of her body, being very careful not to hurt her tender breasts. Twila reached for his hands as they were stroking her there.

"Have I hurt you?" he asked.

"No. Pull me up."

"But I'm not done."

She pulled herself up and then he helped her. She looked at him and saw that he wanted her. Twila touched him, but Jona stepped back.

"What's the matter?"

"Nothing. I'm just not used to being touched there."

Twila was surprised. "You have never been touched there by a woman?"

"No."

"Are you a virgin?"

Jona looked at her with the same expression as he had the first time she saw him.

Twila pulled his robe apart.

Jona closed his eyes and shivered at her touch.

Twila pushed the robe off his shoulders and with her feet, she slid his briefs down his legs. Without hesitation he stepped out of them.

"Make love to me, Jona."

"I am not supposed to."

"I won't tell anyone." Her eyes never left his. She had reached him.

Twila slid off the table and guided him to her white bed. She lay down and he climbed on top of her.

"Kiss me, Jona." He did. It was succulent and desperate, and while he was kissing her, he found her. The feeling was excruciatingly wonderful.

As he felt the end bounding toward him, he heard Twila whisper, "Jona, I love you," and for the first time in his life, he felt complete. He had connected with someone, made love to someone, and it wasn't just sex – ugly or distorted like when the devils did it. This was like nothing he had ever dreamed.

Twila lifted his head up in her hands and looked into his eyes. "Tell me you didn't feel that."

"I felt it," he said with a fervency in his voice that had not been there before and uncommon for even him to hear.

"You could feel other things, too. Like happiness, love, excitement, pleasure, sadness. Jona, you could be a human being."

"They would never let me."

"Who?"

"Ethel, Mother, the devils."

"I must finish your grooming," he said, his voice back to normal.

Twila cried, not for herself this time, but for Jona.

❦❧

After lunch with Reed, William tried to contact Detective Dickerson. The interrogation of the picket guard who let Leo Trinket walk right out the front grate didn't prove to be any more useful than the one with Security Officer Cunningham.

He was grasping at straws, and he was well aware of it. Perhaps that's why getting those fingerprint sheets from Cody Dickerson was so important. He didn't have anything better to go on. He had looked at Ethel Fletcher's printout for relatives and friends, and it was his plan to go talk to them and try to get some kind of feel for Ethel's whereabouts, but she hadn't listed any relatives or friends when she had her fingerprints made for her Windham teaching position. Her parents were deceased.

William got back in his patrol car to comb the county, knowing it was like looking for a toothpick in a woodpile, but it wasn't going to stop him. He couldn't just sit at home or up at the office and wait for something to fall into his lap. He had to try. He had to search. Maybe he would get lucky and find the car or see Ethel or Leo. He knew dozens of back-roads all over the county, and just maybe Hannah was down one of them.

But Sunday came and went, and Hannah was still gone.

Chapter 42

The list of questions Detective Stone had for Jack and Elaine Tyler were going to piss them off. He was going to question two of the state's most prominent and highly regarded citizens. Jack Tyler ran the Texas Department of Criminal Justice, one of the largest and most prestigious prison systems in the world, and his wife ran the school district within that system. Hopefully it would help them find Hannah and at the same time, wouldn't cost him his job.

It was nine o'clock in the morning and Jeff had already had six cups of coffee, a sweet roll, and two Rolaids. William had wanted to go with him, but after his outbursts at the Estelle Unit yesterday, Jeff had convinced him that he would be able to get more out of the Tylers alone. With notepad in hand, he grabbed his London Fog, a Christmas gift from his mother, and went to his car. It was still colder than a well-digger's backside.

He decided to visit with Ms. Tyler first, anxious to see her reaction to questions about Ethel.

Elaine was in a meeting at the central office when Jeff arrived. Her secretary looked pleasant yet strict when he approached her.

"Good morning, I'm Detective Stone with the Walker County Sheriff's Department, and I need to speak with Elaine Tyler please, ma'am."

"I'm sorry. She is in a meeting right now. Maybe you could come back this afternoon."

"Miss Baker," her name was displayed on a convict-made nameplate at the front of her desk, "I am here in an official capacity and need to speak with her now. So, please tell her I'm here and that I want to talk with her."

Brenda Baker stood up. "I will not disturb Mrs. Tyler while she is in that meeting. There are some very important people in there. You have shown up here without an appointment, and you'll just have to wait."

This girl is stunning, Jeff thought, as she stood there in a black leather skirt, arms folded and having no intentions of changing her mind.

"Miss Baker, I am investigating a kidnapping by an escaped convict. Now, either you go into that meeting and discreetly tell Mrs. Tyler that I want to talk with her immediately, or I'll go in there, flash my badge, embarrass her terribly, and tell her myself that I want to talk to her immediately. It's your call."

Brenda walked out from behind her desk to the meeting room. Her legs were a mile long in black stockings, black high-heel shoes, and the short leather skirt.

Wow, Jeff thought. Then he smiled remembering last night. Stella cooked him his first home-cooked meal in months, then they snuggled up on the couch and watched some television and one thing led to another. But if he thought about the another part, Miss Baker and Mrs. Tyler might notice more than just his badge.

The secretary quietly eased into the meeting room and found Elaine Tyler sitting at one end of a large oval table. Brenda whispered distinctly, "Mrs. Tyler, Detective Stone is waiting by my desk. He wants to speak to you immediately."

Elaine knocked over her water glass as she tried to get up,

praying her legs would stay fastened beneath her.

Elaine strained to regain her composure and said, "You'll have to excuse me. Something has come up that I need to attend to."

Elaine opened the door that led into the front office where Detective Stone stood by Brenda's desk.

"Detective Stone, I'm Elaine Tyler. How can I help you?"

"Do you have a place where we can talk privately?"

"Of course. We can go into my office,"

Jeff scanned Elaine Tyler's office to get a feel for her personality. The state office was not even as nice as his office, but the way in which it was decorated made it seem elegant. The predominant color was a rich teal green. The plants in the room were healthy and vibrant, cared for weekly by a convict horticulture student. A valance made of expensive fabric bore a paisley pattern of green, lavender, pink, and gold. A swag of fabric was draped in front of the valance on a separate rod with an ornate spiral of fabric in the center; drapes hung to the floor on either side of the window. A sheer in front of the window delicately softened the state-issue mini blinds. The chairs were upholstered in the same fabric as the drapes.

"Please, sit down, Detective. Can I get you some coffee?"

"No, thank you. I've had way too much coffee this morning."

"So," she clasped her manicured hands together, "how can I help you?"

"I'm here investigating the disappearance of one of your teachers, Hannah Douglas. I'm surprised you wouldn't have assumed as much."

"Well, of course I knew the reason you were here, Detective, but I'm wondering how I can help you."

"Ma'am, one of your teachers has more than likely been kidnapped by an escaped convict. I want to know what you know about it."

"I don't know a thing. We are all worried sick about Mrs. Douglas. The meeting you called me out of was on that very subject. I'll do anything I can to help, but I really don't know why you think I'd know anything about it. I first heard about the situation from my husband, and he knew only that Mrs. Douglas was missing and somehow an inmate that escaped from Estelle was involved. And, oh yes, something about a name tag. Her name was on the name tag he wore when he walked out the front gate."

Jeff sat still and listened intently; it was his intensity that made her even more nervous.

"Tell me about Ethel Fletcher."

"What do you want to know?"

"How long did she live with you?"

"Just a few months. She kept house for us and cooked. We needed a housekeeper and she needed a job and a place to live."

"Was she your first housekeeper?"

"No, we've had several different ones over the years."

"Did they all live with you?"

"No."

"How many?"

"Only her."

"Why her?"

Elaine stumbled for a story that would sound believable and somehow came up with, "She came to our church one Sunday, homeless and penniless, asking for help. We let her stay with us until she got on her feet. That's all."

"That was very generous of you. What church do you attend?"

"Why? I don't see where that's any of your business."

"No, ma'am. It's not, but most people who attend church are very willing to say where. Do you still go to church?"

"No. Do I need my lawyer present?"

"I don't know. Do you?"

Elaine picked up a pencil from her desk and started tapping it unconsciously. "It's just that these questions sound so personal."

"Just routine, ma'am. I'll be questioning a lot of people. That's how detectives find answers."

"Yes, yes of course. I'm sorry. I didn't mean to sound rude."

"So, how did Ethel Fletcher end up being your house keeper?"

"The girl we had was caught stealing from us, and I had to let her go. Ethel asked for the job," Elaine explained.

"So, the previous maid was fired after Ethel moved in. Is that correct?"

"Yes."

"And what was her name?"

"Whose name?" Elaine's face defied her again.

"The maid whom you fired?"

"Why does it matter?"

"I might want to ask her some questions about Ethel."

"Of course. Let me think," Elaine said trying to sound nonchalant. "Oh yes, it was Libby."

"And her last name?"

"Angus."

"Libby Angus," Jeff repeated. "Why does that name sound familiar?"

Elaine shrugged.

"Isn't that the girl who went missing about a year ago?"

"Yes. I believe she did. We all assumed she ran off with some man," Elaine said casually. "She was that type."

"What type is that?"

"You know. Cheap. Looking for a good time. The kind that sleeps around."

"Did she tell you that about herself?"

"Of course not."

"Then how did you know that about her?"

"I could just look at her and tell."

"My goodness, Mrs. Tyler. You'd be one hell of a good detective if you can just look at someone and then just know what kind of person they are, and what all they do. You would really be an asset to our team.

"The fact is, Mrs. Tyler, foul play was suspected, but her body was never found."

Elaine could feel beads of sweat trickling down her back beneath her blue cashmere sweater. Her skin began to itch, and she could feel her face changing colors.

"I understand that Ethel Fletcher teaches at The Walls Unit. Did you help her get the job?"

"What if I did? She has a teaching certificate. What has any of this got to do with Hannah Douglas? Forgive me if I'm a little confused."

"The two women didn't get along, did they?"

"No, they didn't," she answered.

"The Fletcher woman didn't get along with anyone, did she?"

"I wouldn't say that."

"What would you say, Mrs. Tyler?"

"The girl has had a hard life. Anyone that knows her can see that. I've just tried to help her. That's all."

"I had a talk with Ethel's principal, Earl Cowen. He told me about all the problems he has had with her, as did the principal before him. He told me about Ethel being caught in the janitor's closet with an inmate, the same inmate that escaped from Estelle on Friday the thirteenth. He told me about the grief she caused Hannah Douglas. He told me about coming to you just the other day for the sole purpose of trying to get Ethel Fletcher fired and how you responded. I think Ethel Fletcher just might have a lot to do with the whole ordeal, Mrs. Tyler, and I also think you know a lot more than you are letting on. Are you still confused, Ms. Tyler?"

"Hannah Douglas was transferred to another unit at her own request and with a much higher salary. I'd say she came out all right."

"Until Friday, Mrs. Tyler. She was doing all right until Friday when Leo Trinket took off with her. You transferred Trinket to the same unit as Hannah Douglas."

"I don't believe this! Am I under suspicion? I mean, do you think I planned any of this?"

"I think you have let Ethel Fletcher get away with everything but murder." Jeff thought for a moment about Libby Angus. "Or just maybe you let her get away with murder after all?

"I'll get to the bottom of all this. Have a nice day, Mrs. Tyler," Jeff said. He stood up to leave, then looked at Elaine sitting behind her desk in her elaborately decorated office and actually felt sorry for her.

෨෭

William went to juvenile services to see if he could find anything in Ethel's background that would help him get a feel for where to look next. He was hoping she would have a juvenile record. Anyone as crazy as Ethel Fletcher probably had some trouble as a child.

Ron Conover, a man William had worked with on countless occasions, was in his office. He was in his mid-forties but already had a row of false teeth as a result of ice hockey during his younger days. He was still in good shape, but William felt like he could probably kick his ass if need be.

"Conover, I need you to do me a favor."

Ron looked at him suspiciously. "That's not like you, William. Forgive me if I'm wrong, but you are about to ask me to do something against the law." He had a hint of a Yankee accent.

William closed his eyes for a long second. "I need to see if you have a file on Ethel Fletcher."

"You know as well as I do that I can't open files up to you on juveniles. They are sealed. Like it never happened."

"I don't want to do anything with that information except see if there is anything that might give me some clue as to where she is, who she is, what she is."

"What did you say her name was?" He gave no indication that he was going to help William.

"Ethel Fletcher. I am almost positive she helped that escaped convict abduct my wife."

Ron Conover drew his mouth to one side, giving a pondering thought another few seconds to congeal. "William, I've got to go across the hall for a few minutes. I need to look up some information on a run-away before I forget it. Why don't you wait here for me, and we'll talk about this when I come back. I won't be gone but about ten minutes." His eyes never blinked; his expression never changed.

"I can do that."

Conover stood up. A map of the state of Texas was framed on the wall behind him as if to validate his chosen homeland. He reached into his Wrangler slacks and brought out his keys, placing them on top of his unsullied desk and left William alone in the room.

William wasted no time. He picked up the keys and quickly found the one that opened the inactive alphabetized filing cabinet. *F-F-F,* he said to himself. *Here it is. Flack, Flanagan, Fleming, Fletcher. Ethel Elizabeth Fletcher.* William looked behind him, making sure no one was looking over his shoulder. What he was doing was against the law, but he didn't care. The envelope was not actually sealed shut as he was afraid it might be. It was just an ordinary file folder.

There was a copy machine in the far corner of the room. He looked at his watch. There were several pages of information on Ethel Elizabeth Fletcher, so he was right. For there to be that much in her juvenile file, she had to have had an unstable childhood.

The machine made a considerable amount of noise. Of course he had never used one while breaking the law before either. Three more pages.

Finally the last page. He gathered his information, folded it twice and stuffed it in the inside pocket of his jacket. He returned the file back to its slot, shut the drawer, locked the cabinet, replaced the keys and went to the door and was about to turn the knob when the knob turned on its own. Ron Conover had come back.

"Decided not to wait?" he asked.

"I decided not to waste my time. I know I can't get anywhere with you on this matter. You are too much of a 'go by the book' man, and I respect that. I'll go another route."

"You could always get a court order."

"I thought about that, and I think that's the way I'll go."

"That would be best."

William nodded his head. "I'll see you later, Conover."

"Take care. And William?"

"Yeah?"

"I'm sorry about your wife."

"Thanks."

Next stop was The Walls. God, he hoped he wouldn't have a hassle getting in. Not today. He was going to try to be a little more civilized to the picket guard. He wasn't going to take his weapon with him. He left it locked up in his squad car.

A different guard was in the picket today, and that was a stroke of luck. The security officer at the ID booth called Mr. Cowen's office to tell him that Detective Douglas was on his way up.

Virginia Deigo was waiting for him at the top of the ramp just like before. She didn't even try to hide the anguish she felt for both him and for Hannah. Once he thought about it, he figured he might be able to get more out of her than he would Earl Cowen. He would go to him first, but if he didn't get what he wanted, he would seek help from Virginia. It wasn't like him to use people, but things were different now. Hannah was in danger, and he didn't care what he had to do to get her out of it.

"How are you, darlin'?" Virginia asked.

He decided it wouldn't hurt to prime her, so he told her the truth instead of ignoring the question as he had from the five hundred other people who had asked it. "I feel like somebody has ripped my heart out of my chest and squeezed every single drop of blood out of it."

"Oh, you poor thing. If there is anything I can do, all you have to do is ask."

"You mean that, don't you, Virginia?"

"Yes, I mean every single word."

"You are a sweetheart. Thank you."

"Come on. Mr. Cowen is waiting for you." She took hold of his arm and escorted him into the principal's office.

Earl stood up. "Any news?"

"No. I need your help again."

Earl looked at Virginia. "That's all, Virginia."

"Wait," William said. "Could she stay? If it weren't for her, I wouldn't have this lead to go on, and I have a feeling that it's the lead that's going to help me find my wife."

Earl Cowen applauded William's words. Even if they were true, not everyone would have given someone like Virginia the satisfaction of feeling blessed by them.

"Mr. Cowen, I think if I could see Ethel Fletcher's personnel file, it might help me to understand her a little better. As it is, I don't really know anything except what we have on her at the Sheriff's Office. I thought maybe if I could find out where she went to college, where she lived, her former jobs, her references, that kind of stuff, it might help me figure out where she is. Who she is."

Virginia slipped out the door.

"That's against regulation," Earl said.

"I know it is. It's just that if I have to get a court order to look at every single shred . . ."

Virginia cut him off. "Here you go." She presented William with the file.

"Virginia. You can't . . ."

"Hush, Earl. I just did."

Earl looked down and scratched the back of his head. He didn't have a prayer and he knew it.

William opened the file and got out his notebook to take notes.

"No need in that," Virginia said. She snatched the file and took it straight to the copy machine. "This won't take but a minute, sweetie."

William looked coyly at Cowen. He knew what must be going through his mind. "You have a treasure working for you," William said.

"I have a rogue working for me." He laughed in spite of himself and in spite of the seriousness of the situation.

"You two make quite a pair," William said, hinting at Earl.

That idea struck a chord with Earl. He supposed they did.

Virginia, in her red voile dress and rhinestone buckled belt, danced into the office with document in hand. "What else do you need?"

William stood to leave. "This will do for now. I don't know how to thank you enough."

Virginia reached up and kissed him on the cheek. While rubbing the red lipstick off his face she said, "You find that sweet little Hannah. That's the thanks I want. Isn't that right, Earl?"

Earl knew when he was defeated. "That's right."

William glanced at Earl. He didn't want to rub it in, so he headed out the door. He stopped and hugged Virginia. "You are precious, and when I find Hannah, I'm going to tell her that she has a guardian angel by the name of Virginia."

A million dollars would not have meant more to Virginia Deigo, and Earl Cowen saw honor in that.

Chapter 43

He was ashamed to admit it, but in some ways he dreaded Blair's session today, and in other ways he was curious about what would come out of it, or in this case, who would come out. He found a book after their last session titled *Satan's Children* by Dr. Robert S. Mayer. It was a book about some of the patients Mayer had treated who suffered from multiple personality disorder. Apparently the disorder was a result of abuse inside Satanic cults, and it was shocking to say the least. Biscamp found some of the accounts to be so similar to Blair's that he wondered if perhaps she had read the book and was retelling some of the events as if they had happened to her. But, in fact, Mayer stated that he had misgivings at first about his patients who told about these episodes.

Biscamp decided that it wouldn't be fair to his patient if he just outright didn't believe her, so he would give her the benefit of the doubt but watch her closely for any signs that she might be fabricating her story.

When Blair came in, she looked haggard, like she hadn't had any sleep in days.

"You look tired today, Blair. Do you want to tell me about it?"

"No."

"All right then, why don't we talk a little bit about your family?

You have never mentioned your family."

Blair looked suspiciously at the doctor as if he were trying to trick her.

"I don't even know if you have any children."

She didn't say anything.

"Do you?"

"I don't want to talk about family."

"You know, Blair, last week you let me do some regression therapy with you. I felt like we really made some progress, and I'm convinced that it would be a good place for us to start today."

Blair began wringing her hands. She was ridden with anxiety, more so than he had ever seen her.

"Blair, I'm not going to hurt you or make you tell me anything that you don't want me to know, but you are going to have to learn to trust me." He leaned forward and put his hand over hers to stop them from moving. "Have I ever hurt you or lied to you?"

"No."

"And I'm not going to today. I am here to help you, and that is why you came to me, isn't it? For me to help you?"

"Yes."

"I want you to lie back on the couch and relax. That's it. Just relax."

It did not take her as long to go under as it had the time before. Her hands had ceased moving and her face had relaxed.

"Blair, I thought we could talk about Leena today. You let me meet her last week." Blair stayed still. "Who is Leena?"

"She is my friend."

"How long has she been your friend?"

"For a long time."

"Where does she live?"

"She lives at Thirteen-Thirteen Belial Road."

"What does she do?"

"She protects me."

"What does she protect you from, Blair?"

"From everything."

When Blair first became his patient, she had refused to put her address or phone number down on the forms to fill out. Since she did not use an insurance provider, she always paid for her sessions in cash. Biscamp had asked her why she was afraid to tell him where she lived, and she said it wasn't anyone's business, so he left it at that. But this was a golden opportunity for him to gain that much needed information for her own good.

"And where do you live, Blair?"

"Sometimes I stay with Leena."

"When I last talked to Leena, she cautioned me about asking you questions that could cause you to get hurt. Do you know anything about that?"

"It's okay now. All the people who could hurt me are dead, and I am in charge now."

"How did they die?"

"I'm not sure. They died after I left."

"And where did you go?"

"I ran away to have the baby."

"The baby?"

"Yes, the baby from the devils."

"Do you still have the baby?"

"No, I gave it away."

"What did you do after you gave your baby away?"

Everything about her appearance made him think she was telling the truth.

"I got a job and I went to school at night."

"What kind of school?"

"I was working to get my GED."

"And did you reach that goal?"

"Yes, and then I worked my way through college."

"What did you do after college?"

"I became a person."

That is a very sad answer, he thought.

"Now that you are a person, how do you feel?"

"I felt good until Ethel came."

"Who is Ethel?" He was expecting Ethel to be another personality like Leena.

"Ethel is the one who helped me become Mother. She said it was my destiny."

"Whose mother did you become?"

"The Mother of the foster home?"

"Oh, so you run a foster home for children?"

"Well, it used to be for children. The government brought children to the home who didn't have anywhere else to go, and Mother and Father took them in."

"So there are no more children at the foster home."

"No."

"And who are you the mother of now?"

"The women."

"The government brings women to your home?"

"Not exactly. We have to go out and get them."

"And where exactly do you find these women?"

The voice changed, the posture became more refined, and the attitude was completely different. She sat up on the couch and opened her eyes.

"Those women are none of your business."

"Hello, Leena. Blair told me that she wasn't afraid to answer my questions. I asked her."

"Blair is an idiot."

"Why don't you tell me what you mean by that."

"It's just that she doesn't know when to shut up." She dug in her purse for a cigarette.

"Maybe you could tell me about these women."

"Not on your life."

"What would you like to talk about?"

Leena blew smoke out the side of her mouth and cocked her head.

"Nothing. I don't want to talk about anything."

"You know, you gave me a lot of insight into Blair's condition last week. If you were telling me the truth, I can understand now why she has trouble sleeping and eating."

"If you had eaten the kinds of things that Blair has eaten, you wouldn't care about putting anything else in your mouth to eat again either. The only reason she eats is to stay alive. She gets no pleasure from it. And I can tell you that for a fact."

"You said she had been forced to swallow eyeballs."

"That's nothing." She sighed and took another drag on her cigarette. "You moved your ashtray. It was on the left side of the coffee table last week."

"I'm sorry. The cleaning lady probably just cleaned it and put it back down." It was not uncommon for severe patients to notice the slightest change in things and not like it one bit. Leena moved it to the spot where it rested last week and flicked ashes into it.

"Now what were we talking about?" she asked

"Things Blair was made to eat."

A pallor seized Leena's face that had to have been real. If the events she was about to describe were false, they were very real in her mind.

"Do you remember the babies I told you about?"

"Yes."

"Well, during the ceremony, a newborn baby was placed on the altar. The devils would sing these chants to Satan and then one of the devils would force a knife into the chosen child's hands. That child had to lift up the knife, above the baby and . . . above the baby and, and . . .," Leena caught her breath, "stab it into the baby's chest." She lowered her head and sobbed.

Biscamp could actually feel her pain, and the story, whether it was real or not, was horrifying.

"The devil that put the knife in the child's hands then took the knife and used it to cut out the baby's heart." Her eyes were glazed over. She was reliving the nightmare in earnest. "He held the baby's heart up for everyone to see. Dripping blood. Bright red." She screwed up her mouth in horror. "He took the knife and cut the baby's heart into pieces. He made each child eat a piece. And then he drained blood from the little baby's body into a shiny gold goblet. They each had to drink from the goblet."

"Leena, did you ever have to take part in those things?"

Her demeanor changed.

"Of course not. I was talking about Blair."

"Why didn't you have to do those things if Blair did?"

"I just didn't. I have my limits. I am there for her – don't get me wrong. But I couldn't do the rituals for her. They would have known, and then she would have died."

"Is that why Blair ran away to have her baby? To keep it from being killed?"

"Yes. And I admired her for it."

"Did you go with her when she ran away?"

"Yes, but after awhile she didn't need me anymore, and that was fine with me. I was still there in case she ever did."

"And why are you back on the surface?"

"Because of Ethel. Like she said."

CଔБO

Martha and Edward Brooks called Detective Stone Monday morning at the Sheriff's Office. They wanted to know if the woman kidnapped by the escaped convict was the wife of the Detective Douglas who was working on Twila's case. He told them that she was.

Martha asked, "Does her disappearance have anything to do with our daughter's?" She sounded both hopeful and fearful. In part she wanted desperately to know who had Twila, but on the other hand, she prayed to God that it was not the ax murderer who had abducted Mrs. Douglas. Jeff understood.

"Mrs. Brooks, I don't have any proof at this time one way or the other. We do know that Leo Trinket did not pull off his escape without help, and we have some suspects that we think may have helped him. One of the suspect's names came up when we were questioning a man about one of the other missing girls."

Martha interrupted, "That sounds like you may know who took my daughter."

"Like I said, Mrs. Brooks, it's all speculation until we get some proof, but we're working around the clock to find your daughter and the other missing women."

"Detective Stone, please tell Officer Douglas how truly sorry we are that this has happened to him and his family. He seemed like such a nice caring man. I know how devastated he must be."

"Yes, ma'am, he is. And as you have probably guessed, he has thought of nothing else but finding his wife, but that doesn't mean that the rest of us aren't still looking for Twila."

"Maybe if Officer Douglas finds his wife, our daughter will be with her."

"I hope we find them all."

"He and his wife are in our prayers."

"I'll tell him."

It was almost two o'clock and Jeff's stomach reminded him that he had worked through lunch. He had the urge to call Stella before getting something to eat. She answered the phone in her sweet southern accent that reminded Jeff of a lazy afternoon on the banks of a cool clear pond.

"Hi, Princess."

"Hi, yourself."

"Have you had lunch yet?" He was sure that she had, but he wanted an excuse to talk to her for a few minutes.

"No, actually. I didn't have to work today, so I'm cleaning house."

"Yeah, your house looked like it needed a good cleaning."

"You are incorrigible. My house looks clean because I clean it! That is how a house stays clean."

He laughed. "Okay, okay. Listen, since you haven't eaten, why don't you let me come by and take you out for a quick lunch."

"I have a better idea. Why don't you come over here and I'll make us some lunch?"

"Twist my arm."

"You'll have to come over in order for me to do that."

"I'll be on my way in ten minutes."

This was great! She was going to cook for him. He liked the feelings she had awaken in him so much that he was almost afraid to pursue this budding relationship. *What if she got tired of him? What if she didn't want a steady boyfriend? What if she did and then someone took her away like they had Hannah and the other missing girls?* He couldn't think like that. His paranoia was getting growing pains again, and if he wanted to ever have a full life, with love and excitement and meaning, he would have to stick his neck out.

Now that he had imposed upon himself a lecture on life, he drove to Stella Perkins's house. Just walking inside her home gave him a feeling of well-being. *Was she too good to be real?* He wondered.

Smells like those from his grandmother's kitchen took him back to childhood summers and country cooking. Cornbread, black-eyed peas, and chopped steak simmering in onions and brown gravy. The growl in his stomach grew into a full blown chorus.

"Go wash up," she urged. "It will be ready in a minute."

He didn't have to be told twice.

The meal was as delicious as it promised to be when he walked through the front door and smelled it cooking, and he overindulged. He couldn't help it.

"Why aren't you plump? I would be the size of the Goodyear Blimp if I could cook like that."

"Silly, I don't cook like this for myself. I usually just get something at the hospital. I don't really enjoy eating by myself much."

"Maybe we can change that." He leaned across the table and stole a kiss. "I need to get back to work."

"How much sleep did you get last night?"

"Oh, about four or five hours."

"Go lie down on the couch while I clean this up. I'll wake you up in an hour."

He started to protest.

"I don't want to hear it. Nurse's orders. Scoot!" She popped him on the back side.

The thought of a cat-nap after that huge meal sounded tempting. He was definitely tired. He surrendered. "One hour," he cautioned. "I've got to question someone this afternoon."

"Okay! I promise. One hour. Now go."

Stella watched the clock and woke him exactly one hour later, and the way she woke him up delighted him. She sat down on the couch and put his feet in her lap, then she rubbed each foot with the skill of a trained masseuse.

Jeff couldn't speak while she was rubbing them because it felt too good, and frankly he needed it.

"Better?" she asked.

He managed an "Un-huh." He opened his eyes and looked at her. "I really do feel better. Thanks."

"You're welcome."

He got up and found his shoes. "I'll call you tonight, if that's okay."

She just smiled.

Chapter 44

Jack Tyler was in his office, but like his wife, was armed with an "attack secretary" out front. Jeff heard the same song only the second verse. He didn't have an appointment. Mr. Tyler was a very busy man. Make an a appointment and come back. And, like this morning, Jeff pulled rank. "Ma'am, I am here on official police business. I don't need an appointment."

"If you want to talk to the Director of the Texas Department of Criminal Justice you do."

Jeff pulled out his radio from underneath his sports coat.

"823 S.O."

"Go ahead 823."

"823 S.O. Could you have a unit check by with me. Reference: interfering with a peace officer."

"10-4."

"What are you doing?"

"I'm getting some deputies over here to haul your ass to jail. Interfering with a peace officer in the performance of his duties is against the law."

Her already fair complexion turned three shades paler. Jeff was concerned that she just might faint. She got on the phone. "Mr. Tyler, a detective is here to see you."

Jeff couldn't hear his response, but could guess what he was saying.

"Yes, sir, but he won't take no for an answer. He is very, uhh, serious."

She looked up at Jeff and then said, "Yes, sir."

"Go right in."

"Thank you."

"Wait! Did you cancel that call for deputies?"

"No."

Her mouth dropped open.

Jack Tyler tried his intimidation tactics on Detective Stone, but Stone wasn't amused.

"I'm a busy man. What is it that you want?"

"I am a busy man, too, Mr. Tyler. At the moment I am busy investigating the abduction of a teacher from the Estelle Unit."

"We have internal affairs looking into that. It's not your concern."

"The husband of the lady your convict kidnapped is my partner, you son-of-a-bitch. Don't tell me it's not my concern."

Tyler looked as though he had been slapped in the face. Who in the hell did he think he was? Just a little piss-ant cop. A nobody.

"My boss is the sheriff. In case you don't know, he is the supreme law enforcement officer in this county, and since you reside and work in this county, you are under his jurisdiction. And since this all appears to be news to you, I'll give you another news flash. I've not come across anyone yet that Sheriff Applegate believes to be above the law. So why don't you crawl out from under that title you hide behind and talk to me man to man?"

"I'll have you thrown out of this office so fast it will make your head swim." He reached for his phone.

Jeff Stone walked over to the door and motioned for the two

deputies he had sent for. They, of course, were in full uniform and looked very serious.

Jeff approached Jack Tyler. "We can do this here, or we can do it at the Sheriff's Office. How do you want to play it?"

"This is preposterous. The sheriff is going to hear about this."

"The sheriff knows about this. Who do you think sent me?"

Tyler finally took a deep breath.

"Now, why don't you have a seat and we can get this over with. I have other people to see this afternoon. Like I said, I am a busy man."

Jeff pulled his chair up close enough to the desk so he could lean on it if he wanted to. He didn't, but invading Jack Tyler's space was a ploy that seemed to be working. Jack's body language told Jeff so.

"What can you tell me about Ethel Fletcher?"

"I think she is crazy."

"Why?"

"I don't know. A lot of reasons. The look in those hideous eyes of hers. Her personality. Just her way." He glanced over at the officers still standing behind the detective.

"So why did you let her stay on as your housekeeper?"

"I didn't. That was my wife's doing."

"So, your wife cares more for Ethel than you do?"

"That's understandable. She is her niece."

"Niece? How's that?"

"Elaine had a twin sister. Ethel was her daughter."

"Was?"

"She died."

"Were she and your wife close?"

"To tell you the truth, I didn't even know she had a sister until Ethel showed up at our house one night."

"Close family, huh?"

Jack was not amused. "Elaine and I have only been married five years. All of her family is dead. I never knew any of them, and she doesn't talk much about any of them."

"How do you and your wife get along?"

"And why, may I ask, is that any of your business or the sheriff's?"

"Because I'm investigating the disappearance of seven young women, and the both of you have a way of turning up in the middle of things."

"How on earth can that be?"

"Tell me about Libby Angus."

The size of his desk, the title in front of his name, nor the Great Wall of China could have protected him from the mention of Libby's name.

"She was our maid for awhile and that is all. I don't know a thing about her. I was never interested in her." He toyed with the gold pinky ring on his left hand. "She worked for my wife. I never had a thing to do with her."

Jeff thought, *he doth protest too much.* "Your wife seemed to know a lot about her. Said she was cheap – the kind of girl who would run off with a married man. Loose."

"You talked to my wife?" Jeff wished he could have checked Tyler's blood pressure and used it against him in a court of law.

"Yes, does that alarm you?"

"No, of course not. It's just that I hate you had to bother her. You are not the nicest person to deal with."

"We got along fine. Funny though. Her story and your story don't sound a thing alike. Let's get back to Libby. Why would your wife think she was loose?"

"I have no idea."

"I have a theory. Would you like to hear it?"

"No, I wouldn't."

"I think you and the maid were having an affair."

Jack drew his hands off his desk and put them in his lap.

"Well? Were you?"

"Is that important?"

"I could care less who you bang except for one minor detail. Libby Angus was the first girl to turn up missing out of the seven."

"That has nothing to do with me."

"But it seems to have something to do with Ethel. She didn't like Libby. Libby disappeared. Ethel argued with Mary Brown. She disappeared. Ethel couldn't get along with Hannah Douglas. She disappeared. Do you see a pattern here?"

"The Douglas woman ran off with a convict."

Jeff leaned up so close to the director that he could feel his breath on his face. "That convict was having sex with Ethel at The Walls."

"What?"

"You heard me. And you can put the idea of Mrs. Douglas running off with Leo Trinket out of your head. She is most definitely not loose."

"So, were you having an affair with Libby Angus?"

He dropped his head. Not one hair was out of place. "Yes."

"What happened?"

"Ethel and Elaine walked in on us at our lake house. We were in bed."

"Ooops!"

Jack did not appreciate Jeff's sense of humor.

"What happened?"

"Libby got dressed and drove home. I never saw her again, and then I read in the paper where she had disappeared."

"Weren't you the least bit suspicious?"

"No. I thought she had just up and left because she was devastated about our affair being over."

"Damn, director! You must think that dick of yours is magic for a girl to leave everything she owns, including her car, her clothes, without even a change of underwear, and just disappear because she can't have it anymore."

"When the next girl disappeared and then the next, I thought some psycho was out looking for young beautiful girls with long hair."

"What was your sister-in-law's name?"

"Elsa."

"Her last name?"

"Fletcher, I guess. Elaine wouldn't talk about her. Ethel Fletcher ruined my marriage."

"Funny how you look at it." Stone raised his eyebrows. "I was thinking you ruined your marriage when you introduced Dick to Libby Angus."

Chapter 45

The woods surrounding the farmhouse were thick and heavy with ice. The needles of the lofty pines seemed to whisper down to the under-brush, giving it warning of the evil that would bite the air tonight.

It would be the fourth night in a row that the temperatures were below freezing and the trees were weary of their unwelcome load. The sky remained gray, dense with humidity, frosting the branches and needles with yet another layer of already burdensome ice.

The weaker limbs had already succumbed to their unaccustomed weight, snapping before crashing to the ground. With the colder air and moisture in the forecast, the forests of southeast Texas would sound like a war zone during the night and resemble the aftermath by morning.

Leo wished he could go home, but he couldn't remember exact-ly where that was. He had been in many homes growing up – one after the other, but the last place he had been was different. He remembered that all of his clothes were white and that most every-body had worn white. It wasn't as scary as here.

Leo had been hearing gunshots in the forest all of last night and even today, and thinking that Mother must be out there hunting down little stray girls.

"Run!" he shouted. "Run as fast as you can! Don't let her catch you." Another pop boomed from the woods. "Oh, no!" he cried. "She got you. You have to hide." His hands were trembling; his face dripping with beads of sweat as he cowered in the closet underneath the clothes that were the wrong color.

The doorknob turned. "Oh no!" he whispered. He squinted his eyes shut as tight as they would close, but he couldn't shut his ears. He put his hands over them. *Hold them tight,* he thought.

The door opened, but not the closet door. He kept thinking she wouldn't find him in there.

"Leo?"

Don't answer.

"Leo, I know you are in here. Come out." Her voice was calm but firm. It never got loud. It never got soft. Always the same. Always the same.

Don't say a word. Don't even think the words. She'll hear them. "Shut up!" he mouthed.

The closet door flew open.

Stay very still, he said to himself. *She won't see me if I am very, very still.*

"Leo. You can't hide from me. I am your mother."

"Shhh!" he whispered. "Be still!"

"Come out of the closet, Leo. It's time to eat."

"Yes, ma'am." He looked. She didn't have a gun.

Ethel, Jona, and Mother were seated at the table when Leo came down. "Leo, sit here, next to me," Ethel said.

"Okay." He was trembling.

Rare T-bone steaks were heaped high on a large pewter platter in the center of the table. Mother stabbed one first. Red juice dripped from the meat and onto the lace tablecloth. Bloody spot, Leo thought to himself. He was the last to get his. There were baked potatoes and corn on the cob on the table as well, but Leo only saw the meat, the flesh of a once-living cow. He hacked into his T-bone as if it were still alive and might possibly try to defend itself. Leo conquered it quickly though. He cut it into a dozen different pieces, bloody chopped up pieces – just like he had chopped up Mother and Father. He had chopped them into a dozen bloody pieces. He smiled.

"Eat your dinner, Leo," Mother ordered.

His smile quickly faded. Mother had come back. He put a piece of the rare bloody flesh into his mouth and chewed it. He swallowed it down and thought to himself, *the next time I kill you, Mother, I'll eat you piece by piece. Then you won't come back.*

His smile returned.

"Are the girls ready, Jona?"

"Yes. I'll take them their garments a little while before the ceremony."

"Good. I'm going to call for them at eleven o'clock tonight."

"I'll help you with that," Ethel said.

"No!" It was the first time they had heard Mother raise her voice. "I'll do it." In the back of her mind she remembered the tapping of the shoes, coming up the stairs, down the hall. Tap, tap, tap. And her door would open. Her door would open and her mother would say, "Get up and get dressed." This time she would be the one tapping up the stairs and clicking down the hall. She would open the door and say, "Get up and get dressed." And they would have to go to the wicked place. They would have to wait in the cages. They would have to dance for the devils and . . . and if they did not, they would have to lie on the altar and get stabbed to death.

Libby had finally given birth to the baby. Jack's baby. Elaine was sending Jack an invitation for tonight that he could not refuse. She wanted him to see his Libby again. He could watch his baby be put on the altar and stabbed to death, and then he could swallow one of her eyes and eat a piece of her heart. And then he could burn in hell.

Elaine looked up, coming out of her reverie: "Ethel, do you know all the words yet?" Mother asked.

"Yes. I'm ready. I know every chant, every part, every word. I never thought I would look forward to the ceremonies, but now I can hardly wait."

"You are a child of Satan. He has made it clear to you why we do what we do, as he has with me."

Mother turned to Jona. "Are you prepared for tonight?"

"Yes, Mother," Jona said.

Leo was too busy with his meat to hear anything. Mother opened a tiny silver box that was resting next to her plate. She took a pill out of it and handed it to Leo.

"Take your medicine, Leo. It is time."

He did as he was told.

CR80

Gabriel filled Hannah's fitful dreams that afternoon in the solid green room where she was being held captive. She could see him running towards her in the pasture, his splendid mane illuminated by the sun as he tossed his head in noble fashion. He came right up to her so she could breathe into his nostrils as she had done a hundred times before. Then he took off hurriedly as though he had been summoned to the pond. She watched as he drove his golden body into the water, disturbing the lily pads. He splashed around playfully for only a few seconds before he started to whinny. Hannah noticed a change in his frivolity. His eyes had a frightened look about them. His expression had changed completely, and he was desperately trying to climb out of the pond, but the water lilies were holding him. They had wrapped around him like ropes. He became frantic. Hannah ran as fast as she could towards her beloved horse. Finally, she reached the water's edge as Gabriel tore himself free from the stalks of the pond flowers. She looked out into the water, beyond the menacing water lilies and saw the body of a girl, but she could not see her face. The girl was dead, and she floated on the water like one of the lily pads. The girl looked familiar to Hannah, but she couldn't tell who she was. Her hair was covering part of her face and the rest of it floated behind her like an open Japanese fan. It was long, dark hair, not unlike her own. Horrified at that thought, Hannah backed up, away from the pond and the water lilies and the dead girl, and walked over to where Gabriel was grazing. When he saw her, he got frightened. He neighed and stomped and tossed his head, then ran away, terrified of Hannah. Of course, she thought, he thinks I was the dead girl in the pond. She turned around to look at the girl, but the body was gone. What was that dripping sound? She looked down and noticed water dripping onto her boots. It was coming from her shirt tail. Only then did Hannah realize that she was soaking wet.

Cʒ℘

Another treetop broke and fell. The noise that resembled gunfire woke Hannah up. She closed her eyes once again and thought about Gabriel. William and Reed had given him to her for her birthday just a few years ago. She loved him to death. *Death.* That is what her dream had been about, and for the first time, she realized, without a doubt, that she was about to die.

Chapter 46

The Sheriff's Office was overflowing with people. The Department of Public Safety had been swarmed with wrecks due to hazardous driving conditions, and the county was being dispatched to the overflow. Huntsville public schools had been canceled and some businesses were shut down because vehicles this far south were not equipped to handle the iced-over roads. But there were those people who had to get out, just for the hell of it, and slip and slide their cars and trucks into poles, ditches, road signs, bridges, and each other.

William got to his office and closed the door anxious to look over the file Virginia had copied for him. Ethel had gone to Stephen F. Austin State University for her teaching degree. Her records noted that she had done her student teaching twice at Riley Elementary. He dialed information and asked for the principal's number at that school. He called. No answer. "Damn!" Nacogdoches was also in a deep freeze. Their schools would be canceled too.

He scanned the paper work and found the principal's signature. William called him at home.

"I am Detective William Douglas with the Walker County Sheriff's Department. I need your help."

The principal had hated Ethel Fletcher and was more than willing to tell William about the events that led up to Ethel's final days at Riley Elementary. He told him about all the children who had been involved in freak accidents while she was their student teacher. He told about the two supervising teachers who had failed her, and then about how they died. He didn't know how, and he couldn't prove it, but he was convinced that Ethel Elizabeth Fletcher was responsible for it all.

Finally the principal asked why William was calling about Ethel.

"I think she has kidnapped my wife."

"Then God help her," he said. "And God help you."

William was about to wade through Ethel's juvenile records when the phone rang. It was Jeff.

"I think I might know where Hannah is. I'm on my way to pick you up. Meet me outside."

"I'll be there. Hurry!"

William slammed down the phone. He felt for his guns, the one in the holster and then the one strapped to his ankle. He put on his coat and hat and ran for the front door. He heard Jeff's siren before he saw the lights. He was driving a patrol car since he wrecked his unmarked car. That had been less than a week ago, but to William it seemed like forever and a day.

William walked down to the street so Jeff wouldn't have to turn into the parking lot. The car skidded into a slide as Jeff applied the brakes to pick up his partner.

"Damn this ice!" William said. "Did you call for back up?"

"I've got three units waiting for us at Sycamore and Eleventh. This place is out in the woods on Lake Livingston. They're going to have to follow us."

"How did you find out about it?"

"Interrogating Jack Tyler. He has a lake house where he and Libby Angus used to play doctor."

"Libby Angus and Jack Tyler?"

"Yep. She was the first girl taken."

"What makes you think Hannah will be there?"

"Elaine Tyler and Ethel Fletcher walked in on Jack performing a gynecological exam on Libby Angus with his very own personal probe. I think Ethel and Elaine are hiding all the girls there. It would be the perfect place. Out of the way. Inconspicuous."

"Jesus, help me. I'm trying not to get my hopes up."

Jeff spotted the three other units at Zipp's Convenience Store. They had heard his siren and were ready to pull out and follow him.

"Do you think the five of us will be enough?"

"Hell no. Dispatch has the directions. Two Rangers have been notified as well as the FBI." He looked over at William. "I knew you wouldn't want to wait on them."

"Thanks."

"I just pray to God they are there."

They took Highway 190 East towards Livingston. The ice on the road made it a roller coaster ride, and what should have taken fifteen minutes took them thirty-five.

Jack Tyler had not wanted to write down the directions for Jeff and told him he wouldn't without a warrant. Then Jeff explained to him how fast the news of his affair with Libby Angus was going to spread, and that it would probably reach the governor's office before Jeff could get a search warrant, and that seemed to change Jack's attitude. With the detailed directions to his lake house, Jack handed over the keys with permission to search the place. It would look better for Jack if he helped the police rather than fought them, and even though he still might lose his job, maybe he wouldn't go to prison. Jeff wondered where they would imprison the former Director of the Texas Department of Criminal Justice. He would have to look into that for curiosity's sake.

The house was a beautiful two story, but not very large. The front was mostly hidden by trees and looked beguiling behind their frosted branches. The back was almost solid glass with a view of the lake. It didn't look like a place where someone could hide seven women.

The sirens pierced through the chilled air like shards of glass falling from a breaking window, and the twirling red and blue lights pillaged the serenity of the view, but nothing else stirred.

All four cars stopped and the five men got out. Each drew his weapon and checked to see that a round had been chambered.

William's heart was in his throat. "Please, God," he said. He thought he would be able to feel her if she were here, but he couldn't. With Hannah he could always tell when she walked into the room, even before he smelled her Shalimar. Before he heard her footsteps, he could see her face, he could feel her presence. But he didn't feel it now.

"Oh, God!" he said to Jeff. "I don't think she's here."

"I haven't even opened the door yet, man."

"I'd be able to feel it if she were here. Jeff, Hannah's not here."

"Well do you mind if I take a look? I mean, we made the trip and all."

The five deputies searched the place before the Rangers and the FBI got there. Jack and Elaine Tyler's lake house, as William suspected, was vacant.

A crime scene team was called in to dust for prints and comb the house for strands of hair, blood, and skin tissue.

"Maybe Tyler called his wife and warned her we were coming out here. She could have gotten here before we did and taken them somewhere else." William was grasping for straws.

"He couldn't have."

"Why?"

"Because I left him in the custody of a deputy with the orders that he was not to let him talk to a soul until he heard from me."

"His secretary could have . . ."

"Nope. I had another deputy haul her ass to jail for interfering with a peace officer."

"You're kidding."

"Nope. She made me mad. I told the deputy to have the jailers book her and process her, and put her in a holding tank for the full four hours before letting her make a phone call. I doubt she'll use it to warn Elaine Tyler."

William smiled. Amid all the pain, anger, frustration, and fear he felt at this very moment, Jeff had managed to squeeze a tiny little bright spot in, and he was grateful for it.

On the way back to the Sheriff's Office William started going through Ethel's juvenile records. "She was in foster care. Looks like she went from one family to another. She couldn't have stayed long in any one place for there to be so many."

"That reminds me," Jeff said. "Jack Tyler told me that Ethel was Elaine Tyler's niece."

"Niece?"

"Yeah. He said Elaine never talked about her family and he didn't even know she had a sister until Ethel landed on their doorstep. Turns out it was a twin sister."

"Where is she now?" William asked.

"Dead. I guess that explains the foster care."

"Why didn't Elaine take her?"

"I don't think she knew about her. Jack said his wife hadn't had anything to do with any of her family as long as he's known her, but they've only been married for five years."

"I'll bet you anything Elaine knows where Hannah is. Take me to her office. I'll get it out of her if I have to pull it out tooth by tooth."

"I talked to her this morning. She told me a completely different story from Jack's."

"She's the key. Step on it."

"All right, but let me do the talking. We won't learn a thing if you go in and start extracting all her teeth."

"That's not funny."

"Yes, it is ."

"No, it's not."

The two detectives drove over to the Central Administration Office for the Windham School District. Elaine Tyler, the superintendent, wasn't there and her secretary was gone as well. In fact, the building was almost deserted and of the few still there, none of them knew where Mrs. Tyler was or when she had left.

The Sheriff's Office was directly across the street from Windham's administration office, which sat in the front yard of the Wynn Prison Farm. Jeff and William decided to go there and have the deputy that was holding Jack Tyler in custody at his office, bring him to the Sheriff's Office. Meanwhile Jeff called Elaine Tyler at her home, but as he suspected, there was no answer.

Director Jack Tyler was livid when he walked into the Sheriff's Office, and he made that very clear as he cursed Jeff Stone for outlandish disrespect for his position and for defamation of his character.

"Relax, I could have had him cuff you, then people really would have been suspicious. And as for defamation of your character, you'll have to blame that on Dick."

"Where is my secretary? What have you done with Sally?"

"I think you need to be more concerned about the whereabouts of your wife. Where is she, Mr. Tyler?"

"I don't know where she is."

"That's not a good answer."

"Well, it is the only answer you are going to get." He picked up Jeff's telephone and dialed zero. "Yes, operator, I need the number for Tommy Hearn, Attorney at Law, and ring that for me, please."

William eyed Jeff with a look that said, *He is such an arrogant ass.*

Jack pressed the flash key and dialed zero again. He asked for the number of Tommy Hearn's residence and again for the operator to ring the number for him. No answer. He slammed the phone down as if trying to break it.

"Careful, I'll add vandalism to your charges."

"I'll have your jobs for this."

"Well, one thing is for sure, Mr. Director of TDCJ. You won't have them today."

Looking at the deputy, Jeff said, "Book him for conspiracy of kidnapping. Oh, and Deputy Masters, he's already had his phone call."

"Wait just one damned minute here. I didn't reach him and you know it."

"I guess you're just out of luck then."

Jack sneered at William. "This is all your doing, isn't it? You're sitting there so smug as if you had nothing to do with this."

William stood up and got within a foot of Tyler's face.

"You'd better believe that I have everything to do with it, and believe this. If I find out that you and your wife are involved in the kidnapping of my wife, you won't need your attorney, you priggish little bastard. Not the governor, the president, not even God himself will be able to hold me off you."

"I take that as a threat, and I have two witnesses that will have to testify to such."

Deputy Masters looked at Detective Stone. "I didn't hear anything. Did you?"

"Not a word. My eyesight's not what it used to be either. Lock his ass up."

William walked down the hall to the dispatcher's booth. "Nate, put out an attempt to locate on Elaine Tyler. White female. Thirty-nine years of age. Short dark hair. Brown eyes. Approximately one-hundred forty pounds and five feet, five inches tall. Drives a yellow, late model Mercedes.

"Who is she?" Nate asked.

"The superintendent of Windham School District."

"As in the prison schools for TDCJ?"

"That would be the one."

Chapter 47

Jeff came up behind William. "Partner, you look like you have been swallowed by a fish, puked up, and washed ashore."

"Gee, thanks."

"I'm serious. You are going to have to get some sleep. Go home."

"I can't just go home and tell Reed and the Richeys that I am going to bed because I'm tired. His mother, their daughter, and my wife is missing. I don't have time to waste on sleep."

Jeff picked up the phone and dialed William's home number. "Hello, Mr. Richey. Listen, I'm sending William home to get some sleep. Will you make sure that he does that?

"Thank you, sir."

William lowered his head and glared up at Jeff. "You didn't have to do that."

"You made me do that. You aren't going to be worth a damn to Hannah or Reed if you kill yourself trying to find her. You haven't had a decent amount of sleep since this whole thing started. Tell me I'm wrong."

William couldn't tell him he was wrong. He had tried to sleep, but he couldn't. How could he sleep when Hannah was in danger?

"What about you?" William retorted. "How much sleep have you had?"

"For your information, I had a nap this afternoon, and I am good to go for another several hours. Look, I promise I will call you if there is a reason to."

"I wanted to go over Ethel's juvenile records some more before I quit."

"I'll do that. Go home. If not for you, then for your son."

William yielded. "Okay, but you call me."

The strain and stress from losing Hannah had indeed taken their toll on William. He stayed up with Reed and his in-laws for a little while and told them about what had happened that day. His eyes had the hollow look of a Picasso subject during the artist's blue period. He was so tired that his eyelids felt like sandpaper. Maybe Jeff was right. Some sleep would make his head clearer.

He said goodnight to his family and went to the bedroom that brought Hannah even closer to his heart. Her hats perched on the hat tree he had made for her. He closed his eyes and pictured her wearing one with her long and flowing black hair cascading down her back. The crystal perfume bottles on her dresser brought the smell of her skin as close to him as if she were there. Dainty Victorian purses hanging from her floor length mirror reminded him of her femininity. He opened her jewelry box and it tinkled out the tune *Somewhere My Love,* and William grasped at his heart. *You are somewhere, my love, and I'm going to find you.* "Dear God, please help me find her."

Meredith had put the comforter back on the bed and made it up from the last time he tried to sleep. He took it off the bed again and laid it back down on the floor. He could not possibly sleep in their bed without her. Not now.

A heavy sleep clutched him almost as soon as his head hit the pillow, but heavy dreams came with it. Hannah and he were together at the farm riding Banjo and Gabriel. The sun was shining and the warm afternoon air felt like silk against their faces as they floated through its breeze. It was a relaxing and peaceful afternoon, but when they came close to the pond, a dark dense cloud boiled out of what had been a blue and tranquil sky. Lightning streaked across the dark – one strike and then another. The lightning melded into one enormous bolt that struck at the ground in front of them. It had happened all of a sudden. One minute it was beautiful and sunny, and then the next minute all hell broke loose.

The horses screamed in terror and both reared up high enough to pitch them off. William hung on, but Hannah could not. She hit the ground and lay there. Gabriel took off for the pond. As William tried to reach her, her body kept moving farther away. The lightning struck again, catching the grass on fire. The fire formed a circle around Hannah, not letting William get to her. The flames rose up like orange walls of evil daring him to rescue her. He tried to reach her, but the fire was too hot and strong.

The horses started screaming again. He looked beyond the fire and saw Gabriel coming out of the pond with eyes full of terror. William ran over to the pond and saw someone floating in the water. He rushed in, thinking it could be Hannah. He turned the body over to find that her face had been burned away. Looking back toward the fire, he saw that it was gone, and so was Hannah. He looked back at the woman in the pond. Her arm was floating out beside her. William raised her hand up out of the water and saw Hannah's wedding ring – the one he had placed on her finger the night they were married. His Hannah was dead.

Overwhelming grief jolted him out of his fitful sleep. He looked around frantically for Hannah, rubbing his face hard, trying to restore his senses. "No! No! No!" he cried. "It can't be too late. God, don't you let her die. Don't you let her die!"

The clock showed 9:00 p.m. He got up and put his clothes back on then charged out of the bedroom and down the hall. Hannah's parents were still up, but Reed had gone to bed.

"Good Lord, William. What's the matter?" Henry asked. William's urgency startled him.

"I can't sleep. I've got to find my wife. I've got to find my wife." He put on his gun belt, slipped his boot holster inside his boot, put on his coat and hat and left without another word.

CX8D

Driving to the Sheriff's Office, William thought about the night they were married. It was the most magical night of his life; even more magical than the morning Reed was born. It was the beginning of their lives together as one unit, one soul, one being, and together, because of that union, they had made Reed, and Hannah had brought him into the world.

He remembered the surprised look on her face when he slipped the diamond wedding ring on her finger because she thought she was just getting a gold band. She stared at the ring and then up at him. She had never looked more beautiful.

The dream. The nightmare. It had seemed so real. William felt like his blood was draining out of his body. Hannah would be gone forever. He had to find her. He had to save her life. He had to save his own.

Jeff was exhausted, but he couldn't quit after sending William home to rest. He was sorting through his notes on Elaine and Jack Tyler and comparing them to the report on Libby Angus's disappearance. But Stella kept popping into his overworked mind. The phone rang, giving him a slight start.

"Sheriff's Office, Detective Stone."

"Hello, Detective Stone. This is Nurse Perkins."

A big grin broke out of his tired face. "How do you do that?"

"Do what?"

"Call right at the very minute I am thinking about you?"

"Psychic, I guess."

"That sounds interesting. Can you guess what I am thinking?"

"Yes, and it's indecent."

He laughed out loud. "You really are psychic."

"What are you still doing at work? It's after nine o'clock."

"I had a nap this afternoon. Remember?"

"A one hour nap. Jeff, you are going to run yourself ragged and be of no help to anyone if you don't get some rest."

"I could come over there, but then I sure wouldn't get any rest, at least not with what I'm thinking about right now."

"You're incorrigible."

William stormed into the office.

"Princess, something just came up. I've got to go. I'm sorry. I'll call you later if it's not too late."

"Okay. Bye."

"Partner, you look like you could use a drink."

"There's got to be something we are missing. We have got to do something and fast. Time is running out. I can feel it, Jeff. I know what I'm talking about." He sat down in his chair. He looked at Jeff in a way that begged Jeff to understand. "Hannah and I . . . we are like that. We can feel each other. Sense each other. I'm telling you, man."

"Okay, okay. Just calm down." Jeff was trying to think of something that would get William onto another plane. He was close to the edge and about to fall off. "Why don't you get Ethel's juvenile records and I'll get Leo's. We can go through them together and see if something turns up."

"Good. Let's do that."

Cody Dickerson walked by their office and noticed their lights on. "Hey," he said as he poked his head in the door.

"Cody, hey," William said. "I tried to get hold of you to see what you found out about those prints on Leo's mother."

"Nothing. It came back to a couple of possibles, but that's sketchy with just thumbs."

"What were their full names?" William asked.

"Hold on. I wrote them down in my notebook. It's out in the car."

William shook his head. "I can't believe he's up here this time of night."

"I told you, partner. Everybody is working on this. The machine doesn't quit just because you grab a couple of hours of sleep."

Cody came right back in. He had parked just outside the front door of the building. "Okay, we have one Elsa Beth Johnson. Deceased. And we have an Elaine Blair Compton."

Cody looked up and into two frozen faces. "You want to tell me what's going on?"

Jeff spoke up. "Elsa. That was the name of Elaine Tyler's twin sister."

"Elaine Tyler. That's right. She is the Superintendent of the Windham School District. Surely you guys don't think that . . ."

William looked at Jeff in disbelief. "Elaine Tyler is Leo Trinket's mother. That explains it."

"Jesus! That means that Ethel and Leo are first cousins. But something doesn't jive," Jeff said.

"What?"

"They were both in foster homes."

William flipped back to the page in Ethel's folder that gave her parents' names. "Ethel's birth parents are Albert and Sharon

Fletcher. She was taken out of the home because of child abuse, drugs, alcohol, neglect, you name it."

The sheriff came in.

"Sheriff, come on in. We just discovered who Leo Trinket's birth mother is," Jeff said. Cody was still trying to catch up. "Elaine Tyler."

Sheriff Applegate removed his hat and shook his head. "I'd say its about to hit the fan, boys."

Nate's voice came through on the radio. "S.O. 801."

The sheriff responded, "This is 801, S.O., go ahead."

"801, you have an urgent call from a Dr. Biscamp out of Houston. He's on hold."

"10-4, S.O. I'm in Jeff's office. Patch him through."

"10-4, 801."

Sheriff Applegate shrugged his shoulders. "Don't know him," he said. The phone buzzed. He picked it up and put it on the speaker.

"This is Sheriff Applegate."

"Sheriff, this is Dr. George Biscamp. I have been stewing around all afternoon and all night about something one of my patients told me today while under hypnosis."

"Yes, sir. Did you want to tell me about it?"

"Well, the problem is, I am not supposed to divulge that information because of the patient-doctor privilege thing. You know – ethics and all."

"Yes, sir."

"The problem is, see," he stumbled around, "I think what she told me may have something to do with those missing women in your county."

Every face in the office perked up. William didn't even breathe.

"Well, I guess Dr. Biscamp, you'd have to decide whether it would be more ethical to keep this patient's secret or perhaps save the lives of seven innocent women."

"It is not that simple."

"Yes, sir. It is that simple."

Biscamp took a few seconds and the sheriff allowed him that. "My patient told me that when she was a little girl, she was forced to be in this satanic cult. Her parents ran a foster home. From what she told me, well, it sounded like those people used the children in foster care as objects for their horrific rituals. So horrible, in fact, I'm not even sure I believe it."

"And what exactly does that have to do with our missing women?"

"My patient told me that the place is no longer a foster home because she didn't like children, and now that she is running it, they use women for their rituals rather than children."

The sheriff began to feel hopeful. The rest of the men in the office could barely contain themselves. The seconds seemed to turn into hours, but not for the missing women. Their hourglass was seeping sand.

The sheriff asked, "What is your patient's name?"

"Oh, really, I couldn't tell you that."

"Can you tell me where the foster home is located?"

"I'm not sure that I can do that either."

"So, you're sole purpose in calling me tonight was to tell me that the women who have been abducted may have been taken to a home where they are being used for horrible satanic rituals. You know where this home is, but you won't tell us. You know who the kidnapper is, but you won't tell us."

"You make it sound like I . . ."

The sheriff interrupted him, "I'll tell you what it sounds like. It sounds like to me that you are getting off to this."

The doctor tried to argue, but Applegate would not let him.

"And I'll tell you something else. If you don't tell me where the fuck this place is, I'll have some of my men come and arrest you as an accessory to seven counts of kidnapping and possibly murder."

"You won't be able to get away with that." Biscamp was outraged.

"Maybe, maybe not. But in the meantime, I can cost you a hell of a lot of money in attorney's fees, not to mention the kind of damage your practice will suffer. Talk like this has a way of snowballing, if you know what I mean."

"This sounds like blackmail. I won't tolerate it and neither will the courts."

"Let me tell you a thing or two you might not be aware of. One of my detectives is sitting right here in this room with me and listening to our conversation. His sweet, beautiful, precious wife is the kidnapper's latest victim. Now you may not like it, but the fact is, every judge in this county knows him, and they are all just heartsick about what has happened to his wife. Where do you think that will leave you?"

"All right, all right." Biscamp had wanted to spill it all along, but he needed some sort of permission.

"Will you promise me that I will not be brought up on charges for divulging confidential information?"

"I promise you that."

"The address is Thirteen-thirteen Belial Road." The sheriff reacted as if he recognized it, but with trepidation.

"Thank you, good doctor, and your patient's name?"

"Really, I can't . . ." He could hear his father spitting and sputtering at him. *That's right, you little weasel. You'll never amount to anything. You don't even have the guts to save the lives of seven innocent women by spilling a name. You make me sick. You're as bad as the people that took them. You're as guilty as they are, you little pervert.*

"It's Blair Comptom."

"Thank you, good doctor. You may have just saved seven lives. The sheriff hung up the phone and immediately called Judge Rothlander for a search warrant for the premises.

"While we're waiting on that search warrant, William, what were you saying about Ethel?"

"Elsa Johnson was not Ethel's real mother. She was her foster mother."

The sheriff spoke up. "Elsa Johnson! That's the woman Leo Trinket killed with an ax. She and her husband. I worked the case. Found him in the corner of their barn still holding the bloody thing in his hands. He had the strangest look on his face that I had ever seen in my life. It was like he was relieved and petrified all at the same time."

William jumped in, "Do you remember how to get there?"

"It was way out off Richard's Road. I remember telling my wife about it and I must have mentioned the address because she said it meant something wicked. Something from the Bible."

Everyone in the meantime had put on their coats, hats, and guns. Cody ran down to the dispatch booth and gave Nate the address. "Get everybody you can find on this to back us up."

Nate asked, "Do you have directions?"

"The sheriff has been there before. We'll keep you informed from the car and you can tell the others as we find our way. We've got to go by and pick up a search warrant first."

Nate said. "Can do."

The sheriff grabbed a Bible from his office before running then sliding out to his car. *Damn this weather!*

"William, you ride with me. Cody, you ride with Jeff." The sheriff stopped dead in his tracks.

"What?" Jeff asked Applegate.

"It's been bugging the hell out of me, but now, I finally figured out who Elaine Tyler, the Windham superintendent reminds me of."

"Elsa Johnson?"

"How did you know?" Applegate asked.

"Elsa Beth Johnson and Elaine Blair Compton Tyler were twins."

"It's hittin' the fan, boys. It's hittin' the fan!"

As soon as they got in the car, the sheriff picked up his car phone and called his wife for the passage in the Bible that she remembered when he mentioned Thirteen-thirteen Belial Road.

He handed the Bible to William. "Look up Deuteronomy 13:13, and read it."

William found it and read, *Verse 13: Certain men, the children of Belial, are gone out from among you, and have withdrawn the inhabitants of their city, saying, Let us go and serve other gods, which ye have not known;*

"Keep going. Read on."

"Verse 14 says," *Then shalt thou enquire, and make search, and ask diligently; and, behold, if it be truth, and the thing certain, that such abomination is wrought among you;*

15 Thou shalt surely smite the inhabitants of that city with the edge of the sword, destroying it utterly, and all that is therein, and the cattle thereof, with the edge of the sword.

16 And thou shalt gather all the spoil of it into the midst of the street thereof, and shalt burn with fire the city, and all the spoil thereof every whit, for the Lord thy God: and it shall be an heap for ever; it shall not be built again.

17 And there shall cleave nought of the cursed thing to thine hand: that the Lord may burn from the fierceness of his anger, and shew thee mercy, and have compassion upon thee, and multiply thee, as he hath sworn unto thy fathers;

18 *When thou shalt hearken to the voice of the Lord thy God, to keep all his commandments which I command thee this day, to do that which is right in the eyes of the Lord thy God.*

The sheriff raised his eyebrows. "You know, after hearing what the psychiatrist said about that being some kind of satanic cult, it makes you wonder if Leo Trinket was trying to stop what was going on out there when he butchered his foster parents. Stop it for good."

William bent forward and hugged himself. "Maybe he won't hurt her. He may even be her salvation."

Chapter 48

Chants filled the night air with haunting strains. Still frozen and draped in ice, the trees of the forest offered their own baleful melodies; branches tapping and clicking against one another in an ominous chorus.

The torches were lit and the candles glowed while the altar lay in wait for the ultimate sacrifice. Whispers of evil escaped from the gargoyles that guarded the walls.

Among the whispers of the house and the symphony of the forest, the tap, tap, tap of Mother's shoes was the most foreboding sound of all. One step, two. One step, two. And on and on against the hardwood floors. Clean, sharp, acute. Tap, tap, tap. And then the tapping stopped in front of the first bedroom door. Resolutely, Mother turned the knob and opened the door. "Get up and get dressed," On to the next door. "Get up and get dressed." And on and on until she delivered her message to all the women she held prisoner in the bedrooms on the second floor of the farmhouse. Being on the other side of the door made all the difference.

Libby Angus, Linda Woodrum, Beverly Peters, Vicki Cockrell, Terry Mooney, Twila Brooks, and Hannah Douglas were terrified. The women were wearing dark red velvet capes with hoods. They were lined in fine soft satin and trimmed in gold brocade; a long gold tassel dangled from the hood of each cape. Beneath the capes the women were naked and beneath the hoods their heads were shorn. Their eyes were wide with fright and consternation while their hands were bound with gold ropes that had tassels hanging from them like the ones on their hoods. One behind the other, they filed down the hallway and the stairs looking like captive angels being led to the slaughterhouse.

"Where are you taking us?" Hannah asked loudly.

There was no answer.

"I said, where are you taking us?"

The others in front of her turned their heads and peered out of the deep red hoods. Their eyes begged her to be quiet. They looked defeated, hopeless, as if they had resigned themselves to the fact that there was no way out, all except for Twila, that is. Her aqua-blue eyes still had life behind them. She had not given up. Twila was the woman right in front of her.

Hannah whispered, " Do you know what's going to happen to us?"

Twila shook her head slightly to indicate that she did not. Her tassel bounced about like a puppet doing a dance.

"My name is Hannah. What's yours?"

She turned slightly and whispered, "It's Twila."

"We could try to run. They couldn't catch all of us," Hannah said.

"No talking!" Mother scolded. Her dark eyes glittered with hatred as the flame from her candle cast reflections in them. She was wearing a velvet cape as well, only hers was black with a scarlet satin lining.

Mark Casey had not been able to bring Jack Tyler. Elaine was so disappointed about it that she had wanted to postpone the ceremony, but he was in jail. Obviously the police had gathered enough evidence to implicate her in the kidnappings, and they were going to include Jack as an accessory. That would be somewhat of a just reward for his philandering.

As Hannah passed by the woman in the black cape, she looked into her face. "Oh, my God! Mrs. Tyler? Is that you?"

Elaine gazed upon her with hatred.

Hannah asked incredulously, "What are you doing here?"

"You will see, my dear. All in good time." Her voice was cold and as dark as the black velvet cape she was wearing.

Jona was waiting for them at the end of the dark corridor as they walked single file toward him. Twila felt herself begin to melt inside as she got close to him. When she reached him, he looked deep into her aqua-blue eyes. Even in the somber hallway they were luminous. He wanted to take her into his arms and run with her, to get her out of this den of iniquity and away from the devils. Away from the altar. Away from Mother and Ethel. But he could not wrangle with destiny. He had always known that.

Twila saw love in Jona. She knew she did. There was no mistake for what love felt like or looked like, and it was radiating from him like heat from a furnace. She felt it. She wanted it. Why wouldn't he help her? Why was he letting this happen to her? Why? The tears began to flow. The powerful feeling of sadness overshadowed even the stark terror that confronted her. And when they entered the black room, all she could see was Jona's face when she had made love to him.

The cages were lined up in a row. There were seven of them. The women were led to the cages by Mother and told to get in as Jona assisted each one. He did not look into the faces of any of them. Across from the altar was a row of chairs cushioned with black velvet. Placed around the room were five-foot-tall candlesticks, each holding a black burning candle. Reflections from their flames flickered about on the black shiny floor.

Mother walked to one of two thrones next to the altar. She picked up a mallet and struck a huge round disk suspended from the black ceiling. The clang reverberated, splintering the blackness, and then the chanting started again. It came from a distance and got closer and louder as its bearers approached the threshold of the black room – the wicked place.

Hannah was freezing cold, yet beads of sweat seeped out of her skin. Her heart was racing and soaked in fear. She had read a little about satanic rituals and had even seen some portrayed in movies. As she looked down the row of cages at the other women, all boxed in like rag dolls draped in expensive velvet, they showed little emotion – all but the girl next to her, the one with the aqua-blue eyes. Twila. She was weeping. *Strange,* Hannah thought. *She doesn't seem to be as scared as she is sad.*

What happened next stopped Hannah's heart.

෯෯

"Where in the hell is this place?" William asked anxiously. The hairs on his arms, legs, chest and head were standing on end. With every move he made, they agitated his skin.

"It's hell and gone from nowhere," Sheriff Applegate replied.

"Do you remember exactly how to get there?"

"It's been seven years or more." He saw the concern on William's face. "But I think I can find it. At least these dirt roads aren't as slick as the pavement."

"I'm afraid we're going to be too late." Desperation tinged his voice.

The sheriff wished he could carry some of his detective's burden for him, but he couldn't. Not really. No one could.

"You're just probably feeling that way because we are close to finding something – hopefully Hannah and the other ladies."

"No, sir. It's not just that. I've been feeling this way all night. Something is not right. I mean, I've been scared senseless since I discovered that she was missing, but tonight, it's different." He looked over at the sheriff, his eyes liquid pools. "I feel like I have lost her forever. Part of me feels like it is about to die, and . . . oh, . . . God, . . . I'm afraid that part is Hannah."

"Not if I can help it."

ᘓᘔ

The chanting continued. Hannah felt dirty and shamed. She wanted no part of this. It was wicked. It was vile. It was sacrilegious and unholy. Panic seized her. "God!" she shouted. "Help me. God! Help me."

There was complete silence at her outburst. Everyone looked at her. Hannah didn't care. She wanted God to storm through the door with a band of his angels and sweep her up and away from the pure and unadulterated evil that permeated everything in the room. It was crawling up her legs and consuming her flesh. She could not imagine what forms of depravity and debauchery were about to play out here, but she wanted no part of it. She would rather die.

Hannah spotted the long braids of hair hanging on the wall behind the altar. Then she recognized the silver ponytail holder that Reed had given her. Her hair was on that wall.

"God!" Hannah cried softly. *I would rather die than be a part of this. Take me now. Please God. Stop my heart from beating and take me to heaven. Please, God. Don't let them desecrate me.*

The chanting stopped suddenly again and a softer, much more human sound, entered the room. Hannah looked up and saw Ethel Fletcher in a purple velvet robe trimmed and lined in gold. She was carrying a baby. The hood of the garment covered her red frizzy hair, but her colorless pellucid eyes cauterized the room when she entered it. There would be no God in here. Not now. No angels from heaven would enter this wicked place.

The baby was crying and flailing its tiny arms and legs. Ethel placed the baby on the altar, then took her place next to Mother, Elaine Tyler, in front of her waiting throne.

The infant was screaming. Hannah looked down the row at the other women. The one at the end looked desperate. She tried to move, but her hands were bound and she couldn't. "No!" she screamed. "Not my baby! Please, God, no! Not my baby!"

Mother spoke, "There is no God here. Only Satan. He is the master here."

The chanting began again and Mother approached the baby. She brought out a dagger from underneath her robe. Twila recognized it. It was the one used to cut off her hair.

The chanting continued, "Hail Satan! Hail Satan! Hail Satan!"

Mother raised the dagger up high above her head. Silence.

"We offer this pure and unsanctified child as a sacrifice to you, Satan. Accept this offering, master of the earth." She brought the dagger down and plunged it into the baby. The baby fell silent. Libby Angus lowered her head and cried the cry of death.

Ethel joined Mother at the altar. She held the dead infant in place while Mother opened up the baby's chest. Ethel reached into the child's tiny body and pulled out its heart. She held it up high. "Satan, we offer this to you so that you may grant us the things that we ask of you. Save us Satan and cleanse us with this sacrifice as we partake of your blood."

Ethel put the tiny heart on the altar and cut it into pieces. Mother arranged them on a platter before serving them to the masked devils. One by one they took a tiny piece of the heart and held it between their fingers until each had received his portion.

Ethel continued, "Save us, Lord Satan. Use us as your servants. Beat within us as we take your heart into our bodies." They ate.

Hannah could not watch. She tried to think of something else. Another time, another place. Anywhere but here.

Music came out of nowhere. Erotic music. Hannah wanted to disappear.

Jona came forward and stood in front of the seven women.

"Which one of you will dance first?"

Twila looked at him in disbelief.

He bowed down in front of Mary Brown.

"Dance for us," he said in his soft buttery voice, almost like a song.

"No," she said. "I can't dance."

"Yes you can. Just move for the devils. They will like you. You are so pretty."

"No."

Jona helped her up out of the cage, untied her hands and unclasped her cape. It fell to the floor. The music was erotic, disturbing. Jona guided her to the center of the white circle on the floor.

Jona told her to dance.

She tried, but she was so scared.

"Dance for me," a devil said.

Mary started screaming uncontrollably.

The devil didn't say a word. He picked up the dagger and thrust it into her heart, and then she became as still as the baby.

Jona went to the row of women and asked for one of them to dance.

Beverly nodded her head up and down. She didn't want to do it, but she wasn't ready to die.

Jona unclasped her cape and it fell to the floor. She walked to the center of the circle.

Sirens, dozens of them, warbled in the distance.

Mother ordered, "Quick, take them to the barn."

The sirens sounded like an angel choir to Hannah. She knew that her angel was in one of those cars and behind one of those sirens.

Leo Trinket unlatched her cage and easily picked Hannah up. His mind was almost clear. Mother had given him his medicine, and he felt better. He was glad the ceremony was over. He had always hated the ceremonies. This was the first time he had been told to wear the devil mask. He headed for the barn behind the others.

Hannah knew somehow that she was being delivered to her death, but it was a better death than what she would have endured in the black room. The wickedness was smothering her slowly in there. She would not have danced for the devils, and she did not want them to see her naked. Her body was not for their eyes. God had rescued her from that, and she was thankful.

She looked into the face of the man who was carrying her. "I recognize you from somewhere. How do I know you?"

"I used to be in prison until Ethel got me out."

"Yes, now I remember. Your name is Trinket."

"Yes." He was breathing harder now. The trek to the barn was not a long way off, but it was freezing cold outside and he wasn't dressed for it.

"What will happen to us in the barn?"

He looked at her blankly, "You will burn in hell."

C3 80

Jona grabbed Twila. She was crying again.

"Oh, Jona. I loved you with all my heart, and I think you loved me. You were going to let them rape me and kill me, weren't you?"

Jona looked into her beautiful eyes. "I didn't want to."

She believed him.

"Then why?"

"I had no other choice. I have never had a choice."

The sirens were getting louder.

"What will happen in the barn, Jona?"

"They will put all of you in a room beneath the floor and close the door."

"What will happen to us?" she cried.

"You will burn to death. It's an incinerator." He said it almost casually.

"I love you, Jona. Look at me. I love you."

Jona did look at her. "I love you too."

Everyone else was already in the barn. The sirens were almost to the winding drive that led up to the house.

Jona looked into Twila's aqua-blue eyes and kissed her. It was warm and passionate. He put her down. "Run," he said. "Run toward the sirens. Stay in front of the house so no one will see you from the barn. They will think you're already in the room."

"What about you? Come with me."

"I can't. I have to do something first."

"Jona, please."

"Go. Now. You must hurry. If Ethel sees you, she will shoot you down like a wild dog. Run!"

"Okay. I love you, Jona." She ran around the house and toward the sirens. They still sounded far, far away.

They were all in the barn now – all but Twila. Mother told Ethel to start the incinerator.

The sirens were coming up to the yard. They would see Twila. Jona smiled. He had saved Twila. He had saved someone who loved him.

He went to the shelf and picked up the can of kerosene.

"They're in the barn. Hurry!" Twila screamed. She was out of breath and freezing cold in her bare feet. Her hands were still bound. No one stopped to untie her. They all ran for the barn.

William felt a tiny spark of hope, and it was big enough to make him run faster than he had ever run before.

He was less than one hundred feet from the barn when fire began shooting flames through the roof. "Hannah!" he screamed. "Nooooooo!" Hannah!" He reached the door. He could hear the crackling of the fire consuming everything as it grew larger.

He took off his coat. He was about to use it to open the door of the barn when Jeff pulled him back.

"Stop it."

"No. You can't go in there. No one could survive that. It's too late."

Twila fell to the frozen ground, still wrapped in the red velvet cape. She screamed from the torment that was in her soul. She screamed for the innocent women who had just burned to death. She screamed for Jona.

William ran to her. "Was Hannah in there?" He took her by the shoulders and shook her. "Was Hannah in there?" Fury and fear had engulfed him as completely as the fire had engulfed the barn.

Twila thought back to them coming down the stairs. The woman behind her had said her name was Hannah. She looked up at the desperate man in front of her and could not answer him.

"Talk to me!" he yelled.

Bright orange, yellow, and blue flames torched the frozen night and branded it with the malignity of the evil that had fed it.

Jeff came up behind him. "William?"

Twila finally drew up the courage to tell him. "Yes, Hannah was in there."

Chapter 49

Jeff lifted the girl up from the ground. She was shivering. "We've got to get her out of this cold."

Jeff picked her up into his arms to get her feet off the icy ground and headed for the house. "Don't take me back in there," she screamed. "No. I won't go back in there."

The sheriff rushed over to them. "Who is this woman?"

"My name is Twila. Twila Brooks."

"Are there any others?"

"They're all dead. All of them."

"How did you get out?" the sheriff asked.

"Jona saved me." Her tears had subsided. She was spent; her energy gone. Too much had happened for her to be able to remain lucid for another moment.

"Get her into my car," the sheriff ordered one of the deputies. Then his attention turned to William. "Did she know Hannah?"

"She said Hannah was in the barn. But she could have been wrong. She was delirious. You saw her. She could be anywhere, if she was ever here at all."

He turned to Jeff. "I'm going to look in the house. Come with me."

Jeff followed him.

Applegate had been in the house before and did not relish going inside it again. It spooked the hell out of him. But he had to. There were things to do.

It is all just a nightmare. I will wake up from this, and Hannah will be at home with Reed and everything will be the way it's supposed to be, William thought.

An FBI agent poked his head out the door of the black room as William, Jeff, and the sheriff were coming into the house. "Detective Douglas?"

William's heart started beating again. They had found Hannah. Why else would they be calling him? "Here I am."

"Could you come here a minute please?"

William entered the room. He was not ready for what he saw. The blackness, the cages, the chairs, the demonic masks, the altar, the dead mutilated baby. *And oh, God. The woman. The dead naked woman.*

The FBI agent said, "That is not Mrs. Douglas. One of the deputies already identified the body as that of Mary Brown."

William's knees went out from under him. Jeff caught and steadied him before he hit the floor. "Come on partner. Let's get you out of here." Jeff threw a look of disgust at the FBI agent who called William in there.

The agent said to Jeff, "I just wanted him to look at those." He pointed to the wall.

It was then that William spied the hair – the seven braids of hair hanging on the wall. Hesitantly he walked toward them and stopped. Lovingly he picked up the braid that was secured by sterling silver animals: a giraffe, a lion, a zebra, a hippopotamus, and a cheetah. It was time to go home. He had to go home to Reed.

Chapter 50

"How do I tell Reed? Do I wake him up?"

"Partner, I don't know. I'll come in with you," Jeff said.

"No. I'll manage."

William got out of the car and somehow made it to the front door. Neiman was waiting up for him.

The collie got excited like when Hannah would come home after having been out for awhile. He turned back and forth, backed up, then reared up and barked.

William thought that was odd since he had never acted that way for him before.

Then Neiman sniffed at William's coat pocket and began to whine like he didn't understand.

William reached in his pocket and pulled out the braid of hair. Neiman could smell Hannah. Realizing that Hannah was not with him, he cried the way a dog does when he is locked up and can't get out.

William knelt down on the floor and buried his face in the collie's ruff and cried with him.

"Dad?"

William looked up and into the face of his son.

Reed reached for the long black braid in his daddy's hand, and recognizing the little silver animals, knew it was his mother's hair.

Meredith and Henry watched as Reed tried to find comfort with his daddy, and they knew then that their daughter was dead.

CR&O

Jeff went home and got as far as his front door, but he couldn't go in. He needed someone to talk to. He needed for someone to hold him. He was empty.

Getting back into his car, he drove to Stella's house. The lights were off. He knew she would be asleep. It was almost four o'clock in the morning.

Jeff walked up to the porch and knocked. After a couple of minutes he looked in her garage and saw that her car was gone. He realized that she was at the hospital giving care to some poor fool that needed it. But he was the poor fool that needed it now.

Jeff sobbed.

CR&O

The next couple of days were all a blur for William. Forensic data came back. Hannah's fingerprints had been found in one of the bedrooms.

Twila Brooks had been given a sedative in the hospital. After a good night's sleep, she was ready to tell Detective Stone and the sheriff what had happened to her.

She looked at photographs and identified Elaine Tyler and Ethel Fletcher. She also identified Leo Trinket as the man who carried Hannah Douglas into the barn.

She told them about the ceremony and the baby. She recognized photographs of the missing women as the ones who were at the farmhouse. Even though she only saw them that one night, she would never forget their faces: the one whose baby was murdered, the girl who was stabbed on the altar, the one who about to dance for the devils, the woman who sat next to her and had told her that her name was Hannah.

Twila told them about Jona, but not everything. She told them that he saved her life, but she didn't tell anyone that she had fallen in love with him or about the single red rose that helped her to keep her sanity in the white room. She needed to keep some secrets for herself, memories to cherish when visions of the devils and Ethel and Mother crept up behind her.

She told them about the cages. She told them about how she had first met Ethel at The Kettle Restaurant – how she had been a customer and when she left had said, "My mother had long hair and wore it in a braid like yours" – and then about how she came into her house and cut off her hair. She told them about Ethel's freakish eyes. She told them about the baby's heart, and about the room under the barn.

They had found the room beneath the barn. There was nothing left but ashes, bone fragments and teeth.

Meredith and Henry helped William plan Hannah's service, not a funeral, but a memorial service. There was nothing left of her to bury except for her hair – her beautiful long hair, and William could not part with that. He would keep it the way he found it, bound by the silver ornament that Reed had given her.

Reed. He knew something had happened to his mother before anyone ever realized she was even gone.

He hadn't picked up his fiddle since he found out that his mother was dead. There was no music in his heart. Not now. There was despair, resentment, and the deepest kind of sadness. There was no room for music.

People came to the house to offer their condolences and their respects. It was a steady stream of well-meaning friends, loved ones, co-workers, and family, each bringing food as though it could somehow minimize the pain.

Neiman had to stay outside. He moaned and wailed as though he realized fully what had happened. Reed put on his coat, gloves, and hat, and stayed outside with him, offering comfort and getting some in return.

The memorial service was scheduled for Thursday, February the nineteenth, at two o'clock in the afternoon. It would be held at the First United Methodist Church.

William's and Hannah's relatives and closest friends would eat lunch at the house before the service. William was concerned that the collie's wailing would disturb everyone. It disturbed him. He called Jeff.

"I need a favor, Jeff."

"You name it."

"Neiman, Hannah's collie, is still carrying on outside, and I am afraid it will make everyone uncomfortable while they are eating. Do you have a place or know of a place we can keep him until this evening?"

"I'll take care of it. I'll be by to get him in just a few minutes. I just got out of the shower. But it won't take me long to get dressed."

"Okay. Wait. Hold on," William said.

"What is it, son?" he asked Reed.

"Dad, what are you doing with Neiman?"

"Nothing. Jeff's just going to take him somewhere until after the service this afternoon. A whole lot of people are coming over here to eat lunch, so we will have to keep him outside."

"So?"

"So, people aren't going to be able to eat with him crying like he's been doing."

"No, Dad." Reed teared up.

"Hang on a minute, Jeff. Reed, there's going to be a lot of people here and he makes them nervous crying like that. He's making me nervous, and I don't know if I can stand it. Not today."

"I'll stay outside with him."

William didn't want to deal with this. "Jeff, Reed doesn't want him gone, so . . ."

Jeff interrupted, "I tell you what. What if I come get the dog just while people are eating? Say twelve-thirty. That way Reed can eat, too."

William gave the suggestion to Reed and he conceded.

"That sounds good, Jeff. Thanks. And after the service I want you to take some of this food."

"How are you holding up, Partner?"

"To tell you the truth, I don't know."

At twelve-thirty Jeff went in William's back yard and found Reed sitting on the deck petting Neiman. The weather had finally warmed up some, and the ice was mostly gone. The sky was a brilliant blue after all the days of gray.

"What have you got there?" Jeff asked Reed.

"It's my valentine from Pretty."

"What's inside?"

"The best chocolate fudge in the world."

"The best, huh?"

"Yes, sir." Reed held the heart tin under his arm like a little girl might carry her only doll.

"Will you help me put Neiman in the car? I promise to bring him home this afternoon."

"I guess so."

"Good. And I want you to tell him everything is going to be all right, so he won't be afraid."

"But everything isn't going to be all right." Reed's sad eyes broke Jeff's heart. He would have given anything at that moment to take the boy's pain away.

Neiman sat quietly in the seat next to Jeff. He was grieving for William and for Reed, but more than that, he was grieving for Hannah.

It was so unfair.

Jeff knocked on Stella's door. He had Neiman beside him on the leash.

"Hey, there. I'm not quite ready yet," Stella said. Then she saw the dog.

"With all the company they have at the Douglas house, the dog was creating a problem. Could he stay in your back yard until after the service?"

"Sure. Of course."

"They said he's been crying and whining. Do you think it will disturb the neighbors too much?"

"My neighbors are at work. Nobody is around to hear him if he does."

"Great. I'll put him back there."

"Okay. I'm just going to go finish getting dressed and fix my hair."

"There's no hurry."

Jeff took Neiman to the back yard. He took his leash off and petted him for awhile. "You be a good boy. You'll get to go home in a little while."

Jeff left Neiman and went into Stella's house. As soon as he did, Neiman started whining. *Man, that is sad,* he thought. *No wonder William didn't want him there this afternoon.*

Jeff went into the kitchen to pour himself a glass of water and something caught his eye. A gray pearl ring. Neiman started barking.

Chapter 51

Deputy Masters and Deputy Sweet rang the doorbell. William answered it.

"William, I'm here to escort you and your relatives to the church. Sweet will bring up the rear."

"Thanks, guys. I didn't even think about all that."

"You shouldn't have had to," Masters said. "Just let us know when you're ready."

"Let me tell everyone, and we'll be right out."

"Take your time. They aren't going to start without you."

☙❧

Neiman was scratching, barking, and yelping. Jeff thought he ought to go outside to see what the dog was after, but the ring on the windowsill had him puzzled.

The ride to the church was slow. Oncoming traffic pulled over to the side of the road and stopped to pay their respects.

Jeff had seen that ring before, but where? He didn't remember Stella wearing it. She didn't wear jewelry on her hands or arms.

The traffic lights were red, but the procession went right through. The lights on the patrol car were swirling and flashing. Hannah used to play with William's lights when he took her riding through the neighborhood in his car. She was like a kid about it.

He picked up the ring. *It looks like a flying saucer. Spaceship. Reed. Hannah. The portrait of her with her horse. Oh, God!*
Neiman was going crazy.
"Jeff?" Stella had come out of her bedroom. She saw the puzzled look on his face.

The town square was covered with cars. The First United Methodist Church was filled to capacity except for the reserved spaces for the family. There were people standing outside.

"Why don't we let the dog stay in the house? He looks like a house dog to me."
Jeff just stared at Stella. His eyes were blank.
"Jeff? Are you all right?"

Flowers were everywhere. All kinds and all colors. But by and large the room was filled with white Shasta daisies. Hannah's favorite. The entire county had sold out of white Shasta daisies.

Jeff opened his hand. In his palm lay a gray mabe pearl ring. Stella's eyes got large and round.

There was a choir in the choir loft. William didn't realize that there was going to be a choir. Hannah would have loved that. She used to close her eyes on Sunday mornings when the choir sang. She said it polished her soul for the coming week.

Neiman was digging furiously. Jeff could hear his claws scraping against wood. He was hoarse from barking so hysterically.

The organist was playing a hymn. "What a Friend We Have in Jesus." William remembered the first time Hannah heard it played on the grand pipe organ. She had wept.

"Where did you get this, Stella?" His voice was raspy, broken. His throat was tight with anguish.
Stella didn't answer.

The minister walked up to the pulpit and everyone stood. It was time for the family to walk down the aisle.

Neiman was going to hurt himself. Jeff needed to tend to the dog, but he couldn't move. He could barely breathe.

William remembered Hannah walking down the aisle to be his bride. She was the most beautiful sight he had ever seen.

Stella's eyes began to blink.

They had not found Hannah's wedding ring. William asked that they look for it while investigating the crime scene. It should have gone to Reed.

Jeff took Stella by the wrists and yanked her hands from her face. "Look at me!" He was crying. Something brown was on her eyelashes. He plucked it from them. It was a contact lens.

Finally they reached the front of the church. Light filtered through the stained glass windows. The colors reminded William of the poem Hannah had written to him for Valentine's Day. Dear God, how he loved her. He really could see her and feel her in the colors.

Jeff took his thumb and pulled at the corner of Stella's other eye. A brown lens popped out of it, also.

Neiman was going to hurt himself if Jeff didn't stop him.

Everyone in the church was seated. The service was about to begin.

"Look at me, Stella." Jeff prodded up her chin. "I said look at me, damn it!"

Her demeanor changed. Defiantly she opened her eyes and cast a look on him that could have come from the devil himself.

Jeff was shocked. Her eyes were almost clear. Just two black pupils.

The minister spoke. William tried to listen, but all he could think about was Hannah.

Jeff grabbed her by the hair and pulled. The wig came off and left a head full of red frizzy hair. "Ethel? You're Ethel Fletcher? My God!"

The choir sang. Their voices were huge and grand. The melody was beautiful. Reed put his head on his father's shoulder. His valentine was under his arm. Hannah's hair was in William's pocket.

"To hell with you!" Ethel screamed. She searched for a knife in the drawer next to her and found one. Jeff tried to stop her. Neiman kept barking and digging.

The minister said, "With William's permission, I want to read to you a poem that Hannah wrote for him for Valentine's Day less than a week ago. It's called 'Colors of a Valentine.'"

The knife went up in her hands just like at the ceremony. She came down hard before Jeff could stop her.

The poem brought tears to everyone's eyes, even the minister's. It wrenched William's heart hearing it again. William didn't know if he could stand another minute of life without her. All of this. The people, the poem, the flowers, the music, the windows, everything was closing in on him. It was supposed to be comforting, but it was choking him. He wanted to go outside and scream as loud and as hard and as long as his lungs would allow. He wanted to hit something, smash something. He wanted to die and be with her. And then Reed tugged on his sleeve, and he came back down to earth.

"Dad," he whispered. "I just can't believe Pretty is dead. I don't believe it."

William wrapped his arm around his son and kissed him on top of his head. "She's alive in our hearts. I can see her when I look at you. You are so much like her," he whispered.

Blood dripped on her spotless kitchen floor. It was deep red, and she yearned for a taste of it.

Jeff stumbled back and regained his wits. He pulled the knife out of his shoulder and threw it on the floor. Without hesitation he whipped Ethel around and forced her against the counter. He yanked his handcuffs out of his pouch and cuffed one arm. Then he ran the other side through the handle on the refrigerator and cuffed Ethel's other arm behind her. Pure hatred was smeared across her face.

Reed would be his reason to live. William could not let him down. William looked down the pew at Meredith and Henry. They had lost their daughter – their only child. And then he thought of Edward and Martha Brooks. How thankful they must be to get their daughter back. Seven women taken and only theirs came back.

Jeff had to get to Neiman. The dog was in a frenzy. "Neiman, what's the matter, boy? Come here."

Neiman would not come. He kept right on digging. There was a cellar door in front of him.

The minister told about the kind of person Hannah was, her vitality for life, her love for her family, her accomplishments. William knew all these things. He couldn't concentrate. He just wanted to hold his wife again. He wanted to feel her face against his. He wanted to hear her laugh. He reached in his pocket and stroked her braid of hair. He took a deep breath. *God, this can't be happening. I can't be sitting here at my wife's funeral.*

Jeff pulled at the door. It opened. Neiman whimpered, got his bearings and trotted down the narrow steep steps. He lost his footing and fell the rest of the way to the floor of the cellar. Jeff was right behind him.

The choir sang again. It was sad and sweet. Reed tugged at his daddy's arm again. "Pretty can't be dead. Dad! I can't stand this."

William hugged him tightly. They would get through it together. Somehow.

A prayer was lifted up for Hannah's family. It was strong and stirring. Surely God heard it. William wondered if there really were angels around to comfort them, because he had not felt one yet.

Reed's fiddle teacher, Matt Brice, walked up to the center of the chancel. He was carrying his violin. "Dad, did you know Matt was going to play?"

"Yes."

Reed sat up straight as Matt began playing "Amazing Grace." There was something not right. Reed's trained ears tried to tune in to Matt's perfect pitch, but something was in the way. He cocked his head. It was sirens. Several of them. Dozens of them.

Matt stopped playing. Surely all the police in the county knew that William Douglas's wife was being remembered today.

"Dad?"

William shook his head. "I don't know."

The sirens got louder, stronger. It sounded as if they might blow right into the sanctuary. No one said a word.

Everyone turned to face the front door of the church.

Blue and red lights were flickering through the stained glass windows. The front door of the church opened and William saw Jeff Stone standing there with the full bright sun glaring behind him. It was blinding.

One peace office after another filed into the church as if making the way for some dignitary who had come to pay his respects, and when the last one stopped, Jeff reached for someone behind the door. He brought her to his side to give her support.

Reed and William were standing in the aisle. They didn't remember getting to that spot. They just ended up there.

The front door closed and the glaring sunshine was shut out. Coming down the aisle towards them in a red velvet cape was the most beautiful sight William had ever seen. He could not move, mesmerized by the vision of her coming down the aisle to capture his heart once again.

When she reached them, Hannah said. "Can you believe it? I was late to my own funeral."

Epilogue

Spring exploded in Huntsville, Texas. The dogwoods and the azaleas bloomed. The air was filled with the sweet fragrances of flowers and fresh air.

There were flowers outside Leo's window, and they let him tend them. He wore his overalls when he worked in the dirt.

The nurses gave him his medicine, just like when he was in prison, but they were kinder here. No one hollered at him to get in line, or to shut up, and he never again had to wear white. He did, however, have to empty the trash. That was still one of his chores.

He hoped he could stay at Garden Terrace forever. There were no devils here. He looked for them occasionally. He even caught himself looking for Mother, but he knew deep down that she was really dead. The fire got her this time, and she couldn't come back from the fire. No one came back from the fire.

He wondered if the policemen found his tunnel. It was how he escaped with Mrs. Douglas. He didn't tell them about it, and he didn't think Mrs. Douglas would tell his secret. She was nice like that.

CB&O

Detective Jeff Stone was having dinner at the Douglas house

tonight. Brenda Baker, Elaine Tyler's former secretary, was going to be there, too. He hoped she wore that short black leather skirt. He still couldn't get that out of his mind. Nor could he get Stella out of his mind. Of course she never really existed. She was just a figment of Ethel's twisted mind – a way to deal with the atrocities that were her childhood, the atrocities that shaped her life. Like Elaine Tyler, she dealt with it the best way she knew how.

He wasn't going to let it destroy years of his life like Debra had. Life was too short and too precious. He could move on, and just maybe Brenda Baker could help him.

Ethel was too emotionally disturbed to be put in prison. She was sent to an insane asylum where hopefully they could help her. It was clear that she had some goodness inside of her. Stella, after all, was a part of her.

Before going to Hannah and William's house, Jeff had a couple of stops to make. He had gotten the addresses from county records.

Earl Cowen came to the door and gave a wide grin when he saw that it was Detective Stone. "Come in. Good to see you."

"I can't stay. I have to run by Virginia's house after I leave here."

"Never you mind that," he heard Virginia holler. "I'm right here." She came prancing out of the den and into the foyer. Then she latched onto Earl.

"What is this?" Jeff asked. "Are the two of you an item?"

Earl blushed.

"We are indeed. Aren't we, hon?" Virginia said.

Earl couldn't say a word, but Virginia was handling the situation fine all on her own.

"I have something for the two of you."

Virginia clapped. "Well, what is it, Sweetie Pie?"

Jeff opened up the box and took out a medal for Earl and a medal for Virginia. Each hung on a purple ribbon. Inscribed on the front was the word "HERO." On the back, their name. "It's not much. But I told you that if your information helped us to find Mrs. Douglas, I would get you both medals. And in my book, you really are heroes."

For once Virginia was speechless. She could not think of one word to say. Nothing.

Jeff pinned the medal on her frilly blouse and kissed her ruby red cheek. He shook Earl's hand and left.

He could smell the steaks cooking on the grill when he got out of the car at William's house. It was one of spring's rights of passage, steaks cooking on a grill. Brenda's car was already there. He felt his heart skip a beat.

Neiman met him at the gate to the back yard. He was outside with everybody. He treated Jeff like a member of the family now.

Hannah greeted him with her bright glorious smile. "Jeff, you remember Brenda."

"Yes, I remember Brenda. She's that sassy little lady I thought I was going to have to take to jail not too long ago."

Everybody laughed. It broke the ice.

Brenda sat in the swing with Jeff and watched William and Hannah love each other with their smiles, their touch, and even the air they breathed. It wasn't just a feeling with them. It was a living and thriving entity that was beautiful and contagious.

Neiman got the first steak. He liked his a little rare. As the rest of them waited for their steaks to get done, Jeff asked Reed to get his fiddle.

"I thought you'd never ask." And with that he ran in to get his great-grandfather's old violin.

"I want to play a tune for you that I composed myself."

"Really?" Hannah asked, surprised. "What's it called?"

"*Colors of a Valentine.*"

Zaner Grace

The End

www.ingramcontent.com/pod-product-compliance
Lightning Source LLC
Chambersburg PA
CBHW020836030726
47496CB00001B/247